Praise for
THE YEAR SHE LEFT US

A *New York Times Book Review*'s Editors' Choice
A NPR and *San Francisco Chronicle* Best Book of the Year

"Haunting. . . . The foundling may be a familiar figure in the history of the novel, most prominently in Dickens and the Brontës, but Ma gives us a striking twenty-first-century iteration. . . . Like Philip Roth and, more recently, Chimamanda Ngozi Adichie, Ma is unafraid to generalize about her culture and explore its snobberies and social codes. . . . The most vivid characters in the book are Gran and the troubled Ari. They're shimmering and unforgettable. . . . One of the stunning accomplishments of this book is Ma's tonal range."
—Mona Simpson, *New York Times Book Review*

"Kathryn Ma's first novel is electrified by the enraged tenderness of its alienated young protagonist. Part mystery, part odyssey, *The Year She Left Us* heralds the arrival of a fierce, subtle new American voice."
—Jennifer Egan, author of *A Visit from the Goon Squad*

"A sparklingly original fiction debut."   —*O, The Oprah Magazine*

"A deft, raw dissection of an American family. . . . With great cleverness, Ma injects her Chinese family with American realism."
—Rebecca Liao, *San Francisco Chronicle*

"There's much to enjoy in *The Year She Left Us*. . . . It's Ari's voice that sets this novel on fire. She seethes and broods with a furious wit. . . . [A picture] as full and vexing and self-contradictory and transcendent as any human life."
—Laura Miller, Salon

"Full of secrets and obsessed with identity, this story of an adopted Chinese girl comes closer to the complexity of things than any other account I have read. It is moving and well told, and rings perfectly true."
—Gish Jen, author of *World and Town*

"In a first novel etched with grief and conviction. . . . Ma addresses the complicated questions of what family means with clarity and empathy."
—Jane Ciabattari, a NPR Best Book of the Year selection

"*The Year She Left Us* is unlike any novel I have ever read. With remarkable clarity, Kathryn Ma understands the weight of the unspoken—how it can tear away the tenuous tissue that holds together a family—and the tender mercies required to heal. I savored every rich, masterful line."
—Dolen Perkins-Valdez, author of *Wench*

"The characters of Kathryn Ma's glittering debut novel are complicated, infuriating and hugely sympathetic. I couldn't wait to find out what they'd do next; I envy readers coming to these pages for the first time."
—Margot Livesey, author of *The Flight of Gemma Hardy*

"Ma is a clear-eyed but compassionate storyteller. In telling Ari Kong's quest, Ma succeeds in creating a deeply intelligent heroine as compelling as Holden Caulfield and Alexander Portnoy. . . . *The Year She Left Us* is a fresh, compelling look at the ties that bind among all the kinds of families that we create."
—May-Lee Chai, *Dallas Morning News*

"In this provocative tale of a family pulled apart, Kathryn Ma proves herself a powerful storyteller and an astute observer of the complexities of human experience and the perils and possibilities of love."
—Karin Evans, author of *The Lost Daughters of China*

"As tough and tender a book as I can remember reading. I'll never forget eighteen-year-old Ariadne Bettina Yun-Li Rose Kong, raised in San Francisco but born (and abandoned) in Kunming, China. Add to the world's great literature of orphans and adoptees this stunning new novel by Kathryn Ma."
—Ann Packer, author of *The Dive from Clausen's Pier*

THE
YEAR
SHE
LEFT US

THE
YEAR
SHE
LEFT US

A NOVEL

KATHRYN MA

HARPER ● PERENNIAL

NEW YORK ● LONDON ● TORONTO ● SYDNEY ● NEW DELHI ● AUCKLAND

HARPER PERENNIAL

A hardcover edition of this book was published in 2014 by
HarperCollins Publishers.

HarperCollins books may be purchased for educational,
business, or sales promotional use. For information,
please e-mail the Special Markets Department at
SPsales@harpercollins.com.

FIRST HARPER PERENNIAL EDITION PUBLISHED 2015.

Design by Fritz Metsch

The Library of Congress has catalogued the hardcover
edition as follows:
Ma, Kathryn.
The year she left us / Kathryn Ma.—First edition.
p. cm
ISBN 978-0-06-227334-5
1. Orphans—China—Fiction. 2. Adopted children—
China—Fiction. 3. Adoptive parents—Fiction. 4. San Francisco (Calif.)—Fiction. 5. Domestic fiction. I. Title.
PS3613.A13A613 2014
813'.6—dc23   2013026100

ISBN 978-0-06-227335-2 (pbk.)

15 16 17 18 19   OV/RRD   10 9 8 7 6 5 4 3 2 1

For my mother

and

In memory of Dad and Chris

PART ONE

The Year of the Sheep

CHAPTER 1

ARI

———

Lucky girl. That's what I was told from the first moment I can remember. Another stranger, smelling unlike my mother, would swoop in low with a scary-wide smile to ruffle my hair or pinch my cheek. I would shrink and scamper, hide my face in my mother's knees, hear them laughing at my baby shyness. Later, I stared, black-eyed and baleful. I hated to be reminded. Hello, Ariadne. What a lucky little girl. Now you have a family. I'm the one who's lucky, my mother would always chirp. She knew my fell looks, was afraid of my eruptions, my locked face and the storms that followed. When left alone, I would say please and thank you. When prompted to be grateful, I went gleefully mute.

I had other labels, too. A miracle, a blessing. An ironic twist to a long family saga. That one made me laugh, since I wished I had said it myself. A colossal mistake. That's what Gran called me until the mistake had arrived and couldn't be gotten rid of. Some people bundled me with all the others, for there are thousands of girls like me, like us, who were carried away to the richer nations and raised into families gobsmacked with love, swollen with good intentions. The Lost Daughters of China. The Unwanted, the Inconvenient, the Unhappy Outcome of the One Child Policy. *Rescued* is how my mother, Charlie, sometimes put it. I have a better word. *Salvaged*.

She's hardly worth noticing, that lucky little girl. Most people think they already know her, since she can be found all over

3

America, growing up in cities and towns and suburbs, from the most ordinary places to the unlikeliest of locales. They spot her at the mall, strolled by her white mother and father, and on the swings at the playground and in their child's classroom. She's smaller than her playmates, with hair as shiny as a beetle's back. One quick look at her sends their minds to swift conclusion: *Asian kid, white parents, must be adopted, probably from China.* There are so many of us now that the sight of a mismatched family is as ho-hum as baby's breath tucked into a clump of roses. *Cute kid,* is what they're thinking. *Well behaved. Early reader.*

They wouldn't be wrong for a lot of the girls they see. My Whacka-doodle group was full of that kind of charmer: the unfussy baby, the adorable child, the soccer midfielder who played the flute and loved her golden retriever. A well-adjusted girl, despite the bleak beginning. A lucky girl with a brief, predictable story.

That wasn't me. I fixed my sights on that bleak beginning and ran straight toward it while the rest of them scrambled away. My story was mine to demand, holes and gaps and secrets and silences and all. Some of it was told to me; some I lived or guessed at. I'm writing it down for all the mothers who wave at us in the grocery store and jangle their car keys and try to get us to smile. For the fathers who glance our way and think, *That's what we would've done, if we hadn't been able to finally get pregnant.* But most of all, I'm talking straight to you: the dropped-off daughters, the loose-change children, the thousands upon thousands whose lives branched when we were hours new. Though we're older now—the oldest of us have grown from babies to girls to women—we can't shake that feeling of *what if* and *I might have been.* My story is as much yours as it is mine, full of the unanswerable questions that invade and claim us, turning us inward until we lose ourselves completely. It's an act of self-preservation, writing down what scraps I know. I'm trying to skirt boggy disaster, the swamp that surrounds us, the dark water that refuses us a clear look at the bottom. I have no idea whether my words will save me. Whether, in the telling, I can flail my way out. I know only that I'm very tired and ought to stop and rest. Like the traveler who swaps a tale in exchange for a hunk of bread and a warm place by the fire, I sink to the ground and begin. I'll leave for you the crucial question: Must I be grateful? Is that your idea of luck?

KNIFE OR SCISSORS. Scissors or knife. The question was in my mind even before I knew it was there. Knife was sharp, and quick. Scissors snipped. Snip, snap. A cleaner cut, a chicken bone sheared. Knife was swift: one downward motion. Scissors were careful: no room for mistakes. Knife might bounce. Scissors might slip. Knife might miss. Scissors might not cut through.

The artist used a knife. He used a knife and a taxi. The knife was from his kitchen. The taxi was from the street. He paid the driver up front. If I don't come out, come in and get me.

Which hand, left or right? Easy question. Left hand. Right hand writes. Right hand dribbles. Right hand is the only hand that can hold the knife or scissors.

Palm up or palm down? Empty or at rest? Up, up. Let me read your future. Down, down. Hello and then good-bye.

Knife: on a surface. Scissors: in the air. Knife: aim well. Cover up the other fingers. Stretch wide between the one and the rest. Mr. Spock, ha. Live long and prosper.

The artist's hand was beautiful. Soft and smooth. The hand of someone young. A perfect cut. A yawning gap. Lack, emptiness, less, fewer. Less is more. Absence speaks louder. Negative space. Wiggle-waggle. As wide as the sky. As vast as the ocean. Count backward from ten. Ninepins left standing.

Knife wants steady. Ready, aim, chop. Scissors want strength. Powerful grip. Elbow grease. Clamp shut. Put your back into it.

Afterward, what? Blank, blank, blank. Blankety-blank. Fill in the blank. Soft as a blanket.

Knife or scissors? Scissors or knife?
Both.

CHAPTER 2

ARI

I was born in the Year of the Sheep, though where I was born and into whose arms I slid—I was little, a slip of a thing—and who my mother was and who was my father are not known to anyone but the woman who birthed me and then left me on the middle step of a local department store, or let somebody else do it, which is practically the same thing. At the orphanage they pinned a crudely drawn picture of a sheep on my blanket. "Sheep," A.J. used to read to me off the paper place mat at Panda Panda. "Wise, gentle, shy, pessimistic." What a joke. None of that's me except for maybe the gloomy part. "Often puzzled about life." Yes, but who isn't? "Sometimes called goat, sometimes ram. Not well spoken." Well, you'll be the judge of that.

At the Kong family gatherings—George Kong was Gran's first husband; Herbert Hsu was her second—at the family roundups, part mud wrestle, part on-demand tribute, and in our Whackadoodle playgroup, how I longed to be a Monkey. Monkeys were intelligent, nimble, inventive. Very impatient, which I consider a virtue. My friend A.J., she's a happy Monkey. All the Whackadoodle girls were Monkeys; all born, like me, in 1992, but I was born three days before Lunar New Year, on January 31, if you believe the one page in my onion-skinned orphanage file, and so I missed out on being like all the rest. You'd think, since she was going to dump me, my mother would have lied and stuck a note in my basket—not a basket, actually, but a plastic tub; this wasn't Moses in the bulrushes or some other romantic shit—stuck a note on my blanket or wedged into my grasping hand a letter claiming a birth date after Lunar New Year so that I could enter life as a clever Monkey, not a woolly-headed Sheep who clods about, waiting for slaughter. She didn't leave any note. She didn't even leave a birth date. The orphanage guessed at it, based on the pull of my greedy suck, my pinked-up coloring, the fuzz on the rims of my ears. Ten days, they guessed. Ten days from birth to the middle step of a fine department store in Kunming, China, in a plastic washing tub. And so life began for me, Sheep/Ram/Goat/Not Monkey, one girl among thousands set down and then picked up.

Of the orphanage, there is nothing I remember, and it is gone now, moved, reorganized, expanded, absorbed into a social welfare institute, which means orphans and old people housed together in a jolly happy place, built in a redeveloped section of Kunming, City of Eternal Spring, Yunnan Province, China, seven thousand one hundred ninety-seven point oh-three miles from where I was raised, which was San Francisco. A pockmarked nursemaid at the orphanage claimed me as her favorite. She cried when we parted. I like to imagine that I left her behind, just as my mother left me, although I was five months old and didn't do much under my own steam, save for eating like a horse, or maybe a sheep or ram, and squirting my brains out—apparently I went through a lot of diapers. This was reported to my mother, Charlie, by that ravaged nursemaid, scar-faced, saw-toothed, with hands, Charlie said, like a football receiver's: Auntie X, who then fell to weeping. There was a string around my neck, to Charlie's horror. She snatched it off the minute she got me out of the sight of Mr. Zhu, the orphanage director, and Auntie X, who had probably tied the string out of simple kindness, a note from one ersatz mother to the next. On the string a little card in English dangled: "Like eating. Like the Bowns." A mystery, that word, though I have my theories. A foodstuff, maybe, that I couldn't get enough of, or a toy that rattled, drawing my hungry gaze. Maybe it referred to my crib buddy, whom I like to think of as my first and only sibling—I make him out as a brother, though statistics run against me. I have three mothers. Four, if you count the one who threw me away. No father. I'm due a brother, don't you think?

A brother, then. Baby Bowns. They laid us two by two in little burrito bundles, no mother's breast to smell but at least another human, whose every kick was a kind of comfort. Or was "the Bowns" a place outside in the garden where they let me sun in a wheeled bassinette parked with all the other bassinettes between the plastic flowers and the spittoon? I made up the flowers. The spittoon I added because I've seen them in Beijing's public places, and I figure there must have been one bent brass spittoon in the orphanage garden for the use of Director Zhu and the occasional visiting official. There aren't many men in orphanages other than the shadows of the anonymous breeders.

"Not worth ruining your life for," Gran told Charlie when Charlie put in the application. Gran is Charlie and Lesley's mother. Once I came into the picture, everybody called her "Gran." Aunt Lesley is Charlie's older sister. Charlie calls her "Les"; she's a bigtime judge in San Francisco. Everyone's afraid of her, except for Gran and me. Charlie is a lawyer, too; she works for the poor and downtrodden. Great-Aunt Rose is Gran's younger sister. She married Bennett Kong, George Kong's younger brother, and had four boys—a host of sons, a wealth of riches, a triumph for Rose and an elbow in the face to Gran. Charlie and Les never married, much to Gran's eternal disgust.

So "not worth ruining your life for," Gran told Charlie. "The cart before the horse. A burden you can't afford." She didn't want Charlie to adopt a baby and ruin her chance of finding a husband. Charlie was thirty-three when she got me, an age at which plenty of men were already divorced with dangling children of their own, but it was different for a man, said Gran. Their children had mothers. For a woman, dragging along a kid was worse than bad credit. "You've still got time," she said to Charlie. "You're all alone. What business do you have adopting a baby?"

"From your homeland, Ma," Charlie tried to tell her. "A way for me to connect to you and Dad."

"Who asked you to do that?" Gran flicked her huge hand like she was batting away a pigeon. "We made you American. All that *Roots* stuff is nonsense."

"But this is a chance to help a child."

Gran groaned. Where on earth had it come from, her daughter's zeal for doing good? "If your father were alive," Gran threatened, and Charlie interrupted her to say that Dad would have loved having a granddaughter, and Herbert, too. Both doctors, both dead. Gran was used to losing husbands.

"Besides," Charlie argued, "work is okay with it. Work is anyway all about families and children." "Work," Charlie named it, like her job was a person, which to Charlie it was, and a most beloved. "I'll still have time to take care of you."

Gran thrust out her jaw. Her skin was soft and papery, with little hairs like cactus prickles stuck on the point of her chin.

"I manage fine by myself." It was true. She did. Nothing got in her way. She's eighty-four now—eighty-two at the time I ran away—and I'm pretty sure that she's going to live forever. Gran's a Dragon. The zodiac got that right.

They argued the whole time that Charlie was waiting to get word that her baby was ready for pickup. Les didn't help. She didn't come to Charlie's rescue. "It's your life," was her only wisdom, "though it's a game changer, that's for sure." After the phone call finally came, Charlie received a tiny picture, but Gran refused to look at it.

"They fake those pictures. They show you the prettiest one and give you a different baby. You don't have to tell me she's small and scrawny. Not like you girls. You were healthy from the start. You'll have to take that iron-fortified formula, the small cans, which are more expensive, but you won't have a refrigerator. Very inconvenient. And then she'll get constipated. Iron does that. So you better take prune juice, too. You'll need it anyway, with all that travel. Why can't they bring her here? Why do you have to go and get her? You're doing them a favor. They should pay you to lessen their burden."

She wrote out more instructions, which she faxed to Charlie five days before the journey. "Keep her covered at all times. If she gets sick, don't go to a Chinese doctor. Call your cousin the pediatrician, the one who lives in St. Louis. George's medical school classmate was your cousin's professor, so we know he got good training, though why he's in St. Louis, I cannot imagine. Wait till you come home to buy her toys or clothing. Don't buy the cheap stuff. That's all they have in China." Two days before, she called again to rail. "You don't know what you're getting. Her mother is poor; she's probably a peasant. She never went to a doctor. Who helped her to have the baby? Maybe there's a birth defect that they're not telling you about. How do they know anyway? The really big problems always show up later. What are you going to do if she takes after her father? He couldn't be any good or he would've prevented the mother from leaving her baby like that."

I'll say this for Charlie. She was stubborn when it counted. After I was grown, she could hardly face me: my waiflike body, my raggedy hair. The piercing at my eyebrow, which made her wince. She didn't want to see the stump of my little finger, the two missing joints like the ache in my breastbone, unmet, unmatched, unshriven. When I abandoned her to go in search of my father—the trail stone cold, the scent long faded—we turned away as strangers. Trouble spilled, just as Gran predicted. But in the beginning, Charlie was full of love.

CHAPTER 3

CHARLIE

Most days she couldn't believe her luck. She not only had become a mother, the baby they gave her was Ari. As light as a teacup, with a big cartoon smile, she was born to be gazed at and sung to and carried, her pert head fitted into the crook of Charlie's arm like a child in utero, presenting its crown for passage. Her first word was *book*. Her first smile was exclusively for Charlie, their union two hours old. She had a grip so strong it felt like desperation, though the chuckle she emitted whenever she grabbed for Charlie's finger gave Charlie a shot of pure joy. Les hired an artist to paint a mural in Ari's bedroom and paid a handyman to install safety latches in Charlie's kitchen, and then, since she determined that he'd done a neat, professional job at her sister's apartment, she had him come to her own house to make baby gates for the bottom and top of the stairs and build a custom toy box and put in shelves at toddler height. More than once, Charlie and Les caught each other doing very un-Konglike things, babbling or kissing the air or crooning. Blowing raspberries on Ari's belly, which produced gusting laughter. Charlie and Les would laugh with her: who knew it would be so much fun?

Gran flew up from Los Angeles, intending just to take a quick look, and a one-day trip became a five-day festival, celebrated with extravagant meals, a monogrammed blanket, embroidered shoes, additional instructions. She allowed as to the child's apparent good health and noted the possibility that the baby came from parents of aptitude if not education, pointing out Ari's alertness, and how her expression brightened at the sound of her grandmother's voice. "She follows me with her eyes," Gran said over and over, and Charlie and Les joked between them that Ari had already figured out that one should, at all times, know exactly where Gran stood.

"She looks just like you," people often told Charlie. A Chinese person never said that, but lots of others did. In fact, mother and daughter didn't look much alike. Ari had short legs; Charlie, long ones. Ari's nose was a rounded bump; Charlie's, for a Chinese, was Roman. Her baby's hair was silky while Charlie's sprung to unwelcome, crackling life whenever she hastily brushed it. Gran had scrutinized Ari, wondering aloud if she came from one of the ethnic minority populations scattered over the poor rural areas outside of Kunming. No, she decided, Ari was Han Chinese. They would never know for sure, of course, but she had classical features. A delicate face, a smooth brow. A neck of the proper proportion.

"She's perfect," Charlie replied, dabbing milk from her daughter's chin. She felt she had the right to boast, since the credit was in no way hers. It gave her comfort to know that, when Ari was old enough to speak for herself, it would be for Ari to decide whether to tell people she was adopted. Nobody would know unless Ari told them. *She's fortunate*, Charlie thought. *She has that clear advantage.*

Their skin tone was exactly the same, not that it mattered.

To Charlie's relief, she shifted more easily than she expected into juggling work and motherhood. She had had long years of practice taking on more than she reasonably should. It wasn't easy, but it didn't overwhelm her. There was a brief moment when she thought, foolishly, that she would give Ari a father, but that moment passed, and she banished the notion for good. She and Gran and Les were all that Ari needed.

Once in a while, worry crept in. Adoption was such a complicated matter. The road would have bumps, but they would travel it together. She calmed her worries by marking her small achievements:

a home haircut, a treated fever, a first swing on the playground with Ari clasped in her lap. *Remember this moment*, she said to herself, meaning savor the happiness, though her instinct also took it as a kind of warning. She had noticed with unease that Ari's own happiness was sometimes arrested by a puzzling stillness. In the middle of a string of syllables or a warm bottle or an urgent, five-fingered wave, Ari would stop and aim a hard look at something Charlie couldn't see. In those moments, Charlie imagined another woman standing just behind her shoulder, looking down at the baby—half in guilt, half in rapture. The way Ari stared made Charlie think she was listening, and Charlie would make herself be quiet, too, so that her daughter could hear whatever it was she strained for. At other times, Ari would give a sharp cry of protest and throw her bottle or thrash her tender feet. Then Charlie would scoop her up and do her best to soothe her, getting a kick in the mouth, if she wasn't careful, or a sharp little fist near the eye. The next morning, Ari would greet her with a dazzling smile, standing at the bars of her crib like a passenger at the rail of a gleaming ship, ready for grand adventure. Charlie would clap her hands and return the winning smile. *Remember this moment*, she would say to her daughter, storing their joy like a peasant parcels rice, saving it up for winter time, down to the last gleaning.

CHAPTER 4

ARI

My passport (U.S.) reads "Ariadne Bettina Yun-li Rose Kong," a mouthful of moniker, a free-for-all for a foundling. The name in all its glory doesn't fit on any form—Charlie went overboard with deliberate purpose. My naming provided her a special thrill, a belief in the future that appealed to her positive nature, like labeling desk files or cartons stacked in the garage. *I know what's in here. If I can name it, I've got it under control.*

At the orphanage, they named me "Zhu An-li," of which "li" was the only part that trailed me to San Francisco. We all were given Director Zhu's surname, a favorite practice of slaveholders in the South. I mean the American South, not southern Yunnan Province, and God, how offensive, comparing myself to a slave. It's hard to keep track of one legacy over another when you don't know which country's history you belong to. I'll stick for the moment with China, eons old. Maybe at the orphanage they were just following tradition, putting Director Zhu in the robes of the gentleman scholar—rich, proud, influential, boasting a powerful first wife, a string of concubines, and a household filled with children. The idea pleased me. The usual explanation of why we'd been dumped at police stations, public parks, factory gates, hospitals, school yards, dormitories, and the middle step of a fine department store in Kunming, China, hit hard those phrases that preordained forgiveness: "too poor to raise you" and "wanted you to have a better life than they could give." But it was all a guessing game. Nobody knew a thing. If you could make up your family, why wouldn't you make up a good one? I'd rather I had a rich father than some dirt-poor loser who couldn't afford a condom. A wily financier or a corrupt government official. A man of power with an eye for the pretty ladies. I would have even settled for Director Zhu, who had a unique kind of household at his disposal. My father took what he wanted. And he had money to burn.

That's how I see it, now. It steadies my hand to look at my life that way, to peel off the gauze to check the wound beneath. Better to know what pain you're facing than to cover up the damage, but I'll admit that when I was little, I wanted the happy story. How Charlie named me was my favorite bedtime tale. We would curl up together in my painted pine bed, and she would tell me where each part came from and how perfectly it suited. I can't remember if it made me feel loved or empty or anxious—probably all three, and Charlie knew it—but anyway, I asked, and Charlie told me.

Zhu An-li. "An" meaning "peaceful." All the girls at the orphanage who were born in the Year of the Sheep had the name "An" as the first part of our given name. It was a quick and easy way to organize us by birth year. "Li" means "beautiful." They were being generous; I wasn't anything to look at. In the first baby picture that they sent to Charlie, I was scrunched and scrawny, just as Gran predicted, with my eyes shot open, as though I'd just heard a noise go *pop*! Charlie cried when she got the phone call and they read her the particulars of what she'd been waiting months to hear: baby's name, age, location, dates of travel. It was part itinerary, part Annunciation. Three times she had to wipe her teary face and ask them to repeat the name and then ask how to spell the alphabet version. Not being able to speak or write Chinese— she was born during the Cold War, when educated immigrants like the Kongs didn't want their children to speak anything but perfect English and respectable French—Charlie had to wait till she got her referral packet to see the written Chinese characters of my orphanage name. She cried again when she showed the name to Gran.

"What does it mean?" she asked.

"Peaceful and beautiful." Gran wasn't impressed. "Not very original, but it doesn't matter, since you'll have to change it."

Change it she did, though not enough to please Gran. She started by giving me a Western name so that teachers and other children would accept me as one of them.

"I knew right away that you were very brave," Charlie always told me. I liked to spread her hair on my pillow. "You didn't cry at all when they gave you to me. That's why I named you 'Ari.'" A whopping lie, though I didn't know that until later. "'Ari' means 'lion.' You were my little lion, afraid of nothing." My very own creation myth, meant to make me strong. My bed overflowed with stuffed lions, some that roared when I squeezed them around the middle. A bright green jungle print streamed across my walls—another myth, since lions don't live in the jungle. Ceramic lions danced on my bookshelf. There wasn't any room for a Sheep to shelter.

Les didn't approve. "'Ari's' too short," she objected. She told Charlie that I needed a bigger name, in case I would someday rise to address a jury or run a large company from behind a polished desk. "You want her taken seriously. 'Ari' can be her nickname. Come up with something else. Something longer."

"I like 'Ari,'" Charlie said.

"At least give her the option." Les was a big believer in keeping one's options open.

Charlie listened to Les, as Charlie always did. She stretched the name all the way to "Ariadne," and then tacked on "Bettina," the way a gluttonous diner passing through the buffet line throws extra mashed potatoes on his plate though he knows he won't have room to swallow another bite. It's a heady thing, naming a little baby. Creating for her an identity that she'll be sure to grow into.

"Bettina" came from Gran's name, "Betty," though that was all wrong, too, because Gran's name isn't short for "Bettina." Her name is simply "Betty." She picked the name when she came to the U.S. and cast about for a Western name—a Christian name, Gran called it—that was close to her given name, "Pei-nan," meaning north *and* south. The perfect contradiction.

"But Gran," I once said when she told me that she was mistress of her own fate, right down to choosing a name for herself. " 'Pei-nan' doesn't sound like 'Betty' at all."

"Ha," Gran said. "What name would you have had me use?"

"I don't know," I said. "How about 'Penny'?"

"Exactly," Gran said. "The cheapest name in the book."

"Penny" wouldn't do for Gran; "Betty" wouldn't do for Charlie. She dressed it up to "Bettina," and then had only my Chinese name to choose.

"Get rid of the whole thing," Gran insisted. "Don't leave a trace of 'Zhu An-li.' Who knows what they really know? What records they have that they aren't saying? Change it completely. Don't let anyone come looking." Gran didn't trust that my real mother wouldn't show up, along with fifty or sixty relatives, to ask for money or sponsorship or worse. She had left during the war. She knew what it was like among the hordes of the hungry.

But Charlie had read all the adoption manuals. She had studied the books, pored over the articles, surfed the Web, wept as she read the memoirs of all those blessed, transformed, humorous, humbled, rueful adoptive parents who told in unstinting detail of their own personal journeys, not to brag about their children or hear themselves talk, but to *share their experiences* and *build community* with the many other parents choosing international adoption. They were Charlie's gurus, her Sacagaweas, her faithful familiars who led the way into the fraught unknown. *Keep your daughter connected to her heritage*, they all advised. That was the wisdom of the particular cultural moment into which we were born and then transacted.

Charlie had a Chinese name; so did Les. Adopted or not, her

baby would need one. She decided to keep "li," meaning "beautiful." "An" she dropped and replaced it with "Yun," meaning "cloud."

"Does that work?" she asked Gran. "'Yun-li'? Cloud beautiful? Would a Chinese person think those names go together?"

Gran sniffed. What did it matter? It wasn't the baby's real name. It was all made up after the fact. There was no need to have the geomancer, a feng shui expert, count the brushstrokes or consult the astrological charts to choose the best day for naming the child. No need, for a baby who had started so unlucky in the world, to place the furniture, arrange the fish tank, remove the mirror, hang the proper scrolls. Bad luck was bad luck. One might hope for a tolerable outcome, but the beginning couldn't be altered. Besides, Gran didn't hold with the old superstitions. She admitted only to true-blue American ways.

"Just be done with it," Gran said. "A long name like that, for such a tiny baby?" She was mad that the baby wasn't called outright "Betty." Her sister, Rose, had a grandson named "Rosen." What was this "Ari" name that sounded uncomfortably Hebrew? But then, to Gran's greater displeasure, Charlie at the last minute added "Rose" as well, because Auntie Rose had traveled with Charlie all the way to Kunming to pick up the baby. Gran ground her teeth, too proud to admit she was jealous. At least the child would carry the Kong surname. Even Gran couldn't complain about that.

"Yun-li," Charlie told me as she tucked the blankets tight. "Cloud beautiful. There were beautiful clouds above the Golden Gate Bridge the morning I flew to get you." She taught me how to write the American parts of my name, my crooked letters taped to her bedroom mirror and hung in her office for everyone to see. Together, we learned how to write my Chinese name, taking turns with a thick pencil on a big pad of paper we propped on her knees in the bed. Sometimes I practiced with my finger on Charlie's back, drawing big sweeping lines as we counted the strokes together, bumping my fingertip across her spine.

"I was so happy for us both," Charlie liked to remember, "that

I cried every time I saw your name in print." The doctor's certificate of vaccinations. The adoption order, signed by a California judge. The U.S. passport, stiff as the wings of the eagle emblazoned across its plasticky blue cover, with the bearer's new name officially stamped inside: ARIADNE BETTINA YUN-LI ROSE KONG. It's a heady thing, renaming a baby.

CHAPTER 5

CHARLIE

C an I come in with you?" Charlie begged at the doctor's office. It felt strange to be asking her daughter for consent, but now that Ari was eighteen and a half, she had the right to shut Charlie out. To her relief, Ari didn't answer, and when Charlie followed her tentatively into the examining room, Ari didn't stop her.

"Tell him exactly how it happened," Charlie said. "Tell him everything that the Chinese doctor said."

"If you don't shut up, you can wait outside," Ari said.

"Don't say that," Charlie said, more firmly. She had to make Ari understand that she wanted to make things right. She wished for the thousandth time that she had been there in Kunming when the accident happened. A.J. had handled it well, getting Ari to the ER quickly and then back to Robyn in Beijing, but it was the mother's job to keep her child safe. Of course, Ari wasn't a child anymore, a point Ari kicked home every chance she got, but how could Charlie not worry?

The doctor breezed in and raced through the preliminaries. He was a young guy, last name Bowker, wearing running shoes that squeaked. He spoke so fast that Charlie got the impression of a white coat flying.

"What happened to the finger?" he asked. "Why didn't they try to save it?"

Ari shrugged. "It was an accident," she said. "The rest of it was pretty mangled. And it was bleeding pretty hard. I didn't stop to pick up the pieces."

"Too bad," the doctor said. "The Chinese are brilliant at micro-surgery. They could have reattached it. It's a cultural thing, you know," he said, turning to Charlie. "The Chinese place great value on the wholeness of the body. A Chinese patient would've insisted on reattaching the finger, even though the finger wouldn't be all that functional. Here, in America, we usually let it go. But you being Chinese"—he gestured to them both—"I figured you'd want to go for the replant."

Charlie stared at him. She had no idea what he was talking about. "Are you saying that her hand won't function properly?"

"I didn't say that." He manipulated Ari's left hand forward and back and bent each finger in turn. If it hurt, Ari didn't show it.

"Will she have full use of her hand," Charlie asked, "even with-out a pinkie?"

"Great," Ari said, "let's have the same question over and over. How many times does he have to say it? It's perfectly fine. I've been telling you that all morning. It didn't get infected. It's heal-ing on its own."

"We don't call it a 'pinkie,'" the doctor said.

Charlie felt herself contracting. She was already folded into a chair against the wall next to lurid charts of the nerves and mus-cles of the human hand, but she gathered in her elbows tighter and drew back her feet so as not to take up one more inch of room than she needed. She hated the doctor. She had never met him before; he was the only one she could get Ari in to see on such short notice, but he had barely looked at the wholeness of Ari. If he had, he would have noticed how thin and tired she looked. True, she had just flown thirteen hours from Beijing to San Francisco, but it wasn't her daughter perched on that table. All the dips and dots of anger and unhappiness that Charlie had glimpsed in her before seemed now to be pooled in the dripping sarcasm of Ari's tone, in the dark circles under her charcoal-lined eyes.

"I don't see how that's helpful," Charlie said to the doctor with as much dignity as she could muster.

"Are we done here?" Ari said.

The doctor held up Ari's right hand as a demonstration model. "Thumb, index, long finger, ring finger, little finger," he intoned. "Distal, intermediate, and proximal phalanges. In your daughter's case, accidental amputation, leaving a small section of the proximal phalanx on the little finger, left hand."

"A stub," Ari said. "I wish the whole thing had come off. It looks like I've got a tiny flipper." She twitched the half-inch piece in a disturbing wave.

Charlie swallowed hard. She recalled another man, another finger. Only once in her childhood had Ari needed a trip to the ER, after she'd fallen against the coffee table and gashed the back of her head. Aaron had scooped her up, quickly stanched the bleeding, and calmly driven them to the hospital, Charlie trying not to hyperventilate. Ari had cried, waiting for the doctor, until Aaron had sat her in his lap and held out his finger. "Squeeze as hard as you can," he told her. "Squeeze until you hurt me." She couldn't have understood him; she was only a baby, but she stopped crying instantly and stared into his face. Charlie, remembering, fused her own fingers into a tight fist. She wiped her mind blank, as empty as she could make it.

The doctor rebandaged Ari's finger, all the while chatting. He could remove that piece, he said, but he advised her to leave it alone, at least until the swelling was down. It was healing nicely. The stump would shrink up some. She might have pain, numbness. Physical therapy would keep her other fingers nimble. The more he said, the more Charlie despised him. At the sight of Ari's injury, his eyes had shone like a gossip's. He didn't care about her daughter, only about his own liability if he didn't guess right on this one. She knew, dimly, that in hating the doctor she was angry at the wrong person, but she hurried away from that thought.

"And you say it was a metal door," the doctor said. Charlie's chest tightened.

"Yes," Ari said. Her tone was casual, her expression profoundly bored. A heavy metal door that swung the wrong way, which Ari wasn't expecting. Her friend was coming out, and Ari, stupidly, had her hand in the wrong place.

"It's a very clean cut to have been made by a door," said the doctor. "But I've seen stranger things. I had a guy in here last week who lost his thumb in a waterskiing accident. It's a whole different thing, losing a thumb." He grinned at Ari. "You're a very lucky girl."

"Don't I know it," Ari said.

"BUT WHY DIDN'T you call me?" Charlie asked, unable to muzzle herself when they were out on the sidewalk. Ari sped up, outpacing her to the car, and jumped into the driver's seat before Charlie could get there.

"Things were really busy. I was going to call as soon as I had the chance. You didn't need to send Les to come get me. She was really pissed that she had to cut her trip short."

"She was glad for an excuse to leave Hong Kong early," Charlie said. "Her part was over. She said the conference was only half useful." She looked at Ari's hand, the heavy white bandage wrapped like a knob around the tip of her little finger. "Shouldn't I drive?"

"I've got it," Ari said. "You made a big deal out of nothing. They have doctors in China, you know."

Charlie reached up slowly to buckle herself in. Ari steered through jerky traffic with her right hand and two fingers of her left. She had the radio on, tuned to the baseball replay, Jon Miller describing a pitcher's three-fingered grip.

"Maybe I have a career as a closer," Ari said. She held up her mummified finger. "Better ball control. Better pitching."

"We can go to a game if you'd like," Charlie offered—they had used to love going together, Ari cheering from the bleacher seats and Charlie keeping book—but from Ari's cold silence, she might as well have asked, "What are your plans for the rest of the summer?"

Once home, she followed Ari right to the bedroom doorway.

"Would you like something to eat? I can make you a sandwich before I leave."

"Go away," Ari said, "go away, go away, go away." She flung herself facedown across her bed, wallowing like a piglet, returned to old habits just by smelling the pillow.

"Oh, honey," Charlie said. "You've had such a time of it. It won't be so bad, just hanging out for the next few weeks. The time will go quickly. You can get organized for college, buy your sheets and towels, that kind of thing. Say good-bye to your friends." She told herself not to look at her watch, though she had some prep to do before her next client, a father who, if Charlie didn't help him, might disappear for good and leave his kids stranded. Now that she knew that there wasn't any infection, she could leave Ari to get some sleep. Ari would settle down after a nap and a good meal. She glanced at her watch, asked herself if she'd gotten back the car keys.

Ari sat up, her hair spiked around the crown of her head. "I'm going back to Beijing," she said. "I had stuff going on before you and Les dragged me back here."

"But there's only another three weeks. You ought to be getting ready."

Ari shook her head. "I can't stay here," she said.

Charlie allowed herself a stir of impatience. She had thought that, in letting Ari go to China after graduation, her daughter would better appreciate her own home and family. She would find out for herself that she shouldn't take those things for granted. She didn't want Ari to be grateful, exactly. Just thankful for what she had, and able to express that thankfulness once in a while.

"I want you to rest, get some sleep, do your laundry," Charlie said. "When I get home from the office, then we'll talk."

"Robyn needs me," Ari said. "Her biggest tour group gets to Beijing in three days."

"A.J. is there to help her."

"You don't get it," Ari said. "I need to go back. I was figuring things out there."

"You had the whole summer for that," Charlie said. "It's time for you to focus on your future." She looked at her watch again. "I've got to get to work. I've got people coming in."

"Go ahead." Ari rummaged in her bag. Her hands shook slightly as she pulled out a pack and a lighter.

"Oh, Ari. Please don't do that."

"Everybody smokes in China." She opened her bedroom window.

"Not in the house at least."

"It's like one big cloud," Ari said. "*Da kun.* One big cloud of blue smoke." She slipped past her mother out the bedroom door.

"Honey, wait," Charlie called.

In the hallway, Ari glanced back, her face white with exhaustion, her mouth trembling.

"Stay here and talk to me," Charlie said, but Ari turned and tossed the car keys into the bowl on the table. Quickly, she left, boots clattering down the staircase, surprising Charlie all over again that her light-as-a-feather daughter could make such an angry noise.

SITTING AT HER DESK AT WORK, Charlie tried to think clearly. She understood how difficult transitions were. Ari needed time and space to process her two months in China. She was tired, and upset at being summoned home, but beneath that, Charlie wanted to believe, ran Ari's familiar pluck. Les had alarmed her, saying, "She needs help. She's way out there. You've got to reel her in," but Charlie wouldn't hear it. In a day or two, Ari would relax and tell her all about her summer—the job with Robyn in Beijing and her visit with A.J. to their orphanage in Kunming. Robyn had convinced Charlie to let the girls go to Beijing together. "They'll learn so much," she had said, "and be all that more ready for college." *I ought to call Robyn,* Charlie thought, *and tell her that the doctor said everything was fine.* Instead, she dropped her phone into her briefcase. A part of her, the same part that hated the doctor, blamed Robyn for Ari's accident, though she knew that wasn't fair: Charlie herself was to blame. She should have listened to her misgivings when Robyn proposed that the girls come work for her this summer, but it was hard for Charlie to say no to people she admired.

Robyn had been a magnificent friend from the moment they'd met at the airport, the beginning of their journey to bring home their daughters, Ari and A.J., born just days apart. Eight families had traveled together to the orphanage in Kunming. Robyn and David brought David's son, Brent. Auntie Rose came, too, an indispensable helper. Charlie was sad at the time that Gran didn't want to go, though it had turned out for the best, because Auntie Rose was kind to all whom she met. What would Gran have made of those families gathered nervously at the gate with their mountains of luggage, their money belts full of cash? The start-over dads, the infertile mothers? Their earnest attempts to thank the nursemaids at the orphanage while pulling out alcohol wipes to swab everything down? Even Charlie had had to keep from rolling her eyes when Robyn told her the name she and David had chosen for their baby: Asia Jade. Thank God they'd shortened it to "A.J."

As soon as they got home to California, Robyn made sure that the girls would be friends. The Reises lived across the bay in Oakland, but Robyn organized playdates, swim lessons, birthday parties, adoption playgroup, and she handled the driving, too. Working mothers like Charlie, especially if they were single, owed a huge debt to stay-at-home moms like Robyn.

Later, when the girls turned twelve, they took Ari and A.J. for a heritage visit to China. The trip had gone badly. "I can do better than this," Robyn had said, and started her own nonprofit business arranging tours for adoptive families who wanted their daughters to see China. Now she worked full time on the business and spent every summer in Beijing. Her Web site was a treasure trove for thousands: "How to Talk to Your Three-Year-Old About Adoption . . . Your Four-Year-Old, Your Five-Year-Old, Your Teenager, Your Neighbors." Charlie found the resources incredibly helpful. There were books to buy and Listservs to sign up for and recipes to download and tips on celebrating Lunar New Year. A cottage industry had sprung up around adoptive families, a global village, complete with its own vocabulary, therapists, and gurus.

Ari had jumped at the chance to go when Robyn offered.

"They're only eighteen," Charlie had objected.

"A mature eighteen," Robyn answered. "They're both so capable, and they'd have such fun together. A.J. loves Susan and the tour staff." Susan was Xiu Xiu, Robyn's Beijing partner. She had a staff of six young women who led the tours; she had let them choose English names: Cricket, Willow, Nan—Charlie couldn't remember them all. One was called Pony. Every tour group began in Beijing, then went to Xi'an to see the terra-cotta warriors, and on to Chengdu to visit the captive pandas. From there, the guides took small groups of families to their various orphanages in different parts of the country. Robyn wanted Ari and A.J. to help staff the office and welcome the families when they arrived in Beijing. Most of the girls were between eight and fourteen, though some were as young as four.

"Remember what it was like the first time we took our girls?" said Robyn. "So bewildering and scary. We've got much better language now around the whole experience. The girls aren't afraid anymore that they might be left again for good. Ari and A.J. can tell them what it's like to visit the orphanage, and they can help with the cultural activities—brush painting and the cooking classes. We never have enough hands. The younger ones start crying if they have to wait too long for their turn."

"It's fine for A.J.," Charlie said. "She goes every summer. Her Mandarin is good. But Ari's like me. She knows two phrases: 'Menu, please' and 'Where's the toilet?'"

"So she'll improve," Robyn said. "David's not coming at all this time. He's like you: he loves the office. And he refuses to miss another baseball season."

"Where will you live?"

"I lost my old place, so I rented a new apartment. Rents have gone up—all those damn foreigners." Robyn laughed. "It'll be tight, but we can manage."

Charlie wasn't sure. She said she wasn't ready to give up Ari yet, especially with college looming.

"You're never around anyway," Ari argued across the table, the two of them sitting down for a rare family supper. Between senior year and Charlie's job, they hardly saw each other. "If I don't go, A.J. won't, either. She'll be lonely without me. You're the one who's always saying we should know something about where we came from. Gran and Grandpa George, blah blah blah. You're not interested in going. Les isn't, either. I *have* to go. I have to go *this summer.*"

Charlie wavered. Her daughter looked fierce to her, fiercer than usual. She had gotten a new, lopsided haircut that curved like a spiral staircase around her head, and when she decided she didn't like it, she had cut off the longer strands herself. Her eyes, as always, were smudged with dark makeup, and her blunt, unplucked eyebrows emphasized her obstinate look. She wore a man's shirt carelessly pinned together over a pair of someone's discarded blue jeans. That foot that Charlie had kissed with abandon when Ari was a baby looked bruised at every toe, the same as her fingernails, painted purple-black. Two small tattoos had sprouted on either wrist: a Keith Haring crying baby and, inexplicably, a barking poodle. From the small of her back upward, a third tattoo tendriled. A mum, Ari said, where I can't see it. Charlie had tried to smile. Ari had stopped calling her "Mom" when she was only eight.

Ari drummed the table. "I'll learn Mandarin. I'll be with A.J. every second. I'll do everything that Robyn tells me. I can pay for my own ticket"—her part-time job at Pen and Parchment—"and I'll totally get ready for school when I get home."

"It's not the money," Charlie said, though it was, in part. Les might offer or maybe Gran, though Gran and China—Charlie never knew what to expect.

"I want to help those other girls," Ari said. "The ones going back to their orphanages." That was the clincher. It was in helping others, Charlie believed, that a person came to know herself. Her natural gifts and inner strength and passions. How, in service, she could find her highest calling. Les offered to pay for half the ticket. Ari took off for Beijing.

Once there, Ari quickly moved out of the apartment.

"I was crowding them so badly, we had groceries stacked in the hallway. It was way awkward. Cricket told me about a room with a family she knows in her building. It's perfect. It's really cheap. I'm paying for it myself. I'm *fine*. Robyn came over."

Yes, said Robyn, she had checked out the place, and it was legit. There was a landlady who stood guard like a foo dog. Apologies, she said. It was a bit crowded in Robyn's apartment. The pictures on the Internet had made the place look a lot bigger. Ari was great, a huge help, great on the marketing side because she was such a good writer. Robyn never changed a word she wrote.

"Don't worry about a thing," Robyn assured Charlie. "The girls are having a great time. The weeks are flying by. The younger girls love them."

"She never picks up when I call," Charlie said.

"E-mail is better with the time difference. Or you can call here. There's always someone in the office."

"I'm fine," Charlie said. She shouldn't breathe down Ari's neck. Robyn was sending pictures, and Ari e-mailed now and then when Charlie beseeched her.

"China photos" was there on Charlie's desktop; she clicked on the file to watch the slide show that Robyn had sent. Ari and A.J. at the airport, dozing on top of their duffels. The two at the gate of the Forbidden City. Ari at the Beijing office, studying the binder where Robyn kept the list of the next group of families due for their heritage tour. Ari and A.J. at the orphanage in Kunming, A.J. smiling wide and pointing above her head to a red-and-gold banner: WELCOME DAUGHTERS HOME. Ari stood beside her looking stiffly into the distance. A faded yellow blouse drooped like a pillowcase from her shoulders, and her black skirt, before so tight that Charlie had objected, looked like bunting come loose from its tacks. In none of the pictures was her daughter having fun. *I didn't notice that before*, thought Charlie.

I was figuring things out there, Ari had told her, but the opposite looked true. China had made her miserable, as miserable as A.J. was happy. Charlie's head sank. She had hoped, without saying so to Ari, that letting her daughter go to China would bring home a happier child. She missed the little girl who had let Charlie hold and soothe her; in her place was sometimes a stranger. How relieved Charlie had been at Ari's departure! The fighting had stopped; for eight whole weeks, the house had been mercifully quiet. She'd caught up at work with time left over for walks and agreeable meals, even a couple of casual dates with a friend of a friend from the office—a pleasant change from rushing home to deal with a prickly Ari.

She turned off the computer. There had to be a way to fix things between them. She texted Ari, knowing she wouldn't answer, then packed her briefcase and passed uncertainly out of the office. They would need bread, eggs, milk, yogurt. Chicken, if Ari had gone back to eating meat. She would cook a nice supper. She would stay up late if she had to. Tonight, they'd start over again.

CHAPTER 6

GRAN

When all else changes, Father used to say, your family stays the same. They might take away everything you have, everything you've worked for, and you might in that moment believe you've been good as murdered, but if you've got one member of your family left on this earth, then you know who you are and where you came from. That's what Father told me when he sent me out into the world. Oh, I was a hopeful one, full of dash and adventure, and I lived an exciting life, nothing like the quiet one you see me living now. I lived in the best cities and had two husbands and three big houses, but I never stopped racing to get where I wanted to be. To make something of myself like Father predicted I would. War separated us, and strife and sickness. Sickness of the spirit and strife of the soul. Fear invaded but didn't defeat me because I had people who needed me to be brave. My every breath I drew for others. Every crevice of my thoughts I filled with plans for their welfare. I have never stopped doing that, all the hours of the day. I keep my family close, as close as the lungs to the heart.

This is not my story. I'm just here to keep things straight. I'm the pilot light, burning low and constant. This is my granddaughter's story. She's been told that family isn't everything, that parentage doesn't count because it's who you are yourself that matters. That's wishful thinking, not mine. The least I can do is correct the family record. I have no interest in crowding the picture. I'm not taking over, as my daughters so often accuse me of. Ari needs to know the things I have to say. "Go ahead, Gran. Give it context," she said the last time I saw her, a year and a half ago now. I laughed at the way she drew out the word *context*, soaking her voice with spite. It's her mother's favorite word, that and *background* and *circumstances*. Charlotte's so good at making excuses that she does it for a living. A professional justifier, that's what she is.

I want Ari here with me. More wishful thinking.

Ari went to China and then came back and ran away. Surely I'm not spoiling anything by telling that little bit. She went to Kunming, where she had been abandoned. "We don't use that word," Charlotte likes to correct me. As though words hurt more than history. More than fact. She's a sharp one, my granddaughter—my only grand-child, the only one my daughters gave me. She remembers people and events and conversations clearly and says what she's thinking, even what should be forgotten, but I have to warn you: her story is full of bitterness, and there's no happy ending. It's not finished yet because Ari is incomplete. She's twenty now, but as uncreased as a fresh sheet of paper. At her age, my life ended, so I picked myself up and started again.

Here's the context. We're American. Ari's like me; she was born in China, though she's a Sheep and I'm a Dragon. Nobody will tell us who her real parents are. They say they don't know, though I don't believe that for a second. They know everything; they keep everything secret. She was left at a store where somebody stumbled upon her and drew a crowd so he wouldn't be accused of being the father or uncle or neighbor. Those luckless Chinese stuck there for good, they have to be careful to show the world their business, and even if they have witnesses to every blameless moment because they know that the government is watching, always watching, those witnesses might lie to save their own skins. That's how it must have happened, if it's true that she was abandoned. The man who found her shouted to others, "Whose baby is this? I just found this baby!" People gathered, gaping and mostly silent. A woman might have cried that in the park across the street she had seen a figure hurrying, carrying a bundle, a bundle wrapped up so, a parcel or maybe this baby. The department store manager ordered everyone away. It wouldn't be good for business, for the store to become known as a good place for discards.

They took her to the orphanage. They have a whole system; they're used to that sort of thing. Five months later, an orphanage auntie gave Ari to Charlotte, who couldn't control herself and promptly broke down in public. She showed me the video; her eyes squeeze shut like sand is flying. She's crying so hard that she almost drops the baby. If I had been there instead of my sister, Rose, the transfer would have gone far more smoothly because the orphanage auntie would have fastened on me first, the only one who was calm and collected, and passed the baby straight to me.

Ari made not a peep when she was handed over because she's braver by far than Charlotte. She's not one to cry while Charlotte is weeping. She took leave of her birthplace, as I once did, and, like me, she did well with her fresh start. At school she excelled, so maybe her real parents were clever after all, giving me high hopes that my grandchild wouldn't disgrace me. Look forward, I told her, look forward, look forward, look forward. She looked back, a fatal error. She never should have visited that orphanage full of bad associations. I told Charlotte and Lesley not to let her go, but when did either of my daughters ever listen? George, Charlotte's father, believed the same as I do, and he didn't know half of my reasons, only the part I told him. The future holds promise while the past is full of ghosts. But Ari looked back, and that's when the trouble began.

Ari is young, almost too young to look at. She has a future of mistakes ahead of her. I am old. My mistakes are all behind me.

"GOOD AFTERNOON." A woman in an ugly black blazer is bearing down on me, a fixed smile on her face. Her dentures have that dull look of man-made materials, like artificial countertops or the handle of your toothbrush. A petroleum product, that's what her teeth are made of. I have all of my choppers, every last one, including all four wisdom teeth that grew in straight when I turned twenty. Upheaval was good for me. My wisdom came on strong.

I nod coolly. Cool is why I'm here, in the Woodhaven common room, where they run the air-conditioning morning, noon, and night. All summer long, the ladies and gents of Woodhaven retreat into their condos and blast the icy air. Their utility bills must be a fright. What's wrong with a fan and an open window? I like the dry heat as hot as an oven. It's not like Taipei, where Herbert and I lived, so hot and sticky that the bread molds and the towels mildew. But even I have my limits. On days like today, ninety-two degrees and higher, I bring my book to read in the common room. I raise it now to block out that crow of a woman.

"May I help you?" she asks. "Are you here to pay your respects?" She is eyeing my leopard footstool and my volume of Dickens. *Hard Times* for the meek and mild.

"I'm not leaving," I tell her. "And the food hardly tempts me." She's worried that I'm going to poach her meager outlay of cold cuts and potato salad. As if I needed funeral meats to stock my larder. I have plenty because I've husbanded well. That's a pun. I may not have been born here, but I was top of my class at Bryn Mawr.

"But it's reserved," she says. Her voice trembles. The smile has vanished. She can't be the widow, so she must be a sister or cousin. A family member sent on ahead to make sure things are set up for the postfuneral reception. I saw a little notice on the bulletin board when I came in: RESERVED FOR THE FAMILY OF WILBERT TOWSON. I didn't know the gentleman, though I'm sorry for his widow. Imagine having to explain the name "Wilbert" all your days.

"What do I pay my dues for?" I say. "I have every right to sit here. I'm only taking a corner."

"It's reserved," she repeats, "for a memorial service." The last two words intoned gravely. Does she think the specter of a final crossing will get me to leave my cool comfort? I wave my book to dismiss her. A memorial service, ha. That's a fine dodge of a phrase. Nobody has funerals anymore, and nobody gets buried. It's fallen out of fashion, and though I carry a smart handbag and always dress for an occasion, that's one modern trend I refuse to follow. There should be Scripture and hymns and deacons and mourning. I had the university organist for George and a whole choir for Herbert. Death can't be cheated or softened with funny stories and family pictures. There should be a hole, dug by men with bent backs and expressionless faces, and a casket not on wheels but lifted to the shoulders, a long and polished coffin almost too heavy to bear.

"Your guests are arriving," I inform the stingy hostess. She flounces off to chivvy them to the table. The bereaved are fagging in, their tongues hanging out for a drop of whiskey, poor things. They're more likely to get warmish wine in a plastic cup, or water drawn from the city tap and then bottled and gussied up with mountain scenes on their labels. At least some of the guests are decently attired in black suits and, on one, a lovely short black veil. The she-crow is still glaring in my direction, impertinent conduct at Wilbert Towson's last hurrah. Her outfit is helpfully laying to rest the age-old question: Are there, indeed, different shades of the color black? Yes, by the looks of her ensemble, in three shades of faded black—dredged up, no doubt, from the depths of her closet after she, more than anyone else in the family, sat vigil at the deathbed.

I wait another thirty minutes reading my Dickens. Then I hoist my footstool and march through the crowd to the door. I stayed to make my point, but that wasn't the only reason. Maybe I was hoping that someone would say hello.

I MOVED HERE three days after Ari's seventeenth birthday. Somebody had to look to her future. Herbert had died the previous summer, and I had remained in our Taipei apartment until Lesley told me that Ari had been suspended for showing up drunk at school. I knew about Woodhaven from an old college classmate who had lived here briefly until her husband died and her daughter insisted she move to Harrisburg, Pennsylvania, like a company transfer, convenient for everyone but my friend. I bought the place unseen but used a good broker who dispensed with brochures and Web site descriptions and instead e-mailed me photographs and room dimensions.

I wanted a corner unit but the prices were scandalous, and so I settled on a third-floor condo with an extra three feet in the kitchen. It has two bedrooms and a view of the courtyard. Squirrels leap in the trees, the closest I've lived to wildlife. I'm hoping to see a deer one day, though it's been three and a half years and none has made an appearance. There's no staff assistance or nursing care here—that was one of my requirements; I don't approve of the conveyor-belt program—only senior independent living in six buildings, with a common room and a pool. There is no doorman, but this is Millbrae. There wouldn't be a taxi to hail even were a doorman posted, uniformed and ready.

I didn't inform my daughters of my plans to move to Woodhaven until the deed was recorded. Lesley and Charlotte objected; if I were going to move, they said, they wanted me close to them in the city, but I know better than that. Their lives are their own, and it's too late to mend them. If I had to give up the globe, I might as well choose Millbrae. What would runty San Francisco be next to Shanghai, Manhattan, Los Angeles, Taipei, teeming cities where the world spills through the gates? I like things shiny—shiny and new. Next to Woodhaven, a new development curls in on itself with curb cuts and sodium streetlights and broadband cabling into all the houses. And everything at Woodhaven gives off the cheer of the recently retired who are determined to be content at the prospect of their depletion. The people and properties have all been resurfaced—hips, faces, putting greens, pathways. The gents' pink pates are scrubbed free of carcinoma. My Benz sails the pleasant streets like a tour boat gliding placid waters. Lesley complains that if I weren't going to plop myself down in San Francisco, I should have moved closer to Stanford, that sprawling suburb of a school whose bland perfection thrills her. Ha, I said. Give me fieldstone and climbing ivy. I never liked Stanford, with its nouveau pretensions, though George was very proud when both girls attended school there.

"It's just like Ma to buy a place almost convenient to us but not really," I overheard Lesley say to Charlotte after I moved to

Woodhaven. They were in my living room; they thought I was in the bathroom. I was enjoying the privacy of my extra three feet of kitchen.

"It's closer than Taipei," said Charlotte, always looking for the bright side.

"We don't want her driving into the city," said Lesley. "We've got to come down here to see her every week or she'll be using us as an excuse to motor all over the place." It's hardly a drive—twenty miles in twenty minutes.

"I wish work weren't so busy," said Charlotte.

"That's such bullshit," said Lesley. "You leave me to deal with her most of the time." And then they moved and I couldn't hear the rest. I should have emerged and assured them that they didn't need to visit. I wanted only Ari. For her, I had big plans.

YESTERDAY I SENT YAN to buy Ari a notebook. Yan is my servant, whom I brought with me from Taipei. When I was growing up, "servant" is what we called them. Here in Millbrae, I'm not allowed to say that. She's my caregiver, my housekeeper, my live-in companion. I don't like her dogging me twenty-four seven, but the alternative is worse: Lesley threatened to move down here herself.

"Somebody has to look after you. I'll buy the unit next door." Naomi's place. How I miss her! Naomi lived in Shanghai at the same time I did, though of course we didn't meet, since she lived in the Jewish quarter. Her father was a doctor the same as mine. Lesley could never replace Naomi—she's too high principled, being a judge and such.

"Your visits are enough," I told both my daughters. Lesley has no reason to move—she has a very nice house at the top of Telegraph Hill. If she had a better car, she wouldn't resent coming down here. Lesley drives a Prius, Charlotte a hybrid Civic, cars with no pickup and precious little style. Nobody loves to drive as much as I do.

"Just keep Yan happy," Lesley told me, "or I'll have to move down there and harass you into behaving."

My husbands were never as bossy as my daughters.

I gave Yan ten dollars to take to the store. Buy a good one, I instructed her, with sewn binding and a sturdy cover. What she brought back was no good, the paper was limp and the coil snagged at my sweater. A little more money? she suggested, looking away. She didn't want me to lose face that I had been tight-fisted, but I don't embarrass, especially when I'm making sure I'm getting value for my money. Some people call that cheap, but it's a fool who is parted soon from his fortune. I gave her fifty dollars and sent her to buy another. Not a coil ring notebook but a leather-bound book from a fancy store because Ari needs a notebook as tough-skinned as she is.

Yan chose well. She brought back a handsome journal, eggshell blue with a thin leather strap that cleverly cinches. Made in Italy. Next to the Chinese, the Italians have the best food and the nicest things, though Paris, not Rome, is a city I adore. With Naomi I could joke, "The third time I marry, I'll choose a Frenchman who'll sweep me off to Paris to live out my golden years." Naomi would have laughed and named the best contenders. It's not out of the question that I will marry again. I'm eighty-four years old, but there are gents who are ninety. They'd be lucky to have me. I'll bet I could keep them kicking.

If I ever see her again, I'll give the journal to Ari. I want her to keep writing, not on the computer, but on paper, by hand, so that the story moves through her, and when she's done, I'll make her throw it in the garbage. In our final talk, the last time we were together, I told her to do exactly that.

"Then what's the point of writing it down?" she asked, but her index finger twitched like a miser who spots a gold coin on the table. The middle finger of that hand, her right hand, the one she didn't despoil, has a freckled bump at the first joint raised by years of her pressing a pencil and bearing down too hard, as though she were cutting to bone. She's had a pencil in her hand since she was two years old. Before kindergarten, she could read a whole book. Before she could cut shapes out, she was typing on the computer.

Her teachers were in awe of her. So was her mother, which was certainly part of the problem.

"It's up to you," I said. "And when you're done, that part of your life will be finished." I wrapped the blanket more tightly around my shoulders. Morning clouds misted the mountains, and the chill air had turned my clothing damp.

"Are you giving me permission to tell everything?" she said. In her rosebud mouth, a half laugh lurked. She raised her eyebrows, two furry burrs that needed only a little tending to have shaped them into lovely curves like moon peel framing her pale and delicate face. A metal shank bisected the right brow. It hurt to look at her. Her questions annoyed me, delivered as they were in her most defensive mode, far too ironic to ever catch a husband.

"Don't pretend that you're waiting for my permission. You don't know where to begin? Start with their finding you, poor abandoned baby. You love reading stories. Without much history, yours should be easy to tell."

"I'll think about it," she said. She rubbed at the bump on her finger. I saw a blue stain there, ink from the fountain pen, water from the well, leaving a mark where pencil never did.

CHAPTER 7

ARI

would have gotten away with it if not for a slipped bandage.

It was an accident, I explained, when Robyn called me the day A.J. and I got back to Beijing. It was just as A.J. had told her. Stupidly, because I wasn't paying attention, I had gotten my finger caught in a heavy metal door at our hotel in Kunming. It was only the tip of my finger. It wasn't a big deal. "I've got it bandaged so it won't get wet," I said. "I'll keep an eye on it. You don't have to worry."

"Do you need stitches?" Robyn asked. I was sure I didn't. Robyn put down the phone. "Maybe I should go over and take a look at it myself," she said to A.J.

"No," A.J. said, as I'd asked her to do. "Ari just needs to rest. We hardly slept on the plane, and the food was awful." She started to cry. That part was real, she told me. She didn't have to fake that. "I miss California. I miss Daddy and Brent. I want to go home. I'm tired of this place." I imagined Robyn hugging A.J. tightly, smoothing her long hair, freshening the bed for her to lie down with Robyn next to her, a worried mother holding her daughter close. Once upon a time, I had let Charlie do that for me. Maybe Robyn was feeling guilty that she had brought A.J. with her, making her swelter away her last carefree summer tending to all those orphans. Like a lot of the mothers we knew, Robyn was sure that her own enthusiasm for Chinese culture would give A.J. a boost of ethnic pride, nurture in her an identity she could own. It was all very well for Ari, I once overheard her tell Charlie, Ari, who was adopted into a Chinese American family and didn't have people coming up to ask their ludicrous questions: *Where did you get her? How much did you pay?* But now she had to wonder: Had she pushed too hard on the whole China thing?

"She asked me if you were the problem," A.J. reported. "Was it okay having you here? Did it make me feel awkward? Was it weird to be with Ari, who comes from a more Chinese background? And who, these days, isn't exactly getting along with her own mother?"

"I hope you milked it," I said. We both laughed wickedly.

"I got her to take me to the Hard Rock Cafe."

I listened to her talk, trained my thoughts on a flame-grilled burger. A.J. made me promise that I wouldn't do anything else crazy. I said everything was fine now. I just needed a little rest.

WE DIDN'T TELL ROBYN about the Kunming hospital visit. A.J. took me there; we waited for hours. The doctor didn't ask a single question. "It's going to be fine," I told A.J. over and over. "I'm sorry. I was being stupid. I was thinking of that picture. . . ."

A.J. nodded. The photo of the artist who had cut off his little finger.

"Please don't tell," I said. "Please, please don't tell. Charlie will go ape shit. Les will kill me."

"But this is big," A.J. said. "Not like getting drunk at a party or kissing some guy you don't like. This means something."

"It doesn't mean anything. I can't explain it. It was like somebody else was making it happen, and I was just watching. Please, please. I'm counting on you." I leaned close and sang:

> You're like me, and she's like me, and
> we're in this to-ge-ther
> We'll be friends for-ev-er
> Whackadoodle! Whackadoodle!
> Tic! Tac! Whack!

A.J. didn't sing with me.

"'Whackadoodle,'" I sang. We were sitting on plastic chairs in the Kunming airport waiting for Pony, who was buying gifts to take home. Pony, like the doctor, hadn't asked any questions about where we'd been the day before, or why my finger was bandaged. She'd been too busy getting all the families in the heritage tour group on their flight to Hong Kong or off to other tourist destinations. I turned to face A.J. She looked pale with fatigue. Grease and soy sauce had soiled her white shirt, and red bug bites dotted her hairline. Stand next to me, her father, David, always said, so I won't get bitten. You're so sweet, the mosquitoes love you.

"Here," I said, "put your head on my shoulder." She lay her head down. I draped my arm around her shoulder and twisted a strand of her hair around my finger, the finger on my good hand, the one that didn't hurt. My jaw ached the same as my bad hand because I was grinding my teeth like a madman.

"They're going to find out," A.J. said, "as soon as you take off that bandage. They're going to know it wasn't the tip of your finger."

"I'll deal with it then," I said. "Right now, nobody has to know." She looked so young that people couldn't believe she was headed for Cal in the fall. I sang to her some more, "'Whack! Whack! Whack!'"

"Stop it," A.J. said, but after a moment she joined in softly. "'Whackadoodle! Whackadoodle! Tic! Tac! Whack!'" My face relaxed; I could trust her not to tell. I breathed in and smelled myself, rancid.

Pony returned and we had to stop singing.

AFTER ROBYN CALLED, I took the pills that I got from the hospital doctor and fell asleep in my heat-stifled room. My afternoon dreams were short and skittish. When I woke up, I couldn't remember a single image, but I felt panicky, as if I had lost one of the little girls in our tour group and didn't know where to find her. The room lurched; I didn't want to stay there and have to think about what I'd done, so I snatched dirty clothes off the furniture and floor and bumped a duffel bag down to the corner laundry. My landlady,

Mrs. Du, brought me a small pot of soup with dark, bitter greens, and I slurped it down, swallowing the leaves quickly. I thanked her profusely in my lousy Mandarin and gave her a packet of digestive biscuits, which I'd scored at the 7-Eleven. Later, I heard Mrs. Du through the thin wall, snoring. Mr. Du worked the graveyard shift and often came home late. Lots of nights I envied Mrs. Du sleeping while I sat up smoking and writing in my journal and listening to the soft scuffing of the other neighbors.

I closed my eyes. I had taken out my contact lenses and put on my snake-green glasses, and when I reopened my eyes, I saw dizzying ovals of green. My jet lag had felt permanent the whole time that I had been in China. I craved sleep but fended it off with drinking black tea all day long the way the Chinese did, out of a fat glass jar, and smoking in bed and watching movies on my laptop. To stay awake was a nightly competition, me pitted against myself. I knew I needed sleep and tried to dip down but couldn't. The ceiling floated toward me; I blinked, and it lifted. I sat up and opened my laptop. I was blogging for a travel Web site and writing freelance articles for a student-run publication that believed my story, when I dropped the name "Harvard," about being a college student living in Beijing for the year. They had already paid me enough to buy what little I needed.

I shifted my hand and gingerly raised the finger. My whole hand felt fat and heavy. It looked like a hand that belonged to somebody else. The bandage had slipped; it was wet and sticky. I could see the wound, beef red and oozing. My good hand felt heavy, too, as though it still held the knife, the kitchen knife I had borrowed. The knife from the kitchen, the scissors from the street. A peddler had sold them to me—his largest pair, with big, looped handles and blades he had sharpened at my request just before he took my money. The knife was plenty sharp, it almost did the trick, except for the skin, the flap of stubborn skin, hanging fast, keeping me to-gether. Blood had pumped out from both sides of the finger. Blood and skin, an instant fascination, less blood in my finger than in any single Tampax that I had ever tugged out of my body, but plenty enough to spritz me.

Curious how it had looked. Bright red blood, so bright it was truly pretty. Red marrow, dark as mud. White tendon, yellow fat, the white bone of a chicken. That flap of skin like cured leather. There had been one thing left to do. The scissors did it.

WHEN I OPENED my eyes again, I was still in my airless room. I wiped my face. Mrs. Du was snoring. I felt more dizziness and fought it. I wanted to call A.J., but it was two o'clock in the morning, and I was afraid to wake her. No way could I go home to San Francisco. If they sent me back, I would go certifiably crazy. I was probably already crazy, but going home would seal it. The pain in my hand spiked up my arm to my head. The laptop slid off the bed, then I fainted and fell to the floor. Mr. Du rushed over at the sound of the crash. Two days later, Les arrived fuming.

HAND ABOVE MY HEAD. Pain above my heart. I remember how angry I was that my cut wasn't perfect. The artist in the photograph hadn't made my same mistake: where his finger was severed looked smooth as a baby's bottom. A.J. and I had gone to a café after the orphanage visit, where a man we didn't know came right up to our table and talked to me as if he knew me and showed me the artist's photo. I can't recall what I did after that, though in recent months I've tried to, for Charlie's sake and mine. I must have borrowed the knife, bought the scissors, found a clean T-shirt for mopping up the mess. That last step means I was thinking clearly, though how can that be, since the day was such a jumble? A.J. said that when she found me, I was sitting on the bathroom floor in our hotel room in Kunming, my hand wrapped tightly and raised high above my head. She heard me swear that, someday, I'd cut off the rest of my finger.

CHAPTER 8

ARI

I t was WeiWei who named us the Whackadoodles. We were WACD—Western-Adopted Chinese Daughters, corralled on a monthly basis at a playground or a park so that the girls with white parents could see girls who looked like themselves, who also had white parents—a klatch of the mismatched.

That wasn't the reason, Charlie told me more than once. It was for *support*. Affinity groups mattered.

Whatever. I went. And so did forty others; the swing sets could hardly hold us. The Bay Area was lousy with Whackadoodles, cred-carrying members of a group that was still going strong last time I heard, all of us part of China's grand experiment in crib-time crowd control. At the beginning, it was mostly about making friends. Later, mothers like Robyn brought in outside speakers—adoption specialists, culture bridgers, researchers who reported on the mounting numbers of abandoned girls and the Fates of Those Left Behind. The parents would assemble for lectures and discussions, leaving us with finders and minders. A group of Russian women from San Francisco's western end had serendipitously tapped into this steady source of employment and showed up every month to make sure we didn't crack heads. They fed us piroshki and stale cookies out of a Costco tin. Their big bosoms were the best mothers one could hope for. I loved their brusque voices, their knit pant legs I grabbed onto, the wattles they let me swat. When Charlie showed up to fetch me,

I screamed and ran from her until one of the babushkas put me firmly into my car seat.

A.J. was in the group. So was Becca Kamin. We were the same age, though Becca was from a different orphanage and she had a younger sister, adopted three years later. The three of us ran the Monkey playgroup—I threw in with the Monkeys, who let me be the boss. I sent them all scrambling, some to dollies, others to building blocks. A.J. was my enforcer. Becca reported the names of anyone who didn't do what I said. It felt good, behaving badly, knowing that our mothers and, later, our kindergarten teachers would have made us share and talk through our feelings. The babushkas didn't care as long as we let them stroke our hair and chuck us under the chin. Their own grandchildren—I saw them occasionally in the backseats of the crummy cars that dropped off their grannies—were fat little boys who made rude faces at us. No wonder the babushkas enjoyed our pretty smiles. We were everybody's pets. To see us nourished and laughing made everyone feel good. We stood as proof positive of fundamental goodness, that race didn't matter, that a baby was a baby no matter from what part of the world.

In first grade, no more babushkas. Instead, they trucked in specialists at handling orphans, eager women in long, loose skirts and shapeless sweaters who studied adoption trends and wrote articles for magazines. They had a great deal of experience counseling families and children.

"Draw a family picture," they said, passing out paper and markers. "If you could draw a picture for your birth mommy, what would it look like?"

"How was group today?" Charlie asked me.

I showed her my picture. An empty house, a garden thick with weeds. "That lady was gloppy," I reported. There was something sticky about her that I didn't want to go near. I missed the babushkas with their tins of stale cookies. I distrusted trust builders, shut my mouth as they attempted to apply their listening skills. The next time, I threw a fit on the sidewalk. Charlie hurried me home while I yelled for A.J. to follow. The month after that, Charlie tricked me by saying it was Becca's birthday and there would be cupcakes with a candle in each one. The cupcakes showed up; so did a beskirted lady. I angled for the door as soon as I saw her warm smile. A skinny arm shot out and grabbed my T-shirt.

"You have to stay here," a tall girl told me. I gazed up at her, saw her glinting braces. She had me hoisted up on my tiptoes with her fist next to my windpipe.

WeiWei Chang.

A crush bloomed in my chest.

SHE WAS EIGHT years older than us and, by that fact alone, a demigod from the start. Tall and skinny, with blue and yellow rubber bands in her braces. "Cal colors," she announced. "That's where I want to go." That immediately made WeiWei the object of love from A.J., whose father, David, was a Cal grad and a diehard Golden Bear. She came with her own mythology, for we had already heard from the older groups, the Dragons and the Snakes, about the Girl Who Put Her Hand Up. To us, she was a legend. Our fates had been decided by central agency bureaucrats who had matched us up with our parents' dossiers. Our parents of course described the process in more golden terms—"You were waiting for me but we didn't yet know it"; and "We were meant for each other, that's why they joined us together"; and, for the faithful, "God moves in mysterious ways"—but WeiWei had chosen her future, which gave her the glow of a hero.

Her parents were American-born Chinese from San Rafael, California. Her mother, Michelle, a fluent Cantonese speaker, was working in Guangzhou in the late 1980s. She wanted to adopt a Chinese baby. She had heard of a few Chinese American couples who had worked U.S. State Department connections to get the Chinese to let them adopt girls out of orphanages that, the rumors said, were chock-full of children, mostly girls, many of them healthy. China didn't have a program yet for international adoption. Michelle, schooled by her mother in the fine art of *guanxi*, worked her own connections, generous with gifts and relentless with questions.

Her husband sent daily faxes from home: proof of their citizenship, their marriage, their childlessness, their income. At last, Michelle found herself in one of Guangzhou's many orphanages, holding out her arms to the five-year-old girl who'd been selected.

"Don't cry, don't cry," the aunties chastened the girl. "This is your new mother. You're so lucky that this lady wants you. You're going to America. *Gam Sahn*, Gold Mountain. Life is good there." And when she didn't stop screaming, "Don't be a fool. Run away from this place."

Michelle cajoled the girl in her own language; the officials joked and offered candy, but the girl kicked and hollered. She clung to two aunties and bit a third one who was trying to unloose her. A crowd of children gathered, looking impassively on the chaos. They had never seen a Westerner before. The lady looked Chinese, but she wore funny clothing. Her hair was cropped and curly. She towered over the aunties.

"Let me stay, let me stay," the girl heartbreakingly begged. Michelle was almost crying at the cruelty of her own need. The aunties began to look helplessly at one another; two started crying themselves, and the eldest drew breath to apologize to the American and the officials from her government who were no longer smiling.

"Hi lady, hi lady," a voice called out in English. A girl stepped forward, a seven-year-old scarecrow in a Harrah's Reno T-shirt, her hand straight up in the air like a miniature radio tower. In Cantonese she volunteered: "I'll go with you." Michelle and the aunties gaped. The officials frowned and muttered. The girl's hair was cut short, one-inch long around her whole head, so they all could see her scalp crusty with ringworm and a boil or two along the side of her neck. Her feet were bare; a front tooth was discolored, but the smile was confident and altogether dazzling. "You look like a very nice lady," she said. "I would like you to be my mother. What do you say?" she petitioned.

Michelle said yes. The officials weren't so sure. Michelle apologized to them for taking so much of their time, but she felt she had to say again how impressive their orphanage was, such a well-run facility and the children looked so happy. Wouldn't it be wonderful, she mused aloud, if they could put their heads together and do even more for the children? More books and paper, art supplies and music. Formula for the babies and better refrigeration.

The officials left the room for an agonizing ten minutes. When they returned, they were beaming. They said they were certain that Michelle and her husband would be very good parents. It was clear they understood Chinese ways. This little girl—WeiWei was her name—was actually the child they had first chosen for the Changs, but they didn't introduce her earlier because they weren't certain that the Changs wanted a child as old as seven.

Oh, but they did, Michelle assured them. Any child of China would be welcome in their family, but with this child in particular she felt an instant bond.

Twenty minutes later, they shook hands all around. Michelle thanked the aunties with gleaming jars of L'Oreal face cream. She promised to bring WeiWei back to visit. WeiWei didn't even say good-bye to the other children. She walked out the door proudly, leading Michelle away.

"I feel bad for that other little girl," her father said later. They were in San Rafael, making pancakes together.

"She was a stupid girl," WeiWei said. "She believed everything that I told her."

"What was that?"

"That the American lady and her husband were going to eat her. The aunties chose the fat ones for foreign devils to dine on."

Her father laughed. By then he was in love with his daughter. He told his wife the story; Michelle wondered, but she was in love, too. Who could blame WeiWei? They were meant for each other. They just didn't know it until WeiWei put her hand up.

"YOU HAVE TO STAY HERE." WeiWei let go of my shirt and punched my shoulder lightly. "Get a name tag," she ordered. "Look, I've got one." I obeyed her. She watched me try to scrawl "Ariadne," and when I botched the job, she got me another name tag and said, "Don't you go by anything else?"

I found my tongue and told her. "It means 'lion,'" I said.

WeiWei approved. "Stick with the nickname," she said. "'Ariadne,' huh?" I nodded back. "Weird name for an orphan," she said.

I clutched the hem of her shirt, delighted. She had said the word *orphan*, a mysterious word that made grown-ups shush and stammer. I knew what the word meant but didn't know the source of its power; it didn't seem like a potty word, like *pee* or *penis*, but it carried some secret I hadn't yet figured out. I felt that WeiWei would tell me if I asked.

"Her mom's name is Charlie," A.J. informed her. I had forgotten all about my friend. With my second hand, I held on to another piece of WeiWei's shirt. "It's a boy's name," said A.J., "but her mom is a girl." I glared at A.J., who was making me out to be different.

"That's cool. You got a father?" WeiWei asked.

I shook my head.

"Well, we can share," WeiWei said. "Right?" she asked A.J.

"That's what my mom says," said A.J. sourly. She inched closer to WeiWei, but I body-blocked her, stepping on WeiWei's toes. Out of the corner of my eye, I saw the lady with the paper pad and markers coming to fetch us. This one was named Linda. She had the Sheep, Monkeys, and Roosters all sitting together in a circle. She had a guitar, which boded badly.

"Bend your arms," WeiWei said. "Tight, like this." Her fists were at her shoulders, and her elbows pointed at her toes. We held ourselves stiff as fence poles, and WeiWei carried us upright, her hands cupped under our elbows, first A.J., and then me. I felt the other kids' envy as she tacked across the room and then casually hoisted me higher before "Elevator down!" and lowering me to the circle. *WeiWei Chang*, their wide eyes told me. *The Girl Who Put Her Hand Up.*

AFTER THAT. I never missed playgroup, and neither did WeiWei, because she was getting paid, she told us, "to keep you little mutts in line." She started calling us the W-A-C-Dees, the Wads, the Wick-eds, and finally the Whackadoodles. She made up our song and told us to be nice to the younger girls and not let the older girls boss us. She read to us from a children's book she had written—"for girls like us," she said—a real published book starring WeiWei on a visit to the orphanage she came from. The ladies in skirts, she told us, deserved our attention.

"Some things they tell you are kind of helpful," she said. "Some of it you know, like that China got so crowded that they couldn't let people have more than one kid, and so parents had to give up their second baby, or maybe they gave up their first kid because they were peasants and needed a son to work in the fields. You've heard all that already." We'd heard it, yes, but to hear it from WeiWei's mouth made it thrillingly ordinary. Her matter-of-factness made us believe those things we'd been told from our earliest ages, explanations delivered in such hushed tones of concern and regret that they sounded as false as fairy tales. When WeiWei said it, it didn't sound like a lie made up to protect us.

"There's some other stuff, though," WeiWei said. "Like what to say to people who ask stupid questions about why you're Chinese and why your mother and father aren't, and how to talk to people who don't like China." Magnificent with scorn in crop top and jel-lies, WeiWei surveyed us, infusing us with her courage. She leaned in; we held our breath. "A lot of people are afraid of China, because it's a huge country and it's basically taking over the world. Well, if China takes over the world, none of *us* has to worry. And you'll get nasty kids at school saying stuff to hurt you, like your mother put you in the garbage, or she was a prostitute, or your parents bought you off the black market from the guy in Chinatown who sells the restaurants their frogs and turtles. They're ignorant. That's bullshit."

"WeiWei," the lady in the skirt objected. "A little at a time. At age-appropriate levels."

"A bullshit detector is appropriate at any age," WeiWei told us. We asked her, what was a prostitute? She grinned and wouldn't say. The next time the lady asked me to draw a picture, I put

WeiWei in it, lifting me to the ceiling. At the last minute, I added a tiny A.J.

"That's A.J.," I told Charlie. A smear of pink waiting her turn to be lifted. A.J. hated pink, so I wanted to see her wear it.

"And who's that?" Charlie asked. By then, I'd heard from WeiWei all about her father. How he'd laughed when she told him what she'd said to that five-year-old girl. Charlie was pointing at a large figure in my picture, a man with curly hair and a wide smile, who was standing next to a bushy green tree. He wore a blue and gold jacket with a matching baseball cap on his head. He looked a lot like A.J.'s father.

"That's my father," I said. "WeiWei said it was okay to put him in."

"Of course it is," Charlie said quickly. "Your father, like your birth father? Do you want to put in your birth mother, too?"

I held on to the top of a kitchen chair and kicked the rungs as hard as my sneakers would let me. "My father, like your husband. Like if you had one. One for both of us," I said.

"Oh, honey," Charlie said, pulling me in for a bony hug. I drew my fists up to my shoulders and locked my legs, but Charlie didn't get it, and my feet didn't leave the floor.

CHAPTER 9

ARI

wanted to go away again the minute I got home from Beijing. Charlie dragged me to the doctor, a total prick who exhaled coffee breath all over my finger while lecturing me about keeping the wound clean. He totally bought my accident story, or if he didn't, he figured it wasn't his problem. I was right to let Charlie come into the room with me to hear what the doctor said. When he asked about the accident, I could tell she wanted to believe me. It was too scary for her to think that I had cut off the finger myself. Next to the doctor, she looked older and grayer; with her hair pushed back, the frown line between her eyebrows looked like a scalpel nick, though the rest of her looked younger. She was wearing skinny pants I hadn't seen before, a big improvement over her baggy old ones. She'd told me that while I was away, she'd hit the gym and been out every weekend with friends. Seeing those pants—black jeans, tight at the ankle—I didn't know how to feel. I was glad, I guess, that she'd been taking care of herself, but it was strange to think of her having a life without me. At the first chance I got, I left her mooning in the apartment with my luggage exploded from one doorway to the next, grabbed the bus, and rode to Pen and Parchment.

Niall was working and so was Katie O.; they grinned when they saw me and motioned to meet in the stockroom. Niall set down the box he was carrying and folded me in a hug that smelled happily of cigarettes and bike sweat. He was wearing his leather vest with the broken zipper and the two patch pockets he had slashed with a Cutco knife that he was trying to sell to a Presidio Heights house-wife who had asked him to verify that his knives were better than Macy's. His streaked hair was shorter and blonder; he'd gone surf-ing, he said, in Southern California, where the water was actually warm, not like the crazy cold of Ocean Beach and Pacifica.

"My God," said Katie. "You look like a stick. Didn't they feed you in China?"

"It was hot," I offered. "But I really loved it. You can't eat in weather like that. All the women carry these frilly umbrellas to keep the sun off their faces. They don't want to get tan. They prize whiteness." Katie laughed. She worked in the framing department. We used to recite the names of the mats people could choose from: stone white, Caribbean sands white, snowdrift white, true white. Prize white. That was the one she pushed on customers who brought in professional photographs of their children, the kids arranged in front of beach houses or vineyards, the teens always guarded, the babies doing that funny gummy smile with a couple of teeth like tiny tablets. I worked in paper and sometimes in blank books. Once in a while, Kurt told me to help Ines in the fine pens department, where Ines grudgingly let me handle a Parker or two.

"Let me see you," I said. I twirled Katie halfway around and admired her new tattoo. She had added a florid hummingbird to the back of her arm, a ballsy choice, since she was kind of pudgy and, over time, that hummingbird might grow to look like a pigeon. The greens made her skin tone look even pinker. She couldn't see it herself except in a mirror. But Katie didn't care. Gaze upon me, was her message to the world. You can do my looking for me.

"You're home early," Niall said. We'd agreed before I left to keep things loose between us.

I told them about the accident. I showed them my clumsy ban-dage.

"Then you need med-i-cine," Katie suggested. "Come back at six o'clock."

I looked at Niall. He was glancing out the stockroom door, but he turned and nodded and said he'd stick around if I returned after Kurt left. I went out the back and walked ten blocks to a taqueria, hoping some of my favorite food would revive me. Starting in Beijing, I hadn't been able to swallow very well. My throat felt tight all the time, like I had buttoned myself into a shrunken blouse or struggled into a hooded sweatshirt that didn't fit me anymore. I ordered chicken and black beans and an *agua fresca*, but after a few bites, I had to push the plate aside. I checked my phone: it wasn't yet time to walk back to Pen and Parchment; Kurt wouldn't leave for another hour. I stared at my hand; the bandage I wore reminded me of the silk cocoons we'd been shown in China, our tour guide narrating the miracle of it all. I wished I could feel my finger aching or throbbing instead of what was coming on: an emptiness, a loneliness, a kind of rising panic, the fleeting sensation of what I had felt in Kunming right before I shut myself in the bathroom.

I checked my phone again. The time had barely budged. I stared out the window and prayed for the hour to pass.

KURT, THE MANAGER, left at five minutes after six. From the corner across the street I watched him lock the front door. I scooted around to the back, and Katie let me in while Niall turned off the rest of the store lights. The summer fog hadn't yet reached this part of the city, downtown and close to the Mission, and late-afternoon sunlight brightened the store near the windows. Pads of creamy paper and pens of every color filled the long shelves, beckoning to be handled. Far back from the windows, the center of the store was dark, but the glass cases up front that housed the fine pens glowed faintly like displays in a museum. I wandered down the aisles looking at the prettiest things, the handmade papers and the silk-covered books. Katie called me over to the children's department, where she had pulled up four stools in primary colors and the low art table we used for rolling joints.

"This is Drue," said Niall. "She works in the art department. This is Ari. She used to work here."

My eyes adjusted to the dim, and I saw a blonde girl standing next to a children's easel. I said hello, and she gave me a tentative smile. She wore a flowered dress over frayed blue jeans. Her face had the petaled look of the unsexed. Behind her, Katie rolled her eyes at me and pointed to the box of a large jigsaw puzzle, the lid showing kittens and puppies, but Niall stayed standing next to Drue until Katie pulled him down and demanded that he start rolling. By the time we were done—and the four of us, laughing, had traced ourselves against the easel and then jostled our way toward the back door—Niall's tanned arm was glued around Drue's shoulders.

Katie O. tripped, cursing. It was after eight, and the fog had rolled in, so that even the fine pens department had disappeared into gloom. In the darkness, I got confused and turned toward the paper department while the others went straight. I heard Katie laughing and calling, "Ari, you dumb shit, where are you going?" I stuck out my good hand and tried to feel my way to the others. The friendly feeling of the earlier hour had collapsed, and I felt the black center of the store yawn wider.

When I had jumped on the bus to escape to Pen and Parchment, I suppose I had been thinking in the back of my mind that I might spend the night with Niall, but in the end, with nowhere else to go, I rode the bus back to the marina and crept into the apartment. Charlie was asleep. She'd left me dinner in the oven. I had a few bites and then stretched out on my bed, strangely wired. Despite my exhaustion, despite the pot we had smoked, I was wide awake, because in Beijing it was the middle of the afternoon. I thought about calling A.J., but she'd be full of questions that would send me stumbling further into the dark. Then I thought of WeiWei, and before I could stop myself, I texted, *hey*, and waited five minutes, then ten, then longer. We hadn't talked for many months— her time was precious, her orbit crowded—but maybe, seeing my name, she'd know, as she always had, that I needed someone to talk to. I sent a second message, just in case she didn't see the first one. The bed was too soft after my thin mattress in China. My eyes hurt from the glare of the screen on my phone. If Charlie had awakened and come out of her bedroom, she would have seen flashing light coming from under my doorway as I checked and rechecked to see if WeiWei had answered. But WeiWei didn't call, and Charlie didn't come looking, and I couldn't rise to tap on my mother's door.

CHAPTER 10

CHARLIE

C harlie waited for the conference room door to open. It was four o'clock in the afternoon; she had booked the room for a client meeting, but her boss, Hal Nugent, the public defender, was in there with two senior deputies who handled felonies. She could see them arguing through the smudged glass. Hal's white shirt was stained and rumpled. Danny and Paula were leaning against the table, Danny drinking from the mug he carried around the office with a picture of his kids holding butterfly nets. Hal stabbed the air and started yelling at Paula, who threw up her hands and yelled right back. The best advocates, Charlie believed, were the ones hard-wired for combat, who brought the fight to the other guy and gave no quarter. She wasn't that kind of lawyer. In her twenty-three years of being a public defender, she had learned how to raise her voice and when to pound the table, but tenacity, not fireworks, was Charlie's secret weapon.

She had realized early on that she would have to figure out how to stand up for herself without imitating the men. It was years ago in a courtroom, before a grumpy law and motion judge. Her supervisor at Legal Aid, a wily lawyer named Marcus with twenty years on Charlie, had brought her along to see how things were done. She stood nervously, ready to speak if asked. The case was routine; the bailiff was yawning, and the courtroom clerk was on the telephone right in front of the bench, but Marcus bulled ahead, loudly complaining, to the enjoyment of the lawyers waiting their turn in the gallery, that the landlord's attorney was willfully obstructing the process.

"You're wasting the court's time," the judge said. He glared down at Marcus, ignoring Charlie. "This is a simple matter, and yet you've managed to make this file"—he looked over at his bailiff, who was standing close to counsel table—"what is that, Fred, six inches?"

The bailiff held up the fat file. "Looks like that to me, Judge," he said.

Marcus grinned. He muttered just loudly enough for the bailiff to hear. "What do you know about six inches, Fred?"

Charlie was shocked. Had she heard him correctly? She expected Fred to turn and tell the judge what Marcus had just said. Instead, Fred grinned back and replied with a brief hand motion for Marcus's entertainment. The judge ruled against them, but Marcus was undaunted. He clapped his hand on the client's shoulder and sent the guy home with fifty bucks from Marcus's pocket.

"What do you know about six inches?" Charlie tried it out a couple of times in her office. She'd be skewered, probably fired from her job and hauled up for misconduct. She decided to watch and learn from the senior women attorneys, but there were only two, and both of them were vicious. Les, her sister, was in trial all the time, but Charlie couldn't duplicate Les's cool command of the courtroom.

Over the years, Charlie had learned to follow her own instincts. She left Legal Aid and became an assistant public defender, choosing, after a few years, to handle parental abuse and neglect cases. Sometimes she was the kid's attorney; other times, she represented a mother or father whose kids might be taken away. Where Hal Nugent might bellow and bluster—to good effect; he cowed a lot of opponents—Charlie mastered the details. She would never be a performer. Instead, "I object," became the essence of Charlie's practice. What she brought to the game was the strength of her convictions. Stubbornness was her method, and indignation her bulwark against cynicism, burnout, humorlessness, and despair.

Les was different. She spoiled for a fight. Before she became a superior court judge, she'd been a cowboy litigator in a small downtown law firm known for its stable of pugnacious trial lawyers. The brain trust, the local courtroom reporters called it. Plenty of people were put off by Les's manner. Some called her arrogant; others assumed she was a lesbian, and most of her opponents at some point had accused her, behind her back or to her face, of being a righteous bitch. Charlie hated such talk. Since childhood, she had looked up to Les for her keen mind and her sense of fairness. It was Les who had inspired Charlie to become a lawyer, even though she knew that Les had more natural talent for the job. To Les, arguing was as necessary as eating a meal or walking. She was hardly aware of her bulldog aggression, and Charlie loved her and pitied her for it, for she felt that Les was unhappy to be alone while Charlie was content. And of course she had Ari.

Now, waiting in the hallway, Charlie heard through the glass the muffled name "Wilson" and suddenly wished she weren't standing by the door. Maybe she could retreat casually back to her office, but Paula had already spotted her and held up a pinch of air. Charlie hugged her sheaf of papers. Her client, Va, was already ten minutes late. She hoped that Va would show up alone, not like at her detention hearing a week ago, when Va had brought her twelve-year-old son to court. "I didn't have no one who could watch him," Va had said. If she brought him again today, he'd have to wait in the lobby. Va's younger son, four-year-old Manu, had been detained by the court and ordered to live with his aunt for a while. Now Va, like any mother, wanted her four-year-old back.

The conference room door opened. Hal and Danny and Paula walked out smiling and joking, so Charlie knew they hadn't really been fighting. Probably Hal had been venting about an overreaching prosecutor or a judge screwing a client.

"Hey, Kong," Hal said. He clapped his meaty hand on Charlie's shoulder. She saved her suits for the courtroom, but she had three loose blazers, one black, one beige, and one navy, which she wore around the office. Today, in her beige jacket, tan shirt, and unbelted brown pants, she looked as washed out as she felt. In the two weeks since Ari had come home, she hadn't said more than a few words to Charlie. They hadn't had a meal together or sat down for a conversation. She was either out all the time or asleep when Charlie left for the office. Charlie was determined to sit her down for a talk.

"Your sister's killing me," Hal said. "On this Wilson Ng case. She's got a bug up her ass, and it's biting me in the balls. What the hell's she thinking?" he turned to ask Danny and Paula. He knew that he shouldn't talk to Charlie directly, that she wasn't permitted to discuss the matter with Les, but he wasn't finished complaining. Hal was trying the case himself with Danny and Paula. Les was the judge assigned to the preliminary hearing on whether the attempted murder case against Wilson Ng, a local plumber, could go to trial. There was a hate-crime charge, too. The media were going crazy.

"She's giving the D.A. all the time in the world to blow this thing out of proportion. So Wilson let fly a couple of racial insults. Who could blame him? The guy was frightened for his life. That's why he picked up the pipe in the first place. His boss was a bigot. A total asshole."

"Riordan's the asshole," Paula said. "He's playing up to the media, appearing with the Pied Piper's family, yammering on about race-blind justice." Patrick Riordan, the district attorney, had assigned the case to a deputy to try until Hal announced that he would handle the defense himself, shaming Riordan into taking first chair for the prosecution.

"Who's the Pied Piper?" Charlie usually made it a point not to learn much about cases in front of Les. After a trial ended, they sometimes talked about the issues, but never before, while a case was pending.

"That's Wilson's boss, the guy he beat with a pipe, but as far as I'm concerned, Wilson's the true victim here. Ronald 'the Pied Piper' Porter, so named because of his alleged connection to a copper-stripping operation that goes on all over the city. They go onto construction sites and strip the pipes and sell the copper.

Porter is one of the middlemen, but the cops haven't caught him yet and the witnesses have clammed up. They had an investigation going. With Porter out of commission, they've pulled the whole thing off-line. All the public sees is an unemployed Chinese guy who beat up his white boss with a pipe. Never mind that his boss abused him for years or is a criminal himself or made the first move against Wilson."

"Did he?" Charlie asked. "Have you really got self-defense?"

Hal shrugged. "If that's all I'm left with, yeah, we got it. But it gets a helluva lot harder if your sister lets that hate-related sentence enhancement stand. For the D.A. to charge this thing as a hate crime, Jesus. You don't stick a Chinese guy with a hate crime against his white boss! Nobody's going to end up happy. We're in the largest courtroom, and there's a crowd out the door. Reverend Yeung and Reynold Low are calling me up every hour." He jerked his head at Charlie. "I bet you've heard from them, too."

Charlie nodded. She had known Reynold since her Legal Aid days when he was an advocate for Chinatown low-income housing. Later, he started the Chinatown Housing Project, which he and Reverend Stanley Yeung had built into a multiservices provider, a key nonprofit that served thousands, not just in Chinatown but all over the city. Charlie had served two terms on the board of directors; her term had ended two years ago, but she still showed up for all the fund-raisers and for Reverend Stanley's legendary dumpling-making parties. She had e-mails from them both asking for her to come to a benefit for Wilson Ng. She had sent back an apologetic message: I can't get involved; my sister's on the case. They knew that, of course. Like Charlie, they were tenacious.

"What a mess," Hal said. He sounded almost sympathetic. "It's warfare out there in our fair city. You could Google map the factions in this thing: Chinatown versus the unions versus me, Hal Nugent, foot soldier in the Norman Conquest." He turned to Danny, who rolled his eyes at the boss. "I'm serious," Hal said. "Afghan warlords are going to start showing up next. Your sister, where does she live?" His shrewd eyes were back on Charlie.

But Charlie wasn't a twenty-five-year-old baby lawyer anymore. "She's a judge," she replied. "She lives on Mount Olympus."

VA FINALLY SHOWED up with her son Joseph in tow.

"Hello, Joseph," Charlie said briskly. Triage was essential to Charlie's work, and Joseph didn't qualify for emergency treatment. He was a young-looking twelve-year-old, with light-brown skin; dark, curly hair; and long black lashes. He wore basketball shorts and high-tops. A heavy baseball glove swallowed his left hand.

"Hi," he said. His smile was uncertain. He reminded Charlie of another child, the son of a mother she'd represented, the mother a drug addict, the son who'd missed months of school. That boy had never smiled, but, like Joseph, he had carried a baseball glove. A present from his missing father, the social worker had said, when the judge commented on the boy wearing the glove in court. Charlie remembered how the boy had refused to remove it.

"Your mother and I have to talk, so I'm going to ask you to wait in the lobby," Charlie said.

Joseph smiled again but shook his head.

"He wants to stay here," Va said. "He can't talk anyway."

"He doesn't speak?" Charlie said. Hadn't he just said hello?

Va's shrug could have meant many things: he was dumb, he was troubled, he was scared, he wanted attention. *We don't have time for this*, thought Charlie.

"Sit here," she said to Joseph, and moved a chair into the hallway. She went back into the conference room and took up her legal pad. The laptop was efficient, but the notepad was friendly. It built trust to let her clients see what she was writing. She wanted them to know that, to her, though at any given time she handled two hundred cases and more, the people she represented were more than numbered files. "I don't see how you manage the caseload," Les often said, which Charlie knew meant, "I don't see why you stay in that awful job."

"Now, Va," she said, "let's go over your situation."

She did not leave Manu in the car for very long, Va insisted. Her boyfriend had wanted to play *pai gow* poker at the card club. It was a Saturday night; they always partied on Saturday night, and Ela, her sister, usually watched the children. But Ela was busy and Joseph was at a friend's and Va figured that Manu would sleep because he was tired. She meant to leave him for fifteen minutes. Twenty minutes, tops. She had only wanted to say hello to her friends and party with her boyfriend and have a quick refreshment. They had rolled down the two front windows but didn't roll down the back ones so nobody could reach in and take him.

"The police report says you left him for over three hours." An August night. Hot in the car, even after dark. A Good Samaritan had called the police around ten.

"Noo, noo," Va said. She was a twenty-six-year-old Fijian-born woman in a bright print dress who lived in the southern part of the city. She had relatives in the area. Va had used to work for San Francisco Unified until budget cuts eliminated her aide position, but she had her own apartment in Section Eight housing, where she lived with Manu and Joseph. Charlie felt drab sitting across from Va and thought she might have something to learn from the younger woman's bright dress and unhurried movements, which showed how comfortable Va was in her large and beautiful body.

"Here is Manu," Va said, showing Charlie a picture. In the photograph, Manu was squashed into a stroller. His feet dangled heavily, touching the pavement. Yellow grocery bags hung from the stroller's handles. Joseph stood beside, holding one handle and hoisting his baseball glove. Manu had darker skin and a broader nose and fuller lips than Joseph. Charlie knew from the file that Manu had a different father, and she wondered if he was black and whether that was frowned upon in Va's community, a Fijian woman with a black American man. Neither father paid child support. Va made a little money working as a home health aide.

"When will he come home?" Va asked. She had visitation rights but only at her sister's house. "Her children aren't very nice to Manu. They call him 'black boy.' They eat all the treats I bring him."

Charlie explained that the court had ordered temporary detention and that Va had to show that she could take good care of Manu before they would let him come home. It was a very serious thing, leaving a child alone in a car. There would be another court hearing in about two months. In the meantime, she was going to help Va get signed up for counseling sessions and parenting class, and Va was going to have to demonstrate to the social worker, who would make a report to the court, that there'd be no risk of danger if Manu was returned to her care. Fortunately, there was no drug or alcohol or gambling addiction involved; if she did as Charlie advised, Va would have a good argument that Manu should come home.

"When?" Va asked. "When? When? Joseph wants him."

Charlie glanced through the window. Joseph hadn't moved. He sat staring at the opposite wall, exactly as she had left him.

"Excuse me for a minute," Charlie said. She went out of the room and got from her office a basket she kept there of children's books and an old Game Boy.

"Would you like to look at these?" she asked Joseph. He picked up the Game Boy then put it down, not wanting to take off his glove.

"I want to see Manu," he said softly.

Charlie knelt beside him. "I'm sure he misses you, too."

"I can take good care of him." His eyes filled. "I shouldn't have gone to my friend's house. If I'd been home, I could've watched Manu."

Charlie gave him a pen and paper. Maybe he'd like to write Manu a letter, she suggested. She went back into the conference room.

"They're very close, aren't they?"

Va nodded. "We are very unhappy without Manu at home."

"What about your boyfriend?"

"He's gone," Va said flatly. He had run off when the police came to look in the *pai gow* club for somebody responsible for Manu.

She wasn't to worry, said Charlie. "I think things will go fine. I'll do everything in my power." She shouldn't have said that. She hadn't exactly promised, but she knew that, to Va, those words sounded like a guarantee that Va would get Manu back. *How can*

you do that job, people always asked her, *representing all those terrible parents?* Everyone is entitled to representation, Charlie would say. It made her angry that women like Va, raising children on their own with no help from the missing fathers, were treated like criminals when they were just trying to get by. It wasn't Va's fault that she had lost her job and had no money for child care and had become a mother at fourteen, far too young to be a parent. Charlie imagined the worst: rape or incest, poverty, no schooling. She didn't have to imagine it. She saw it every day.

"I'll do my best to help you," Charlie repeated. Power worked both ways. The state had a lot of power, but individuals had rights, too. Those better off in society had a duty to protect the rest. Every Saturday, no matter how many cases he had handled the week before, Charlie's father had volunteered at a public health clinic. He wasn't doing surgeries or putting in stents or even checking EKGs but listening to airways and lancing pus-filled boils. Charlie used to go with him and watch his sure, quick hands at work. He took hospital shifts on Sundays as well, exhausting himself with work.

"The social worker is coming for a visit. Have you written down the date?"

"Yes," Va said. "I've written it in my book." She rummaged in her purple handbag. The air had gotten stale; Charlie smelled Va's perfume and sweat and was glad they were almost finished. Va showed Charlie a flowered notebook where she'd written down the date in red marker.

"And you should let Joseph know that, once school starts, the social worker will visit him at school. Plus, she might drop by the house at other times."

"No worries," Va said. She smiled at Charlie. "My Manu is coming home." She found her comb and ran it through her thin hair. Her fleshy upper arm, as firm as a thigh in a wetsuit, reminded Charlie that Va was young. She would have more kids after Manu and Joseph. "My brother's car isn't working, so we got to catch the bus," Va said. "I got a job to go to tonight."

"And you've arranged for somebody to stay with Joseph?" It

wasn't her responsibility to ask that question, but now that she'd talked to him, Charlie wanted to know. She reminded herself that if Social Services had been concerned about Joseph, they would have asked the court to send him to Ela's also.

Va chuckled. "Nighttime," she said. "Any boy sleeps. Do you have kids?"

"I have a daughter," Charlie said. She didn't talk about herself unless a client asked directly, in which case she shared sparingly. It wasn't a matter of trust. It was just good practice to keep her personal life to herself.

"She live with you?" Va asked.

"Oh, yes," said Charlie. "For another few weeks. Then she's off to Bryn Mawr." She stopped herself, feeling foolish. She looked over at the top of Joseph's bent brown head. He was crouched over the paper, writing.

"But you don't work at night," said Va.

"Sometimes," said Charlie. Va looked at her, amused. "From home," said Charlie. "I work from home at the kitchen table."

Va stood and, walking out, motioned for Joseph to follow. He stood up immediately, leaving his paper on the chair.

"Manu," he had written in chains across the paper, row after row in careful script. At the bottom, a single phrase, "I am waiting." It was signed boldly: "Joseph."

"Wait," Charlie said, following them to the lobby. "I'll give you a ride. Wait here for a minute."

OPENING HER FRONT DOOR, she knew right away that Ari was out again. The apartment seemed emptier than when Ari had been thousands of miles away in China, its silence downright reproachful. Charlie hurriedly laced on sneakers and headed out for a walk. The fog had burned off midday but was flowing back in over the bay, blanketing the channel while the shoreline remained in sunlight. She walked one block to the Marina Green, nodding to people she passed whose moving mouths she thought were saying hello until she drew close to them and saw that they were wearing white earbuds and

talking to somebody else. She was far too old to be living in her neighborhood, which was populated by young professionals—*We used to call them yuppies*, she thought. She herself had been a yuppie, without money, and Les, too, with money and all the rest. On weekends, the neighborhood swelled with beautiful singles in their twenties and happy couples in their thirties, and all week long, young mothers in workout clothes pushed twins in strollers outfitted with cup holders and sunshades, like mini-minivans motoring down the sidewalk. The shopping street, which used to have an independent drugstore and a stationery store and a rambling old movie theater, now offered little more than what she could find at the mall. Les had long urged her to move out of her apartment and buy a house on Potrero Hill or in the East Bay, Oakland or Berkeley, where Robyn and David and A.J. lived. "I'll help you," Les had offered, though they both knew that Charlie wouldn't be able to pay her back. But Charlie loved living by the water. Les had a view. Charlie had a connection.

Aaron had thought she lived in the best spot in San Francisco. They used to walk together along the marina and look at the boats that notched the bay and watch the brown pelicans flying low over the water. He had said that he would one day buy a sailboat and berth it just steps from their door. For the first time since she'd rented the apartment, her home hadn't felt like more space than she needed, or too elegant, with its large picture window and arched doorways, for a single woman to claim. She had almost given it up after the Loma Prieta earthquake—she should move to bedrock, Les advised her, and get off that liquefied landfill—but she had stayed and then started the adoption process and then met Aaron, a big, late surprise. She passed another walker pumping her arms to the beat of a private playlist and wished that she, too, had a sound track at her command to drown out all thought of Aaron.

"On your left," a voice called out, and a girl in shorts whizzed past her on a bike, steering with one hand and tapping a message on her phone with the other. Ari's absence gnawed in Charlie's head. It was Ari, not the neighborhood, who had aged Charlie. She felt the wind pick up and chill her, but she pressed on toward the bridge.

She had lost all confidence in how to talk to her daughter—which questions it was okay to ask and what was intrusive. There was too much advice out there full of conflicting rules on how to be a good parent. She was supposed to give her child space but set limits and define expectations. Boundaries made teenagers feel secure, but too many restrictions drove them underground. All teenagers lied—that was part of growing up; but some lied more than others. She wanted to know more about Ari's visit to Kunming, but when she had raised the subject Ari had cut her off.

"I wish you'd drop it," Ari had said. "I'm so done with talking about it."

The outburst had bewildered Charlie. They'd hardly spoken since Ari had come home. Though she was used to clients swearing fervently to one set of facts when witnesses swore to another, Charlie weighed that behavior in its proper context: when people were afraid, they consciously or unconsciously lied to save their skin. But what on earth was Ari afraid of? She wasn't poor, like so many of Charlie's clients. She wasn't alone: she had Charlie and Les and Gran. It would have been better if their family had been larger— she refused to think of it as "more complete"—but it was fruitless to dwell on what she couldn't provide. Still, A.J. had a brother and Becca a sister, and both those girls had two parents, whereas Ari had only one. Even WeiWei had discovered that she had a sister, a wonderful surprise.

A mother walked down the pathway hurrying her toddler, a little boy in a green fleece cap snugged tight against the wind. Charlie stopped to smile at the child, but he plunked to the sidewalk and began to wail. Charlie's smile faded. She knew that her daughter suffered in some deep, unreachable way from not knowing the mother who bore her, but how long was Ari going to cling to that ancient hurt? She watched the pair struggle, the mother lifting the little boy off the pavement by the hand. Charlie shoved her own hands deep into her pockets. She didn't need a touch or a mirror or another person to tell her that her features were as rigid as that mother's retreating back.

CHAPTER 11

ARI

When I was a child, there were three people willing to say the A word to my face. One was my best friend, A.J. One was Gran. And the third one was WeiWei.

In second grade—I was eight; WeiWei was sixteen and soon bound for television glory—the Whackadoodles went on a field trip to Angel Island, California's Ellis Island in the San Francisco Bay. Thousands of Chinese immigrants were processed at the immigration station there, some held for months or even years in detention camps, but in second grade that story didn't matter; we were too young to absorb the history lesson on offer, and although this was another attempt to connect us to our culture, all we knew was that we were traveling by boat to a cool—*See that?*—island.

The day was hot, and there wasn't much shade; after an hour of walking around behind the grown-ups and collecting pebbles in A.J.'s backpack, A.J. and I sat down on a rock and held out our hands for another Jolly Rancher. WeiWei had been doling out the candies to keep us walking.

"You cleaned me out," she said. "I haven't got any more to give you."

We protested and hung on to her pockets. Her cutoffs were frayed at the hems and so short that I was looking straight at bare leg. WeiWei peeled us off and let us try on her big mirrored sunglasses, which slid down our bridgeless noses.

"Do you girls want to stay here with WeiWei for a while?" Robyn asked, smiling down at us from under a baseball cap. She had slathered sunblock on both of us in the morning, but we got browner while Robyn's nose turned pink. I remember the heavy crunch she made on the path when we walked behind her that day, so she must have been wearing her hiking boots. She was quick and springy in her step; the whole family hiked and camped and skied, sometimes taking me with them. Robyn knelt and drew off A.J.'s shirt, and I saw with envy that, underneath, A.J. had on a stretchy tank top like the one that WeiWei was sporting. Charlie let me choose my own outfit every day; I was wearing my favorite corduroy jumper and jelly shoes that were chafing. Charlie hadn't come, but she had packed me a lunch big enough for three, which she did whenever work called her away.

"I don't mind," WeiWei said. "We'll wait down there." She walked us to the water. I showed A.J. how I didn't have to take off my plastic shoes to stick my feet right in the ocean. I passed my lunch around, and we sipped at juice boxes while WeiWei told us the difference between a peninsula and an island.

"Ariadne got stuck on an island," WeiWei said. "You can pretend you're waiting for Dionysius."

"That's her name," A.J. said, pointing at me.

"It's Greek," I said. "She was a goddess."

"She was a troublemaker," WeiWei said, "and a hero." And then she told us the story of Ariadne, how she gave Theseus the thread to find his way out of the labyrinth after he had killed the Minotaur.

"When he sailed away, he took her with him a little ways and then abandoned her on the island of Naxos."

"He left without her?" A.J. asked.

"Abandoned her," WeiWei said. "Took off and left. Just like what happened to us."

"On an island?" I asked. I was confused by what she was saying. Had I, Ariadne, lived on an island at some point? Anything was possible, my past was so unknown.

"Your mother had you, then abandoned you someplace. Where was your Finding Day place?"

"The police station," said A.J.

"A department store," I said.

"I was worse," WeiWei said proudly. "Probably they tried to kill me. Somebody found me in a burlap sack on the roadside." A.J. and I were silent, trying to figure out what she meant. Could a baby breathe inside a sack? What about cars, how come she didn't get run over? I didn't know what burlap was, but I could imagine it, rough and smelly.

"But I screamed so loud that I got found and taken to the orphanage, and then I got adopted. I was oh-ohld," she drew the word out. "Almost as old as you are. It was my last chance."

"Tell that story," A.J. said.

"Did Ariadne die on the island?" I asked.

"No, the god of wine, Dionysius, came and got her. He married her and made her immortal, so it all turned out okay." She lay back and let me arrange her long hair in a fan around her shoulders. "You should read the Greek myths," she said, wiggling her toes in the sunlight. I twisted off her silver toe ring and put it on my thumb.

"Tell your Gotcha Day story," A.J. asked.

But WeiWei shook her head. "Not today," she said.

We couldn't see her eyes behind her mirrored glasses. We lay down next to her, afloat on our island bed.

AFTER THAT, I borrowed from the library all the Greek myth books I could find and put them on the shelf next to the book by WeiWei. I had looked at her book so often I knew every photograph and could recite every word, though she left out the part about being stuffed in a burlap sack. Now I had Ariadne on Naxos, a story I read over and over, imagining myself in her place. When she heard from Charlie what I was reading, Gran sent me a big box of books for Christmas. I got the d'Aulaires' volume with its homemade-looking drawings, and Edith Hamilton—"a Bryn Mawr woman,"

Gran declared—and a stack of arty picture books that played up when the gods were helpful and played down their sex romps. By the time I was nine, I had figured out that when Zeus "fell in love" with a nymph or a maiden, he was bound and determined to rape her. Everyone, it seemed, used sweetened language to talk about ugly subjects. One day, when Gran was visiting from Taipei, where she lived with Grandpa Herbert, I overheard her say to Charlie, "All these foreign adoptions are making the problem worse. There were five thousand children adopted by Americans last year. Five thousand! It makes me sick that they're throwing away their daughters."

"They're poor and uneducated," Charlie said. I was sitting on the staircase at Les's house; Gran stayed there when she came to San Francisco, and they were in the living room waiting for Les to come downstairs. "They don't see any other option."

"That's my point," Gran said. "You're giving them the option. They see all these rich Americans carting away the babies and think, 'Maybe my baby will have a big American future.' So then they abandon her and make her somebody else's problem."

"We don't use that word," Charlie said.

"I didn't mean problem," Gran said. "Ari's not a problem. I mean responsibility. A child that must be raised."

"I'm talking about the A word," said Charlie.

"A, what A? Be clear," said her mother.

"'Abandon,' 'abandonment.' It's a scary word to a child."

"Aha," said Les, coming out of her bedroom. I smelled her jasmine-scented body lotion, which I helped myself to whenever we came over. One time, I snuck home a whole bottle, but Les never called me on it, though she must have known that I took it. "Are you spying on those two?" She leaned over and patted me down across my stomach and my back. "Wearing a wire I see," she said. "I hope you got some good stuff."

If I had asked her to let me stay and eavesdrop, Les would have said yes. We had a little joke between us that we were the only sensible ones in the family. Charlie was full of nervous desire, and Gran was single-minded. As far as I could tell, all Gran ever talked about was getting an education. She lived too far away from us to know much about our daily lives, and I thought she was way too old to see things the way I did. Les and Charlie talked about her all the time and rushed around whenever she came to visit, but a lot of what they said had to do with Gran wanting things from them that they didn't want to give. Husbands came up a lot, as in why it was unreasonable for Gran to demand they marry, and the words *career* and *choices*. I, taking my cue from Les and Charlie, hadn't thought of Gran as somebody who could help me. But now here she was, saying out loud my secret feelings: that I had been abandoned and it was enough to make you sick.

Les smiled at me and toed down the staircase, so she must have guessed that I wanted to hear more of their conversation. But Charlie came to the bottom of the stairs, surprised to see me there, and told me to come down; we were all going out for dim sum. When she brought me into the living room, I saw that Gran's face was creased with disapproval. She had more to say on the subject, and I had a lot to ask her.

THE NEXT DAY I got my chance. Charlie dropped me off at Les's house for a visit with Gran while Charlie ran Saturday errands. It was the first time I was left alone with Gran; later, she told me that she hadn't wanted to be used as a babysitter when I was little, but at nine years old I wouldn't need minding, and my company was finally of interest. Les wasn't home, and as soon as I got there, Gran told me to keep my jacket on; we were going out. I wondered if Gran knew her way around on the city buses as well as Charlie did, and then Gran walked straight for the stairs to Les's garage, lifting Les's car keys from a hook beside the door.

"I haven't driven in months," Gran said with satisfaction. She frowned when she saw dried bird shit on Les's windshield. "Neither has Lesley, I'm bound to say. Get in. How do you get that door up?"

I pushed the button that raised the garage door, pleased that Gran had asked me. Charlie usually did things for me, and Les did things for herself; for a grown-up to assume that I knew what to do made me stand up straighter. I scrambled into the shotgun seat and showed Gran how to push back the driver's seat so she could unscrunch her legs. Sitting close to her, I noticed that she was a lot bigger than I had thought; the steering wheel looked small in her hands, and the top of her head almost reached the sunroof. She wore a loose bracelet of black and green jade and a gold pin of a poodle with a big pearl for the poodle's topknot. Even with Gran sitting down, her large bosom bobbled and wobbled, but the poodle didn't budge.

"In Taipei," Gran said, "one of course has to use a driver. Taking the car for a spin is what I miss most about not living in L.A. That, and my beautiful restaurant." I didn't know anything about a restaurant, but before I could ask her, she slung her arm over the back of the seat and backed rapidly out of the garage.

I don't remember what kind of car Les drove in those days, but I know that as soon as we got going, Gran stuck in a CD of opera music that blared loudly. Did Gran not want to talk to me? I was worried that my being there was a chore or a duty, not for me but for Gran, who clearly had a plan for the day that might or might not include me.

"Turn that down," Gran said. "And tell me how to get to Divisadero."

All my bus riding around the city had given me a pretty good idea of how to direct her, and soon Gran was pulling into a car wash on the corner. She got out and ordered the works then asked me to sign her name on the credit card slip—she didn't have her reading glasses, and how could anyone see such a tiny scrap of paper, no bigger than a tea bag and curled up like a snail?

"Where I come from," she informed the balding Chinese lady behind the cash register, a woman as old as Gran but only half as tall, "we give a proper receipt for payment rendered."

"Maybe you go back. You happy there. No room for you here." The woman pushed her pen in my direction. "You granddaughter. She speak English?"

"Better than you," Gran said. She waited patiently while I

considered. I could tell she didn't care if I took all the time in the world.

"Do you have a pencil?" I finally blurted. I didn't like pens; I used only pencils, a rule I had that worried my teachers but didn't bother Charlie, who excused my peculiarity as "an exploration of identity and boundaries." I didn't know what she meant. I knew only that ink stayed put on the page, but if I wrote in pencil, I could erase everything and start all over again.

"You sign," the woman insisted, and shoved her pen at me again. "Hurry up," she said. "People waiting." Behind us in line, several people inched forward. Gran calmly opened her handbag and took out a slim leather case.

"You may use this," she said. I opened the case and slid out a pen and a matching mechanical pencil. I'd never seen one so beautiful before. I had a collection of mechanical pencils that I kept in my pencil box with my yellow No. 2s, but this one was silver and heavy in the hand. I bent my head to write.

"Mrs. Betty Kong Hsu," Gran instructed.

"What you doing?" The woman was practically screaming. "This a credit card slip! Use pen! Use pen!" The girl in line behind us offered me her Sharpie, but Gran refused it while I wrote Gran's name as clearly as I could, running out of room by the *y* in *Betty*.

"No good!" the woman said. She ran around the counter and out into the lot, yelling to the crew in broken Spanish, but it was too late: Les's car had been sudsed and waxed and polished. The foreman twirled a red rag in the air. Gran sailed past the yelling woman and handed the man a ten-dollar tip as if bestowing a jewel on a subject. The car smelled of pine. The windows sparkled.

"That's more like it," Gran said. She pointed the car west, and we drove out to the Great Highway and then along Ocean Beach, where the sand blew across the road and we saw the waves crashing. Once on the freeway, Gran cruised in the middle lane. I didn't ask her where we were going. I could tell that she didn't have a destination; she wanted speed and the open road and enough traffic so that she could flash her lights at a trucker to let him know he could pass, or give a thumbs-up to motorcyclists speeding by. The CD ended, and Gran ordered me to put in another. The pen and pencil were back in their case in her handbag, but Gran said to wait; I could look at them again later.

After an hour of driving, first south and then back toward the city, we headed downtown. Gran parked in the big lot near Union Square and asked me where we should go for lunch. I didn't know how to answer. Charlie and I rarely ate out.

"Chinatown?" I asked. I knew how to walk there because every year the Whackadoodles met at the Grant Avenue gate to watch lion dancers or eat special cakes or buy willow or forsythia or flowering quince branches for Lunar New Year and the Lantern Festival and Qingming and the Moon Festival too. None of which, Les pointed out to Charlie, they had ever bothered to celebrate growing up in Palos Verdes.

"Oh, it's so dirty there," Gran said. "Isn't there somewhere better?" She marched into a fancy hotel, talked to a man, and came out. We went for *steak frites* at a white-tablecloth restaurant.

"We are not Chinatown Chinese," Gran told me over lunch. "We come from Hangzhou, a beautiful city, and we speak Mandarin, not Cantonese. The people who live in Chinatown came from mostly one part of China. Through no fault of their own"—she speared a piece of meat—"their ancestors were uneducated, and they speak a different language." I already knew the difference. A Mandarin tutor came weekly to Whackadoodles to teach us driblets of vocabulary and once in a while a song. Only the girls who went to the private Chinese American school or had after-school immersion could write characters and say whole sentences. One girl attended a public elementary school with a Cantonese-language program, but none of the rest of us did. Adoption was one thing; class was another. We might visit Chinatown, but we weren't *of* Chinatown. Cultural heritage had its limits, and that, too, obstructed me. Here I lived in a city full of Chinese, but I was still an outsider, set apart from most.

"My father belonged to the intelligentsia," Gran continued. "He was a very important doctor who owned a hospital in Shanghai. He was rich for a while, and he took care of the wives of all the important officials."

I worked on my steak and fries. Each time I had met her on her annual visits, Gran had told me about her father, ob-gyn to the stars, whom everyone in Shanghai in the 1930s and '40s knew as Dr. W. W. Wu, the world's most charming man. She went on boasting while I waited for my chance. If I didn't speak up soon, she'd be on to Bryn Mawr College, and how Charlie and Les had refused to go there, but how I, her only granddaughter, would make the better choice because Bryn Mawr would be perfect for me: it was filled with brilliant women.

"My father made sure that Rose and I had the best education," Gran said. She paused to spit out a piece of gristle and then move it, unembarrassed, to the edge of her plate.

"I wonder who my father is," I said.

"Ha," Gran said. "Wouldn't we all like to know." She looked at me across the table, the first time she had studied me all morning. I was wearing a dress that I hated, scoop-necked and pretty, but I was too small to fit into the teenage clothes I was dying to wear.

"Well," Gran said, "in asking that question, I see you're finally old enough to engage in a real conversation."

I nodded, thrilled that Gran could see past my peach-colored dress. *She* wasn't going to nervously change the subject.

"I guess my parents abandoned me," I said. The A word in my mouth felt dangerous and thrilling.

"They did indeed," Gran said, "and a very wicked thing it was, too. They had their reasons, as I'm sure people have insisted, but as far as I'm concerned, no reason is good enough. I was a nurse, you know." I was surprised; I hadn't known that, either. "I saw a lot of babies being born, some good and some damaged. You do what you can for the damaged ones, and you don't throw away the good. It's a human duty to raise and educate your children, or if you can't do it, you ask your family to step in. Your parents should have known that. No matter how poor they were, they should have found a way.

My father did, even in wartime. When the Japanese invaded and bombs were falling and China was in chaos, my father took care of us and made sure we got schooling, with tutors during the war, and then on to college. So no, I don't excuse your parents."

I nodded, dumbly. It was and it wasn't exactly what I'd wanted to hear.

"Nor will I excuse you if you don't make something of yourself. Look at you. I never saw a brighter button. You're smart as a whip and full of fire. Never mind about that mother who abandoned you or that father who didn't provide. You belong to the Kong family now. You're *Han* Chinese; your ancestral home is Hangzhou. You've got a huge advantage over all those other girls adopted by Americans"—by "Americans," she meant white people, I guessed. "Your mother is Chinese. Nobody has to know you're adopted."

"But that's all we talk about in Whackadoodles," I said. "They want us to say how we feel about being adopted." Just that week, I'd been encouraged in playgroup to write a letter to my birth parents. While the other girls were writing, I'd escaped to the bathroom.

Gran's jade bracelet clinked against her plate. I thought of the sound that Charlie's heavy key ring made when she tossed it every evening into the cloisonné bowl on the altar table in the hallway. Sometimes our house seemed to me like a kind of jail that I needed to escape from.

"In China," Gran said, "adoption is no big deal. Children are passed from family to family according to supply and demand. If one man has three daughters and his cousin has none, the first man will send one of his daughters to help take care of the cousin. Or if the parents can't take care of all of their children—maybe the mother is sick or the father hasn't got enough to provide for everyone—another family member offers to take an extra one or two in. Everybody did it, whether rich or poor. That's how it used to be, and it made a lot of sense. What's the expression?"—she laughed—"a win-win situation."

I remember how she looked in our booth in that grand restaurant. Her face wasn't old but soft and mobile, her mouth moving pleasantly and her eyes bright and inviting. Her voice was low and forceful, and the way she spoke to me without apologizing for causing me pain or recasting the dire circumstances of my birth into a feel-good children's story fell as warmly on me as the square of sunlight that moved across our table. She held my gaze steadily as we talked and ate.

"Can you think of yourself that way?" she said. "Simply transferred from one family branch to another?"

"Is that how it worked in your family?" I wanted confirmation that what she described was real. But Gran frowned and didn't answer. Had I asked the wrong question? I didn't want her to clam up the way other adults did, so I hurried on to reassure her. "I don't mind being adopted," I said. "I like the way you describe it. It's very Chinese, switching parents."

"Good," she said. I saw gold at the back of her mouth when she rewarded me with a smile. "It wasn't only the Chinese. In the old days, everyone made adjustments. You'll read about it soon enough in Austen. *Mansfield Park*. You have such pleasures ahead."

"I like Greek myths. You picked out really good books for me," I added.

She waved away my manners. "The daughters got such ill treatment by the gods," she said. "Abandoned, raped, blamed, punished. Always some drama and always the victim." She leaned across the table. "Father taught me: don't feel sorry for yourself. You have advantages. Thank God you turned out as smart as my daughters. At least there's that. When a child can't keep up— What's the matter? You look like one of Rose's boys who's lost again at tennis."

"I don't like it when people tell me I'm lucky."

Gran hooted. "I'd hardly say that," she declared.

WE STOPPED AT a gas station on our way back to Les's. Gran taught me how to pump the gas and how to check the oil. I didn't think that filling the tank to exactly where it was when we started out that morning would fool Les, but Gran assured me that Les wouldn't notice that her car was clean and her odometer higher.

Her daughters, she said with annoyance, thought more about other people than they did about themselves. Grandpa George Kong had been like that, and to what end? All his do-gooding wore him right out.

We made ourselves a pot of tea and called Charlie to come pick me up. While we were waiting, Gran let me rummage through her handbag. I didn't scrabble right away for the mechanical pencil. I thought if I didn't show too much interest, Gran might let me have it. I had noticed that the things I wanted most—cooler clothes, harsher music, better answers to my unanswerable questions—adults tended to withhold for my own good. I took out a handkerchief that Gran said Rose had embroidered and a thick book and a pair of Chinese scissors, the kind with short, sharp blades like a mouse pirate's dagger and big, looped handles like the ears on Mickey Mouse. We didn't own anything like them, and they looked playfully harmless; but when I stuck the point into my open palm, I could tell that if I pushed harder, I would puncture a hole in my hand.

"Can I have these?" I asked. In my art box at home, I had only safety scissors.

"You may not," Gran said. "I need those."

"Can I have this then?" I drew out the leather case and sniffed it deeply. It smelled not of leather but of Gran's complicated scent—deep, rich, and potent. Its fold-over flap was imprinted with faded initials; I picked out a *G* and a *K*. My hand closed around the case. I told myself that I deserved a reward for spending all morning with an old person.

Gran held out her hand, and I reluctantly gave it to her.

"George Kong, your grandfather, was a very precise man. He always had the instruments he needed. I was never in the operating room with him, but the nurses told me they never saw such elegant work. Of course, Father was better. He had the touch. His father and all his uncles were Hangzhou tailors, and he learned to sew when he was a little boy. Look at my hands." She held up her hands for my admiration. I had my eyes on that case—I had to make it mine. "Big enough to catch a baby, but they didn't let the nurses do that. You may look again," she said, handing it to me.

I drew out the precious contents and tucked the case into my lap. My hand had turned into a magnet—first I tried the pen and then the pencil, which fitted my hand neatly and lodged along the raised bump on my middle finger. Gran handed me a notepad, and I wrote my name over and over with lead so fine it might have been made of rabbit whisker—at Whackadoodles that week, our Chinese-brush-painting teacher had passed around a brush with just one delicate whisker. *If she gives them to me*, I thought, *I won't tell Charlie because she might want them as badly as I do.* She missed her father—she kept his hat in her closet; I had tried it on during one of my long snoops—and I worried that if I showed his things to her, Charlie might suggest that we split them between us. She was always going on about the virtues of sharing. I hated sharing, unless it was with A.J., who liked the pencils I collected and who shared her stuff freely—her hair clips and her gum and her father.

Gran leaned across the love seat toward me. The powder she used made her face look very white. Scooped flesh pouched under her appraising eyes. I wasn't afraid of her, and I could see that my boldness pleased her.

"In wartime," she said, "Father taught us: 'Ask for what you want but take what you need.'" She sat back. "Rose never understood the distinction."

I hesitated. Was I supposed to ask or take? It was a test. Gran waited. I put the pen and pencil back in their case and set it on the coffee table.

"I'd like to have something of Grandpa George's," I said. "Can I have that?"

"Quite right," Gran said. "As badly as you wanted it, you didn't need it, did you? Need is when your life depends on it. When you think you might die or lose everything you've worked for. Need means *there are no other options.* Yes, you can have it." She watched me snatch it up again. I didn't want her noticing that it wasn't exactly wartime, so her rules didn't apply. I wrapped the case inside my wadded-up jacket and went home with Charlie. Within a week, I'd given the pen to A.J. The pencil I treasured, never telling Charlie where I'd got it. It used lead as fine as capillaries that I bought with money I took from Charlie's wallet. I couldn't bear down hard, but it served its purpose well. Whatever story I wrote with that pencil, I could rub out completely and start all over again.

CHAPTER 12

ARI

A. J. flew home and came straight over, grabbed my hand, and inspected the bandaged finger.

"I've been worried. Does it hurt? Is it healing?"

I had readied myself for her visit with a morning cigarette and a pull of vodka and by dressing in boots and a man's sweater, heavy as chain mail, in black from head to toe; but for all my armoring, I felt twin constrictions in my throat and my belly. "It's nothing," I said, and pushed up my sleeves to show her my forearms, untouched by cigarette or razor. An odd gesture, I could tell by the look on her face. I didn't know why I showed her. I'd never cut or burned myself. I didn't purge or binge or pull out my hair, though there were times I wished I did. We knew two dozen girls between us who had fallen sick and dragged themselves, step by baby step, down those elegantly prescribed, formal pathways of destruction, but I was the only one who had used a butcher knife.

"Let me look," A.J. said. I waggled the finger at her, then flapped my whole hand like a bird around her head looking for a place to alight on her messy topknot of hair. The bun made her taller than me, but we were the same size and had the same urchin build, with hips as straight as a drain pipe. We swapped clothes easily, and people had often asked when we were little if we were twins, until they looked again and saw that A.J. had a white mother, and I a Chinese one. When David took us to Cal women's basketball

games and then to Top Dog for kosher dogs with an extra bun, A.J.
and I had faked being sisters—"You're the freak of the family" and
"I'll race you home!" The charade meant that I could get away with
calling David "Dad." He didn't mind. He didn't pay it any attention, but when Robyn came with us, she crouched and corrected
me, each time giving me a long hug and a longer explanation of
how she knew it was hard for me, but it wasn't fair to let me delude
myself. Maybe not "delude." Maybe not "You know damn well he's
not really your father." I'm not crediting her kindness, her carefully chosen words, her hugs of some real comfort, but her basic
message stung. Each time she made me take back the "Dad" for a
"David," she drew the line darker between the other Whacks and
me. I wanted A.J. and me to be different in the same way, but I
was way out to sea with a Chinese surname and a single mother.
I know that's crazy, that a Chinese girl adopted into a Chinese
family would be more unnatural than one with white parents, but
that's how it felt—as if I were on a leaky boat chugging in the
wrong direction, looking back at the other girls firmly anchored
along the shore. I finally cut out the "Dad" stuff. I cut out "Mom,"
too, and took up "Charlie."

"I'm fine," I repeated. I retreated to the kitchen to have a drink
of water. My mouth felt ashy, the water body-warm, like a sip of
blood in my throat. A.J. followed. I could feel her concern like a
needle in my neck. "I look like shit because I lost my tan," I said. "I
hide all day in the P and P stockroom waiting for Niall and Katie to
get off work."

"Are you guys back together?"

"God, no. I'm so over Niall. What about Jamie?"

"He left for school already. We're definitely taking a break." A.J.
found the bread and put two pieces in the toaster. She took out the
honey and put the water on to boil.

"Uhh," she said, stretching. "Let's go out and do something. I
want to *walk*. I sat on that plane for *hours*." She was always happier outside, moving, and I guessed that she didn't want to run into
Charlie, who might start interrogating her about the accident.

"Why do you hide in the stockroom?" A.J. asked. "Don't they still love you at P and P?"

I tried to face her. She wore a coral-and-silver pendant on a black cord around her neck and a new white blouse I'd never seen before—summery, billowy, gauzier than the bandage I had to change every night. That was good: she was not the old A.J. Not the A.J. who'd been with me when I fissured apart in Kunming. That A.J. lived in a Cal T-shirt and canvas flats and pinched her bottom lip when she was thinking about a boy, and if she weren't here, I wouldn't have to dwell on the last time we'd been together. I watched her glance again at the big red wall clock and reach up to her heavy bun. She pulled out the fastener and quickly retwisted her hair into a rope, then wound it and secured it, a sailor tying off a line. Seeing her sweep through the familiar gesture—elbows in the air, hands flying—opened a door in me; the cold flooded through.

She froze, her hands above her head. "What's wrong? Are you okay? Does it still hurt? Can you take something for it?"

I let her lead me to my bedroom, where she mounded up clothes, books, crumpled wrappers to make room for me on my bed. I lay down, fetal, the mattress like a dog's bed hollowed out for my curl, the pillow already dented by my oily head. For two weeks, I had faked my way with Charlie, making her miserable with my glowering resentment that she and Les had ordered me home from Beijing. With Niall and Katie, I'd lived each day for six o'clock, and in between those bouts of bravado, I'd huddled in my bed, too heavy to eat or shower. The room had gone suddenly black. I kept my eyes squeezed shut and pinned myself to the feel of the pillowcase against my face. *Bed, bed, bed,* my heart was drumming, saying the word, a child's word, a fairy-tale incantation to tell myself that I was here, now, where I could manage in the safest, most known-to-me existence. I wasn't in Beijing, that teeming city, staring at the faces of strangers who might be kin, or at the orphanage with A.J., or in the hotel bathroom in Kunming with the kitchen knife in my hand.

"It's okay," said A.J., rubbing circles on my back. She started talking a steady stream, telling me little stories, the beat of her voice calming me the way it had in high school when I'd drunk too much or fought with a boy or argued with Charlie about why I hadn't come home. There'd been two more tour groups after I'd left, she said, and Willow had dropped out of the final tour to take care of her father, who'd been injured at the bus station where he worked. Robyn said that A.J. could go in Willow's place, and so she did it all over again, the exact same trip we'd made in July—Beijing; Xi'an; Chengdu to see the giant pandas, those big, spoiled babies. We had a joke between us that with their specially trained nurse-maids and white-coated doctors and government-sponsored habitat re-creators, the baby pandas had a sweet life compared to a million orphans. A.J. said she enjoyed redoing the trip; she could take in more history and her Mandarin was getting better. A cute little girl named Stacey had tripped on the Great Wall and cut her lip; she had needed stitches. I didn't move when she said that, but I could tell by the way A.J.'s hand stopped its circles that she was thinking, as I was, of the emergency room in Kunming.

"I went back to Beijing from Chengdu," she said. "I didn't go on any of the orphanage visits."

"But you did the final dinner," I said into my pillow. I rolled over and found I could meet her worried gaze. "Didn't want to miss that extravaganza."

"There was one girl, I felt so sorry for her. She was fourteen and really big. I gave her the biggest outfit we brought—X-X-X-L—and it didn't fit her. She had huge boobs—remember Bree's sister?" Bree was a Whackadoodle girl whose older sister, Ireland, had a pair so big that I told Bree they could have their own reality-TV show, and when her mother found out, I was banned from her house until Ireland left for college.

"This poor girl could barely squeeze into the top, and the pants didn't fit her at all. You should see the group photo. It looks like an angry giant stomped in to terrorize the village."

The final dinner, a banquet with live entertainment, was a tour highlight. It was held the night before the group split up to go on their homecoming visits to their individual orphanages. Before dinner, the guides handed out red pajamas for the girls to wear—tourist clothes, not worn by anyone in China except for visitors pretending to go native. You might as well put on a coolie hat and a pigtail if you thought that red pajamas made you authentic, but when I was little, I desperately wanted a pair of those pajamas. The Whackadoodle girls gathered for the Lantern Festival every year—Monkeys and Sheep and Rabbits and Roosters, all of us carrying glowing lanterns into the wintry dark. We wore our hair in pigtails twined with white blossoms. Robyn got the idea that we should dress alike, so she sent all the parents a link to a Web site where they could buy red pajamas.

"What do you think?" Charlie asked Les. We were in our kitchen, where Charlie was making lunch.

"I'll pay with my own money," I said. I was maybe seven. I didn't have any money, but I thought that might persuade her.

"I think it's bizarre that all these white families celebrate Chinese holidays that hardly any Chinese Americans pay attention to."

"We didn't—we were supposed to blend in. But isn't it better now, with people embracing Chinese culture? Adoptive families are part of that; they want their daughters to know those traditions."

Les snorted. "Merchants figured out it's good for business and got everybody excited. I'm glad we grew up without it. Remember Christmas? Christmas was the best. Dad dressed up like Santa Claus—"

"—and Ma cooked a goose and made stuffing with chestnuts. We should make that this year." Charlie smiled wistfully at me. "I wish you were old enough to still hang a stocking."

"Ma kept the Santa thing going forever for us," Les said. "Why did you have to ruin it so early for Ari?" I was four when Charlie sat me down and told me. I wasn't supposed to tell A.J.—my first official secret. Les was more mad about it than I was. She loved the sneaking around. She spent weeks choosing things for my stocking and wrapped my big presents in special Santa paper. Charlie told me that it didn't matter that Santa didn't exist because the important thing was that the spirit of Christmas was real—another myth, another likely story—but Les insisted on putting out milk and cookies and carrots. She nibbled the carrots before I came downstairs in the morning. If she couldn't have Santa, she still wanted the reindeer.

"I had to tell Ari," Charlie said. "It's kind of a balancing act. You want them to have the fun of it, but you don't want them to lose trust in you when they find out that Santa is all a big lie."

"Do you have to do everything the books tell you? Where does common sense come into it? Why not let kids be kids?"

"Like you have so much experience in the field," Charlie retorted, and they were off again on one of their squabbles. As little earthquakes are said to let off pressure so the Big One never comes, their grumbling at each other staved off a real fight, though it's not true that small tremors guarantee safety. That's another myth.

I'm sure I begged and pleaded, but Charlie and Les ruled against the pajamas. No doubt they used words like *stereotype* and *offensive*, words I heard later and for years to follow. "You don't need a costume to prove you're Chinese," Les said. The other girls avoided me in my limp skirt and red sweater, except for A.J., who stuck loyally by my side. The group looked unforgivably adorable, forty-some girls lined up like matching dolls, while I was the troll who ruined the photo, scowling into the camera, my mouth a dangerous fault line. If WeiWei had been there, she would have taught me a new swear word. Instead, I stomped on Becca's paper lantern and tore mine to shreds and broke the stick in two.

"I felt sorry for that girl," A.J. said, "too big for her red pajamas. She hated the whole thing. She refused to go to dinner."

"She's a lucky girl," I said. "Didn't anybody tell her?"

"Ha. You're feeling better."

I sat up and nodded.

"Let's go then. Up! We're doing Steep Ravine." A.J. hauled me from my bed.

WE RAIDED THE KITCHEN for cheese and crackers and stuck a couple of water bottles into a backpack. A.J. bought apples on our way to the bus stop. Steep Ravine was a trail we knew well from hiking excursions with David and Robyn. We caught a bus that took us across the Golden Gate Bridge, and a second bus to the Pantoll parking lot on Mount Tamalpais. From there, we would hike down to Stinson Beach.

We started walking. A.J. reported on her family—her brother, Brent, David's son by his first marriage, working his first real job at a start-up in Boulder, and her crazy uncle Saul, who was off looking at rocks in Ecuador and Honduras. A.J. wanted to visit him next summer, though she said she'd be glad to work with orphanage groups again. The trail left the road and sloped down through dense forest of pine and redwood, which blotted out the weak midday light. A.J. trudged happily; this was the very best cure for jet lag. She wouldn't go to bed until the sun went down, she said, so she wouldn't wake at three in the morning, worrying about how, as a lowly freshman, she would get the classes she wanted. She was a gnat on the undergraduate food chain, a lower-than-a-gnat, a larva. I breathed in moist air, smelled the loam of the forest floor. Every few steps, my sneakers slipped on wet leaves and tree roots. The thick, yellow bodies of banana slugs stapled the path. The wind high above us made a rushing noise through the trees.

"My dad saw WeiWei on TV," A.J. said. "Getting some kind of award for East-West relations."

WeiWei on TV again. I was glad I'd missed it. For more than a year, we had heard her on the radio, seen her on the news. Bought *People* magazine and pored over the pictures. WeiWei had a sister. The Whackadoodles were abuzz. A Swedish couple who had adopted a Chinese daughter had learned about WeiWei from her TV show. It wasn't on in the U.S. anymore, but old episodes were still playing in other countries. They had contacted the producers to say that their fifteen-year-old daughter looked a lot like WeiWei. They sent photographs to prove it. The girl, Anna, was much younger than WeiWei, but she had come from the same orphanage. Was it possible they were related? It wouldn't be the first time that a countryside family gave away more than one daughter. WeiWei was in Guangzhou, filming a documentary about her orphanage and her journey. She invited Anna and her parents to join her. Together, they arranged for a Chinese lab to test their DNA. The lab confirmed that the girls were full sisters. WeiWei had written a memoir. A movie was in the works.

"Let's call her," A.J. said. "Maybe she'd like to hear about Beijing."

"Let's not," I said. WeiWei hadn't bothered to answer any of my texts. I'd gotten one e-mail from her assistant assuring me that WeiWei would be in touch at some point.

"At least let's call her before school starts," A.J. said. "It's coming up so fast. When do you sign up for classes?"

"I haven't a clue." I gripped the backpack at my shoulders; its weight was beginning to drag. "I don't want to go at all." She had heard me say it before. I hadn't applied anywhere else because Gran was paying, as long as I went to Bryn Mawr. Gran had practically filled out the application. All I did was defecate a bogus essay and upload the document and push a few buttons. My essay topic? My illustrious, colorful, famous, talented, tragically persecuted great-grandfather: Dr. W. W. Wu, denizen of Shanghai, International Concession.

"If you didn't want to go there, why didn't you tell them?" Sometimes A.J. could be as absolute as her mother.

"Don't take their side," I said.

"Stick up for yourself," said A.J. "That's what WeiWei would tell you."

"I don't need you, or her, giving me advice. She's got somebody else to worry about now. I can take care of myself."

In the half-light of the forest, I saw A.J. cast two quick little glances my way.

"She's just busy is all. She'll want to see us next time she comes to San Francisco."

"She can't stand not being in the spotlight. It's like the rest of us don't exist."

A.J. paused to look up into the redwoods. "I wonder what it's like, finding out you have a sister."

I shook my head and walked on. WeiWei Chang. The Girl Who Put Her Hand Up.

THE TRAIL DROPPED steeply through the trees. A creek ran beside us; in late August, the water was low, but ferns grew thickly along its banks, and moss grew bright on big logs and downed branches. I tried to focus on the beauty around me, but it jumped and wavered, a jerking curtain of browns and greens. The backpack was heavy with apples, water, and wine, a bottle I had smuggled from Charlie's closet. I felt sweat spread at the small of my back and tugged at the straps again.

"I'll carry it," A.J. offered.

"No, I've got it." She had noticed that I was walking with my left hand raised in a wave to the forest. When I let my hand dangle, the blood expanded my fingertips until they felt like they would burst.

"Let me take it for the ladder," she said. The ladder was coming up, a ten-foot climb straight down to where the trail continued.

"You don't have to take care of me," I said. "I get really tired of you mothering me."

"Well, you're not taking care of yourself. That much is obvious."

"If it's so obvious, why do you keep bringing it up?"

"You're leaving soon. I want to know you'll be all right."

"Maybe I should leave now."

"Maybe you should," she said.

We walked in sudden silence, stunned by our exchange. Ugly words jumped into my mouth, but before I could speak, A.J. made me madder.

"Your mother is really worried about you."

"I don't care. I don't want to hear it."

"I don't believe you," A.J. said. "You're better than that. You do care about your mother. She only wants to help you."

I grabbed her arm. "It will kill me if you start talking to me like that."

She shook herself free. "You need to talk to someone—if not me, then somebody else. You're right; I can't look after you, and nobody else can, either. What's going on with you? Why did you do that in Kunming? We'd been to the orphanage before. It wasn't so awful, was it? The kids have clothes, they have food, they get attention. You need to get over it, or you'll drive yourself crazy. Please, Ari, go to your mother or Les or your gran or somebody who can help you. Stop hanging out at Pen and Parchment. You're really scaring me, and I don't like it."

I ran. I should have dropped the backpack with its bouncing water and the bottle of wine like a brick between my shoulders. Twenty feet ahead of me, the trail dropped into the ladder. The only way was down, and I flung myself onto it and stepped blindly, my feet slipping on the wet rungs, my left hand unable to grip. I missed the last rung; I fell on my back and cracked against the bottle. A.J. was yelling, sliding down the ladder, oh God, oh God, oh God. It was just like Kunming, the whole drama repeating itself to remind me just how fucked up I was. The backpack, she cried, was dark and soaked through with something, and she didn't dare move me, and her cell phone had no signal. When I finally could move, the wet turned out to be water. I was badly bruised, but the wine bottle hadn't broken. We sat in the middle of the trail, A.J. sobbing. I didn't speak. Maybe twenty minutes later, a young couple came along and fed us trail mix and walked us gingerly to the beach.

As we waited for the bus, A.J. quietly said: "I want you to tell Charlie what happened in Kunming. That it wasn't an accident, that you cut off your own finger. I don't want to see you again until you've told her."

I stared ahead. I pictured A.J. in her red pajamas, singing in Mandarin the song that our teacher had taught us, a song about happy children that we accompanied with hand motions and the stomping of little feet in matching Chinese slippers. *Clap, clap, clap. Stomp, stomp, stomp. Clap, stomp, clap, stomp, twirl in your red pajamas.* We weren't children anymore.

I WENT STRAIGHT to Pen and Parchment. I was hungry by then; it was four o'clock in the afternoon, but I didn't have any money, so I sat on a box in the corner of the stockroom and shook out a cigarette.

"There's no smoking in here," said a mocking voice. Kurt, the manager, stood over me, looking down. I quickly got up, but Kurt didn't step back. I felt my heels pressing against the box behind me. Kurt looked me over, his pupils unnaturally contracted, as if he were in a bright room and I was in a dark one. I could see the rims of his contact lenses, the plastic disking his eyes.

"You've been hanging around here," he said. "Weren't you supposed to go off to college? Improve your mind? Make something of yourself?"

I had no answer. I couldn't breathe very well. He had his hands in the pockets of a new leather jacket, an attempt to look Niall's age, ten years younger. He constantly made fun of Niall, calling him "surfer boy" and "Master Niall." Kurt had colored his hair—the gray that before had speckled his beardlet and his sideburns had been replaced by an even sheen of black.

"You can't be looking for Niall," Kurt said, "now that he's got someone else in his pocket. So what do you want?" He shifted and let a little space come between us. Katie and I had had a rule that we would never be alone in the stockroom with Kurt. He never tried anything, but he checked us out every day, dropping remarks about a skirt one of us was wearing or the color of our tights. He didn't get why I was with Niall. "You're not blonde enough for him," he'd said, and I'd felt the scrape of his envy.

But I found, staring back at him, that I wasn't afraid to be alone with Kurt. He was harmless, I could see that, a narrow man in a narrow job whose own fantasy life didn't take him further than a grope and a fiddle between the boxes with any girl. His leer was more comical than creepy.

"I'm not going to college," I said. It was as simple as that. I had passed through a door I didn't even realize was there. "I need to make some money so I can get back to Beijing." I had no idea what

I'd do when I got there, but I pictured myself in my room, or walking the crowded streets, or drinking Mrs. Du's soup with the taste of dark greens in my mouth. "Have you got anything for me? Anything you can think of?" It was my turn to leer at him.

He looked nervous to be faced with what he had halfheartedly fished for, so I suggested we leave and go someplace to talk.

"Wait here," he said, and he backtracked into the store. Katie appeared, frowning and squeezing her forearms.

"What are you doing?" she asked.

"I'm taking Kurt out for a drink."

"That's not a good idea. You should go get something to eat"—she pulled her wallet out of her backpack and tried to give me some money—"and come back here in a little while. I'll go out with you. You don't need to go with him."

I shook my head. I knew what I was doing.

"Jesus," said Katie. "Don't be stupid. If you need a place to stay, you can come to my house. Drue and Niall won't be there. They're going to Oakland tonight."

"Did they move in?" I said. The upper shelves, I noticed, were full of neon-colored boxes—green, harsh yellow, and a screaming pink that offended me all of a sudden. We weren't supposed to put heavy things on top. I grabbed the stepladder, dragged it over, and set my foot on the bottom rung. Steep Ravine had sent me sprawling, but I was going up and no one was going to stop me. Katie grabbed the ladder and gave it a shake. I swore at her.

"Well, fuck you, too," Katie panted. "You're really crazy these days, you know that? You said you wanted the room, but the first of the month's coming up, and you haven't claimed it. My housemates offered it to Niall, that's all. He hasn't decided yet."

I kept my eyes on those boxes. "Go ahead and give him the room. I'm going back to Beijing. Why would I want to live with you? All you do is work in this stupid store and put ugly tattoos all over your ugly body."

Katie slammed out of the stockroom. The hanging lights swayed above me. I went up rung by rung. Kurt came in and pulled off his jacket. I turned around to face him. I let him reach for me while I clung to the ladder. When I opened my eyes, I saw Niall looking in, his face white and passive against the dark of the doorway. I stayed right where I was. I had only to get the money. I'd stopped thinking of anything else.

CHAPTER 13

CHARLIE

Ari didn't come home that night. Charlie texted and called but got no answer. She tried not to worry, telling herself that it wasn't the first time that Ari had spent the night over at a girlfriend's house or with a group of kids crashed on somebody's floor, though who those friends might be, Charlie was uncertain. Now that A.J. and Robyn had returned, she hoped that Ari would put Beijing behind her and turn to matters at hand. There were only ten more days before Ari left for college, and though Charlie had agreed months ago that Ari could take herself to school, Charlie had thought—before Beijing, before Ari's freeze-out—that the two of them might spend these last days together. "See you for supper," she wrote in blue on silver paper and tacked it to Ari's door where her daughter would be sure to see it.

It was a Saturday morning, and Charlie was due at Gran's. She drove first to Japantown to buy her mother a present. Her neighbor kept on his balcony a collection of bonsai trees that Charlie often admired, and when Charlie had asked him about it, he gushed for twenty minutes about the thrill of raising bonsai. She had in mind buying one for her mother that she hoped might spark a lasting interest. Gran was happiest or anyway the least amount of trouble when she had a project and a goal to strive for, preferably one that didn't involve Charlie or Les or Ari, and though her mother had never been a hobbyist, maybe she was ready to slow down and develop an interest in something harmless. She was a good cook, but her sense of smell had dulled and her pride no longer allowed her to cook for others. She went to church but didn't like the other ladies. There was no garden to tend, and she had never liked needlework. Rose was an excellent handicrafter who made darling strawberry hats and sweaters for her eight grandchildren and the grandchildren of all her friends. "She's Madame Defarge," Gran declared, "always with her needles, knitting."

The Japantown shop had specimens galore. It was hard to decide which one her mother would like. Charlie finally chose a pine tree with a gracefully curved trunk and added two little charms to the moss beneath its branches: the tiny figure of a white crane and a small ceramic tortoise, "To honor old age," the Japanese saleswoman suggested. The gift was expensive, over a hundred dollars; she couldn't let Gran find out how much she had paid or she'd be chastised repeatedly for wasting her hard-earned money. She drove to Millbrae with the tree tucked in tissue.

"How are you, Ma?" Charlie asked, kissing Gran on the cheek. Her mother looked well in a pair of navy slacks and a bright pink silk blouse with a bow around the neck. She wore low navy pumps with flat black ribbons across the toes. Charlie had on scuffed brown boots, a stretched-out green T-shirt, and worn jeans. The chunky heels on her boots made her feel substantial, but between her mother's big-boned frame and superior posture, Gran stood a good three inches taller than Charlie. Gran had played every sport well—badminton, field hockey, volleyball when they let the girls compete—unlike Charlie, who ducked when a ball came flying. In recent years, Gran had lost a modicum of height, but her thinning hair and the hollows under her cheekbones had given her head a sharper, more angular look, which defied anyone from observing, even silently to themselves, that old age was causing Gran to shrink.

"Lesley called," her mother said. "Apparently, it's more convenient for her to come for lunch today." Usually Les and Charlie alternated their weekend visits.

"Shall I put this in the window?" Charlie showed her mother the bonsai in its dark green polished dish.

"Oh," Gran sighed. "Something else to take care of."

"I thought you might enjoy learning about it," Charlie said. "Bonsai is an art form."

"I hope you didn't pay too much for that. Put it on that shelf. Move that picture"—a snapshot of Charlie and Les in matching Easter dresses—"put you girls over there, next to Father."

Charlie set the smaller snapshot next to the large silver-framed wedding photograph of Gran's parents, W. W. and Eugenia. From her half-white, half-Chinese mother, Gran had gotten her big hands and broad shoulders and a mouth full of horse teeth, Eugenia's slightly bucked but Gran's straight and strong. Her father, Wei-Wen, was the handsomer of the couple, a young man in a dapper Western suit, with black hair combed back in a low pompadour. He wore a confident grin that Charlie and Les agreed was downright sexy, and, instead of a boutonniere, there was a trout fly pinned to his lapel. Gran had saved one of his favorite fishing reels as a keepsake, which she had let Charlie play with like a spinning toy when she was young.

"This looks good," said Charlie, taking from the refrigerator the luncheon dishes prepared by Yan, who was out running errands.

"Where's Ari?" Gran asked. "When's she coming to see me?"

"She'll be down sometime. She's been catching up on her sleep, getting over jet lag."

"She's too young for jet lag," Gran said. "What happened in Beijing? What aren't you and Lesley saying? You make me feel old, like I need protecting. If she's unhappy, I'm sure I can help her. Sometimes it's better to keep the mother out of it and let someone else take over. When you were young and you didn't want to talk to me, you used to talk to your father."

Charlie nodded. She talked only to her father, as best as she could remember. They would drive to the Saturday clinic and stop for hamburgers on the way home.

"I wish you'd tell me what happened with Ari," Gran said to Les, who had used her key to walk in. She was tall, like Gran, and dressed like her, too, in pressed navy slacks and a cream-colored shirt. Her chin-length hair was expertly cut to show off her high cheekbones. Their great-grandmother's Caucasian stock showed up stronger in Les than in Charlie. Les had lighter skin, a higher forehead, and eye folds thick enough for the liner and shadow she artfully applied. In strong sunlight her hair used to flash natural streaks of red, but now it was fully black because she tinted out the gray. "She's my girl with red hair and freckles," Gran sometimes described her, which as a child had infuriated Les, who, as far as she was concerned, was Chinese and nothing else. She, like Charlie, had studied that photograph of Gran's mother and father, and knew that the elegant man with the white teeth and confident smile was the ancestor of choice. Everyone looked up to Les. When she came into a room, the air felt charged, the light both softer and brighter. Even here in Gran's home, where the formality of the furnishings kept visitors stiff at attention, Les's presence altered the room. The tight-backed sofa and chairs upholstered in slippery gold-colored fabric, their tapered legs like limbs wearing silk stockings, seemed to Charlie to relax when Les walked through the door. The lamps glowed a little more warmly; the tied-back draperies breathed and rustled.

"What happened to Ari?" Gran asked again.

"She had an accident," Charlie said. "It's fine now. I've taken her to the doctor."

"So you say," Les said. "It seemed like a strange accident. Why did you let her go back to Kunming? Wasn't one visit to that orphanage enough? I thought you said that if we took her when she was twelve, she wouldn't wonder about it when she got older."

"That's what the experts advise," Charlie defended herself. "Every child is different. Some have issues early; some deal with things much later. You're supposed to expose them over time. They learned that from the Korean kids who had problems when they became teenagers because nobody had talked to them about their birth parents or anything about their adoptions. It became like this burden, a big shameful secret. Secrecy is unhealthy. It bottles up emotions."

Gran scoffed. "I will never go back," she said. "Rose, she can go back all she wants to. There's nothing back there for me. Ari's an American. What good does it do to worry about where she came from? There's nothing to find out. There's nobody to tell her."

"I'd go again if somebody paid me to lecture," Les said. "I'd like to see Hangzhou, where Grandpa Wu was from. Our visit to the orphanage—" She didn't bother to finish.

"Was a disaster," Gran said. "I told you not to take her."

"I'm glad we went," Charlie said to Les. "It meant a lot to Ari that you came with us."

"Is Ari going to come see me before she leaves for school?" Gran asked.

Charlie nodded, moved by her mother's query until she caught a glimpse of Gran's iron frown.

"I'm sure she will," Charlie said. She remembered uneasily her promise to Va that Manu would come home. "And Aunt Rose is nearby, once she gets to Philadelphia."

Gran plunked the luncheon plates on the table. "What does Rose know about girls? I'm the one who has daughters."

"She has daughters-in-law," Les said. "Four of them, in fact."

"And every one a paragon of virtue," Gran said. "But do you know what Rose said to me when you girls were Ari's age? 'I wouldn't know what to do with girls.' She was absolutely right; she would have been hopeless with daughters. Girls are much more complicated to raise than boys. Especially her boys. Who could have predicted that Bennett, almost as handsome as George, would produce such boring sons? No, if we're going to get Ari straightened out, it has to be soon, before she leaves for school."

"Or maybe college will give her the independence she needs," Charlie said.

"You always hope for the best," Gran said. "You didn't get that from me."

THEY SAT FOR LUNCH. Gran served from elegant china. She always said that one should take the trouble. Les poured a chilled white wine she had brought. Retrieving her dropped chopstick, Charlie bumped the table leg.

"Somebody asked me this week about what year you left China," Les said. "I couldn't remember. Forty-eight? Forty-nine?"

"Whose business is it?" Gran said.

"Forty-six," Charlie said. "The year she started at Bryn Mawr."

"And Aunt Rose came later?" Les asked.

"Forty-eight," Charlie said. "I wrote it all down for Ari."

"That's what I'm talking about," Gran said, "wasting her time when she should be getting ready. Bryn Mawr professors have the highest standards, you know. She's going to have to work hard as soon as she gets there."

"But Mu-you died in China, right?" Les said.

Gran glared and huffed into the kitchen. Charlie made a face at Les. They both knew better than to speak of Mu-you, Gran's younger brother. Charlie hadn't known about Mu-you at all until she was in grade school. A friend had stopped inviting Charlie over. Your mother was mean to my mother, the girl said. Charlie asked her father why.

Your mother spoke up, her father said. She did the right thing and spoke up and made the rest of the parents angry. The other girl's mother had complained in a PTA meeting about a boy in Charlie's class. The boy had been in a special program for slow learners and was ready to join a regular class. Your mother stood up at the meeting and defended the boy's right to get the same education as all the other children. The principal called to thank her, but she didn't want his praise. She did it because of her brother, Mu-you.

Charlie had asked, Was something wrong with Mu-you?

He was born the year after Rose, her father said. He wasn't like other children. He was cognitively impaired. Charlie didn't know what those words meant. Severely retarded, others might call him. I don't approve of the label. Mu-you died in the war, around the same time as Grandpa Wu and Grandma Eugenia. But don't speak of it to your mother. She doesn't like to talk about such things.

Waiting for Gran to return to the dining table, they heard her banging pot lids in the kitchen. Charlie made another face at Les.

"I was just asking," Les hissed to Charlie.

"Drop the subject," Charlie hissed back.

SHE LEFT GRAN'S after promising again that Ari would visit. Her spirits rose when she drove down her street and saw the light on through her picture window. Ari must be home. She hurried up the front stairs. There had been times, many days in fact, more than Charlie liked to admit, when Ari was growing up, that Charlie had been impatient for the next stage, the next phase of childhood, but now that it was here, she didn't want Ari to go. I've never regretted it, she said to herself. For all the worry and responsibility and bewilderment—even now, when Charlie's anxiousness dragged on them both like a stone— she had never questioned the rightness of her decision. "What shall I do?" a mother once had posted on a Listserv that Charlie read. "I feel like I've made a mistake. I'm not cut out for adoption." The plea appalled Charlie, who had quickly clicked away.

"Ari," she called. She turned on the lights in the dim hallway. Ari wasn't in the living room or in the kitchen, either. Her bedroom light was on and Charlie's note on the door was missing, but the room was empty. Charlie threw her jacket on her own barren bed and paced back through the apartment. She called again, hearing in her voice the rising note, just this side of panic, that a mother might bleat if she'd lost sight of her child on the playground.

On the splintered landing outside the kitchen door, Ari sat in shadow, smoking a cigarette. Her narrow shoulders were hunched in a man's unfamiliar jacket, and her arms were wrapped tightly over her tented knees. She looked up; her eyes were glassy.

"Here you are," Charlie said in relief. "Did you see A.J.? Did they get home all right?"

Ari stood. Something about the jacket made her look both smaller and older. "I've had a change in plans," she said. "I'm not going to go to school. I've asked for my old job back at Pen and Parchment."

"Not going . . . for the fall?" The jacket—was it leather?—had a peculiar shine. She wondered if Ari had spilled something on it. *If I get a rag*, Charlie thought, *I could maybe wipe that clean.*

"I'm moving out as soon as I make some money. That's it." Her eyes looked dead, but her mouth was nervously twitching. She took a last drag and flipped the cigarette over the rail. Charlie stepped forward to block her from leaving, but Ari didn't move.

"Come inside," Charlie said. "I can hardly see you." She backed away from Ari and ushered her into the kitchen. The lights glared down. Charlie took a deep breath.

"Help me understand. Are you asking to work for a while before you start college? Because if that's what you want to do, we can discuss it."

"I'm not asking anything." Her voice flat and distant.

"Are you worried about money?" Charlie asked in a rush. "I don't want you to worry about the cost. We've already planned for your college expenses. You can help, of course—I won't say no to that." She gave a hollow laugh. "But now's not the time to let money get in the way."

"I don't need money. I—" Ari's mouth clamped for a second into a thin pink line. Her eyes flicked to the kitchen clock and stayed there. "I'm going to get my old job back and look for other work. When I've got enough saved up, I'm going back to China. Like I told you, I was just getting into it there."

"There are good exchange programs—" Charlie began, but Ari shook her head. "Please, Ari," Charlie said. "You have to let me speak. If you don't want to start school right away, we can discuss it. You have to have some sort of plan. You can't just bounce around. What's going on? What's the mystery here?"

Ari buried herself deeper in the folds of the bulky jacket. "I'm good at bouncing," she said. Her head was drawn in so far, Charlie could hardly hear her. "Remember what the orphanage aunties wrote? 'Like the Bowns.' Maybe all I'm good for is bouncing. From one place to another, that's how my life is going to go."

"I understand how hard things have been for you lately, but—"

"If 'lately' means my whole life, then, yes, you're right."

"No," Charlie said. "You were a happy baby! You loved school; you had lots of friends, best friends, who started out the same as you. A.J. and Becca and all the other playgroup girls. They can't wait to get to college."

Ari shrugged, and Charlie saw what the shrug cost her: her daughter's eyes stayed empty, but her face drained to white. "It's that business with WeiWei," Charlie declared. "It's brought up all sorts of feelings. I understand that. I truly do. Every adopted child wonders about her biological family. But at some point, honey, you've got to let that go."

"God!" Ari cried. "I'm so sick of you looking for explanations! Can't we just agree that we won't talk anymore? I can't give you any reason for why I feel this way. There is no reason. So let's just *shut up.*"

Stop now, Charlie said to herself, *this isn't going anywhere*, but she was locked into the skid. "We *will* talk. You won't run away from a simple family discussion. I won't let you shut me out, like with what happened in Kunming—"

At that, Charlie paused. She rubbed at her forehead and felt the hard bone of her brow. Her feet ached; the kitchen light was ghastly.

"You have a family," she started again, "a family who loves you. And I'm sorry that it isn't picture perfect, but believe me, if you saw some of the families I deal with in my work . . ."

Like an officer in the road or a sworn witness, Ari raised her hand between them. The sight of her wrapped finger caught like a hook in Charlie's eye. The evening damp lay heavy in her kitchen. "You're never going to understand me," Ari said.

Charlie had no answer.

CHAPTER 14

GRAN

This morning I awoke thinking of the baby. Still I see the red face, hear his thin cry in my ears. He visits me in my half-twilight moments, shredding my pleasure at the first conscious breath of the day or my contentment after a well-earned nap. His mouth open. His eyes gummed shut. A twisted torso with no proper limbs—in the blurry glimpse I got sixty-one years ago, I saw one arm with a fisted hand moving, or was it a foot, shaped like a concubine's bent and broken lily?

"Shall I clean its eyes, Doctor?" I asked the attending physician, who hadn't given his customary orders. He was turned away, busying himself with his instruments. The mother lay silent in a twilight sleep of her own. Head Nurse hadn't made a motion.

The doctor didn't answer. I didn't know what to do.

"Doctor, shall I clean its eyes?"

"Leave it," he ordered. I looked at Head Nurse. Her cap was tilted downward, her gaze fixed to the linoleum floor. A tray clattered noisily off to the side. I didn't look at the baby, but I heard its cry catch. Next time I looked, its face, not a face, was turning blue. Head Nurse didn't move a muscle. The doctor stayed as he was, turned away and fiddling. *He's doing something about it,* I was still telling myself. *In another second, he's going to turn back around and get started.* I thought of Father's hands—his elegant fingers with clean white nails he kept more neatly trimmed than

Mother's. The clever hands of the son of a tailor. The doctor's hands weren't as beautiful as Father's, but for three months of nursing training, I'd watched them cut and sew and tug. *He knows what to do.* There was something they expected from me, but I hadn't a notion of what. Another minute passed, dragging me into comprehension. *The doctor is waiting. And I must wait, too.*

When no sound rose anymore from the table, Head Nurse looked, then quietly said, "Doctor."

He turned around to make sure that the baby wasn't breathing.

"Clean this up," he said.

I didn't have to do it. Other people came in and took over. I was ordered from the room before I could bend down to take a look.

It was a boy, I'm certain.

YIFU HAS WRITTEN again. I open her letter and read once more about her excessively talented grandchildren—you'd hardly think they were human; one imagines performing seals—and Robert's prodigious prostate. They still live in Pasadena in that big house with the swimming pool and orange trees in the yard. Has anyone mentioned to Yifu that she's old and decrepit? She thinks she's going to live forever. Perhaps she's already arranged it by witchcraft or voodoo or with engineered cell life from Robert's famous lab. I wouldn't put anything past Yifu Yen. "We're coming to Berkeley in October," she writes. "They're giving Robert a special award." She names some prize with an honorific so long that it sounds made up to me. "We were so sorry to miss you on our last several visits. I hope this time you might be less busy. I'll have a free day because Robert is giving a lecture. He's finally learned how to work the PowerPoint by himself. May I come for a visit and take you out to lunch? It's been too long! I'm dying to see you."

She's dying to see me. I should be so lucky. If she hadn't described to me in her last letter the vivid details of her cholecystectomy— she no longer has a gallbladder; her bile was backing up—I'd sit up and applaud her unmitigated gall at keeping up the pretense that we've not seen each other in two years because I was simply too busy. She's deliberately overlooking a perfectly good social slight. My husbands are gone, my children grown. I sold my restaurant, and my nursing days are long over. An exciting day of travel means a trip to the doctor's office. I have hours by the clockful but no yen to see Miss Yen. That's a little chuckle at Yifu's expense. Charlotte would sigh at me—she was always telling Ari that to respect a person's name was to respect the whole person. Solly, Chollie. Some people work hard to earn our disrespect. Yifu is one of them, a woman who can't be trusted. She took eighty years of friendship and, in one blabbermouth moment, poured it down the drain. I haven't forgotten how she turned Rose against me. No, I'll not sit down with Yifu to reminisce about the old days. What's done is done, the bad along with the good. There's nothing to be gained in recounting our schoolgirl years, and I don't see why she would want to since her memories can't stack up to mine. I had many more suitors and was president of all the student clubs while Yifu warmed the secretary's seat. We had mixers every weekend, Bryn Mawr and Valley Forge, or Bryn Mawr and U. Penn. Knowing that Yifu and I shared our every confidence, the boys who fancied her used to ask me for advice. I'd usually mention chocolates, the ones with cherries inside. It was a good way to get the treats we both loved. I was always surprised when a boy hankered for Yifu, but the heart is irrational and its judgment is often faulty. Robert's attentions were the biggest surprise of them all because we could see how intelligent he was and knew he would be successful. Yifu met him at a skating party. She wanted George, but I had spotted him first at a Chinese student holiday party in New York City, two days before Christmas, 1949. We married one year later at a Presbyterian church in Baltimore, with punch and tea sandwiches served afterward at George's professor's house. Rose was my maid of honor and Yifu my only bridesmaid. I wore a beautiful dress from Jay Thorpe on West Fifty-seventh, ivory white with panels. Yifu borrowed it when she and Robert got married, though of course she had to let out the side seams and bring the hem way up. We shared absolutely everything, a mistake I learned the hard way.

She's trying to mend fences. It's a little too late for that.

ONCE ARI WAS old enough to use words as weapons against her ghosts, she asked me questions about my past that I didn't answer. I blame myself for not taking the time to sit with her, for assuming that she was too young to talk to. Maybe, if I had painted her a more complete picture, she would have been reassured that the tree indeed reached back and she was a twig on one of its branches, but I was mean in the beginning with my interest and attention. My neglect was excusable; I had concerns of my own. Herbert was courting me, and he went about it with captivating reserve, waiting for three years—he was George's liver-transplant doctor—before asking mutual friends to invite us both to dinner. I could tell he'd been carrying a torch for me the whole time since George's passing. He proposed over dinner at Huangpu River, the second-best Shanghai cuisine restaurant in L.A. The Pearl was the best—that was my restaurant, a perfect jewel I built and owned for fifteen years. I stole my chef from a Chinatown sty where he was wasting his talent on brown sauce for the masses. He was the heat, and I was the flame, drawing them in with my witty conversation. I played Portia in middle school at Miss Allingham's School in Shanghai. The stage suited me; with audiences, I was a natural, a talent I brought to my restaurant every evening. I had a flair for the front of the house as good as any impresario's under the Big Top and could recall the names and favorite dishes of everyone who came in for dinner, or at least the important ones. I had to close the Pearl when George fell ill.

Herbert could see that I was very lonely. He proposed an adventure: that we move to Taipei, where he'd been offered a plum position, and buy a grand apartment that I would make into a home and a salon for entertaining. We could throw lively parties the way my parents had hosted all the interesting and important people in Shanghai when I was a girl. Herbert had plenty of money; his family was wealthy, so he had even more than George, who'd wasted his earnings and broken his health by working for poor people when it's the rich ones who can pay. I loved George; he didn't disappoint me, but he could have been so much more. Why shouldn't a Chinese head up a major U.S. medical center? Father could have done it had he had George's chances. Herbert knew how to focus on the opportunities ahead. I never knew his first wife, but I could see that before her illness she'd taken very good care of her husband. Their children were successful. Herbert wore good suits and drove a late-model Audi. We were already in our sixties, so there was no mother-in-law to lurk. We married and moved soon after Ari turned one, hardly of an age when she could absorb my lessons. I'll always regret that we left that car behind.

You're correct, Naomi used to tell me. The young people, they're full of questions. Why do they have to know? There's no use living in the past. That was the message we newcomers embraced. Our silence instructed our children not to delve deep, but their children ask away because they weren't taught to keep quiet. They have no model at home of survival and then restraint. They're writing reports for their third-grade teacher or a college short story or a misery memoir. Some of my friends—my old Shanghai schoolmates and our Taipei circle—feel special to be questioned, to be asked to spill their stories before their memories trickle away. Naomi and I knew better than to be flattered into confession. It's why we were friends. We didn't share what was private, though we knew we each had secrets. A secret keeper can spot a kindred lockbox: the maneuvering away from discomfiting topics, the careful explanations and omissions politely deployed. We knew not to tread where our curiosity wasn't welcome.

Ari asked, and I ignored her.

THERE ARE SCRAPS that come to me, stories I might have shared.

When I was thirteen, Father saved my best friend, Yifu, without lifting a finger. It was 1941. Four years earlier, the Japanese had invaded China. Mother had begged Father to let us all live together—she always pleaded for our family to stay united. The year that we had spent in Kuling without Father, right after the Japanese invasion, had been very hard on Mother, though not on Rose and Mu-you and me, for Kuling was our paradise, our mountain Shangri-la. Mother said that we couldn't spend another winter in Kuling in our summer house with no proper insulation, and that Shanghai wouldn't be any more dangerous than mountain life in Kuling, so long as we kept to the sectors where Chinese were permitted. Father agreed that we could return to Shanghai, except for my brother Mu-you, whose condition so troubled Father.

It must not have been a school day, or Yifu and I would have been at Miss Allingham's, the missionary school we attended. I spent many hours at Yifu's house, which was a few streets away from mine. She was a plump girl even then and had a silk scarf from Paris and an English-language dictionary that stood in the parlor on its own piece of furniture. We both liked American movies and went often; there were loads of movie theaters at that time in Shanghai. Yifu was partial to Shirley Temple and my favorite was Laurel and Hardy. We were alone in the house except for the cook and a housemaid. A man came to the door; he said his name was Mr. Wong. His pants were torn, and his eyes jumped about. He said that he had just come from the university where Yifu's father was a professor. Japanese security men had come and taken him away, he said. As he was being led off, her father had asked Mr. Wong to go to his house. He needed money and a family member to help him.

"Where is he?" gasped Yifu. "Can you take me to him?" Her mother was out and wouldn't be home until dinnertime.

"Get all the money you have in the house," Mr. Wong said. "I will take you to him."

Yifu rushed upstairs to remove two gold bars out of the family's hiding place and packed a rucksack with clothes and food for her father. We all lived in fear that our fathers would be arrested and accused of spying, and she knew that the Japanese might detain her father for days. I eyed Mr. Wong. He stood nervously just inside the door, taking care not to stare at the valuable wall hangings or the big shelf of books in Chinese and English.

Yifu is a fool, I thought. *This guy is up to no good.*

"Yifu!" I called, loudly enough for Mr. Wong to hear me. "I'm going to call my father at the hospital. He'll know what to do. Wait for him to get here."

"Who is your father?" asked Mr. Wong, just as I knew he would.

"Wu Wei-Wen," I said proudly. I watched Mr. Wong gulp and go pale.

"Yes, that's fine," Mr. Wong said. "I will just go and check with the taxicab driver, who is waiting to take us to where the professor is."

When Yifu reappeared, we looked for Mr. Wong. He had vanished from the courtyard into the streets of the city.

Just the mention of Father's name was enough to frighten off bandits.

You have to remember that these were the war years. People did desperate things.

SUNDAY AFTERNOONS the world came into our house. First, we went to church—Mother's father was a Presbyterian minister, so we never missed Sunday service—and then we went home to prepare for our weekly open house. The Chinese, French, British, and Americans arrived by pedicab and taxi, sweeping through our front gate. I stood in the courtyard and observed the ladies in their wide-shouldered suits nipped smartly at the waist and clever hats and high heels that clattered. There were Jews, too—I told that to Naomi. A Mr. Ben Cohen, I remember him coming often. Father greeted Mr. Cohen the same as everyone else, with a big laugh and a slap on the shoulder. Father didn't have the narrow worldview of so many Chinese of that time. From humble beginnings to Johns Hopkins University and Peking Union Medical College—everyone saw how remarkable Father was. At PUMC, he met Mother, who worked in the office there. How surprised she must have been that

Father selected her over all the others. She wasn't beautiful. She was tall and broad-shouldered, good for playing field hockey, and she could carry as much as the servants. Her father was Toishanese, her mother an American missionary lady. I suppose, being Eurasian, Mother must have seemed exotic. She was educated, too—she had studied biology and chemistry at Hunter College in New York City—and though it wasn't Bryn Mawr, it served her well enough. Mother declared it her entrée to the world. A sentimental notion, since her entrée clearly was Father.

The foreign guests who crowded our home on Sundays spoke mostly French or English in a babble that grew louder if no clergy were present and the whiskey decanter came out. Mother, having been born in New York City, spoke English readily; it was her Mandarin that was poor. I had to correct her all the time. She served chicken and fruit and cake to the ladies because Cook knew how to procure whatever we needed in the black market, which supplied everybody's larders. Raw clams and mussels were Father's favorites; he would urge the gentlemen to eat their fill.

"Except," Naomi said, when I told her all about Father, "for Mr. Ben Cohen. Perhaps he preferred to eat chicken with the ladies."

Ha, I said. Her point was well taken. My memory is faulty, my stories incomplete.

But there was no shortage of provisions on our table, and Father was the perfect host. The French, especially, loved to come to our house. Father allowed me to sit in the corner and listen to the men talk of politics and war, history and war, the perfidy of the Japanese and the Allies' staunchness. Rose was too timid to hang about with the men, but I was proud to see the guests lean in to catch Father's every word.

At the end of luncheon, Father would stand to offer a toast. I have a photograph of him from one of those Sundays, standing in the courtyard with a group of smiling gentlemen. His collar is open, and his hair is mussed. An easy laugh brightens his round face. On the back of the photograph in Mother's handwriting is a little poem.

Perhaps she wrote it—she was always scribbling—but the words sound more like Father's.

> *Why worry?*
> *All mortals must die*
> *So let's not worry.*
> *Chase our fear away.*
> *Sirens may scream*
> *And shells may rain*
> *And bombs fall.*
> *Let's have a cup of tea.*

Father owned the hospital that served many foreigners and the Chinese in government or university posts. Several other ob-gyns worked there, but all the ladies wanted Father to be their doctor.

"Oh, Dr. Wu," I once heard a woman sigh. She was a pretty young Englishwoman in a blue day dress sitting across from me in the waiting room at the dentist's office. I was ten years old—this was right after Mother and Rose and I had returned to Shanghai from Kuling, and Mu-you had been sent to live with Father's cousin in Hangzhou—and sitting with my ears pricked for the sound of the nurse's footsteps. Rose was with me, and we were both nervous, for we disliked the dentist, though we loved the reward: Mother taking us out afterward for ice cream sodas and an American movie. "He has the gentlest hands," said the young woman. "I won't see anyone else. When my time comes, my husband has promised that Dr. Wu will get to the hospital if my husband has to pull the rickshaw himself."

The second woman, wearing a tented maternity smock, giggled. "You wouldn't be the only one getting special treatment. I heard he took very good care of Lady Brad . . ."

Bradford? Braddock? I didn't hear the name clearly, though I certainly heard the "Lady." I stuck my hands flat on my chair and inched to the edge of my seat. I wasn't guileless enough to keep from staring at the women, but they took no notice of me, or perhaps they believed I couldn't understand English.

" . . . thing ended when his wife came back," I heard. "And then her husband found out and packed her off to Hong Kong."

"Pity," said the first woman, "she was always such fun at parties."

"Who's Lady Bradford?" I asked Mother when we got home. We spoke English at home for Mother's convenience. She was knitting a sweater for Mu-you, which she was hurrying to finish. A missionary couple whom she knew through the YWCA was traveling to Hangzhou and could take money and clothing and tinned foods to Father's family. Mu-you was four. A spinster cousin took care of him. She'd gotten fat, Father joked, from eating her way through our presents.

"Mu-you will like this, don't you think?" said Mother. She held it up for me to see. It was gray wool with a snowflake pattern. We'd laughed in Kuling the previous winter when it snowed for the first time, astonishing Mu-you into running in sweeping circles under the bleak winter sky. Rose had tried to teach him how to catch snowflakes on his tongue, but of course he couldn't do it. "He'll learn," Mother had said. A fantasy. He wouldn't.

"He won't be able to pull it on over his head," I said.

"Cousin Pei can help him," Mother said. She resumed her knitting, the needles clicking steadily, making a quiet sound like soft rain falling on the tin shed roof. Cook was doing our shopping and the *amah* and the housekeeper were busy at the back of the house, so the afternoon was unusually quiet. We were sitting in the parlor where Mother served tea to YWCA ladies and visiting missionaries who came to talk about schools for the poor and improving rural conditions. The chairs were softer in here, not the polished wood of the formal dining room chairs, but I rarely sat for long listening in on their conversations because I found their subjects dull.

"Do you know Lady Bradford?" I persisted. "Is she a real English lady, like a maiden in distress?" I loved the tales of King Arthur and the Knights of the Round Table.

Mother snorted. She paused to count the rows in her snowflake pattern.

"Where did you hear her name?"

"Two ladies in the dentist's office said she was Father's patient."

The needles flashed. "Father has many patients. It's a big job, running a hospital."

"And then he goes on Saturdays to the Red Cross hospital, too," I said, eager to join in Mother's defense of Father, though what he was accused of, I wasn't certain. Mother seemed to be protecting him—her words were ones of praise, but she spoke them to me with an uncharacteristic coldness and turned away, her broad shoulders like a wall between us.

"I wish he wouldn't go on Saturdays," I said. "I wish he would stay home and be with us, like before."

"In wartime, everybody has to do their part. If Father didn't help the Red Cross, many poor women at the municipal hospital wouldn't get proper care. I'm at the end of my yarn. Will you help me with this? Hold up your hands and I'll wind this into a ball."

"*You* hold up *your* hands." Mother did as I said. I drew a loose skein of gray yarn over her rigid hands as carefully as Cousin Pei would be pulling Mu-you's new sweater over his head. This way, Mother would have to look at me. I began winding the yarn into a woolly ball.

"Do all of Father's patients have babies?" I asked. I was ten. I didn't know exactly what an ob-gyn did.

"Some do. But Father takes care of all their problems. Not just delivering babies. For good health, a woman has to have examinations and such."

It was a big skein, more than she would need to finish Mu-you's sweater, but still I wound slowly, fixing her with my eye.

"So they take a test when they go see Father? Like Miss Peek gives us a test at school?"

Mother shifted her big bottom in the chair. I expected her to color, as so many ladies did, but she surprised me. She looked straight back at me and said with a smile, "Father makes sure that a woman's reproductive system is working the way it should. They lie on their backs on his examining table. He reaches up inside them and feels with his hand whether their female parts, like the uterus and the cervix, are in good condition. If they're pregnant, he can tell if the baby is growing nicely."

I stopped winding. The image shocked me. Mother laughed.

"It's not so bad as all that. It doesn't hurt, and it's good for the mother to know that everything is fine, that everything is normal."

"So there's a way to tell if something isn't normal?"

Mother paused. She knew I was thinking of Mu-you.

"Sometimes he can't tell. And even if he can tell, sometimes there's nothing that can be done about it. The baby might be born with problems. Like Mu-you was born different from other children. That baby needs a special kind of love. You find a way to take care of that baby and you keep on taking care of him as he grows older, and even when he's grown up and still needs a lot of attention, you keep on taking care of him because that baby is yours forever. We'll take care of Mu-you for the rest of his life, you and me and Rose and Father. That's our job, to take care of Mu-you. And sometimes we'll get help from other people, like Cousin Pei, who knows how to be patient, but nobody else will love Mu-you the way we do because he's our special boy. He's a good boy, isn't he?"

I nodded. He was a good boy, sunny and often laughing, though he couldn't talk right or feed himself or play games or hold a book in the proper position. I was crying a little bit, but Mother was smiling fondly at me. She might have given me a hug had her hands been free. Mother gave us a lot of hugs, more than regular Chinese parents.

"And he's ours to take care of forever."

"What about God?" I asked. "Will he take care of Mu-you?"

"Oh, God," Mother said. She quirked her mouth and gestured, keeping her hands upright. The yarn didn't budge. I kept on winding. "Who knows the story there?" She laughed. "That's not a good thing for the daughter of a minister to say, is it?" She held me in her smile. "It doesn't matter, in terms of our duty to Mu-you. No, not 'duty.' I don't want you to think that Mu-you is a duty. We do it because we love him and he loves us, and that's all there is to it."

"Does Father love him?"

Her face changed. I saw a shadow cross.

"Yes, Father loves him."

"And it's not a duty?"

"It's love and duty with Father," Mother said. "That's often the way men are. But for you and me and Rose, it's love, love, love."

I couldn't answer her. I was used to talking with Father and doing as Father said, but here was Mother setting out her own law of the land. Her demands were born of love, she said, but they were demands nonetheless—that much I understood. At my mother's insistence, I was to act and feel a certain way. She had given me a job and the emotion to go with it. She had never spoken so frankly to me before, though, looking back, I shouldn't have been surprised that a scientist from New York City would know her own mind and unleash it once in a while.

"Remember this," Mother said. "We act out of love, and we always take care of family. As for Lady Bradford," she added.

I held my breath. I had forgotten all about Lady Bradford.

"There will always be those women who interest your father. Don't worry about it. He knows his duty."

She slipped the last yard of the skein from her hands and watched me finish winding. I handed her the ball of yarn, as neat and round as a pomelo fruit.

"It's perfect," she said. "The perfect tension. If you'd wound it too tightly, the yarn would be stretched and spoiled. Too loose, and the knitting gets tangled. Now tell me." She reached into her basket and brought out a loop of string on which five small buttons were threaded. I recognized them; they were made of jade and cut from a ladies' blouse that someone had given Mother. The blouse was much too small for my hardy mother, but she had saved the buttons—I had hoped for me.

"Shall we sew one of these into Mu-you's sweater?" Mother asked. "A piece of jade to bring him good luck?"

I hesitated. Mother understood.

"One for Mu-you," she said, "and you can have the other four to sew onto your own sweater. Whenever you button it up, you'll think of your little brother."

I nodded and got out my sewing basket, and when Mother was done knitting the last rows of Mu-you's sweater, I sewed one jade button on the inside near the bottom. This was a custom, to sew in a piece of lucky jade, and though we were a modern family and not superstitious, I could see by the way that Mother checked my stitches that the button gave her comfort. She smoothed the finished sweater and then rested her hand on top of my pigtailed head. "You really are a treasure, my Penny Perfect." I grabbed her around the waist and hugged her tightly, her dress soft against my face and her neck smelling of talcum. I felt as mighty as the chair bearers who carried us up the mountain. I had the strength to do anything that Mother asked of me.

Later, that strength left me. I couldn't, or I didn't, do as Mother had asked. In between those two notions lies a dark hole of pain.

I dream of the baby, blue-faced and flopping. His feeble cries fill my restless nights. His veined and ruined body shudders and then lies still. I was a young woman, following doctor's orders. I cannot sleep for thinking of that baby.

SEE WHERE IT LEADS, peering into the past? This is exactly why I never allow myself the luxury of reminiscence. One starts with good memories, and then everything blackens. There's no telling where the path will take you.

No matter. The page will keep my secrets. This is only a kind of exercise to exorcise the ghosts. It's good to have a project, a place to put all my feelings. I put my feelings into words, and then put away the words like I stash spare buttons in a long tin box, which I stick on a shelf and don't bother with ever again. When was the last time I took down that box of buttons and poked a finger through it? If I did, I'd never find anything useful, nothing to replace what's missing or to match my present needs. The jade buttons I never used again, though they turned up later when I least expected. Even so, I find that I can't bring myself to discard a single button. I blame it on the war years and on the Depression. We threw away nothing. I box up the buttons, neat and tidy, and hide the box where nobody can find it. Then I face forward and get on with life again. I've always told my girls to follow my example. Write it all down and then throw it away, or if you can't dispose of it, at least try to hide it. Why nurse the pain of the past? You're better off walking away. There is nothing to be done about it. Some things you must abandon.

CHAPTER 15

ARI

I needed six hundred dollars for a one-way ticket to Beijing, plus three hundred more to keep myself alive once I got there. I worked part time at Pen and Parchment and looked for a second job. Nights I spent at Kurt's place, striving against his slack bulk until he expended himself, his final sale of the day. Afterward, I sat alone in the kitchen, drinking black tea and searching for airfares on the Internet. Katie and I avoided each other, and Niall quit, moving with Drue to Oakland. A.J. started the semester. I told Charlie that I was hanging out with Katie and gave her a made-up phone number "in case you ever need to call the house." I knew she wouldn't. I texted her from time to time to keep her off my back. I said I would think about starting at Bryn Mawr in January, that I wasn't quite ready to leave California. I left clothes and books scattered in my old bedroom to convince her that I was coming back.

Mostly Kurt assigned me to the stockroom, where he could come in for a grope. Sometimes I took a turn in the blank-book section, a hundred square feet of empty journals waiting to be filled. Shoppers spent hours considering their choices: lined, unlined, graph paper, spiral-bound. Plaid cover, animal print, pressed flower, and leatherette. There were hand-sewn leather books we kept locked in a display case. Young women hovered, shyly asking to view the goods. I didn't like them to approach me. I felt outside of their world and immune to their earnest faces. I had no inner thoughts to spill, no impulse to express myself, for all I felt was numb. "This is the kind I use," I told the young women, steering them toward the cheaper versions that were glued and bonded, a bad sales practice that royally pissed off Kurt.

Once in a while I helped Ines at the front of the store in the fine pens department. Those were the only moments when I felt something other than frozen. Ines knew everything about old-fashioned fountain pens, those relics of labored times. I admired how deliberately Ines worked to be out of step. She was an unlikely expert: twenty-four years old and begrudging. She wore black lipstick and hoop earrings and moved her thick body with such deliberate slowness that customers were cowed by her insolent boredom, or maybe by the rows of gleaming wares that she arranged like flaunted jewelry in the long glass vitrines, the ballpoints and roller balls and fountain pens and mechanical pencils. A $10,000 Montblanc Masterpiece with a solid gold nib rested center stage on a raised satin pillow. Ines's uncle Gerardo had given her his grandfather's fountain pen when she graduated from SF State, the first in her family to go to college, and from that first acquisition, she had started to collect. She was writing a couple of screenplays, I think—she didn't say, but I snuck a peek at her notebook.

Most people came in wanting roller ball refills or ink for their Parker Sonnets, but once in a while, an older man or two who shared Ines's passion stopped by to consult her. They had to work hard to get Ines to talk. Hers was a perverse sort of obsession, I decided, since it seemed to give her no pleasure. One guy named Martin came in twice a week to fondle a Visconti Black Ripple, specially imported, that Ines kept under lock and key. He was about fifty-five, sandy-haired, with smooth cheeks and an Irish brogue. He carried a stand-up briefcase with a brass clasp at the top.

"Ines," he said one time when I was helping. He was trying the Visconti again, writing his name on the pad we kept on the counter. "I need your help. I can't make up my mind. Please just tell me to buy it." It cost over a thousand dollars.

"What are the contenders?" Ines asked, and then they were off, talking of the Parker Duofold and the Sheaffer Balance and some we didn't carry. Martin kept stooping low over the display case and bobbing up to exclaim. He produced his phone to show Ines pictures of other models. Ines answered him in her usual military manner, matching him name for name, description for description, without showing the merest glimmer that the subject warmed her, though she must have spent hours poring through catalogs and books. She had taught me a little about what to look for: the barrel, the cap, and the nib.

"The mechanism is important," she said. "How is the ink delivered? Does it fill easily and flow well?" She took out her great-grandfather's pen, a Waterman Red Ripple, to show me. She let me cap and uncap it and write on our scribbling pad. *Ines, Ines, Ines,* I wrote. I couldn't bring myself to write my own name. To see my signature looking back at me made me feel as if I were shrinking. The pen balanced perfectly against the bump on my finger, but then I pressed too hard and scratched a hole in the paper.

"I'm more of a pencil person," I said. I showed her my grandfather's mechanical pencil and the leather case with Grandpa Kong's initials.

"It's a decent design," she said, testing it briefly. "Parker Seventy-five. They sold a lot of those." I liked her diffidence; there was no way we could be friends. "Grid pattern, an excellent writer. It feels instrumental, if you know what I mean. But next to a fountain pen, it's insubstantial. It doesn't announce to your hand that you've really got hold of something. It's less fun to use." She handed it back to me. I thought that "Ines" and "fun" didn't belong in the same sentence, but she probably thought the same of me. "I like the whole business with the inkwell, the nib, the wiping cloth, and the blotter. Using a fountain pen is better than smoking. It gives your hands something to do when you're thinking of what to write."

It was the most Ines had ever spoken to me. I wondered if she was willing to talk because I cherished Grandpa Kong's pencil the way she cherished her great-grandfather's pen. I had noticed that before she slipped it away in its case, she touched it briefly to her lips, the way that Charlie had used to check for fever by brushing her mouth to my forehead.

"Did you notice Martin's shirt?" Ines asked. "You can always tell the true collectors. They have a big blotch of ink on their pocket. Like this." She displayed her right breast pocket. A large stain spread over the area, dark blue and feathered. The heavy spot at the center mimicked the nipple underneath.

"That's your favorite shirt," I said. A blue denim work shirt she often wore as a jacket.

"I don't care. I like things messy. You know how it is." Ines looked at me shrewdly. "You're kind of a mess, I'd say."

That much was obvious. I didn't care, either.

I STARTED LOOKING at fountain pens on eBay, more out of curiosity than as part of any plan. I thought about lifting a couple of good ones and selling them for cash, but it wasn't a good option: I needed the job at Pen and Parchment, and stealing the merchandise would get me fired or worse. It was better to think about domestic sources of funding. Charlie didn't keep cash in the house, so I went through her bookcase when she was at work and filled a box that I took to the Bookdrop, my favorite bookstore in the Richmond District on the western side of the city. The buyer sorted through my box quickly. He set aside a couple of hardbacks and my old childhood favorites—my two volumes of d'Aulaire and the Greek myth picture books—but he put most of the books back in the box with a shrug.

"I can't use these," he said, pushing the carton back across the counter. Behind him were stacks of cat books, cookbooks, graphic novels, and first editions. Ordinarily, I'd browse for at least an hour—in the middle of the store was a groaning table of alluring volumes—but I hadn't read anything for weeks.

"I can take a few," he said. "Do you want cash or store credit?"

I took the cash: sixteen bucks and a few pennies. I was hungry for lunch and standing on Clement Street, where the dumpling and noodle shops could take me to wherever I wanted, Shanghai, Hong Kong, or Beijing, but I had an apple in my pocket that I had swiped from Kurt's. I ate it slowly, nibbling it down to the core. I didn't want to lug the box back on the bus. Katie would have driven me if we had still been friends, or A.J. would have borrowed her parents' car. I could have taken Charlie's car, but I didn't want to smell her deodorant or look at the files strewn across the backseat or see the image of her worried face in the mirror. Instead, I carried the box a couple of blocks to the Goodwill store and dumped it in front, to the protest of a Chinese grocer who wanted the sidewalk kept clear.

By late September, I had saved less than five hundred dollars. Once again, I went to the apartment one morning after Charlie had left for work to look for things I could sell. In the living room cabinets and hallway closet, I turned up nothing, not even mementoes. For all her trembling belief in the vast potential of the human race, Charlie wasn't sentimental. No sterling silver keepsakes or class rings or fake Chinese antiques cluttered our apartment. There was only one shoe box of photos of me when I was younger.

I glanced at the clock; I was due at work in an hour. In Charlie's bedroom, I searched more slowly, going through her dressing table, her cherry armoire, the plastic bins in her closet. There were books stacked on the floor alongside her bed, mostly biographies of modern-day powerhouse women that Les had given her for Christmas. The bed was queen-sized, spread with an old quilt, underoccupied for years. When I was little, I used to snuggle with Charlie and read to her from my book until we fell asleep, curled up together, but I never came in here anymore except to snoop and pilfer. I sat on the edge of the bed to rummage in the bedside table and wondered, not for the first time, what my mother did for sex. Les had someone—someone who was a secret—but Charlie had no one. Whenever I asked, she said she didn't have time for a boyfriend. Had she ever had a boyfriend? I had wanted to know. Oh, one or two, she'd said, but she didn't miss them. It was much more fun having a daughter. She dated occasionally, mostly friends of friends, and once or twice I had stayed with Les for a weekend, but Charlie had always come home saying she was glad to be back in our cozy apartment with just the two of us: I was enough for her.

Crossing the room, I opened the top dresser drawer and wormed my hand through socks, underwear, and bras. I palmed something rough and lumpy. Tucked in a pair of oversized ski socks was a rolled-up, zippered pouch.

Inside were four things I had never laid eyes on before.

The first was a gold ring, the second was a set of jade buttons, the third was a necklace, and the fourth was a picture of my father.

WHEN A.J. AND BECCA and I were twelve years old, our parents took us on a heritage tour of China. We had been promised the trip since we were eight. First we would tour together, and then split up for the orphanage visits—Becca to Guangzhou, and A.J. and I to Kunming.

A.J. and Becca were studying hard for their bat mitzvahs, which were coming up in the next year, and the trip for them was a kind of pre-reward for all their hard work and dedication. Charlie was determined that we should make the trip, part of the generally recommended procedure for international adoptees to come to terms with their adoption. Several of the Whackadoodle girls had already been: Bree and Molly had come home gushing, showing off the butterfly barrettes and knotted bracelets their parents had bought them in the street markets, though another girl, Larkin, came home unhappy. She said that China was dirty, that children wore split pants so they could pee and poop in the gutter, and that she'd never go back again. That didn't worry A.J. or Becca. They had already been on family vacations to Portugal and Israel and Guatemala and said it was cool to check out other cultures. We would take lots of pictures of ourselves doing fun things, like posing in our Whackadoodle T-shirts on the Great Wall and sunning ourselves on a riverboat cruise, and it wouldn't be so bad going to our orphanages. It's not like we remembered anything. The babies would be cute.

I couldn't share their excitement. Except for my first five months of life, I had never been outside of the United States. My Chinese was lousy compared to the other girls'—I knew only a few sentences from our weekly Whackadoodle lessons, while A.J.

and Becca both had after-school immersion—and I wasn't so sure it would be fun to visit the orphanage. What if they found out that they'd made a mistake and weren't supposed to have let me be adopted? Bree and Molly had told us that their parents were allowed to look at their orphanage files. What if, when they pulled out my file, they found something had been overlooked? Would they tell me I couldn't leave the country? Would Charlie have to run around to fix things, or pay money, or prove that she was my mother? Her Mandarin was almost as bad as mine was. It helped a little bit that she was a lawyer, and when she said that Les was coming, I felt slightly better: the two of them together were formidable. But I was so nervous about what we might find out that I couldn't ask myself the scariest question of all: What if my real parents showed up and wanted me back?

I didn't say any of it out loud to Charlie. She was looking forward to the trip, her second visit to China, and Les had never been, so they were in high spirits. "The trip of a lifetime," they called it—whose lifetime, they didn't say. Charlie talked often on the phone with Robyn, discussing the itinerary and the gifts we should take with us. It was important to take little presents for the tour guides, like cable car key chains and American cosmetics and Wisconsin ginseng for the orphanage aunties. They consulted other Whackadoodle parents about what kind of big gift they should bring to the orphanage. Some people gave cash, but that left them uneasy. "Who knows what they'll spend it on?" said Les. "They'll probably blow it on name-brand luxury goods. It's so perfectly absurd: they buy real Louis Vuitton handbags, and the tourists buy the fake ones. They're better capitalists than we are." Experienced visitors suggested things that the babies could use: infant formula and disposable diapers, or picture books for the older children, though whether those should be in Chinese or English, nobody quite knew. Still others said to wait till we got there and then buy a useful appliance, like an air conditioner or a washing machine or a dishwasher for the kitchen.

"Don't tell any of this to Ma," Les warned Charlie. "Can you imagine what she'd say? 'Let them buy their own dishwasher! You paid them enough to get her!'"

"She doesn't want us to go at all," Charlie said. "She says the government is not to be trusted."

I pretended that I didn't hear them. I hoped Gran wasn't right that the government could do things without Charlie's permission. Surely Les and Charlie could protect me. Les was a judge; they couldn't tell her what to do. And there was no way that Charlie would leave me in China. I was hers, that's what she always told me. I reminded myself over and over that my biological parents—we'd been taught in Whacks not to say "real parents"—had given me up for good. It was perfectly safe to go.

Our June departure date drew closer. Instead of practicing my Mandarin, as Charlie had suggested, I hung out with A.J. and Becca, learning their Torah portions. A.J. had the burning bush and Becca had clean and unclean foods. I envied them their task. Since third grade, they'd been complaining about going to Hebrew school and talking about how nervous they were going to be at their bat mitzvahs, still years and years away. I heard the pride in their voices and felt their excitement. Sometimes they missed Whackadoodle events because they had a field trip or a holiday party at temple. It was another way they stood apart from me, another group to which they belonged and I didn't. I wanted so badly to share their every experience that in fourth grade, I asked Charlie if I could go to Camp Haverim summer day camp. A.J. and Becca were signed up for the first session. Charlie agreed, and I spent two weeks learning the blessings, baking challah, and practicing the Hebrew alphabet. I loved the camp and went back the next summer. At the beginning of sixth grade, I told Charlie I wanted to become Jewish.

"Why can't I?" I asked. We were in the grocery store, which had a big display of foods for the Jewish New Year. I had just persuaded Charlie that we had to buy apples and honey.

"We're not Jewish," Charlie said. "Can you hurry up, please? We're having supper at Les's tonight."

"A.J. isn't Jewish," I said. "Becca isn't. But now they are."

"Their parents are Jewish, which makes them Jewish." She unloaded our cart and took out her wallet. "Just be happy you're *you*, okay?"

In Les's kitchen, I told Les that Jews ate turban-shaped challah on Rosh Hashanah and casually mentioned that I was planning to become a Jew.

"Really?" said Les. "I'd like to hear about it." She sat down with me at the table. Sometimes Les took me more seriously than Charlie did. I explained about summer camp and how I practiced the Hebrew alphabet with A.J. and Becca.

"I think it's great that you're interested," Les said. "It's a big decision, though. You probably want to take your time, think about it some more, and talk to others."

"Charlie says no," I said. It always pleased me in a queasy-making way when I could get Les to side with me over her sister.

"She wants you to be sure before you take that step. Like I said, there's a lot to learn about it. Can you think of ways you could do further investigation? Maybe read some books or take a class or two?"

"Ari is not becoming Jewish," Charlie said. She stood over the soup pot, furiously shaking the salt, which she usually measured by the quarter teaspoonful.

"Give her a break," Les said. "She's feeling left out because her friends are getting bat mitzvahed. I don't see the harm in letting her ask questions. Let me do that." Les stood up to take over, but Charlie didn't budge from her place in front of the stove. Her raised wooden spoon was red with tomato.

"They are getting bat mitzvahed because their families are Jewish. Unlike, say, the Kong family," Charlie said.

"She told me no before I even got to discuss it." Thinking that this would be a good time to show how responsible I was, I got up to set the table. "There's classes at the synagogue for people who want to convert."

"For adults," Charlie said. "That's not you." She jerked open a drawer; the utensils rattled.

"Is there anyone you could talk to at A.J.'s synagogue?" Les asked. "Maybe one of the teachers or a youth rabbi?"

"Who's going to drive her to all these classes and appointments?" Rising steam from the soup pot made Charlie's face glisten. "You have no idea how complicated our lives are. In between work, I've got to get Ari to school, make her a lunch every day, help with homework, take her to the doctor, miss work when she's sick, get her to soccer practice, do adoption group stuff on the weekends. There is no room in the schedule for Hebrew school. We don't have one hour more, one minute more, to chase around finding Ari some new thing to try. She is not becoming Jewish. This discussion is over." She slammed the lid on the pot. Les and I looked at each other, Les as surprised as I was.

"I could talk to Robyn about it," I offered. "She became Jewish when she married David."

"Did you hear what I said? You are not talking to Robyn."

"I'm just saying she knows stuff. She's good at being helpful."

"And I'm not?" Charlie fumed.

"You're just being really close-minded."

"Ari's right," Les said. "This isn't like you. You're the original Ms. We-Are-the-World, Ms. Rainbow Nation. You sound positively anti-Semitic."

"You know that's a crock," Charlie snapped.

"I know, so why are you getting so upset?"

Charlie took a deep breath and then, straight-armed, clutched the back of a kitchen chair. "I respect your choices, Ari, I really do, but our family comes from a different faith tradition. If you want to explore Judaism or Buddhism or Islam when you are older, that's fine. But for now, we're going to leave it."

"Oh, please," Les said. "We don't have any faith tradition."

"Our great-grandfather was a Presbyterian minister!"

"Like that ever made any difference. We never went to church except on Christmas and Easter."

"This isn't about you!" Charlie shouted. "This is a conversation I'm having with my daughter!"

Les opened her mouth and then shut it. I chimed in, "So why can't I do what Aunt Les says and go to Hebrew school with A.J. and Becca?"

"I want you—" Charlie took a deep breath. She moved to the stove, turning her back to me. "I want you to be happy with who we are and what we have. You've got a good life. It's not perfect, but it's pretty damn good. For now, that's all I'm asking, that you give this life a try. Stop looking, for once, for a better family to join. I'm trying my hardest, and you need to start trying, too. There isn't anything better out there. This is the family you've got."

"And trust me," Les said. "It's a doozy."

Charlie glared at her and slammed out the front door.

WE ATE OUR SOUP and waited for her to return. I took out the skillet and grilled us each a sandwich. Les occasionally made toast, but grilled cheese was beyond her. I think she subsisted on brie and crackers and pears. There was never any milk, but there was plenty of Diet Coke and beer and a chilled bottle of wine in her fridge.

"Are they really having bat mitzvahs?" Les asked me. I nodded. I was mad at Charlie for overreacting. Usually she liked my self-exploration and encouraged me to ask what she called without irony the "Big Questions." It was unlike my mother to shut me down like that.

Les sipped a beer. "Chinese orphans chanting from the Torah." She paused for a second. "Actually, I think it's great. Their parents are Jewish, so why shouldn't they be, too? It might get a little confusing, but they'll figure it out. They're navigating a lot anyway, having white parents, so they're already doing the whole identity thing. It must be so much easier for you, having a Chinese family."

I studied my soup bowl. It should have been easier, but it wasn't. I felt stupid, alone, and defective.

"It's a brave new world, that's for sure," said Les. "We've got some really complicated cases before us at court—surrogate contracts gone badly, or two couples, one lesbian and one gay, where the biological parents can't agree anymore on financial responsibility or custody arrangements, or one last week where a lesbian couple who adopted a baby from Vietnam have split up, and now the one mother isn't letting the other mother see the baby anymore."

"Is she coming back for me?" I asked. I hadn't touched my sandwich.

Les understood immediately. "Oh, honey," she said. She scooted her chair over and put her arm around me. "She will always, always come back for you." She squeezed me around the shoulders. "That's the first rule of adoption."

I wished that Charlie had been there to hear what Les had said. I wanted to be sure she knew the first rule of adoption—I knew she knew, but when Les said things, they went from "rule" to "Rule"— and, for Charlie's sake, I thought it would have been nice for her to hear Les's promise. It was the closest I ever heard to Les praising Charlie.

I GAVE UP MY PLAN to become a Jew but later that school year, when our orphanage trip loomed, I used A.J.'s and Becca's bat mitzvah preparations as the perfect distraction. I lay on my stomach on the floor in A.J.'s bedroom while she sat on her bed and listened to a tape of her Torah portion, her face screwed up in intense concentration. She wasn't chanting it yet; she still had months to learn it, but the cantor had given her the passage to listen to, to get her ear accustomed to the unfamiliar music, which came out of the ancient boom box in wavelets of up-and-down notes. Strong sunlight patterned the bedroom floor, and I rolled in it like A.J.'s dog, Feng Shui, sending up dust motes into the air. When Becca came over, the three of us made lists of who would be invited and what they should wear to the party and which boys they would dance with. "You can light the third candle," they decided—this would be during the party, they explained, when they got to invite their friends to the front of the room to show everybody whom they liked the best. "We'll invite up all the Whacks, but Ari gets to light the actual candle." We spent hours this way, and whenever A.J. or Becca brought up the trip, I got up from the floor to change the music or get us a snack from the kitchen.

"Are you girls having fun?" Robyn would ask me. "Won't it be wonderful, going to China together? Is your mom getting ready? Have you got your visas yet?" If I pretended to be looking for fruit or crackers, I didn't have to answer any of Robyn's questions and could scoot back into the bedroom and break up the conversation with a rat-ta-tat-tat of questions of my own.

The closer we got to the trip, the worse I felt. I started having bad dreams that woke me in a fright but that I couldn't remember in the morning. I wasn't hungry at mealtimes and then bought bags of cheesy snacks and giant sodas from the corner store, which I wolfed down walking home from school. Charlie was working even more than usual, trying to "get ahead," she said, so that she could be gone for a whole two weeks without putting too much on her colleagues. Now that I was twelve, I was okay on my own for an hour or two in the apartment as long as I called her as soon as I walked in the door. From the very first time she let me stay alone, I loved the freedom and the silence. I skated on stockinged feet across the scratched mahogany floors and read dirty passages in the novels on the bookshelves and pretended that my orange beanbag chair was a huge rock in the middle of the sea and I was Prometheus, chained to it forever, or Ariadne on Naxos peering across the horizon, wailing as she watched Theseus sail away. Charlie had urged me to pack for China, so I put the suitcase ostentatiously in the middle of my bedroom floor and filled half of it with books. I figured that if the trip were horrible, I could lose myself in those pages.

Only one person sensed my deep foreboding. WeiWei called me one afternoon a few days before our departure. It was as if she knew through some mysterious channel that I was in trouble and needed her help. I was home alone, Web surfing and watching TV, anything to avoid packing, while Charlie was out running errands.

"Hey," she said. "This is WeiWei."

"Hi," I said faintly. She had never called me, ever.

"You didn't answer my e-mail."

"Um, I guess not." I was hot with embarrassment. Busy WeiWei, important WeiWei, had sent me an e-mail that I had read three times and then not replied to, not knowing how to answer.

"I hear you're going to visit your orphanage."

"Yeah, with A.J. Becca's going to hers, too."

"So you excited?"

"I guess so," I said. I felt tears spring. I couldn't let WeiWei hear me crying.

"Good," she said. "It'll be a good trip. I've been to a bunch of orphanages. They're okay places, the kids do fine there, there's plenty of food and school books and everything they need, really."

Everything but parents.

"But I know you," WeiWei said. "You take things hard. I know that."

"Is there something wrong with me? That I'm like that?" I said. "Different in some way?"

"We all have our own weirdnesses. Yours just happens to be a brand I get. Orphans have to stick together, right? Nobody knows what's it like for us, though if you think about it too long, you can drive yourself crazy. We don't want that, do we? Life is crazy enough as it is. So look, I sent you something. It'll get to you today or tomorrow. Take it with you. It'll solve all your problems, on this trip anyway. Okay?"

I nodded. The phone felt like a magical object in my hand, delivering me from a fate that was all the more scary because I couldn't imagine what it might be.

"Okay," I uttered, then, "thanks," I managed to say.

"Send me a postcard," WeiWei said. "Have you got my address?" I didn't.

"It was in my e-mail, doofus."

"Where are you calling from?" I asked.

WeiWei laughed before putting down the phone.

"Hollywood," she said. "Where else would WeiWei be?"

THE PACKAGE ARRIVED the next day. Inside was a picture of WeiWei in an unnamed Chinese city, surrounded by a jostling group of smiling Chinese kids. "It'll be fun," she had scrawled on the back of the photo. "In their eyes, you're a hero." Along with the picture were three rolls of film and a plastic camera. It was easy to operate, she wrote, and she wanted me to use it, especially on the day I visited the orphanage. "You won't lose face if you stick your face behind this." Her words made no sense to me, but I put the camera in my backpack to carry with me on the plane.

Robyn had made the travel arrangements, planning the same kind of itinerary that she later used for her touring company: cultural sites first, to get us acclimated, and the orphanages at the end, when we were comfortable with the whole thing, as if comfort could be guaranteed after nine days in the country. We went to Beijing, Shanghai, and Guilin, and then we split up, Becca's family traveling to her orphanage in Guangzhou, and the rest of us to Kunming. There were local tour guides to take us around in each city. I was more relaxed once the trip was under way because A.J., Becca, and I got to share a hotel room. Who cared about the Forbidden City or the Great Hall of the People? We had control of our own TV set and electronic key cards that slid into a slot by the bathroom to make the lights go on. Only the Great Wall caught my imagination, sinuous and potent, like a dragon gliding across the land. I snapped my friends' pictures with Charlie's digital camera; the plastic camera WeiWei had sent me was bulky and it used film—I couldn't check after each shot the picture I had just taken. At night, when A.J. and Becca and I bounced from bed to bed and ate packets of Oreos we'd bought in the hotel shop, I told myself that our day at the orphanage would be just as easy: a quick walk around, lunch, and then shopping. I wondered if our Kunming hotel would be as nice as the one in Beijing.

The night before our orphanage visit, my fears came flooding back. Becca and her parents had departed, so to save money, I was stuck in a room with Charlie and Les. They were sick of each other after nine days on the road and squabbled over whose toothpaste was almost out and whose turn it was to ask housekeeping for a thermos of hot water. Les had brought a bag of freshly ground coffee and a bright yellow cone and paper filters and couldn't leave in the morning without making herself a cup of French roast, which she drank black and piping. Charlie didn't drink tea or coffee. Her stomach was wobbly, she said; she spent a lot of time in the bathroom.

"How are you feeling?" she asked me as we got ready for bed. Les was down in the business center, answering e-mail.

I shrugged. I didn't want to admit to myself or to Charlie how desperately I wanted to skip the whole orphanage visit.

"It must be hard for you, coming back to face it all." She stroked my arm, watching for my expression. Her face looked drawn and tired; dark circles under her eyes showed up like thumbprints. Her voice dropped. She tried for a smile. "I'm a little sorry that I'm putting you through this. It seemed like a good idea, and everybody else was really excited for the trip, but now, I don't know. Is it okay that we're here? Are you okay with going tomorrow?"

This was our particular psychosis, our peculiar pattern that bent us both into unnatural shapes: my mother, unsure of herself, asking me for approval, and I, confused, feeling both old and young, trying to give her the answer she needed to hear. Even at twelve, I understood what she was asking: *Am I a good mother? Are you glad it was me who got you?*

"A.J. and Becca think we'll be happy we saw it," I said slowly, buying time as I tried to figure out how to save myself while protecting my mother's feelings. She wanted me to be as excited as my friends. A.J. had been counting down the hours. Becca had shown us a letter she'd written to her birth parents, which she planned to put in her orphanage file. Charlie, for once, hadn't asked the same of me.

"But how do you feel, honey? We don't have to go. We could wait in the hotel while the others visit, and Les can tell us all about it later. If that would be easier for you. Or we could go out sightseeing, just you and me. That way, you could still get a sense of your homeland"—the word sounded ridiculous; China was not my home—"your city of origin, but the orphanage part, we can skip."

Pride flashed in me; I mistook it for anger. How could I stay back if everyone else was going? What would I say later to A.J. and Becca and WeiWei? And there was something more that I'd never detected before from Charlie. Not just a mother's love or distress or concern for my feelings, but the barest, faintest smell of a trace of pity.

I crossed my arms. I glared at my mother. "Why don't you make up your mind?" I said. "You brought us all the way here, so now we have to go. I don't see what the big deal is. It's just a bunch of kids who don't have any parents. There's lots of kids like that all over the world. I know that's where I came from, but, honestly, it doesn't mean anything to me. You guys are the ones making such a big deal out of it. I'll go, and you can take lots of pictures, and then, can we go home? Camp Haverim starts next week. If we sign up the first day, I can go on the camping trip."

My arrow had struck. Charlie bit her lip and nodded. We went to bed, nobody happy.

THE NEXT MORNING, I couldn't eat a bite. The air was gray and sticky; it had rained hard in the night, and the puddles looked black and oily. A.J. was running a temperature; her cheeks, always pink, looked brightly painted. Robyn fussed but decided it was okay for A.J. to make the visit; she had only a little fever, and when would she get this chance of a lifetime again? A.J. had dressed for the occasion in a spangly tank top and skirt with a sequined belt and sparkly earrings. I had dressed quickly in the same blue capris and yellow shirt that I had worn the day before.

"Do you think they'll remember us?" A.J. asked while we were waiting for the van. Her voice sounded croaky. "Will any of the aunties remember who we are?"

"Maybe," I said, to please her. I didn't want to dampen A.J.'s spirits, A.J., who was up for any adventure, whose eagerness gave me courage, but made me feel superior to her, too. It was better than feeling frightened.

"My mom brought this big photo collage to give them," A.J. said. "It's got a picture of our whole group on Gotcha Day, and pictures of you and me with our forever families." That was Whackadoodle-speak for our adoptive parents, though we hadn't used the phrase since we were little. In A.J.'s excitement, she was talking like a baby.

"That's messed up. What will it be like for the kids who live there, seeing happy pictures of the Ones Who Got Away?"

A.J. paused, tenderhearted. "Maybe it'll help them to hope for a better life." She gave me one of her impulsive A.J. hugs. "Anyway, they'll be happy to see that we're friends."

"They'll be happy when we get to the gift part," I said. After endless debate and consultation, our families had decided they would tell Director Zhu they would buy the orphanage some useful thing it needed for three hundred dollars max. Our Kunming tour guide had scolded them for extravagance—"It's not necessary," she'd insisted, "for visitors to make a big present. If you want to do something, buy three hundred RMB of formula for the babies."

"That's less than forty dollars," Les had objected. "It'll look really cheap if we spend less than two hundred dollars per family." Robyn and Charlie had readily agreed, but David had protested at Les's amount, worried about being taken for fools. "It's a matter of face," Les had informed him, suddenly getting into the whole cultural thing she usually disparaged. China was having an effect on everyone, even Les. David said it was more like a matter of liberal guilt or the foreign trade imbalance. "Then I'll pay two hundred, and you put in a hundred," Les proposed, showing her keen grasp of how the game of face really worked. They settled on a hundred and fifty bucks apiece. I saw the tour guide's eyeballs roll.

"Here," A.J. said, as we climbed into the van. She held out Wei-Wei's camera. "I loaded it with film."

I didn't want it, but I had promised WeiWei. I took it reluctantly.

"I'm so excited," A.J. said. "Do you think they'll remember us?"

She stared out the window on the short drive there while I clutched at the big black camera.

A BANNER HUNG above the door—WELCOME DAUGHTERS HOME— with our orphanage names written in Chinese characters. Three caregiver aunties greeted us in Chinese and pointed to the banner, laughing and saying our names. A.J. ran to stand under the banner, and Robyn and David snapped pictures. I plodded over to join her, obeying all the adults who commanded me to smile. It had been a bad idea to tell Charlie I wanted to come. I should have stayed at the hotel. I could have been eating French toast in the room and watching the Disney Channel. Charlie was telling me to stand next to the sign on the building that had a long description in English—SOCIAL WELFARE INSTITUTE, I read. THIS BUILDING COST $13,000 USD. The rest of the words swam before me.

In the entryway, a group of orphanage children awaited. "Hello, hello!" They waved exuberantly and called out their first names. A.J. answered in Mandarin, and the children and aunties squealed with pleasure. A man walked in, accompanied by a young woman in the same white coat as the aunties, though she was much younger, with briskness in place of their warmth.

"This is Director Zhu," she introduced him. "I am Miss Peng. Director Zhu says welcome to the Social Welfare Institute Kunming. We are very happy you come to make this homeland visit."

I strayed to the side while the adults clustered around. Through a doorway to the left, I saw a dim room with pictures on the walls and toys arranged neatly on shelves. Tables and chairs were lined up in the middle, and stuffed animals hung from the light fixtures, so high up that no kid could reach them. A fluffy yellow chicken peered down. A dingy white bear swung from its neck on a cord.

"Would you care for a tour?" Miss Peng asked. We followed her dutifully through the room I'd viewed, full of toys and books and furniture but no children. The welcoming committee came with us, seven or eight boys and girls in colorful shirts and dresses. I guessed their ages from about six to eight. Some of them looked different—a wandering eye, a cleft palate—but they were all smiling and pointing out pictures on the wall, one after another, of white parents and Chinese daughters: TO THE WONDERFUL CAREGIVERS OF OUR DAUGHTER EMMA; TO DIRECTOR ZHU AND HIS AMAZING STAFF; THE BROWNING FAMILY THANKS YOU WITH ALL OUR HEART. One little boy asked A.J. to stand for a picture in front of another banner all in Chinese, red with gold lettering, framed with the beaming faces of Mickey Mouse and Minnie.

"I don't feel so good," I whispered to Charlie. She bent swiftly, put her hand to my forehead.

"You should have eaten something," she said. She gave me a little packet of soda crackers, which I dropped as we walked, not caring who found it.

Down the hallway we were ushered by the straight back of Miss Peng. The walls were damp from the rain, the dankness no different from other Chinese buildings, but they seemed to me to be dripping. A woman knelt at the end of the passage, wiping the floor with rags. In the next room we entered, a dozen children wheeled merrily around in plastic walkers, their aunties holding them by lengths of cloth tied to the rims. Watching them circle and hearing them cheerily shout our names, I thought I might heave onto the tile floor. Instead, I found my arms stonily lifting the camera I held in my sweating hands.

Click. I took a picture of a toothless baby. *Click.* An auntie cupping a little boy's head. I had found a use for my eyes and my body. I scanned the room, my face behind the camera. I felt my wet breath against its plastic shell.

An auntie separated herself from the group and went up to A.J. to pat her hair and her face.

"This auntie says she remembers you," Miss Peng said. "You were a Monkey baby, very good, very happy." Director Zhu nodded, adding something in Mandarin. A.J. smiled shyly and spoke to the woman, who teared up and stroked A.J.'s hair again and again. Robyn stepped forward, holding a bag open to A.J.

"No, no," instructed the tour guide. "We give all the presents at one time, when you sit down for tea with the director." But A.J. ignored her and reached into the bag and pulled out a little wrapped present that she placed in the old woman's hands. They hugged tightly while David shot video and Robyn snapped pictures.

Miss Peng turned to me. "Another auntie remembers you," she said, but I raised my camera and started clicking away. Charlie murmured something to our tour guide, who called off Miss Peng, who retreated. As we left the room, I kept the camera to my face, able to take in everything I was seeing through the tiny little window that shrank the rooms, the aunties, and the children into unreal miniatures for me to look at, the way I might look at a slide under a microscope or a thumbnail shot on a screen.

I was ready, then, when we finally reached the nursery, to see the rows of babies in their powder blue cribs. With the camera between me and what I was looking at, I wasn't a participant, only an observer. A baby whose eyes followed a passing auntie. *Click.* A baby who smiled when A.J. clapped her hands. *Click.* A baby like me, with a rosebud mouth and a truculent expression. I clicked her twice and named her "Athena" under my breath. I stared at her bright black eyes through my camera, willing her to one day get up and enter her life.

Miss Peng led us into a large room with a long table. The square chairs were so heavy, I could barely move mine to sit down. At each place was a covered teacup and a bottle of water. Wrapped apples and candies and ashtrays dotted the table like centerpieces no one was supposed to touch. Director Zhu spoke for a long five minutes, translated by Miss Peng, whose every word I ignored.

"Eat something," Charlie whispered to me. I was starving by then, but nobody else was eating. Les, on my other side, unwrapped a candy and passed it to me. It tasted sweet and salty; I sucked at it hungrily. Gifts were exchanged; documents were presented; Robyn passed Director Zhu her framed collage of photographs, which, compared to the other ones we had seen hanging, looked small and inadequate—too low on the gushing meter. Without looking at it, Director Zhu thanked her with a slight nod of his head and passed the picture to Miss Peng.

"We would also like to buy the institute a useful gift," Robyn said.

Miss Peng translated. Our tour guide looked disgusted.

"Director Zhu thanks you very much," Miss Peng said. "They very much like a TV for the staff dormitory. After all day, taking care of the babies, the aunties like a little program entertainment."

"A television?" Robyn asked, dismayed. Beside me, Les snorted. David stared at the table. Charlie wore a frozen smile. Our tour guide shot Les a triumphant, told-you-so look.

"We were thinking of something that would benefit the children directly," Robyn said. "A washing machine, perhaps, or a kitchen appliance." They had noticed silent workers washing diapers and dishes by hand.

Director Zhu shrugged and spoke.

"We go have lunch now," Miss Peng said. "After that, I can take you shopping."

LUNCH WAS IN a building next door to the orphanage. I snapped pictures of each dish as it came to the table. Director Zhu vanished, but two other men showed up—I never figured out who they were—and a couple of women who chatted with our tour guide; all of them sat at a second table, along with our van driver. It seemed everybody lunched well when Americans came to visit. I ate from every dish—the food was much better than anything we had at home—but A.J. barely lifted her chopsticks. The medicine she had taken in the morning had worn off; her fever had come back, and she looked ready to drop.

"We'd better take her back to the hotel," Robyn whispered to Charlie.

"We can handle the afternoon," Les said.

"Do you want to go back, too?" Charlie asked me.

"Are we staying at the orphanage?"

"No," Charlie said. "They're taking us to do some sightseeing and some shopping, too, I think."

"I'll stay," I said. I still hadn't gotten my butterfly barrettes. We were flying home the next day; I figured Miss Peng could show me where to buy some.

A taxi took A.J. and her parents back to the hotel. Miss Peng came with us in the van and showed us around a couple of places—a pretty park, an old temple—and then directed the driver to a crowded shopping area where throngs of people bustled in and out of the stores.

"We go there," Miss Peng said, pointing to a large building at the end of the street. I was disappointed; I'd been hoping for a street market, like the other Whacks had been to. This looked like an American shopping district, with clothing stores and pharmacies and shop windows full of cell phones and cameras. We trudged behind her, Charlie and Les hugging their shoulder bags to their stomachs like pregnant women protecting the unborn fetus. At the entryway to the store, Director Zhu materialized with a curt nod. He didn't say a word, nor did Miss Peng explain.

"Huh," I heard Les say under her breath to Charlie. "Johnny-on-the-spot. This is going to be tricky."

"What is this store?" Charlie asked Miss Peng brightly, still trying to make pleasant conversation. Les had given up long before.

Miss Peng rattled off a name. "Before that," she said, "it was called Friendly Nation Department Store Number One."

Charlie stopped. "Oh, God," she said. "This is the store." She looked at me, stricken. "I didn't mean for us to come here. God, Les. What'll I do?"

Les grimaced. "I don't think we can get out of it now," she said.

Charlie leaned down and grasped me by the shoulders.

"Do you understand?" she said. "This is *your store*. Your Finding Day place."

I looked at her and nodded. I raised my camera. *Click.*

UPSTAIRS, DIRECTOR ZHU and Miss Peng steered us straight to Electronics. A salesman came over. Director Zhu said a few words, and the two began walking the rows of TV sets, pausing in front of some for Director Zhu to consider.

Les looked at our tour guide, who shrugged and kept quiet. "Excuse me," Les said, taking Miss Peng aside. "I'm very sorry, but we would like to buy a washing machine. Could you please take us to look at washing machines?"

"This is what you want," Miss Peng said, smiling. She swept her arm in overacted delight. "Thanking you so much. The aunties will be very happy."

"Yes," Les said, more patient than I'd ever seen her. "It's very impressive, how many luxury goods China now produces. Thank you for showing us. We're ready now to look at the washing machines. Shall we find a salesperson who can show us where we can find them? Maybe another floor? The sixth floor, perhaps? I saw a sign when we came in. Third floor for TV sets. Sixth floor for washing machines and dryers." She began moving quickly toward the escalator. Miss Peng, Charlie, and I hurried to keep up. Out of the corner of my eye, I saw a strange man follow. I had noticed him staring at us downstairs. He was a tall, thin man, about Charlie's age, wearing a navy tracksuit and carrying a blue plastic bag by two fingers. His shoulders were sloped, as though he were used to bearing heavy cargo on the long bamboo poles I had seen workers balance with bundles or wooden buckets lashed to either end. He saw me and nodded, breaking into a warm smile. I drew close to Les, unsure whether to smile back. The way he was looking at me made me feel as if I was supposed to know him, though I didn't recognize him from earlier in the day.

"I must tell the director where we are going," Miss Peng said.

"I'm sure he can figure it out," Les said, then caught herself and added, "He's very welcome to join us."

On the sixth floor, no sales clerk came over to help us, though we were the only shoppers. Les found a young clerk lounging by a counter.

"We'd like to buy a washing machine." He looked at her and disappeared. Miss Peng had disappeared, too.

"This place is unbelievable," Les said. "We need a Best Buy or a Wal-Mart."

"Maybe he's gone to get help," Charlie said.

"Let's just pick one," Les said. "How hard can it be? The best washing machine for under three hundred dollars." They looked at each other and started laughing.

"Quick," Charlie said. "Before Director Zhu finds out."

"We need our tour guide," Les said, "so she can tell them where it should be delivered."

I had seen our tour guide come up the escalator behind us, so I told Charlie and Les that I would find her. I started to look but didn't spot her. She wasn't in washing machines or refrigerators. The woman I approached in vacuum cleaners wasn't her, either. By the time I decided that I'd better go back to Charlie, I was turned around and feeling a mild panic. I knew they wouldn't leave without me, but I didn't know which way to go.

"Good afternoon," a man's voice said.

I looked around quickly. The man from downstairs was smiling at me. He spoke in English with a slight British accent. His eyes were clear and his gaze arresting. I saw his thin lips close and draw back in an even bigger smile.

"May I help you?" he asked. He stepped closer. I smelled cigarette and eucalyptus, like the Tiger Balm ointment Charlie smeared on herself for a cold. "Are you lost? Is that your mother over there? The American?" He pointed.

I nodded, not wanting to speak to him but needing his help to find her.

He leaned down. He was very tall, taller than I had realized, and younger than I had thought, with a face as smooth as my forearm.

"I know you," he said. He gripped my shoulder. "I followed you from the orphanage. I am your father."

I MUST HAVE SCREAMED for no more than ten seconds before they came running, because later Charlie told me she had been only steps away. Maybe she was lying to help me feel safe and protected. I don't remember what happened, only that I got away from the man. I made Charlie tell it over and over, all the rest of the day. She said she took me to the van, where we waited for Les, and then we came straight back to the hotel. I calmed down after A.J. joined us. Charlie said store security guards took the man away. He was a local nut, "harmlessly crazy," the store manager told Les, who reamed him out with a blistering lecture on keeping his harmless crazies away from vulnerable young girls. Neither Miss Peng nor the tour guide offered to translate. Les had made her point clear.

"He was not your father," Charlie assured me again and again. There was no possible way that what he had said was true. The authorities knew him; they knew his origins, habits, and methods. He had pulled that trick before, hanging around places where Westerners shopped, picking out adoptive families—there were so many; they visited by the scores—to ask for money. He approached the parents, not the children. He knew that children had no coins to give. They didn't know why, this time, he had spoken directly to me. Maybe because there wasn't a husband, the authorities said. Charlie didn't tell me that part. Les did.

By the time we got home, I believed what Charlie had told me: he wasn't my father, no matter how he had looked at me or what he had claimed. I would never know my father, Charlie said. She cried and held me, but I didn't speak. She apologized for her mistake. We should not have gone into the store. What was she thinking, that she had let that happen? Some people said it was helpful for a child to visit her Finding Day place, but she and Robyn had discussed it beforehand and had agreed that, at least on this trip, we weren't going to do that. It seemed like enough to visit the orphanage, and even that had been hard. Charlie knew that. She had watched me with my camera, and how beautifully I'd borne it, all the emotions of the day. It had been a big day for her, too, remembering her joy on the day she got me, and feeling sad all over again that so many children had not yet found a home. Someday it would help me to have been there and seen it. But we should not have gone into the store. For that mistake, she was sorry.

"Can I call A.J.?" I asked. "I don't want to talk about it anymore."

I remember one thing from the end of our Kunming visit. The final morning, our tour guide met us in the hotel lobby to accept her tip and put us into the van to the airport.

"What did you end up buying the orphanage?" I asked. I had told A.J. the story. We all were standing next to our pile of luggage, waiting for the driver to pull the van around.

"A washing machine," Les said, "despite their best efforts to get me to buy the TV."

"Your aunt Les was brilliant," Charlie said. "It was like some ancient cultural knowledge kicked in, some natural instinct that was in our DNA, waiting to come in handy."

Les laughed. "Director Zhu showed up in the washing machine department with a sales slip all filled out for a flat-panel TV. We started going back and forth all over again."

"Yes," Charlie interrupted, "and you knew exactly what to say to him to get him to concede."

"What was that?" I asked.

Les grinned. "I told him that, if it were up to me, I would be honored to buy the aunties the TV set, but our good friends, the Reises, expected me to buy the washing machine. If I didn't do as I had promised Robyn and David, I would be very embarrassed to see them later and have to explain what I had done."

"It was a matter of face," Charlie said. "Director Zhu didn't want Les and me to lose face before our friends."

"So we bought the washing machine, the best one they had. It didn't cost anywhere near three hundred dollars. Our tour guide was right: we were a little off, there."

"I'm glad my hypothetical displeasure got us what we wanted," David said. "I'm going to try some of that face stuff around the office."

"Thank God, there's the van," Robyn said. "I hope they don't have fever monitors at the airport."

A.J. looked dopey. Robyn had loaded her up with every over-the-counter drug she had toted across China.

"The washing machine is being delivered to the orphanage this morning," Les said.

The tour guide smiled. The two tip envelopes were safe in her pocket.

"I don't think so," she said. "Director Zhu will tell the department store not to deliver. They will switch payment and send the TV instead."

CHAPTER 16

ARI

The man in the photograph I found was not my father.

I will never know my father.

When I was twelve years old and I got lost in the department store, the store in Kunming that was my Finding Day place, and a man came up to me and looked at me as if he knew me and told me that he was my father, and my mother, Charlie, folded me in her arms and told me that I would never, ever know my father, I believed her. Because it was true.

The man in the photograph was not my father.

And yet, because I so badly wanted there to be a father, I said to myself, "There is my father," and I went out to find him.

OF THE FOUR things I discovered in Charlie's sock drawer—the ring, the jade buttons, the necklace, and the photograph—I looked at the last thing first. It was a picture of a man holding me against his chest, both of us smiling at the camera. I was in a dark blue baby carrier, facing outward. I turned the picture over. On the back, in Charlie's clear hand, it said, "Aaron practicing to be a father." She had written a date: August 1992.

I was six months old. I had been home with Charlie for a month.

I studied the photograph. I was wearing a light green, one-piece jumper with little white bunnies scattered across that I recognized from other pictures of me as a baby. The man had hold of my hands and was raising my arms in the air. My legs were kicking in baby pleasure. I had a lot of black hair, some of it swiped across my forehead, some sticking up in back. I was goofily, swooningly happy. We were standing on the sidewalk in front of our apartment in the even light of a San Francisco summer day.

I didn't know the man. "Aaron," I said aloud. I thought that maybe I had heard the name before, mentioned casually a few times by Les, with no response from Charlie. I wasn't sure about that. I hadn't heard it often enough to provoke curiosity on my part, but the sound was vaguely familiar. "Aaron," like "Ari," the first syllable similar, though not pronounced the same. "Aaaaron," "Arrrri." I spoke them into the cloistered air, trying to hear my way into a memory.

He was in his mid-thirties, I guessed, with dark, wavy hair and small, round wire-rimmed glasses. His smile had a touch of defiance, and the way he stood in the center of the sidewalk, his body relaxed, his hands lifted, suggested a man at home with himself in the world. He wore a long-sleeved plaid shirt, blue jeans, and work boots. The shirt was tucked in; I could see that he was fit, with sturdy shoulders and narrow hips. He was white. On his wrist was a leather watchband.

I turned the picture over again. Only "Aaron." No last name.

I examined the other items. The ring was set with a dull red stone. Had it come from Aaron? I had never seen Charlie wear it. It was too big for my finger. The buttons were bright green and showed faint carvings. They were tied together with a piece of black thread. I imagined they'd been snipped from the empress dowager's gown, or smuggled out through Hong Kong by an aristocrat in a hurry. They seemed far too fine to belong to Charlie.

The necklace was cheap. The clasp was broken. Hanging from the chain was the Hebrew word for life, *chai*. A.J. had a necklace like that, in sterling silver.

I searched the other drawers but found nothing more, so I carried the jewelry and the buttons and the photograph into Charlie's study and looked through her desk drawers, which turned up nothing. The file cabinet beside the desk sat black and squat, a creature crouched in the corner. I would have to paw through it, continuing my plunder, and even I, at that point, was feeling sordid. I left the room to get my phone and dialed Pen and Parchment.

Ines picked up. I asked her to tell Kurt that I wasn't coming in.

"He'll be pissed," Ines said. "He's got you down for the front register this morning."

"Tell him I'm sick."

"Are you?" she asked.

I put down the phone. I inventoried what I'd left behind at Kurt's house—a shirt or two, my bathroom things. Nothing I really needed. I knew I wouldn't be going back. I was midcurrent, a body slipping down a stream, half swimming, half carried along by the water. Whatever more I found, I would soon be leaving. I was working blindly, feeling my way in the dark. Reason wasn't part of it, or impulse or desperation. There was only that clear statement: "Aaron practicing to be a father."

Tax files, school files, paid bills, the apartment lease. I went through it all, looking for Aaron. At last, stuck in a folder labeled KEEP, I found an envelope from "A.S., c/o Miriam Streeter." There was an address in Seattle.

"For Ari," the note in the envelope said. "With love from Aaron."

I looked up the name and address on the Internet and summoned a blizzard of pages, none useful. I put everything back in its place, covering my tracks around the apartment. I hesitated over the jewelry—I still needed money—but the pieces looked cheap, and a better plan was forming. I put back the ring, the necklace, and the buttons and kept only the photograph. I didn't think Charlie would miss it. When was the last time Charlie had looked at those things? She did as Gran said: she lived in the present, treasured what she had, and didn't chase after rainbows.

There was just one problem, and I, an orphan, understood it well. When everything you love is yours at the present moment, you live in constant fear of losing it.

My loss was ancient, and I nursed it like a baby.

Their loss was potential, and I played it like a pro.

I decided to visit Gran. If she thought she might lose me, she would give me whatever I asked.

I CALLED GRAN, told her I was coming down, changed into a skirt and blouse, and took the train to Millbrae. I splurged on a taxi from the station to Gran's place. I hadn't been to see her since the start of the summer, before I'd left for Beijing, and I couldn't remember which condo was hers. The names on the directory told a tale of assimilation: Berglund, Cheong, Farhadi, Gomez. I pressed the button for "Mrs. Betty Kong Hsu," and Gran's deep voice answered.

"It's Ari," I said into the intercom.

"Who else would it be? The milkman?"

THE DOOR WAS AJAR. Gran was sitting in her chair, reading a newsmagazine. She didn't look at me until I was standing in front of her. She interrupted before I finished saying hello.

"Why aren't you at school?" she said. "Your mother said you're *deferring*." She pronounced the word with malicious displeasure.

"I didn't feel ready to leave home yet. I just needed a little time to, you know, get in the right mental space for college."

Gran raised an eyebrow.

"Nowadays, a lot of kids defer. It gives you time to figure out what exactly you want to study, maybe get some life experience, so that when you start school, you're ready to take advantage of all that college offers."

Silence followed. I shifted uncomfortably. I had beaten that drum successfully with Charlie; in here, it sounded like I was banging a spoon on a tin pie plate.

"And have you had time enough?" Gran closed her magazine and laid it unhurriedly on the table. "Are you in the right mental space? I suppose it's too late for the fall term, but what about January? You've saved me some money"—she looked about, bored—"which I invested well, but I'd much rather spend it on seeing you get a decent education, which, by the way, if you refuse to do, will mean that there won't be any money from me when you need it."

I looked at her and burst out laughing.

"Oh, Gran," I said, "can't you do better than that?"

WE HAD TEA and lychee fruit and went out for a drive into the wooded hills, Gran palming the wheel like a rancher handling his pickup. She talked to me about her restaurant days and Grandpa Kong and her father. She'd been thinking about her father a lot, she said, and I stopped myself from saying, "Since when don't you?" A neighbor of hers named Naomi had lived in Shanghai during the war, and they had wanted to figure out if their fathers, both doctors, had ever met. Mostly the Jews didn't leave their neighborhood—"their ghetto," I said; "I suppose it was," Gran said with a nod. Mostly they stayed in the restricted sector, but once in a while, some moved about the city. Naomi thought maybe her father had been permitted outside because she remembered his talking about visiting a fine hospital with big tanks of goldfish in the courtyard.

"My father's hospital had koi," Gran told me with excitement, "in big ceramic cisterns in the courtyard, where Rose and I used to play." Her father had welcomed Jews into his home, and maybe one of them who had helped Naomi's family had introduced the two men. I tried to imagine the fathers of two old Millbrae ladies meeting in Shanghai in the 1940s and couldn't. It was so long ago, it had nothing to do with me.

"I was telling Naomi all about it," Gran said. "And how we spent our summers in Kuling, at Lushan Mountain. She'd heard of Lushan—well, everyone has, of course—it's so beautiful and famous, the most beautiful place in China."

I looked at the dashboard clock. I was running out of time to get Gran to open her checkbook.

"I'd like to see pictures," I said. "Do you have any? When we get back, let's look."

Gran shook her head. "Everything was lost once the Japanese invaded. That very last summer, my parents bought a house in Kuling.

The war was on, and so the British home owners finally let Father buy. They wanted to get rid of their houses, you see, and they decided it was okay to let Chinese into the district. Before that, we could only rent." Gran looked wistful, an alien expression.

"Kuling was paradise," she said. "Absolute paradise for Rose and Mu-you and me."

"Who's Mu-you?"

Her whole face tightened, as though someone had cinched a drawstring.

"For Rose and me, is what I meant to say." Then she stopped talking and steered the car toward home.

I WASHED THE TEACUPS and put away the dishes. Her housekeeper, Yan, wasn't home. Maybe Gran had sent her out so she could beetle at me in private.

"Look at this thing," Gran said. She was pointing to a bonsai tree that looked half dead. All the evergreen branches were brown at their tips except for one, which had grown so long, it drooped over the rim of the dish.

"Your mother gave it to me. She knows I hate potted plants. Can you do anything with it?"

"I think you should trim that branch."

"You do it for me. The scissors are in that drawer."

I got a knife instead. Gran watched me. Before I'd arrived, I'd wound a large bandage around the stump of my finger. It was already healed, but I didn't want Gran to see it. She might start questioning me about what had happened in Kunming.

"Your mother says you had a nasty accident," she said, gesturing.

"It's fine now," I said. "This plant looks pretty bad, you know."

"Why did she saddle me with such a thing?"

"To give you something to nurture?"

"Ha," Gran said. "If having children didn't do that, no toy tree ever will. Come help me with this." She went into her bedroom, to the computer on her desk. "It keeps sending me messages I don't want," she said.

"I need to leave pretty soon." Her jewelry box was on top of her dresser. If I couldn't get her to give me some money, maybe I could find the poodle pin with the pearl.

"For heaven's sake, it will only take a minute."

I sat down to look. The desktop was open; I got rid of the annoying pop-ups and put some stuff into folders. "Would you really cut me out of things if I didn't go to Bryn Mawr?" I said. She was standing behind me, looking over my shoulder.

"I suppose it wasn't very original," Gran said. "Especially since I'm going to live forever."

"I'm excited about school." I kept my eyes on the screen. "I'm just not sure about going so far from home. So I was thinking . . . would it be a good idea for me to visit Great-Aunt Rose? Spend some time in Philadelphia, get to know the city a little? I could visit campus." As I spoke to her, I was busy telling myself that I might, someday, visit Gran's beloved Bryn Mawr, and maybe then she'd look back on this conversation as only a partial lie.

"Ah," Gran said, lighting up with interest. "Now we're getting down to it. I know, if you see it, you'll fall in love as I did."

She gave me six hundred dollars from a stash in a hidden safe. "A wartime habit," she said, "in case I ever need to leave in a hurry." Then she drew me a map of all her favorite spots on campus. "Millbrae is colorless, and will be duller still without you." I promised to send her photos of the autumn splendor—the maple and sweet gum and ginkgo trees. When I kissed her good-bye, I clutched her harder than I intended, her oxen back like a slab under my hands.

I SURPRISED CHARLIE twice in the next twenty-four hours. When she got home from work, I had supper waiting.

"How nice!" she said, and I busied myself at the stove and oven, shuttling chili and corn bread and salad to the table. She sat with a sigh, tucking in to the warmth. I settled myself across from her and began to chatter, asking her questions about her work and telling her what I'd learned about fountain pens from Ines, the whole time hearing in my head: *Aaron, Ari, Aaron.* Aunt Les, she said, had that big important hate-crime case that was all over the news, and I nodded my head knowingly, as if I'd read about it and cared.

I didn't ask Charlie, *Who the hell is Aaron?* I didn't have the slightest impulse to put her to the test. She had kept him a secret, and I didn't trust her to begin telling the truth to me now. I was only trying to stay there at the table and listen to her voice over the noise in my head. By the end of the evening, my jaw was so clenched that I thought my teeth might crack.

"Tuck me in like the old days," Charlie yawned after we cleared the dishes.

"You look exhausted," I said, and made to give her a little push, but first, I hugged her.

"Oof," she said, laughing. "You make me feel every bite."

Finally she closed her bedroom door, and her calls of good night fell quiet. I packed a bag and counted and recounted the money. I put half in my wallet and the other half in my shoe, and wound a black knit scarf of Charlie's around my neck, telling myself I was cold.

Dear Mom, I wrote on a piece of notebook paper. *I found the photograph of Aaron and decided I'd like to meet him. I don't want you to stop me, and please don't call him, either. This is something I need to do for myself.* For half a page, I tried to compose an explanation, twisting my mouth harder at every sentence I wrote until the images that had played all night in my head—Aaron greeting me, calling me by name—turned into a bigger movie of Charlie, Les, and Gran huddled together, flapping and cawing, making plans to retrieve me. I stopped writing. It was almost dawn. I ripped up the piece of paper, then grabbed at a scrap on my desk and scribbled: *I have to leave. Don't worry.*

I propped the note on the altar table, dropped my keys in the bowl, and headed out for Seattle.

PART TWO

False Outer Point

CHAPTER 17

LES

All eyes were on the woman in the jury box—young, pretty, nervous. *She looks like Ari*, Les thought, *except for the nervous part.*

"Do you feel you could keep an open mind, listening to all the evidence in the case before deciding?" Les asked, and eighty pairs of eyes in the courtroom clocked from the box to the bench. Les, in her black robe, raised above the rest, looked down at the woman and waited.

The young woman nodded.

"You have to speak up," Les said, "so the court reporter can get it."

"Yes," the young woman said, looking surprised at the sound of her own strong voice.

"'Atta girl," Les said, with a warm smile. Everyone in the courtroom laughed. Those who weren't in the jury box itched to turn on their cell phones. *I had jury duty today,* they'd go home and tell their spouses. *A Judge Kong. She was terrific.*

"Mr. Gordon?" Les asked.

"No questions, Your Honor."

"Ms. Cruz?"

"No questions, Your Honor. The defense is very happy with our jury." Les shot her a warning glance as the D.A. bristled. Ms. Cruz laughed to herself. She knew it was a cheap shot, but hey, why not take it? Judge Kong didn't get hung up on a little gamesmanship in her courtroom. She was a stickler for procedure, though—you better know your rules of evidence—and she protected the jury. Their time is as valuable as anyone else's in this case, she often chided the lawyers. Have your witnesses ready to go, or I'll let the jury know why we're sitting around, waiting. On the law, she was brilliant. Ms. Cruz straightened her shoulders. She wondered if the judge knew her name outside the courtroom.

"Then, ladies and gentlemen, I think we have a jury," Les said. The clerk of court swore them in. She thanked the rest of the group and excused them. They shuffled out, half sorry to go because the case sounded scary—home invasion—and the defendant, a white guy, was a former Saint Ignatius football player (some of the men remembered), and it was going to be fun, watching the judge keep those lawyers in line. It was almost as good as TV.

Les conferred with counsel, then excused the jury, telling them to be back at nine a.m., sharp. "Today and every day that we're together, I'll remind you not to discuss the case with anyone." She surveyed them briefly, making sure their eyes met hers. Except for juror number six, they all nodded. Sometimes there was a man who didn't come around right away. She'd keep alert to him, try for some connection. It was critical for the defendant that juror number six listen to the court, and, more important, to the defense attorney, Ms. Cruz. The D.A. started out at such an advantage that Les worked hard to even the playing field. She'd been an assistant D.A. herself for a short year, but she was known not to play favorites. Ms. Cruz leaned down to speak to her client and put a hand on his shoulder before the jury looked away. Les relaxed. Ms. Cruz knew what she was doing. She didn't need Les's help to wrest respect from the jury. Between the two of them, by the end of tomorrow, number six would be paying attention.

In chambers, Les quickly packed her briefcase and slipped out the door. She had already told her clerk and her bailiff that she'd be leaving at four o'clock. She didn't bother to offer an explanation. She was the boss. They loved working for Judge Kong and protected her fiercely from rivals and reporters. Once, her bailiff, Tony, six feet three and stout, had tackled a man who'd come charging across the courtroom screaming, "I'll kill you!" at the judge. Tony's arm was slashed; the man had gotten a screwdriver past security downstairs. A family law matter. Those were the most dangerous.

Now she was in trials and happier for it, especially in felony cases. The stakes were high and the lawyering was good. She yearned for a spot on the federal bench, where the law was often more complex and the lawyers were sometimes dazzling. There she could match wits with the best the bar had to offer, and she wouldn't have to put up with sharing the turf with her sister. They worked in different courthouses—Charlie didn't often come down to the hall—but both being in state court meant they sometimes intersected. How tiresome it was: "the King Kong Sisters," she'd heard people snigger. A swipe at Asians taking their seats at the table, or maybe it was because they were women, though surely, Les believed, the bar was beyond that now. She didn't consider herself a trailblazer. Those were the women in their sixties and seventies who had mentored Les, her law school professors and the law firm partners who'd opened their tight circle to let Les in. No, the jabs came because Les was a judge and Charlie a public defender, when one should have been a doctor and the other an engineer. People didn't like their expectations unmet; it made them uncomfortable or resentful. Sometimes idiots got Les and Charlie mixed up if Les wasn't wearing her robes. Woe to the lawyer who made that mistake. The next time he appeared in her courtroom, Les would lean down and pin him. "Judge *Lesley* Kong, presiding."

She drove home fast, because Burrell was waiting.

BURRELL JOHNSON made himself a drink and lounged on Les's sofa. From her living room window, he could see rooftops and the bay. A sickly bonsai tree in a dark green dish languished on the sill. The room was cold; it was late November, and the sun was shining, but there'd been early-winter frost on the lawn that morning. His wife, Nancy, had mentioned it when she brought in the papers.

Their sons lived in Chicago and Detroit and laughed at their parents whenever they said it was cold in San Francisco. He sipped his drink, enjoying the quiet. He liked the sparseness of Lesley's home, a welcome refuge after the clamor of the day. His life was noisy. Three times the law firm had merged until it had become an international behemoth. He hated the result, the constant conflicts and endless management meetings, but they'd had no choice—it was a matter of survival. He'd made his money, but the young guys had to have theirs, too, and they weren't content with making a damn good living. Greed had made them crazy. They wanted what their clients in Silicon Valley had, never mind that the profession they'd chosen was to counsel companies and stand up for them in court, not create new markets, new ways for the world to think. The lawyers didn't take the risks, why should they reap the rewards? But his kind of lawyering was just about dead. Nobody cared about service or justice. Lesley was smart to have gotten out of private practice. Her old firm, like his, had cut off its own nuts, morphing from a partnership of some of the best lawyers in town into a bloated business with offices around the country, no more exclusive than H&R Block. They'd regret it, all of them, giving up so much control. At least he could say he'd been master of his own fate, and the master of others', too, with a line to the governor's and senators' offices. How many men, white or black, could say that about their lives? His blood warmed from the pride and the drink and the thought of what they'd do when Lesley walked through the door. He rose to turn on a floor lamp. There was wood in the grate; he could light a fire, but on days like today, when he had a dinner to get to, they always went straight to the bedroom.

Les arrived, and they grabbed for each other.

AFTERWARD, THEY SAT in her breakfast nook, dressed and drinking coffee. They looked like an unlikely pair: Burrell a stocky, bulletheaded black man gone gray at the temples, and Les, wide-hipped, long-limbed, almost fifteen years younger. They didn't indulge in a lovers' interlude, sharing their feelings on damp and tangled sheets.

They had very different habits, imbued with their own romance. Their intimacies flourished when they felt most at ease—across the table, both upright, with hair brushed and shoes on their feet. They had found over the years in their long-running saga—broken off twice, and resumed in urgent surrender—that transitions were difficult, and so they always took the time for quiet conversation. It made it easier for them to reenter their separate lives if they had talked themselves onto a higher plane, like scuba divers rising slowly so they wouldn't get the bends. The lying they didn't discuss. They both knew they had to, once and for all, end it.

"This time next year," Les said, "we won't have any more of this nonsense." She wrapped her fingers around his thick wrist. In bed, she liked holding on to him in little ways: a wrist, a thumb, the lobe of his ear, as soft and black as the tip of a tulip stamen. She had piano fingers, Burrell liked to say, though he was the one who more often wandered into the living room to fool around on the baby grand. Sometimes they sat side by side on the narrow bench, Les playing bass to Burrell's treble riffing. Burrell had said they made a pretty picture, the big, black cowboy and his Chinese sweetheart, like something you'd find in a Wild West whorehouse. There weren't any *women* Chinese back then, Les had objected. It was only men, laboring on the railroads. Well, that's too bad, he'd said. They didn't know what they were missing.

"It's absurd," Les said. "We're far too old for this."

Burrell shook his head. "We're not going to talk about that today." He took a swallow and savored the bitter coffee. After the first fuck, he'd slept briefly, and then turned her over and licked her clean, Lesley gasping. He didn't need a young thing to flatter or cajole him. Les, in her fifties, was as eager to be ravished as the day they'd first gone to bed. He knew himself, had lived for years listening in his head to the skillful arguments of his heart, mind, and needs. Les was the woman he wanted.

"*Mon amour,*" Les said. It was a joke between them. The first time they had met, Les a young attorney and Burrell a lawyer's lawyer, Les had mispronounced his name. "Bur-relle," she had said in the glass-walled conference room that was their combat cage. She was deposing his client in a contract dispute. The depo was easy work, but Les had overprepared, which made her slip up and say his name wrong.

"Are you French?" Burrell had erupted in his loudest baritone voice.

Les had fumbled, off her pace for a moment.

"If you're not French, then try to get the name right. *Burrrl,*" he'd growled, "as in *burly, burnish, beurre blanc, Burton.*" He winked at the court reporter, who knew all his tricks.

Les had doused him with a look. This was 1984, and grim-faced women were clawing their way to the top.

"As in *burial,*" she'd said, "as in, *We're going to bury you in a burlap burqa.*"

He'd had no idea what a burqa was. He had shot her a grin and let her ask her questions.

"I HAD A YOUNG WOMAN in the jury box today who reminded me of my niece, Ari," Les said. The sun had retreated. They didn't look at the clock; they were used to billing their time in six-minute intervals, and so the passing of an hour ticked in their very organs.

"She hasn't come home?" Burrell asked.

"No, and says she won't. They talk on the phone—Ari yells, Charlie cries, they hang up, they get nowhere. If I were Charlie, I'd get on a plane this minute."

"Why doesn't she?"

"Ari said if she does, she'll disappear for good, and Charlie's convinced she means it."

"That's tough," Burrell said.

"I'm furious with Charlie. How could she have let Ari sneak off like that? I'm not saying she's a bad mother. God knows she's managed pretty well. But now's not the time for Charlie to dither. She ought to show a firmer hand."

"Maybe," Burrell said mildly. In his experience, people who hadn't raised children of their own put vast, unwarranted faith in the exercise of parental discipline. *It sounds like a legal theory*, he thought. *The Firmer Hand Doctrine*. One of many doctrines that fell apart in the application.

"You could hire somebody to investigate," he said. "I can get you a couple of names. They'd be discreet; the daughter won't find out, and you don't have to tell your sister."

Les shook her head. "We had a huge argument. She wants me to stay out of it. She says she believes that Ari will come home by herself. Whatever's fundamentally troubling Ari, only Ari can fix. I don't understand it. If I were her, I'd be raging."

"She's legally an adult," Burrell said, "and she has money. You've said she's smart. I don't see her living under a freeway, turning tricks for food."

"This isn't a case we're talking about! Not some messed-up kid in my courtroom, or a client of Charlie's." Les got up to go to the sink for a drink of water.

"Does she have friends?" Burrell asked. "Anyone she could talk to?"

"She has friends," Les said, her back still to Burrell. She glanced up and saw herself in the kitchen window looking so wifely she might have been wearing an apron. Instead of the water, she reached for a bottle of wine. "Good friends, and she liked her teachers, too. But something changed, once she got to high school. She turned really sour and moody." She fetched two glasses and brought the wine to the table.

"Typical teenage stuff," Burrell said.

"It was more than that," Les said, sitting back down. "There was a kind of anger there, mixed with sadness."

"That's not unusual, I suppose. For a kid who's been adopted."

What do you know about it? Les wanted to retort, for she didn't like anyone slapping labels on Ari. But there was truth in what he said. The kinds of questions Ari had asked when she was younger— *Why didn't my parents want me? What if they want me back?*— reappeared in telling ways. She'd been "dumped," not "placed"; her birth parents, Ari cracked, "threw me out with the bathwater."

Les overheard her tell a boy that Charlie had purchased her at a pawnshop. Whenever Charlie tried to lighten what Ari had said by making a joke or giving her a hug, Ari's mood turned darker.

"I wish I could do something," Les said. "It's like my sister has given up. She buries herself in work and says bizarre things like, 'Let's rent a house at the beach when Ari is back next summer.' It reminds me—" She stopped.

"Of what?"

"Charlie had a lover, way back before she got Ari. His name was Aaron. He was an environmental lawyer; he'd come to San Francisco to work on a case, water rights or something, I've forgotten what it was." The memory surprised her. She hadn't thought about Aaron for years. Charlie never mentioned him, and the few times that Les had brought him up, Charlie had turned away in silence. "He was married, separated, but he wanted to marry Charlie. He left one day and never came back," Les said.

"A villain," Burrell said, "who broke your sister's heart. I always wondered why Charlie was single."

"No, not a villain. I liked him. He was funny and passionate about his work and good for Charlie. They were crazy for each other." They had met a few months before Charlie adopted Ari, when Charlie was waiting to find out what child she'd been matched with.

"Did he leave because of the baby?"

"No, he wanted the baby as much as Charlie did. He said that once he was divorced, they'd get married and he'd adopt Ari, too. Be the baby's father. That was their plan." Les had been jealous of Aaron when Charlie first brought Ari home. She hadn't expected to feel such emotion, but once Ari had arrived, she had found herself over at Charlie's apartment all the time, wanting to hold the baby. She had made herself stay home when she saw the little family that Charlie had assembled: Charlie and Aaron and Ari. It wasn't a good memory. Their sudden happiness had made her savagely lonely.

"They were thrilled to be parents," Les said. She could be magnanimous now. "Aaron was like a father to Ari for the first five months she was home. He was a wonderful dad, a real natural with the baby." She smiled. "How about you?" she asked. "Were you a natural?"

Burrell nodded. His boys had been big babies with bowling ball heads. Later, he'd hoisted them high in the air and zoomed them around the backyard.

"I can see that," Les said. Her voice was tender, but she didn't touch him.

"Then he left?" *As I might leave my wife*, Burrell thought, *if Lesley would only say yes.*

Les nodded. "Then, at Christmastime, he told Charlie that he had to go back to see his wife, who was living in Seattle. To settle some things. He'd be back in a couple of weeks. Charlie waited for him. She was sure he was coming back. She waited and waited. Weeks went by; he never returned."

Burrell took her hand. In bed, Les looked twenty years younger, but under the kitchen lights, he saw that age had creased the delicate skin under her eyes and crosshatched her lips into tiny, irregular patterns.

"Is that what she's doing now?" Les said. "Is my sister waiting for something that's not going to happen?"

Burrell stood and pulled Lesley to her feet and put his arms around her. She clung to him briefly. "My mother hasn't been any help. She's usually full of opinions, but now, all of sudden, she's quiet. Aunt Rose says not to worry. She raised four boys—Ari's like a boy, she says. Very independent. It drives me crazy when people say things like that. But Charlie listens to her; she's close to Aunt Rose. She went to China with Charlie to get the baby. She's always had a special lookout for Ari, though she doesn't make a fuss. My mother doesn't like it. She's competitive that way."

"Imagine that," Burrell said. "A competitive Kong woman."

Les gave him a half smile, remembering how bruised she felt, watching Aaron strap Ari to his chest. "Does Ari not know that we love her?"

He stroked her hair. "Maybe you overwhelm her," he said. "All that love. All you women."

She freed herself and nodded. They sat down, their hands touching. "I'm glad I had a father. My mother and me would never have lasted."

"You don't speak of him very often."

"Charlie was his favorite. That was fine by me. It left me the freedom to do what I wanted."

"That's what she's looking for. Freedom," he suggested.

Les shook her head slowly. "I don't think so. She's had a lot of it, maybe too much. No, Charlie used to say that Ari was always looking for a better family to join."

"The Amazing Kong Women. You, your mother, and Charlie. It'd be tough, having three mothers. If I were her, I might run away, too."

"But would you come back, after a while?"

"I would," Burrell said. "I would."

BEFORE BURRELL LEFT, they spoke of other things. He'd gotten no definitive word from the senator's office on Les's chances for the federal judgeship.

"You're still on the list," he said. "At the top, they tell me. If there were a problem, I would have heard." There were two openings in the Northern District, one in San Francisco and the other in San Jose. It would probably be some weeks before a decision was made.

"All the right people are in your camp." Burrell's support was the most important. He sent up the names, and the politicians usually listened. He'd been very strategic in advising Lesley. Nobody knew that they were lovers, not even Charlie. Les was more than qualified for the job, but she knew that she had to keep sharp. The affair—well, there were a million reasons why they should end it.

"What about the Ng case?" Burrell asked her. "What's the status there?"

"Put over," Les said. "It won't go until next year." The attempted murder case against Wilson Ng, the plumber, who'd attacked his former boss and left him in a coma. The D.A. had added a hate-crime enhancement, which Les had ruled at the preliminary hearing could go forward to trial. The victim's family was out for blood. The boss, it was clear, was an unmitigated bigot.

Burrell kept his expression neutral. No trial judge had been assigned yet, but it might end up in Lesley's department. If that happened, she would have to be very careful. Ng had an eighty-year-old mother, well known to Reynold Low because she'd lived for forty years in low-income Chinatown housing. The Chinatown community, led by Low and Reverend Stanley Yeung, had rallied to Ng's defense. With the hate-crime charge, the case was especially ugly. *Wouldn't that be perfect*, Burrell said to himself, *turning the law into a noose around the neck of a poor bastard whose boss had spat on him for years?* But Burrell hadn't gotten to where he was by painting with a broad brush. The law had to be applied on a case-by-case basis, and Lesley had to make her own decisions. She and Burrell were scrupulous about that. They never discussed her rulings.

"When will I see you?" he said.

"Not for a while." They kissed for a long minute but didn't go back to bed. They prized control in themselves and all others. Their affair succeeded—had been kept secret, had not upended their lives—because two months or more would pass before their next meeting. *That*, Burrell admitted wryly, *was the one benefit of growing old*. Your dick was no longer that crazed ferret in a cardboard box that needed constant attention. Their arrangement worked for Lesley, and if he had had to make accommodations over the years, it was better than being without her.

AFTER BURRELL LEFT, Les poured a last glass of wine and made herself a salad. She ate quickly, then sat at her desk to read case files. This week's trial wouldn't go past next Wednesday; she had hearings after that in cases that were likely to settle. After the first of the year, they'd go through reassignments. She wouldn't mind getting assigned to the Wilson Ng trial—she wanted to see her old boss, Riordan, try a case against Hal Nugent. All the media attention brought extra pressure to bear, the kind of challenge Les relished. Whoever presided at trial would get to decide what evidence could come in: the vile and racist remarks Porter had made to Ng for years, Ng's boasting at his boardinghouse that he had a gun to pay back the foreign devils. Ng had lost his job when Porter had laid him off and kept a young white guy instead. No evidence of a gun was found, but there were scrawled notes in Ng's writing that blamed rich, white Americans for his troubles, and Ng had screamed "white bastard" as he beat Porter with a pipe. If Les were a federal judge, she'd have a bright law clerk or two with whom she could debate the issues, but the state court budget didn't fund acolytes. She missed the fun of staying up late for heated discussion with her law partners as they prepped a case for trial.

"You were born a contrarian," her mother had often said. "I say white, you say black. I say go, you say stop. Arguing comes so naturally to you."

Les matched her mother look for withering look. "Oh, right. Like I didn't have to work for everything I've got."

"Don't go looking for praise. You've done beautifully for yourself."

It always comes back to one's mother, Les thought with a shake of her head. And Ari had three of them, as Burrell had said. She remembered that Charlie once had joked that Gran, Charlie, and Les were like the Three Fates, hanging over the world. "I've been reading about them in Ari's book," she'd said. "They were strictly a group act, joined at the hip forever."

Les swiped a finger across her phone and typed in "Three Fates." Clotho, that was Charlie, spinning the thread of life. She was so giving to others that she lost herself in the process. Gran was Lachesis. The name sounded poisonous, like a fatal disease or a chemical waste product. She decided how long a body would live, allotting the length of the thread. Well, that was accurate. Her mother loved to call the shots and hated when others did.

That leaves me, thought Les. She squinted at the screen. Atropos, she read. The one who snips the thread. I suppose that's true. I make the big decisions. Better her than Gran or Charlie because

Charlie was too tender and Gran too abrupt. Les employed reason, and reason, though not entirely sufficient—Burrell's bulk, his cock in her clever mouth—had served Les well.

She put down her phone. Brava for Ari. She had struggled out of the web and escaped from their constant watching. As worried as she was about her niece's future, Les felt a pinch of envy. She had never—not as a teenager, a young woman, or a middle-aged adult—changed course or jumped ship or taken a flyer. Her one transgression, Burrell, she had kept a solid secret, and even that didn't count, since adultery was as common as lying. She wondered what it would feel like to surprise the people who loved her. Both Charlie and Gran would say that Les in her dominion had protected and instructed and once in a while annoyed them, but would they ever say she surprised them? No, never, and that was the sorry truth.

Even Charlie had sprung surprises. Adopting Ari, for one, which Gran had strictly opposed. Les had been skeptical but had tried to keep an open mind. And then, while waiting for Ari, Charlie had met Aaron Streeter.

Les paused, recalling. Look where surprise had landed Charlie. Aaron Streeter had abandoned her just when she needed him most. If Les had had the chance, she would have yelled at him for a week.

But had he really broken her sister's heart? Charlie had said little when he didn't return. Les had suspected that Charlie cried in private, but she didn't confide in Les. She had her daughter by then, and that proved family enough for Charlie. The circle that Les had thought Aaron completed closed in his absence to a ring of two. And though Charlie, like Les, got lonely and needed comfort, they had never needed men to make their lives whole.

"I need to remember that," she said aloud to herself, "when Burrell and I end it."

She turned off the desk lamp and went into her living room. Night had fallen; porch lights and streetlights shone cheerfully on the hill, extinguished at the bottom by the black expanse of the water. Charlie lived much closer to the bay, but only Les had a view. She wished that her window opened so she could lean out and listen, but it didn't matter—from Telegraph Hill, she couldn't hear the sea.

Burrell had asked her what had become of Aaron.

"Did he ever come back? Did she find out what happened?"

Her answer had rung with the same mixture of certitude and righteousness and duty and sadness that she felt whenever she pronounced sentence on a defendant from the bench.

"He died," Les had said, "four months after he left."

CHAPTER 18

ARI

There is a place on the island of Douglas, Alaska, an island across the Gastineau Channel from the city of Juneau, which is called False Outer Point. You cross the bridge from Juneau to Douglas and head north to a rocky cove. The water ripples along the shoreline in low-cast waves. The sky is cement-gray, the horizon the seam of a sidewalk. Bald eagles perch in swaying trees, caught in the act of looking patriotic when you spot a white dot out of place, way high up in the branches. Dall's porpoises glide by in pairs like a holiday cruise line logo. It feels far away from any place you've ever been. The end of the earth, but it isn't.

The island keeps going. There's an "Outer Point" farther on. The first stop you made was journey, not destination.

Seattle, and Aaron, were my False Outer Point.

I HAD KNOWN the name "Aaron Streeter" for forty-eight hours when I found out he was dead. He died in April 1993, when I was four-teen months old. Killed in Juneau while hiking with his friend Steve. Right before he slipped and fell three hundred feet to the bottom, he was talking to Steve about his child.

His son, Noah. Not me.

THE "M. STREETER" I looked up in Seattle turned out to be Miriam, Aaron's older sister. She wasn't happy to meet me. Charlie, she said, had broken up Aaron's marriage. If not for meeting Charlie when he was in San Francisco, her brother would have returned home a lot sooner and been there to help Miriam take care of their very sick mother. Instead, it was Miriam who'd had to shoulder the burden. The cost, the driving, the daily care. She was gone now, three years ago next week. Miriam had her life back, though her own health was ruined.

It wasn't exactly news to me that all roads lead back to a mother.

She talked at me for ten minutes. I stood on her porch and watched her hand push at her scraggly hair. I had left my duffel bag behind the hedge in her front yard and almost forgot it when I stumbled back to the sidewalk.

Steve Ericsson, she said. The guy who got Aaron killed. She went into the house for a name and a number. She was telling me only so that he could see what else he had ruined. He still lived in Juneau. He wrote to her to say he was sorry, but what was that worth to her, once Aaron was dead?

Do you want to meet Aaron's wife? She lives back east. Last year, she moved home. A daughter's duty.

No, I said, I didn't know there was a wife.

Good, she said, because there's no way in hell I'm telling you how to find her.

She fixed her eyes on me.

You're not saying you're his kid, are you?

I shook my head no. I hadn't used the word *father*. I told her I was adopted.

Oh, yeah. Now I sort of remember.

She shut the door in my face.

THE ERICSSONS LIVED in a wood-frame house near downtown Juneau on the side of a steep hill. Steve and Peg. Their four children were grown. They'd gone to schools outside and returned to live in Anchorage and Fairbanks. Steve and Peg had lived in Juneau for thirty years. Steve had gone up there after law school to clerk for a year for a judge on the state supreme court. He stayed. He met Peg, a botany professor at UAS, the University of Alaska Southeast. They had an old dog named Poppy and a cat named Jackson. When I showed up on their doorstep, they took me in.

The first week, I slept in their finished basement on a double bed that dipped like a bowl in the middle. Their two older kids, Lily and Rue, had been born in that bed. Both girls. They had two sons, Wight and Gil. All four named after flowers. It could have been worse, Peg laughed. We might have used trees instead.

Steve was a burly man, six one and solid. He had a square head, peppered hair, and a thick beard streaked with gray. His wide hands spread into thick, fumbling digits. Most of the time he wore bright red reading glasses perched on the end of his nose. He sported a gold hoop in his right earlobe. After years in Southeast, his skin was prize white, that old Pen and Parchment standard.

Peg was delicate, a fern frond, a willow branch. She had straight, long hair tied back in a thin ponytail and reedlike fingers. Her eyebrows were pale, almost undetectable. The blue shirt she sometimes wore coaxed her eyes into color—they turned picture-book blue, like the sky on a sunny day. Otherwise, she looked washed out. She dressed for the weather in jeans and boots. Parkas swallowed her; she belted them on the outside with a piece of rope or a broken pack strap—whatever was to hand; she was a practical woman. She didn't wear makeup or jewelry, but she had four small tattoos on her arms, the flower of each of her kids.

I didn't talk much that first week, and they didn't press me. I slept or read books I found in a box in the basement—Ursula K. Le Guin, Robert Heinlein. The alien worlds were where I wanted to be, places as unreal as where I'd landed. It rained every day. I burrowed myself in blankets and felt almost nothing except the chill in the air when I got up to use the bathroom and the vibration of the clothes dryer on the other side of the wall. I went upstairs for meals and, each time, spilled a little more of my story. Steve said he had always wondered what had happened to Charlie, whom he'd met a couple of times in San Francisco. He hadn't kept up with her after Aaron's death. From the way he dropped his chin when he said that, I knew he meant that Charlie hadn't kept up with him.

And me? I asked. *Did you meet me as a baby?*

He said no. It was just the two lovebirds, waiting for me to arrive.

The house was small for a family of six, as if the rain had shrunk it. Three bedrooms, a living area, a kitchen with a built-in table, and a bay window that looked out onto muddy garden. There was a sleeping loft upstairs, which Steve and his friend Pete had added when Gil was born. The deck on the side of the house was always pooled with water. There was an upright piano across from the dining room table and an oak china cabinet that Steve had built in his friend's garage. On top of the piano and every table throughout the house, there were photographs of their kids fishing, skiing, hiking, sailing. Cycling, snowshoeing, grinning at the camera. Two dark-skinned friends showed up often though not together, one girl and one boy, arms around Rue and Wight. Peg pointed them out to me. They were foreign students who had each lived with them for a year, Marta from Honduras and Pablo from Monterrey. During Peg's sabbatical, the whole family had gone to visit. "They made a lot of good friends at Juneau-Douglas High." I got the idea that she wanted me to know they were used to taking in strangers.

The sun broke through at the end of the week.

"It won't last long," Steve said, "so let's go." He heaved a kayak onto the roof of his rusted wagon and drove the three of us out to Auke Bay. They carried the two-man boat to the water while I struggled into boots and a life jacket, fumbling with straps and clips and feeling hopelessly soft, a tame bunny dropped into a forest. Peg and I took a turn, and then Steve switched places with Peg. We didn't go out very far; the waves slapped the boat, and I didn't know what I was doing, but I worked my paddle until my back and my shoulders ached. The wind stung my face like ice against flesh, at first painful and then numbing. Ahead I saw dark wooded islands and wide-open water, leading to where, I couldn't imagine. The mystery thrilled me. I knew if I fell in, I'd be dead in a matter of minutes, but I wasn't frightened. For the first time in months, I felt my spirits lift.

After about forty minutes, Steve signaled it was time to turn back, but I asked to stay out longer, and he obliged me. When we finally returned to shore, Peg came out of the car where she'd been keeping warm and helped us stow the kayak. We went for battered fish sandwiches and milk shakes in a dockside diner crowded with boaters glad for a few hours of light. Kids slammed in and out of the swinging door, some carrying rods, though Steve said that fishing was mostly over. It had started to rain again, and the place smelled like damp and burgers and fries. Everybody wore tall rubber boots that left thick footprints of mud by the entrance. Ravenous, I finished my meal in five minutes.

"You look happy," Peg said. She handed me a napkin to wipe the grease from my face.

"Can I stay?" I blurted. "Can I stay with you for a while? I'll get a job. I'll pay rent. I know I'm a total stranger, but would you think about it, please? I can help around the house. I'd stay downstairs most of the time and be very quiet."

They exchanged a glance.

"Well," Steve said, "we've been talking about it, too. You wouldn't be the first kid who's washed up on our doorstep. A couple of our kids' friends have stayed with us from time to time when things weren't so good at home or they were taking a break from school."

"We like having extra people in the house," Peg said. "Without the kids, it's way too quiet. But it doesn't work unless we're all clear on expectations."

I felt relief so complete that my lungs unlatched and I took a big breath in. I could stay in Juneau. It seemed the answer to everything—my misery; my confusion; my inept search for the missing, a quest failed before it even got started. I didn't have to go home. I didn't have to face Charlie and Les. Maybe I'd stay forever as Steve and Peg had done, transplants from Boston and Minnesota who'd happily rerooted.

"Rule One," Steve said. "You communicate with your mother on a regular basis. We can't have you staying with us if you don't have the courtesy to let her know you're all right."

I said yes quickly. He had already told me on the very first day I got there that I couldn't stay overnight unless I called Charlie. I had left her a message, telling her I was in Juneau. Since then, we'd talked a few times on the phone, our conversations always ending in a fight. I told her that I'd come to look for Aaron. She said, Why on earth had I left home on such a wild-goose chase? Her question made me mad. Her tears didn't move me.

I didn't tell her right away that I was staying at Steve and Peg's. I said I was at the youth hostel in town. I shrank from the thought of Charlie showing up, pleading, so I said just enough that I hoped would keep her off my back. I even sent her a picture of me standing in front of the harbor, smiling. Like Peg, I could be practical.

"Two, this is a temporary situation. We don't have to decide right now what that means. You can't stay forever, but indefinite is okay. We won't rush you. You can take some time to decide what comes next."

I had no idea of a "next." If I had to leave Juneau, I didn't know where I would go. I didn't have enough money to return to Beijing. Philadelphia meant Bryn Mawr. Home was out of the question.

"We can talk about an amount you should contribute every month to the household," Peg said. "You'll have chores, like Steve and I do."

They'd clearly done this before. They knew their parts in the whole arrangement. I said yes to everything. Their kindness astonished me. Charlie was full of sympathy, and Les worked hard to make things fair, but the Ericssons' invitation, like the sharing of something scarce or money given away freely, was the first time I can remember thinking, *This is what kindness is. It's personal between people.*

"You should think about it some more," Steve said. "Winter will be here in about, oh, ten minutes. The beautiful life you might be imagining—I've seen you looking at those pictures all over our house—doesn't come easy in the winter. It's gray, it's cold, it's dark. It rains more than it snows. There's a wind called the *taku* that'll rattle the teeth in your head. Most of the time, we stay indoors, sleep, and get fat. You'd be better off flying south for the winter and coming back up here in June." His eyes lighted up. "Summers here are magical. It's the opposite of winter. Nobody sleeps. We stay outdoors and play."

"When does winter end?" I asked. "April? May?"

"It depends," Peg said. "April's a little early." Steve fingered his fork, and I remembered too late that Aaron had died in April. Peg changed the subject, and we finished our meal and paid.

Later that evening, when I thanked them, Steve ducked his head. I knew to look for that now, the way I knew to be wary when Charlie wrung her hands or Les laughed sharply. But I was in Juneau, far away from the shut-up rooms where I'd have been worried at by Charlie and cross-examined by Les. Steve wasn't family. I could hear what he had to say.

His chin dropped. His eyes looked hooded. "I owe it to Aaron," he said.

PEG OFFERED to let me have one of the bedrooms upstairs, but I liked the basement, with its musty air of wolf den. Poppy slept on a dog bed at the bottom of the stairs, and Jackson curled in my mattress hollow. Together, we smelled like wet fur. The basement's dark corners and the dripping gutters outside the window near the ceiling matched my tentative mood. I wasn't happy or unhappy. I didn't know what I was feeling, but the edges of the black ditch I pictured at my feet retreated by a few inches. I got a part-time job downtown at the Statehood Café, close to the Capitol building. Starting my first day, the regulars called me by name and teased me for being a *cheechako*, a newcomer who'd probably fall into the glacier or get herself lost hiking. More than one guy offered to teach me how to shoot a bear gun. A couple of tourists asked me if I was Native, though everyone else knew right away I wasn't. The town was mostly white and Native, and no Juneau resident was going to mix up Chinese with Tlingit or Haida.

Then Peg put in a word for me, and I got hired to help in the day-care center at the university. Three mornings a week, Peg gave me a lift to the UAS campus, a collection of low, brown buildings out the valley near the glacier. The roads didn't go much farther than that. I didn't mix with the students but walked, head down, to the day-care center, got down on the circle rug, and played with the little kids. They were divided into groups named after Alaskan mines—the Silver Bows, the Treadwells, the Kensingtons, the AJs. A little furrowed-brow girl in that last group was my favorite; I let her sit in my lap when I read books to the kids, remembering how WeiWei had let A.J. and Becca and me crawl all over her like worker bees tending their queen. When I tried to imitate WeiWei's breezy chatter, the girl stared at me and hopped back to her teacher. I wondered what WeiWei was doing in that moment, then, like all thoughts of home, kicked her from my mind, a stone launched by a boot over the trail edge to the bottom.

The streets of downtown Juneau rose steeply from the water; my legs got strong from walking up and down the hills. The lowest point was the harbor where the cruise ships docked in the summer. In the wintertime, that end of town was practically deserted. I wandered the sidewalks, checking out all the bars and tourist shops, some closed until summer, and studying the totems in front of buildings for Alaska Natives. In a run-down section of town, I saw more Natives than I did anywhere else, and in that way Juneau wasn't different from any other American city that shunted its poor to the shadows. I was ashamed to admit to myself that though I'd run away from home, I was still living in a house on a hill. If I didn't have real problems, why did it feel as if I did? As long as I asked that question, the black ditch gaped open, ready to suck me in.

Above town, the blocks were stitched together with lanes and staircases like a game of Chutes and Ladders. I walked the residential streets, taking in the painted wooden houses that probably looked festive to summer tourists but in October wept gray. Gardens were sodden and side yards full of fishing tackle and boating equipment and humped, plastic-sheeting-covered parts of machinery. Even the prettiest house was crisscrossed with pipes and drains and gutters. The whole place was surrounded by ice fields and water, and everybody went about their business as teachers and cooks and line repairmen and legislators in rubber boots and parkas, always dressed for the rain.

Steve was right. The weather turned colder and the daylight seeped away, as if drawn toward darkness and slumber. I kept close to town on my walks. Like most Alaskans, Steve and Peg owned ice axes and trekking poles and guns, but I didn't know enough about how to take care of myself in wilderness or weather to venture out for a real hike. Every week in Alaska somebody died in a crevasse or a boat or a floatplane. Once again, I was an outsider, though this time I didn't try to fit in. It was enough to be there, to be far away and on my own. I walked through the days, putting one foot in front of the other.

I asked Steve where Aaron had died.

"The Perseverance Trail," he said.

I was surprised. "It's on tourist maps. I thought he died doing something really dangerous."

His brow squinched. "I pegged you for smarter. You should have noticed by now that if you make a mistake here, anything is dangerous." He rubbed his eyes, put his red glasses back on. "Don't ask me about it yet."

"I know you weren't to blame," I said in a rush.

The red glasses stared at me. His eyes glinted.

"Hold up your left hand," he said.

I didn't want to, but I was living in his house, eating at his table. I held up my hand. The stump of my little finger had healed over with pink flesh. There was a little ridge at the top that I sometimes worried with my thumb, though it hurt like hell if I accidentally banged it, and it tingled at the slightest touch.

"Want to tell me how that happened?"

I shook my head no. I hadn't told anyone, not even exactly A.J.

"Then you know how it is," Steve said. His face softened. "I'll tell you about Aaron, though. He was a good man."

I wasn't sure anymore that I wanted to hear about Aaron, but now that he'd begun, Steve didn't want to stop.

"We met in college," Steve said. "BU. Then we both went to law school and became environmental lawyers. Aaron was good at it, better than me by a long shot. He had the passion you need to keep fighting the good fight. He went after everybody—corporations, local districts, state governments, even the Feds. He never met a lawsuit he didn't like. He went for their jugular on a fraction of their budgets; if he couldn't get to their throats, he'd shoot for their kneecaps. The man was fearless. The most creative lawyer I ever met. But I'll tell you what"—he shook his head—"he could be exhausting."

He didn't have to explain. I knew Charlie and Les.

"Was he planning to marry Charlie?" I asked.

"He was, when he was in San Francisco. He and his wife, Wendy, were on the rocks almost from the beginning. He called me, told me he'd met your mother. The three of us had dinner when I was there on business. They were great together; I could see how happy he was. He called again and said your mother had brought you home. Her name is Ari, he said; she named her after me. I hoped he was joking." Steve shifted in his lumpy chair. "He said he was going to adopt you after he and your mother got married. He sent me a picture of the three of you. You were a cute kid. You had a whole lot of hair. I remember that."

I fetched my backpack and took out the photograph to show him. *Aaron practicing to be a father.*

"Yeah," Steve said. "Like I said, he was happy." He got up to feed the wood-burning stove. It was late afternoon; Peg was at school, and Steve and I had dinner duty. We went into the kitchen to make a fish stew with halibut that Steve had caught and frozen.

"I lured him away," Steve said. "I was working on a huge case fighting logging in the Tongass National Forest. We had a coalition of local and national environmental groups going after the big pulp mills and we needed help planning and coordinating. Aaron was brilliant at that strategic sort of thing, plus he was good at getting the most bang for the buck. I asked him to come up for a few weeks, maybe longer; we'd have to see what we needed. He was dying to do it. He'd been asking me for years to get him up here on a case."

Lured him away. "Were you trying to break them up?"

"No. Yeah. No, not really. I wanted him for the case. But once he got here, we started talking. He'd gone home to see Wendy before coming to Juneau, to settle some things. Give me that parsley."

I handed it to him; he took far too long to wash and stem it. When I sat down to wait, he finally turned to look at me.

"He has a son," Steve said. "His name is Noah."

"After he died?" I couldn't do the calculation. Had a son been born after Aaron went to Juneau and died hiking the Perseverance Trail?

"Before. With Wendy. He's two years older than you. Noah was three when Aaron was killed."

"I didn't know that." A stupid remark. He knew it already by my colorless face, bleached clean by the simple fact of a baby. I was a fool for not thinking to ask the question myself. I felt the black ditch yaw open. "He was two?" I asked.

"Just turned three. Aaron had gone home to see him, and then he got here and hung out with Peg and me and saw our family with all the kids running around and knew—" He stopped again.

"What?"

"He'd been a shithead, he said. I said he was right. He'd thrown himself into you and Charlie like he threw himself into everything he did. He'd lied to Charlie. She didn't know about Noah. He didn't want to tell her too early, and then they fell in love and he had screwed the pooch. He said he'd go back in a couple of weeks and figure out what to do. Patch things up with Wendy, marry Charlie, who knows. Then the case got bigger, and he didn't go back like he said. I pushed him plenty to get things straightened out. We argued about it. He told me to leave it alone. He was going to do the right thing. Whatever that meant to Aaron."

"He was three," I said. I couldn't believe it. "Charlie didn't know?" She was a fool, like me, if she hadn't asked him.

"He was going to tell her," Steve said, though he didn't sound convinced. But I didn't care to weigh what Aaron had done. I was thinking only of the awful fact of Noah. There had been a real biological child. I wasn't Aaron's daughter. I knew that, of course I did, but I had temporarily forgotten. Aaron had had a son. In no way was he my father. I wanted to run downstairs to my basement refuge, curl up on the bed, and bury my head in the pillow. I looked again at the photograph of Aaron holding me and would have torn it in two had Steve not been watching.

"I didn't know whether to tell you," Steve said. "Aaron's dead. He fucked up for sure, but I shouldn't have gone around thinking that I knew better. You might even say that my lecturing on the subject was what got him killed. We were arguing about it right before he fell. After that, I learned to shut up about other people's choices. That's why I never told your mother about Noah. We spoke after Aaron's death, but the fact that he had a son—it wasn't my story to tell."

I was still reeling. "Then why tell me?" I asked.

"Noah lives in Juneau. He goes to school at UAS. I've been looking out for him ever since Aaron died. When he applied to college, I got him to come up here. In a small town like this—" He spread his big arms. A hunk of thawed fish flopped in his hand. He looked like a bear standing beside a stream, at once comical and forbidding.

"I wanted to find Aaron, not his kid," I said.

Steve looked taken aback. "I just thought you'd like to know. I didn't want there to be any nasty surprise later."

It was too late for that. To find out Aaron was dead was nasty surprise plenty.

"Whew," Steve said, wiping his hands on a towel. "I've been carrying that around since the day you showed up here. Peg's been pushing me to get it out in the open. I was worried you'd meet him before we had the chance to talk."

I made myself go stony. I reminded myself that cold inside was the only way through it. Steve was done talking. He handed me a bunch of carrots to scrape. For a second, I couldn't move. Aaron had had a son. His name was Noah Streeter. I knew, but Charlie didn't. It was as if Steve had handed me his loaded gun, cocked and ready to fire. I skinned those carrots, afraid of what I might do.

CHAPTER 19

CHARLIE

She had forgotten how to fall asleep. Bed had become a place of suffering, not ease. Nothing helped, though she had tried every adjustment—more exercise, less caffeine, colder room, white noise. Blackout curtains that made the bedroom as dark as a witch's forest. She felt like a two-year-old, exhausted but wide awake. Her daughter's name rode every breath with the puff of an exhalation. When was she coming home? *Ari*.

She began walking at night along the Marina Green. An empty path from one end to the other. Once in a while, a fellow traveler trailed or approached or passed her. It was usually someone from one of the boats tied up in the harbor. In the daytime, along that path, walkers and cyclists exchanged friendly greetings. In the dark, they didn't speak. Their heads were down, their shoulders narrow wickets.

She smoked at dawn, perched on the splintered landing, sitting as Ari had sat, staring ahead, knees tented. She rehearsed what she would say if Ari should call or appear. The words were empty, striving too hard to convince. She would *try* and *attempt* and *make an effort* and *promise*. Speeches that hadn't worked before. Her optimism bankrupt. Her solace defective.

In the afternoons, she napped at her desk or in a chair. On the living room sofa, which left an imprint on her cheek. Sometimes she bounced her head on the pillow in a rhythmic trance that dulled her thoughts to a mindless tapping. *Ari, Ari, Ari*. It wasn't breath anymore. It was only the beat of her head against the pillow.

Baby Bowns. Out there, somewhere.

Come home, she thought. *I am waiting.*

IT WAS LATE NOVEMBER. Charlie reached over to take Joseph's hand as they boarded the Third Street line. They were going to the ball-park, where Reynold Low and Reverend Stanley Yeung had gotten a group of donors backstage passes to go onto the field. Reverend Stanley had called up Charlie to invite her as his guest. "How about your sister, too?"

"Nice try," Charlie had said. She'd accepted, thinking he'd have the class not to bring up the Wilson Ng case. On her next visit to Va's place, she'd invited Joseph to come along.

The day was cold and windy. Charlie drew Joseph closer. He was in his favorite pair of shorts and a Buster Posey T-shirt. She had brought for him an old sweatshirt that she'd found at the back of a closet, but she knew he wouldn't wear it. He was a boy and never cold.

"Next year, I promise, you'll go to a game," Charlie said. Joseph had never been. She had tried to get Va and Joseph tickets, but in a championship season, nobody was willing to give up a single seat. She'd badgered David for weeks until he'd scrounged up a couple of extras, feeling sorry for Charlie that Ari had bolted. Who knows what Robyn had said to shame him into sharing? In the end, the game hadn't been played. The Giants had rolled on to win the Series, and the city had gone wild.

"I told my friends that we went," Joseph said.

"I hope you didn't!"

"They were jealous. Victor said his social worker never takes him places."

Charlie let his words get lost in the streetcar noise. She wasn't his social worker or his lawyer or even a family friend. She wasn't breaking any rules except for the most basic: common sense, self-protection, smell test, Sandra Bullock. That last one was a term they threw around the office to ridicule rich women who thought they were doing good. In the movies, the rich woman was always changed for the better. In real life, she ended up fleeced or beaten.

The streetcar lurched. Joseph fell against her. He wasn't holding on to the pole because his hand was stuck in his glove. The doors opened, letting the riders off.

I'm not rich, thought Charlie, *and Joseph and I are not going to change each other. This isn't the movies. My daughter has deserted me. I don't have heartstrings left to pull. He's just a boy with a baseball glove. There's no such thing as magic.*

Joseph ran to the gate.

I need sleep, thought Charlie.

IN THEIR FIRST phone call, Charlie couldn't believe her ears.

"Aaron?" she said. "Aaron Streeter?"

"He was going to be my father!" Ari shouted.

"He was just an old boyfriend," Charlie said. Ari told her about the photograph, a picture Charlie could barely remember. She had no memory of stashing it in her drawer, a claim that Ari, with her megabytes of memory and lightning recall, refused to credit. Charlie called the whole trip a wild-goose chase, and then the real fighting began.

"Why should I listen to you when you think I'm trivial and stupid?"

"He wasn't your father. You don't have a father. You have me. That's who you're stuck with." By the end of the call, Charlie was weeping and Ari was telling her that she was never coming home.

IN THE SECOND CALL, Charlie tried to apologize. It was true what Steve Ericsson had told her: she and Aaron had talked about getting married. He had wanted to adopt Ari—that was true, too. But things hadn't worked out that way. It had been very hard for her when Aaron died. But Charlie had gotten over it. Life moves on, and we move on with it. Couldn't Ari accept that?

"Why didn't you tell me about him?" Ari demanded.

And Charlie snapped, "Because it wasn't any of your goddamned business."

BEFORE THE THIRD CALL, Charlie wrote out what she wanted to say. She didn't know what it was like not to have a father. She didn't presume to understand everything Ari was feeling. But she did want her daughter to know how much she loved her and that she was trying very hard to both listen and be heard.

She practiced while pacing in her bedroom, hoping she wouldn't yell or cry. On her dresser she'd set out what she'd found in her drawer—a set of jade buttons from Gran and a gold ring and necklace from Aaron. The necklace had been for Ari, sent by Aaron after he'd left. She didn't remember that she'd kept the envelope it had come in, but Ari had somehow found it. When he had proposed, he had put the ring on her finger. It was set with a garnet, Ari's birthstone. She held it up and turned it under the light, tasting metal in her mouth the same as she'd tasted it when, a full month after he'd died, she had sucked at her ring finger to work the band off. A cry escaped; she threw the ring in the trash can, then snatched up the necklace, ready to throw it out, too. But did the necklace belong to her or to Ari? She gently laid it back down on the dresser. She didn't have to decide now what to do about that. She closed her eyes and grabbed the edge of the dresser until the room stopped swaying. A few minutes later, she picked up the trash can and marched it out to the garbage.

The third call didn't come from Ari. It was Steve Ericsson, calling to check in. He wanted to make sure that Ari had done as she promised and let her mother know that she was living with them in Juneau.

"Yes," Charlie said in her deep humiliation, for of course Ari had lied, telling her that she was staying at the hostel. "I hope she'll come home soon, but in the meantime, thank you for looking out for her." They talked at length, Steve telling Charlie how sorry he was that they had fallen out of touch and what a wonderful daughter she had. They were really enjoying getting to know Ari. She seemed to know what she needed—some time on her own terms, her independence. He and Peg had raised four kids and knew how tough they could be on their parents, but Charlie shouldn't worry. Ari was safe and she was healthy. If it were otherwise, Steve would have called sooner. Charlie was welcome if she wanted to visit.

"Do you think I should come?" Charlie asked.

"That's up to you," he said. "Talk it over with Ari. See what she says."

At that, Charlie colored, glad he wasn't there in the room. She couldn't admit to Steve—to Steve and Peg, whose own children had flourished—that Ari wouldn't talk and didn't want to see her. She uttered a final "Thank you." Ari had found a better family to join.

That was two months ago. Winter was settling in.

AT THE BALLPARK, Reverend Stanley drew Charlie aside while Joseph ran the bases and had his picture taken with Lou Seal, the team mascot.

"I want to talk to you about Wilson Ng," he said. Charlie mugged and pretended to look for the exit. But usually jovial Reverend Stanley didn't go along with the joke.

"You know your sister ruled that the case against Wilson can be tried as a hate crime," he said.

"That was the preliminary hearing," Charlie said. "There's no trial judge yet. It might not be assigned to my sister."

"I'm not asking you to talk to your sister," he said. "I'm interested in you. When was the last time you heard someone say that?"

"What a way to soften me up," Charlie said.

"I'm trying to get your attention. I know you. I know what you believe in. Our community needs all our voices to speak out against injustice."

"I can't help you," Charlie said. "But maybe I can offer some assurance. My boss is a great lawyer. If the case goes to trial, he'll try circles around Patrick Riordan."

Reverend Stanley gripped her forearm harder than was polite. *Even a reverend*, Charlie thought as she loosed herself from his hold, *shows his temper like a man.* She smelled his wintergreen breath as he railed against the bullshit media storm that was raining down on Wilson Ng. "That guy Porter, Wilson's boss, abused him for years."

She couldn't help herself. The lawyer in her kicked in. "When you say 'abused,' do you mean actually, physically abused? Or emotionally abused, or verbally?"

"You're splitting hairs," Reverend Stanley said harshly. "I'm not asking for your legal opinion. I want you to stand up, as a member of our community, and join us in telling the D.A. that if he goes forward on the hate-crime charge, we're going to make sure he doesn't get reelected."

His tone stung her. Her forearm smarted. "It's not my role," she said, "and you shouldn't be asking. But just for the record, I believe in the judicial process. If you were a lawyer, you'd understand that."

"If you were from Chinatown, you'd get why this is important."

"Oh, that's helpful," Charlie retorted.

"We need your voice. People respect you. If you speak out, people will listen."

"You're not to use my name," Charlie said. "I can't be seen—"

"I know, I know." He waved her away. "Tell the judge I said 'hi.' We're all very interested in her career advancement."

CHARLIE TOOK JOSEPH HOME on the streetcar. She had parked her car at Va's place. Now that she was a regular visitor, she had learned her way from the freeway to their street. They lived on the second floor of a sagging apartment building strung with twinkling lights on a hill between Visitation Valley and the Portola District, two neighborhoods where Charlie had never been before knowing Va. She was surprised at all the Asian businesses she saw: produce markets, car-repair shops, beauty salons, churches. Black families had used to live there. Now it was Asian and Latino.

Va wasn't home, and she hadn't left a note. *This is not my problem*, Charlie thought. *My duty is to Va, not Joseph. I shouldn't be here. I've done a nice thing, but this is my final visit. I can't come back again.*

"I'm okay by myself," Joseph said, though he didn't sound convinced.

"I've got time. Let's wait for her together."

She looked around the hallway. There were no family photographs or pictures on the wall. Everything looked temporary, as if Va had just moved in. A jumble of plastic sandals sat by the front door. Music leaked from a neighbor's apartment. When Ari was twelve, the same age as Joseph, she had begged to be left alone. *I should have left her alone more often*, thought Charlie, *so she didn't feel overprotected. Or maybe not so often because it gave her too much freedom, or made her feel isolated, or—* She stopped. There were too many pathways to remorse to choose from.

"Is Manu coming home?" Joseph asked. "He doesn't like Auntie's house."

She didn't meet his eyes. "Your mother is trying to make that happen."

"Can I show him this?" He held up the photograph of himself standing next to Lou Seal. "I don't want him to feel bad that I went without him." His eyes filled; his mouth opened wide. Before she could say anything, he was bent over, bawling.

"Joseph! What's the matter?"

"I left my glove there. I took it off and forgot it." He held up his left hand, gloveless.

She would see him again. A tiny beam of gladness struck her in the heart.

"I'll bring it next time I come," Charlie promised the boy.

SHE TRIED NOT TO CALL A.J. more than once a week, usually Sunday nights, when the weekend partying was over and A.J. was in her room, reading. She always asked, "Have you heard from her?" And A.J. always answered, "Not yet."

As soon as I get home, I'll call her, Charlie thought.

Instead, she got on the freeway and drove straight to Berkeley.

"NO WARNING. I'M SORRY." Charlie gave her a weak smile.

"It's okay," A.J. said. She glanced over her shoulder. A boy standing behind her muttered a few words and slipped out of the room. "He lives down the hall," A.J. said. "He's in my econ class." *She's sharing,* Charlie thought, and heard envy for Robyn rattle in her head like stones thrown down a grate.

They went for coffee, A.J. leading Charlie and greeting friends among the students traveling in boisterous packs. She carried her laptop in a drawstring bag that she dumped at her feet when they sat. Charlie feasted on the sight of her—long hair, clear eyes, bright smile. She was wearing an old jacket of Robyn's that Charlie remembered, gray tweed with a Peter Pan collar. It had buttons covered in velvet. White headphone wires trailed from her pocket.

"This is the perfect start to my evening," A.J. said. "I was headed to the library. I can't study in my room."

She's a little too cheerful, Charlie thought. *A little too sweet. I miss my sharp-tongued daughter.* And then, ashamed of herself, her eyes filled with tears. "I'm so sorry," she whispered.

A.J. squeezed her hand. "No problem," she said. "I haven't heard from Ari."

Charlie clutched at the girl's hand. When Ari had vanished and Gran had insisted that she'd gone to Philadelphia, Charlie had called Aunt Rose. *No,* Aunt Rose had said, *Ari isn't here, and she hasn't been in touch.* In the panicky calls that had followed, after that frightening silence fell, Charlie had defended herself to Gran and Les and Robyn and A.J.: *I couldn't have stopped her. All her life she's wanted to go.* A.J., she remembered gratefully, had said she understood.

"I keep hoping she'll call me," A.J. said. "I wasn't—" She took back her hand to pull the clip from her hair. "I'm mad at her, and mad at myself. We had that bad fight right before I left for school."

"She was fighting with everybody." Charlie's own hands felt as heavy as books in her lap. They had called all her friends, starting with the Whackadoodle girls, even WeiWei. No one had any idea where she'd gone. Three days later, Ari had left a message, followed by those phone calls that had gone so badly. Now, she sent only infrequent e-mails.

"I wish she'd answer my texts," A.J. said.

"She's not using her phone." Charlie tried to sit up straighter. Her back hurt, and every time she blinked, she felt the scrape of her eyelids. Three kids next to them were sunk deep in their devices. The girl at the counter called for more milk. Everywhere she looked, they were young, young, young. If only they could see themselves as she did: beautiful, blazing, fully alive in the moment. *You are present*, Charlie thought. *You are loved*.

"She said not to come to Juneau or she'd disappear for good, right? So that's kind of like saying she'll come back on her own when she's ready."

"Maybe," said Charlie. "But when? When?" How many fathers and mothers had asked her the same question, standing outside courtrooms or weeping in Charlie's office? She found herself crying again. A.J. looked embarrassed.

She gathered herself. She smiled at A.J.

"Are you having a good semester?"

"I love it," A.J. said. "So . . ." She reached down and stuck her laptop onto the table. "I wanted to show you this," she said, clicking and tapping on the keyboard. "It's kind of rough, so give yourself a moment."

On the screen was a photograph of an open hand, palm up. A left hand, Charlie saw. In the palm of the hand was a small black-and-white photo of a young Chinese boy wearing a billed cap. The little finger of the hand was missing. *Severed*, she thought. There was a huge empty space where the finger should have been. The owner of the hand might have snapped the picture himself.

"We saw this photograph when we were in Kunming," A.J. said, "the day after our orphanage visit. A man we met in a café tried to sell us a copy. He came up to our table and sat down and started talking to Ari. He went straight to her, almost as if he knew her. Ari freaked and started to get up, but he asked her to sit down and she did. He showed her this picture and then he showed it to me. He said it was antigovernment. Ari started asking him questions, and then somebody in the café asked the man what he was doing talking to us, and the man got scared away."

"This same picture?"

Yes, A.J. said. The hand belonged to an artist. Ari had looked it up.

"She wanted to know more. Who the artist was, what the picture meant. She couldn't find out much, but the picture really disturbed her. He made another photograph, too, of his same hand holding a picture of his mother. One article she found claimed that he'd cut off the finger himself. He ordered a taxi to wait at his door and told the driver that if he didn't come out in five minutes, to go in and get him. He used a butcher knife to cut off his little finger. Then the driver took him to the hospital.

"Ari said it was like a Greek myth. Prometheus or Alcestis. A sacrifice to the gods."

"Is he okay?" Charlie asked.

"The photograph became important. I should have shown it to you before. I'm really sorry."

"I've been stupid," Charlie said. "But—" She looked away and down.

"You knew it wasn't an accident."

"I didn't know. But part of me—" She stopped, not sure that she could explain. She remembered what the doctor had said about the cleanness of the cut. It was terrible to think that Ari had done that to herself. Other parents, were Ari their daughter, would summon the doctors and therapists and peer support and healers in order to cure the patient. Charlie, the old Charlie, would have rushed to fix her, too; nobody had put more faith in the experts than she had as a new and nervous mother. But what if Ari didn't want to be cured that way? "Don't just do something, stand there," was a piece of advice that her old Legal Aid boss, Marcus, had liked to say when he caught her running in circles. Charlie put her head in her hands. She had drained her teacup, but her mouth felt dry as dirt.

She looked up and saw A.J.'s worried expression. "Don't tell Les," Charlie said. "Don't tell your mother." She didn't want them thinking that Ari was somehow crazy.

"No, I won't," A.J. said. "I haven't." They touched hands again.

"What will you do?" A.J. asked.

Charlie shook her head. "I'm not sure," she said. "I think I have to wait."

A.J. nodded. "That will be hard."

"I've done it before," Charlie said. Sixteen months she had waited after her adoption paperwork was in. Sixteen months for word of her baby, every day an IV drip. Later, she had posted comforting messages to other anxious, awaiting parents: if she'd been matched with a baby sooner, she wouldn't have gotten Ari.

"When she gets home," A.J. said bravely, "we'll have a Gotcha Day party."

"When she gets home, we'll do that."

A WEEK LATER. Reverend Stanley left her a message. He sounded jolly again. They'd been unable to find Joseph's glove at the ballpark. He was sending her a new glove, signed by some of the players. "You don't need to thank me. I take care of my friends."

CHAPTER 20

ARI

was endowed by Who Knows with a lousy sense of direction, but I got pretty good at finding my way around Juneau. I started taking the bus to the UAS campus instead of catching a ride with Peg so that she and Steve would think of me more as a lodger than a leech. Free-spirited, not freeloading, that's how I wanted them to see me. Connor and Shawna, the couple who owned the Statehood Café, loaned me a bicycle, a single-speed with colored streamers. I preferred walking the steep and slippery roads. I shortened my way with staircases—they were metal, like fire escapes planted into the hillsides; my boots made them ring like a clanging gate.

Steve was determined that Noah and I should meet. It was as if his talking to me about the misty past, speaking about Aaron and conjuring him in the kitchen, had opened a need in him that wouldn't let Steve rest.

"Let me introduce you," Steve asked me soon after his unwelcome revelation. "We'll have him over for dinner. Peg and you can pick him up on campus. It's been a while since we've seen him."

"I don't know," I said.

"Why not?" Steve said. "I'll bet he'd like a home-cooked meal. You need to meet some young people. He can show you around."

"Let me think about it." I had buried the photograph of Aaron in my duffel. I knew that nothing good could possibly come of meeting his son, Noah. At best, it would be awkward as hell. At worst,

Steve would tell him my whole sappy story. Poor little orphan, who had yearned so for a father that she had come all the way to Alaska, chasing a wild goose. I saw it through the eyes of a skeptical stranger: my grand romantic gesture ending with a whimper. Even if Noah was nice to me, I didn't want his understanding. Compassion, I was convinced, was the first step toward pity.

"Don't be shy," Steve said. I thought of the face that A.J. would have made at Steve calling me shy. "You're a good excuse to get us all together. Peg understands. You let me know when you're ready."

A few days later, he brought up the subject again. The morning was cold and cloudy, and Peg and I were in the mudroom, cleaning. We had piled all the boots and hiking poles and Poppy's dog toys on a tarp in the front yard, and Peg was attacking the mudroom floor with a mop. I moved the bucket for her as she worked. Steve came to the doorway. He had called Noah, he said, and told him I was visiting and that he wanted to get us together.

"Good for you," Peg said warmly. "I hope it went okay."

"I think so," Steve said. He had music in his voice, as though the day had turned sunny. "I told him you were Charlie's daughter. He knows about Charlie," he said.

"Is he coming for dinner?" Peg asked.

The smile slipped. "I invited him, but he said he's really busy with classes."

"I'll ask him again if I see him on campus," Peg said.

They both looked at me. I hoisted the bucket of dirty water and walked it outside to the gutter.

THE NEXT WEEK, Steve came into the Statehood to talk to Connor. They were on the organizing committee for the annual January Dance-Off, a benefit that raised money for local causes. Connor was half Steve's age; he and Shawna had a three-year-old towhead named Caleb, but with his thick beard and barrel chest, Connor looked like Steve's younger brother. Connor took him to the back office, and when they were done, Steve came over to greet me. He glanced around the room and broke into a smile.

"I see you two have met," he said. He gestured to a guy sitting alone by the window. I had served him tea and a toasted bagel and had asked him about the map he had spread on the table. It was a plan of downtown Juneau from 1970, he'd explained. He was writing a paper for a class in city development. When I had passed by a second time to bring him a dish of honey, he hadn't looked up from the map.

"Noah," Steve called. He went straight to the guy's table, beckoning me to follow. "This is Ari," he said, sweeping me in. "Noah Streeter. Ari Kong." He smiled wide. "I told you Juneau was a small-town kind of place."

Noah and I looked at each other, then he quickly looked away. I mumbled hello; he jerked his head in a nod. He had a brush of dark hair that stood up from his high forehead, and he wore black-rimmed glasses. On his face was a tight expression. Aaron in the photograph had looked tall and rangy; I couldn't tell if that was true of Noah, but with his face turned slightly away, I saw that he had the long planes of Aaron's narrow face and his wide, thin mouth.

"This is great," Steve said, "just great. Listen, come up to the house with Ari and me for dinner."

Noah said no, as I hoped, but Steve wouldn't be refused. He told Connor he was kidnapping me ten minutes early and insisted that Noah join us. He paid Noah's bill and shoved a big tip into my hand. "I'll bring her back tomorrow," he called to Connor as we left. He practically pushed us up the hill to get us into the house.

"I'll let Peg know," he said, and disappeared up the staircase. We stood there awkwardly. I didn't invite Noah to take a seat. He dropped his backpack with a thud and shrugged out of his parka.

"This wasn't my idea," he said.

"Or mine," I retorted.

"I didn't know that was you."

"Really?" I said. "You didn't assume that the one Chinese girl waitressing in Juneau was Charlotte Kong's wayward daughter?"

He blanched at that, so I knew the possibility had occurred to him. That was why he had buried his head in his map.

"Your mom made things really hard for my mom," he said.

I opened my mouth to protest, but Peg and Steve came downstairs and bustled us into the kitchen. Steve opened a bottle of wine while Peg started dinner.

"None for me," Noah said. He was tall, like his father, with long, knobby-knuckled fingers. His Adam's apple moved like a walnut under his skin. He held himself so stiffly that a single finger poke in the chest could have knocked him over. In the living room lamplight, his hair had looked reddish; under the kitchen lights, it flattened back to brown. His high forehead and arched brows gave him an inquisitive look, but he wasn't talking.

"Ari?" Steve said, pouring a glass of red wine. I took it from him and sipped, aware that Noah was watching.

"You sure you don't want some?" I asked, extending my glass.

"Can I help?" he said to Peg. "I can't stay long. I've got a paper due tomorrow."

"WELL, THAT WENT SHITTY," Steve said. We were cleaning up. Peg was driving Noah back to his room on campus.

"What did you expect?"

"You didn't help." Noah and I hadn't said more than ten words to each other.

"He was an ass. He told me that my mom and I made things really hard for his mother and him."

"He said that?" Steve shook his head. "I'm sorry." He poured the last of the wine into his glass. Peg had had a glass, but he and I had pretty much killed the bottle. I dried the last pot and set it on the stove. I wasn't sure if he wanted my company or not. Poppy wandered into the kitchen and lay down with a deep sigh. Steve didn't move to take her out, so I reached down to scratch her silky ears.

"When he was growing up," Steve said, "I stayed in touch with him as much as Wendy would let me. We e-mailed, and Peg and I saw him at least twice a year, when we passed through Seattle. I called him on his birthday, and he called me on mine. I really worked on him to get him to come to UAS. I told him how much his father had liked it here, and that Peg and I would be his second family. I even offered to help pay for school, though Wendy's parents gave him the money. That's how he was able to come over Wendy's objection."

"Did he live with you?" I asked. I wondered if he had inhabited my basement room before me. Poppy, I had noticed, had greeted him like an old friend.

"No, he lived in the dorms, but he came over a lot. We talked about his dad; I showed him some of the places where I'd taken Aaron. Spring of his freshman year, we hiked the Perseverance Trail together. We talked about making it a yearly thing. But then he stopped coming. He was busy with school and into his friends and all that. But something had changed. He never said what. It was like all of a sudden he didn't want to talk any more about his father and why he was gone."

I felt a flicker in my gut when he said that. I knew that swing from one feeling to another. Steve shuffled to a cupboard and reached high for a bottle of brandy. He fumbled for his wineglass and almost dropped it. I brought him a clean glass and also a glass of water.

"Aaron's death was an accident," I said. "You said yourself that Alaska's a dangerous place. Noah must know that."

"It's true," he said. He sat down heavily and poured himself a brandy. "Everyone who comes here takes their chances. Aaron made a mistake, same as I did." I sat down beside him. Poppy lifted her head with a question, but seeing us at the table, she settled back down again.

"Will you tell me how it happened?" I asked, hoping I was guessing right that he needed to tell the story.

He hesitated and slumped forward. I could see the top of his head. He lowered his red reading glasses from the top of his head to his nose, as if he were getting ready to read to me from some official report. He'd probably relived it a million times in his head.

"It was April fifth," he said, "and we were stupid. Some years it's okay to hike the trail that early; other years, it's dangerous. I wasn't a complete idiot—I checked the avalanche report. I knew the trail was clear, at least up to the second bridge, because my buddy Debra had run it a few days before and said it was fine, no problem. But it froze again in between, and I didn't account for that. Aaron was leaving soon to go see Wendy or maybe your mother—he hadn't made up his mind. It was the last chance for us to spend some time together before he left. I wanted the hike to happen; I had things I wanted to say. I thought he needed me to hit him upside the head, to get him to make up his mind about what he was going to do and to stop lying to his family and to Charlie." He paused to drink. Poppy's snores and the tick of the cooling oven were the only sounds in the room.

"It was a beautiful day, clear and cold. The sun was out when we started. We went up Basin Road to the trailhead and right away spotted a black bear, which got Aaron excited. The bear wasn't interested in us, but I told Aaron to slow down and keep a lookout. There wasn't much snow on the ground, just patches on the high sides of the trail and up on the mountains. The trail was wet, but the walking was pretty easy. After we got less than a mile up the trail, Aaron wanted to pick up the pace. He was always impatient. He always had a better plan. He said let's run the thing and reward ourselves after with a beer. I said I couldn't keep up with him running, and I was only there to keep his damn ass company, so he'd better stick with me. I wanted to watch for snow slumps, and I didn't want Aaron taking a wrong turn without me.

"I asked him what his plans were, and he had the class not to pretend he didn't know immediately what I was talking about. He said he didn't know. He didn't have a fucking clue as to what he was going to do. He loved Charlie, and he wanted to be with her; but he had a wife and a son, and what kind of father would he be if he left his three-year-old kid? A lousy father, I said, and then we got into it. He said he was thinking, What if he told Charlie about Noah, wouldn't she be fine with it? They could raise the two of you together, Noah and Ari, brother and sister. Noah would live with Wendy some of the time; other times, he'd stay with Aaron and Charlie. I said he was fooling himself to think that's what Charlie would want. 'She just got her kid,' I told him. 'That's complicated enough. She's not going to jump up and down with joy that you're bringing her another.'

"He got mad when I said that. 'You don't know Charlie. She loves everybody. She's a natural-born mother. If I explain the situation to her, she'll understand.'

"I told him he had his head up his ass, where it'd been for the past year. Had he ever stopped to think about why he hadn't told Charlie about Noah? Something inside was holding him back. Some part of him that knew it wasn't right for him to abandon one kid for another, the same part that was telling him to come clean with Charlie. You better be ready, I said. You better be ready for her to dump you because that's what any grown-up would do. And he gave me a funny look and said I didn't know Charlie, and then he took off, running up the trail.

"By then, we had climbed to the part of the trail that runs along a shelf and hooks around a sharp curve. The path was really narrow after we passed the overlook because there'd been a dirt slide at some point, blocking part of the trail. This was April, so the water-falls across the ravine were out-of-control gorgeous. There's a drop-off on the outer edge of the trail that goes straight down to the bottom. The cloud cover had come in and the sun had gone away, and it'd gotten a lot colder. I could see him running. He was moving really fast. He was a bony guy, tall like Noah; his legs were pumping and his feet flying. He had lightweight boots on that didn't slow him down. I glanced up, worried all of a sudden that the morning sun might have loosened a chute above us. Then Aaron hit a patch of ice and he went down and slid. It happened so fast he didn't even shout. He fell on his butt, right on top of an ice slick, and kept on going three hundred feet to the bottom."

I was looking past the kitchen into the dark house. The night felt unnaturally still. I had heard the front door open, but Peg had gone straight upstairs. Maybe she'd heard him talking and was tired of the story. Or maybe she trusted me to sit and listen. Steve took a harsh breath. He lifted his glass and drank.

"It took us two days to retrieve his body. That whole time, we were frantic to contact Wendy. She was traveling in Germany. Noah was with her parents. By the time we reached her, Aaron had been dead for three days. Wendy cratered. She screamed at me on the phone to get him into the ground, but I couldn't find anyone to do it. Finally, I found a guy out in Skagway, a retired rabbi, and our friend Pete flew him into Juneau. We buried Aaron at sundown." He looked at me at last. "I don't visit his grave," he said. "Noah does, but I can't bear it."

I put my hand into his. We both were quiet. I had more questions to ask but, for once, I didn't.

"I've never told the whole story to Noah," he said. "Not the part about his mother. I've tried to apologize for the rest. It was an accident, like you said. I've learned to accept that."

From the strain in his voice, I didn't believe him, or maybe he wasn't feeling guilt so much as raw hurt. I hadn't expected the suffering he was showing. I'd thought eighteen years was long enough for grief like that to fade, but Steve's pain was so present, it felt as if it had taken a seat at the table.

"Wendy blamed me," Steve said. "Blames me. But Charlie never did. She cried when I told her, but she was strong. She said to me, 'Wasn't that just like Aaron? He was out of control, except when he wasn't. That's exactly why I loved him.' I felt bad not telling her about Noah."

"Maybe she knows," I said, hoping it was true. I didn't want the responsibility anymore of knowing about Noah when Charlie didn't.

"Maybe," Steve said, "but whether she does or she doesn't, when she gets the chance to meet him"—he looked meaningfully at me—"she'll be totally kind and totally honest."

"It's getting late," I said. I got up and took Poppy out; when I got back, Steve hadn't moved from the table. His glass was full again, his hand on the bottle.

HE DIDN'T INVITE Noah again, and Peg didn't push him. I worked my two jobs and read books in the basement. I found the public library and started hanging out there. I liked the steady stream of people and the kids lying on their stomachs looking at picture books and asking questions in stage whispers that carried across the room. Big windows looked out onto the water and the mountains. Snow capped the peaks, but the streets were black with rain. It was mid-November; I'd been in Juneau almost two months. My moods were the colors of winter—gray, silver, and white—narrow in range and chilly at the heart. I didn't often let myself think of home, and when I did, it was as though Charlie and Les and A.J. and Gran were on a trip without me. I was the traveler, but I was suspended in motion. Perhaps I was waiting, though it didn't feel like that, either. Winter held me; ice fields hemmed me in. I had bought a long plaid blanket shawl, ugly but cheap, at the Salvation Army, and I drew it around me like a character in my book wrapping up against the damp. After reading my way through the Ericssons' box of science fiction, I had gone to the library and started in on Dickens, Gran's favorite, so maybe I was missing home more than I cared to admit. I had my nose in *Bleak House*, drawn to the title, struggling with the tale. Had I known it was about lawyers, I wouldn't have started the thing, but I liked the feel of the big, fat book in my hands. The light from the window changed on the page I was reading. When I looked up, Noah Streeter was standing in front of me.

"Hey," he said. He looked surprised to find me there.

"Oh, hi." I looked back down at my book, same as the way he'd ducked to his map the day I'd served him at the Statehood.

"I'm researching a paper," he said. "I have to go over to the City Museum."

I peered up at him, curious, and he asked if I wanted to come. He said he wanted to talk to me about something. It was late afternoon; the early hours of darkness stretched before me, so I closed my book and buttoned up my jacket. We walked in the blowing wind, not saying very much. He was writing a paper about historic preservation and wanted to look at old photos. When we got to the museum, it was closed. It was too cold to stay outside, so we went into the closest café—I didn't want to go to the Statehood, where Steve might come in from the rain.

He studied his tea while I hunched over my coffee. His hair had a funny pouf on one side from wearing a watchman's cap. He looked as lopsided as I felt. I pulled my own cap lower on my head. I noticed again his long knuckly fingers as he dragged his tea bag out of its cup like an anchor. Cold seeped under the doorway; a sagging strand of Christmas lights made the place bleaker.

"Steve keeps calling me," he said. "He wants to get together."

I looked at him and shrugged. "He misses you. He's says you're like family to him."

I saw his jaw tighten. "He says it would be nice for me to show you around Juneau."

"I didn't ask him to do that," I said hotly. I was appalled that Steve was using me to get to Noah.

He crossed his arms and settled back in his chair, a fake move if I ever saw one. "He said I should get to know you, because one day, I might want to meet your mother. I must have questions I'd like to ask her. About my father."

I flinched at that, and he noticed. He was wrong if he thought I was worried about protecting Charlie. I had as many questions as he did, but no one whom I could ask.

"In case it isn't clear," he said, "I don't want to meet your mother. If she comes up here, tell Steve I won't meet her."

"Tell him yourself," I snapped. "You already know how to hurt him."

Noah straightened. "I don't know what you're talking about."

"He knows you blame him for getting your father killed."

"Is that what you think? I don't. I never have."

"That's not how he sees it."

"You're lying," he said.

"I'm not the one punishing Steve for an accident years ago."

Noah glared. His face was white with anger. His mouth worked; I saw the rim of his eyes redden. "What do you know about it," he said.

"I'm an orphan," I shot back.

"It's different to lose a parent who wanted you in the first place."

I gave a sharp laugh. "Your father wanted you so badly, he left you for my mother and me."

His eyes widened. He looked like he might throw his tea in my face.

We both got out of there as fast as we could.

HE CAME TO SEE ME the next day at the Statehood. I told him I was working and I didn't want to talk. Give me two minutes, he said, then Connor bustled over, slapped Noah a big hello, took the towel out of my hand, and waved us to a quiet table. Shawna brought us both coffee, and I had to sit down. Noah said that he wanted to apologize, that he'd said things he had no right to say. He owed a lot to Steve, who'd been a friend to his father. He stopped at that. He was calm as he said it. But his face was white. He still had one arm down the sleeve of anger.

I sat silently for a minute, not knowing what I should do. I didn't want to be nice to the guy, but I could see he was trying. Connor was shooting us anxious glances from behind the counter. He'd seen how Steve had begged Noah to come to dinner.

"Hang on," I said, and stood. I wasn't going to apologize back, but I could bring him a cup of tea. This time, Noah thanked me when I put the honey on the table.

"Anyway," I said, "you don't have to worry that Charlie is coming to visit. She knows if she comes, I'll leave before she gets here." Noah took a breath; seeing that, I was able to take one, too. "So you knew about Charlie?" I asked.

"Yeah, sort of. Not really, but . . . the name. I know some stuff. From before."

His mother had told him all about Charlie, he said, the woman who'd messed up his parents' marriage. He knew she'd adopted a baby. His mother said the baby turned out to be a huge mistake—she couldn't raise the kid by herself, and she didn't have any money.

Her family refused to help. She latched onto Aaron, and he, stupidly, went along with it for a while until he got away and realized the whole thing was crazy. He went back home and begged for a second chance.

"They were back together when Dad died," Noah said. "That's why my mom was so destroyed. They had worked things out; he was coming home soon. He promised to get a law firm job in Seattle so he wouldn't keep taking cases all over the country."

I had a red coffee stirrer stick in my mouth, which I chewed ferociously as he talked to keep from jumping up and shouting.

"That's not what happened," I said.

"What part?"

"The whole thing! For one thing, my mother wasn't some greedy gold digger. She works incredibly hard. She's a lawyer, like Aaron. That's how they must have met."

His eyes narrowed. "You weren't there. How do you know what happened?"

"You weren't there, either."

"Did your mother tell you?"

I squirmed and said no. I wanted to correct him, but I held back. Steve had said that he was discreet with Noah, and I knew I shouldn't betray him. Besides, what did it matter? Both Noah and I knew only what we'd been told.

"Your mom was partly right," I said. "My grandmother thought I was a very big mistake. She didn't want my mom to adopt me."

"I grew up feeling guilty that my mom got stuck with me."

"I'm supposed to feel grateful that my mom got stuck with *me*."

At that, he laughed. I forgot myself for a moment and rested my hand on the table. I saw him look at the gap of my missing finger, flick his eyes away, and return for another look. I shifted my arm so that my cuff crept over my hand. No version of the truth would take that hole away.

CHRISTMAS APPROACHED, and I bolstered myself by shrugging off holiday cheer. I would wait it out—I had gotten good at inertia.

Steve and Peg were leaving, going to visit Peg's family in Minnesota. Peg asked if I didn't want to go home; they could find somebody else to take care of Poppy and Jackson, and to check the pipes and the mail. I could tell she wanted me to visit Charlie. "Holidays are a hard time to be apart from those who love you," she said.

I said I'd be fine staying on my own. "I've never had a white Christmas before." She didn't look happy. I wondered how much longer she would let me stay in her basement. Steve didn't mind, though. He said that he loved Christmas in Juneau because lots of people left and things got nice and quiet. I teased him when he said that. He liked his house crowded and his town empty.

I had one moment of weakness, two days before Christmas. Sleet was falling, making it too wet and miserable to go out. By then the sun was setting at about three o'clock in the afternoon, so it was dark way before it was time to go to bed. The week before, Steve and Peg had cut down a spruce tree and brought it into the house; the living room smelled like a Yuletide forest. I'd been reading all day, and my restless mind was seeing alphabet instead of words. I tried writing in my journal but gave up quickly. The first month in Juneau, I had written every day about the strangeness of the place, but it didn't seem strange anymore. I didn't put on music or the TV; I had lost my headphones, and the holiday programs sucked. Poppy lay sleeping. The silence throughout the house felt like smoke coming back down the chimney—a trickling at first and then an alarming presence. I hadn't spoken to anyone in nearly three whole days. I thought about home and how Charlie would be decorating the tree all by herself, or maybe Les would be over to hold the stepladder while Charlie put up the star. Without letting myself think, I picked up the Ericssons' phone, but at the last second I called A.J. instead.

She answered. I hesitated. She guessed right away.

"Ari! Is it you? How are you? Where are you calling from? Is it cold in Alaska? Can you talk? I can't talk. Let me call you right back." I put down the phone; she wouldn't be able to call me because I had blocked the Ericssons' number.

For the next three hours, I tried not to think of home. A.J. was probably on winter break with her parents. Maybe Brent was there, too; he liked hanging out with his sister. Hearing her voice had given me a jolt, the way my finger sometimes shocked me.

Around nine, I called again. A.J. answered right away, her voice muffled. She was in her bedroom, hoping I'd call back. She was whispering, so I whispered, too; it felt as if we were twelve and staying up past our bedtime. I told her that I was good, that I was happy and working. "I'm getting outdoors," I said. "Come up this summer and we'll go hiking." She asked, Did I promise? "Or maybe I'll go back to China," I said, but the words sounded hollow.

"I talked to WeiWei," A.J. said, dropping the whisper. "She says hello."

"You didn't tell her about me, did you?" *About Kunming*, I meant.

"I only said you left without saying good-bye. Nothing about the other stuff." We both fell silent. Finally, A.J. said, "She told me to say she's sorry she never called you. Are you still there?"

"I'm here." Poppy stood and shook herself all over and drew close to let me bury my hand in her coat. When I'd first gotten to Juneau, Peg had told me that Poppy was her personal mood ring: "If I'm angry or upset, Poppy comes to find me. Not like Jackson," she had laughed. "He's your typical royal cat." I bent to scratch Poppy behind the ears, and she lifted her nose to me.

"So WeiWei's good?" I asked.

"*So* good. You can't believe how much they have her doing. Everyone wants her. She hardly has time to sleep. Her sister is really sweet; they Skype'd me together. WeiWei bought a brand-new house; she wants us to visit. She said she'll take us on a personal tour of the studio."

"It sounds like more excitement than I can handle."

"Don't be jealous," she chided. "You should see how happy they are."

"I have to go now. I'm really glad you called."

"You called me," A.J. said tartly.

"Anyway, I miss you."

"Miss you, too. And so does your mom. You should call her."

"Please don't tell her I called," I said. "Please, please don't tell her."

"We'll see," A.J. said. "Don't ask me that again. I'm not going to see her soon anyway. We're going skiing next week."

I spent the next hour on the living room sofa, watching the tree lights blink. I strained to hear sounds of cars or voices, but the only thing to listen to was the click of Poppy's toenails. While I lay there waiting, life was happening to other people. At ten o'clock, I couldn't stand myself any longer. I put on a jacket and trudged through the dark into town.

There were always guys drinking in the bars on lower Franklin, so I headed in that direction, but before I got halfway there, two beer-gut locals smoking outside called to me to come in for a drink and pushed open a saloon door. It had warmed up; the sleet had turned to rain, but it was still wet out. I went in and sat down at the bar. There were four or five other guys drinking in the place; they all looked me over when I shrugged off my jacket.

"You're a tiny thing, aren't you?" one of them remarked, and I answered by pointing at his beer. The bartender gave me a look but brought the beer anyway. Who was going to check for underage drinkers when it was practically Christmas? The two guys who'd waved me in stood sentry on either side of my bar stool and started calling for shots. One was named Rick; he was from Wrangell; I didn't catch the other guy's name. The beer was sour, the music was lousy, and I drank until I got sick.

When I came out of the bathroom, Rick from Wrangell wanted to take me home, but I pushed him off me and staggered into the street. My hand hurt like hell—maybe I'd banged it; I couldn't remember—and my feet weren't working so well, but I kept moving through the dark, heading, I hoped, up the hill to the Ericssons' house. I went six blocks before I realized that the rain had stopped and the sky had cleared. I looked up. I felt the earth tilt. The Northern Lights had appeared while I'd drunk myself stupid. Before tonight, I'd pictured multicolored strands like festive carnival lights, but my imagination was paltry. Vertical swaths—falls and veils of jewel green and milky white—swept in currents across the sky. It seemed to me that the glow was slightly pulsing, though that might have been the beer or the cold against my eyeballs. The fresh night air cleared away my dullness. I thought of how, when I was a child, I had so badly wished to undo the aloneness of my beginnings, and then, once I was in high school, how I had yearned to be left alone, but until this moment, I had not really known what solitude felt like. It was vast and dark and thrilling. My head was back and my breath suspended, and the bright green and milky heartbeat pulsed on above me.

CHAPTER 21

CHARLIE

Charlie was late and Les was fuming.

"I'm sorry," Charlie said, hurrying to the table. "I had to pick up a few things." She squeezed into the open chair, trying to find room for her canvas shopping bags full of bean paste, crackers, and mangoes. Les, as usual, had taken the better seat.

"You look like a bag lady." Les lifted her hands in disgust. A Venn diagram of soy sauce circles decorated the table. "Where did you find this place?" Dumpling Palace, a Balboa Street hole-in-the-wall on the western end of the city where the Asian grocery stores crowded every block.

"Look how popular it is. And everyone in here's Chinese." There were a dozen tiny tables occupied by pairs of slurping diners who looked as if they'd just come from the same barber—they had matching haircuts, women and men alike. At the door, hopefuls jostled. "A sure sign the food is great."

"Or cheap," Les said. "Let's hurry up and order. I've only got an hour."

"A Les hour, or a real hour?"

"What are you talking about?"

"You're like a therapist," Charlie said. "Your hour lasts fifty minutes."

"Are you seeing a therapist?"

"No."

"You should," Les said.

"If I was, I wouldn't tell you." Charlie used to think it was sad that, despite their closeness, she and Les held back from each other, but she had learned that a certain wary distance saved her from being wounded. Very little that she did won her big sister's approval.

"I've got nothing against therapy for other people. You should've taken Ari to a shrink, for example."

"You don't know what you're talking about," Charlie said, her temper spurting. She struggled to get out of her chair, grabbing her bags, but the straps were caught on the chair leg.

"Oh, come on. Don't be a baby. Sit down. Sit down. We haven't seen each other for weeks."

"Because you're always too busy." Charlie sat, deflated.

Les called the waiter over and ordered *xiao long bao*, *shui jiao*, and *dou miao*. "And a clean teacup," she said, holding up her cup with a brown crust on the rim. He clattered plates and chopsticks and threw a single tissue-thin napkin onto the table.

"More napkins, too," Les said as he retreated. Charlie heaved a loud and pointed sigh.

"What, I'm not allowed to get you a simple napkin?"

"I'm not staying if you're going to sit there and criticize me for the way I've managed this thing with Ari."

"This thing? This is not Ari having a few beers and getting suspended from school for a day. She's been gone for almost three months. What are you doing about it?"

"I mean it," Charlie said. "I'll leave if you don't shut up." She felt five years old again, and let the feeling romp, that mixture of rage and impotence best unleashed on one's family. Les didn't understand Ari. Charlie didn't, either, but at least she grasped the completeness of her incomprehension—there wasn't one thing she knew anymore about how to be a mother.

"I've got some names of private investigators," Les said. "Let me hire one to check up on Ari."

"I don't want some ex-cop running my daughter to ground," Charlie snapped.

"You've been working for the P.D. too long," Les said. "Not everybody in law enforcement is out to screw your clients."

"You don't have my permission. She's my daughter. I'm the one who gets to say."

Les raised her hands high, a defendant in the dock. "It's just a suggestion. Burrell recommended these guys. They won't talk to Ari directly. They'll just assess the situation."

"Burrell Johnson? Is he up before you these days?" Charlie spotted him often strolling the hallways of the civil courts like a pasha, but he didn't handle criminal matters, except for the billionaires plucked to be punished for insider trading and pro athletes caught using—in other words, he defended the stuff that people with money did. The rough-and-tumble of state court murder trials or a case like Wilson Ng's were not for a lawyer like Johnson. He called his practice "complex civil litigation"—in Charlie's view, a perfect example of the egregious snobbery of downtown lawyers like Johnson and Les who chose to overlook how most of the world lived. Even the simplest of Charlie's dependency cases was complex. How could it not be, since it always involved a family? Still, he was the best. She'd once slipped into a courtroom to watch Johnson's closing argument in a breach-of-contract case. All the jurors were leaning forward in the box like passengers on a ship lapping into the trough of a wave. Eighty million dollars they awarded his client that week, a figure so outlandish that the trial court had reduced it. Every penny of it, Johnson won back on appeal.

"Mm," Les said. Neither a yes nor a no. Charlie wondered, not for the first time, whether Les saw Burrell Johnson outside of work. Once in a while, his name came up, and Les seemed to retreat inside of herself for a moment. Her expression didn't change, but her stillness seemed furtive, as if she were slipping a tiny package into the bottom of a drawer.

"Ma says when she was Ari's age, she came to the U.S. completely alone, with only forty dollars in her pocket."

"Like that's somehow relevant," Les said.

"Steve Ericsson told me not to worry. He said she's okay. She's got a job, so she's working." She didn't tell Les that Ari hadn't spoken to her since the first week when Ari arrived in Juneau. Charlie had e-mailed Steve to ask him if she could send them payment for rent, but Steve had refused her money. "Ari already pays us," he'd said. Charlie was still carrying a blank check in her wallet.

The waiter slapped their food onto the table, two kinds of boiled dumplings and a plate of dark greens.

"Excuse me," Les said, waving him back. "This isn't what we ordered."

"It looks fine," Charlie said. It smelled delicious. She swiftly took up her chopsticks and carried a dumpling to her plate.

"We ordered that," Les said, pointing to the steam basket on the neighboring table.

The waiter protested. He showed her his order form with its scrawl of chicken marks. "Your Chinese so bad!" he said. Les fired back. Charlie noticed the other diners watching, amused by the lunchtime entertainment of two rich women being dressed down by a working stiff. Les insisted that the mistake was his while the waiter waved his order form, the paper translucent with grease. Charlie finally interrupted. "Bring us what they have, please. I'll pay for the extra dish." The waiter snapped his wet towel over his shoulder and, halfway back to the kitchen, shouted something to the cook that made the other diners laugh.

"You always run from a fight," Les said. "It's the waiter's fault. We shouldn't have to pay."

"What's wrong with you? Can't you be gracious for one lousy minute?"

"You're such a bleeding heart."

"You're a perfectionist. Nobody measures up to your impossible standards. What does it matter?"

"But I'm right," Les said.

"Right and alone," Charlie retorted.

They stared at each other for a horrible second. They hadn't said such things in years. The spiteful words of childhood were dangerous in the mouths of adults.

"Maybe we should start over," Les said. "We're both so stressed. Let's not take it out on each other."

Charlie nodded. She felt a whimper rise in her throat. *Ari, Ari.* The waiter came back with two steam baskets. There were now forty-eight dumplings on the table between them, and a plate of greens swimming in oil. They stared at the food in dismay.

"Next time," the waiter yelled at Les, "you order in English!" At the table next to them, two old ladies picked at their teeth and tittered.

Les checked her watch. Charlie started eating.

"How's work?" Les said. "Have you won anything lately?"

Before she could stop herself, Charlie told her all about Va. She'd gotten to know the mother, who'd had some bad breaks but was getting her act together. Her younger son, Manu, had been detained and sent to live with Va's sister, Ela, but just this week, Charlie had successfully gotten the court to order Manu home under a Family Maintenance Plan. "She has an older son, Joseph, a really sweet boy. He's going to be thrilled to have his brother home. He really missed him. He showed me this comic book he put together of all the stuff they love to do—playing ball, eating ice cream. He's twelve but young. I worry about him in high school. He's not ready to be thrown in with the rougher kids. They live in Visitation Valley. A tiny apartment, but it's clean and decent. Joseph has a friend who lives in the building, a big kid who's kind of his protector. I'm hoping they'll end up in the same high school the year after next."

"You really got to know this family," Les remarked.

"The mother has a job. There was a bad boyfriend, but he's out of the picture."

"I mean, you don't usually get so involved. You've got like, what, two hundred cases?"

"I can handle it. Work has been kind of slow."

"You have your own problems," Les said. "You should be focusing more on Ari, not on some random client."

Charlie, fury rising, shoved her chair back from the table. Les watched calmly. "You're my problem," Charlie said. She stalked out. Two minutes later, she slowed, panting. She shouldn't have given Les the satisfaction, but, oh, it had felt good, running away from that fight.

GRAN WASN'T EXPECTING HER. She looked annoyed when Charlie showed up.

"I thought you were having lunch with your sister," she said.

"Change of plans. Hello, Mrs. Greene," Charlie said. Naomi Greene, Gran's next-door neighbor, was settled on the sofa with a cup of tea in her hand. Gran sat down beside Naomi. On the table were the teapot and a plate full of orange peels. "I'm sorry if I'm interrupting."

"I'm hiding from my son," Naomi said. "He threatened to visit me today."

Gran laughed. "We should make our escape now."

"You drive," Naomi said quickly.

"She has a late-model Infiniti, which drives like a dream," Gran told Charlie.

"Your mother is a good driver. It's too much car for me."

"We'll go to the coast. It's not the Huangpu River, but we can sit in the car if it's windy. Naomi used to live in Shanghai," Gran said to Charlie, who was feeling invisible, as if she were the one who was old.

"I remember," Charlie said. "You lived there at the same time."

"We didn't know each other then, but maybe our fathers met," Gran said. Charlie nodded. They'd discussed it many times before.

"I have my women's group meeting this afternoon," Naomi said.

"That's right. We should leave in an hour." She gave Charlie a meaningful look.

Charlie took off her coat and carried the plate of orange peels to the kitchen. She had come all the way down here; she wanted a proper visit. "Where's the compost bucket?"

"They don't let me put anything in the trash," Gran said to Naomi.

"If it's garbage, it's garbage."

"What did I tell you?" Gran called to Charlie.

"It brings rats," Naomi said.

"Rats as big as houses!" The two old ladies laughed.

Charlie brought a fresh pot of tea and a few chocolate cookies from the cupboard.

"Oh, no," Naomi said, patting her stomach. "I'm watching my waistline." Usually, Naomi dressed neatly in buttoned blouses and tailored skirts, but today, Charlie noticed, she looked like one of the diners at Dumpling Palace, in blue pants, cheap sneakers, and a padded Chinese jacket. Flecks of yellow food scabbed her shirt-front, and her hair, which she always kept curled in a hard, molded wave, was lank on one side, puffy on the other. She had had a couple of ministrokes, Gran had told her, and her son was threatening to move her into *assisted living*. Gran drew the epithet out the same way she said the words *gulag* and *ghetto*.

"Charlotte doesn't worry about calories," Gran said. "She's so busy all the time, she worries the pounds off. And now this business with her runaway daughter."

"She hasn't run away," Charlie said. "She needs time on her own to sort things out for herself."

"But when is she coming home?"

"This is the adopted one?" Naomi asked.

"The *only* one," Gran said. "My other daughter didn't have any children, either."

"That's right, I'd forgotten. I've had some medical problems," Naomi explained. "My memory's not so good."

"Naomi has six grandchildren," Gran said. "Four boys and two girls. The oldest girl went to Smith."

"The boys went to good schools, too, but your mother knows a lot about Smith. She likes those colleges just for women."

"Yes, I know," Charlie said. She tried not to take offense about how they talked about Ari. People often felt free to comment on a child's adoption, strangers and relatives alike. Their bad manners were sometimes shocking. But old people were to be excused on account of their upbringing and their oldness. They had survived war, revolution, genocide, immigration. Charlie had survived disco.

"Adopted children have a lot of problems," Naomi said. "My daughter has a friend who adopted from Russia. The boy got into so much trouble. He died in his twenties. Drugs, they said. And the black children. Even when they get adopted into good families, a lot of them have problems, too. Their mothers used drugs. Crack cocaine. You read about it all the time in the paper."

"Oriental babies are the best," Gran said. "You don't have so many problems." Naomi nodded sagely.

"That's ridiculous," Charlie said. Oldness didn't excuse *that*. "Every adopted child has to come to terms with loss, but you can't make such sweeping generalizations."

"'China gets clean babies.' You said so yourself. Why do you think so many Western parents want to adopt from China?"

"I never said such a thing! It's offensive. Mrs. Greene, please don't listen to my mother. And please don't judge people based on stereotypes. What if a child heard you?" The racism appalled her. She had cheered when Gran had made friends with the neighbor next door. Now they were like a pair of evil crones stirring their brew together. That they themselves had been the victims of discrimination made their atrocious comments all the more upsetting.

"Oriental mothers are different," Gran insisted. "They might be poor, but they take care of their babies."

"It's true," Naomi said. "I tell your mother: Jews and Chinese always put family first."

"Believe me," Charlie said, "there are plenty of bad Asian parents. I see them every day in my work. I've got a client right now who left her four-year-old kid in a car for three hours while she and her boyfriend partied at the casino. I'm shocked at you, Ma, I really am. You and Dad always taught us to treat everyone with respect."

"Is she Chinese?" Gran asked. "This bad client of yours?"

Charlie glared at her.

"I knew it," Gran said. "No Chinese would do such a thing."

"What kind of work does she do again?" Naomi asked Gran.

"I'm a lawyer," Charlie spat.

"Imagine," Naomi said. "How can you defend such terrible people?"

"HER MEMORY'S SHOT," Gran said, after Naomi left. "It comes and goes like a fever."

"Let's hope dementia explains her nastiness," Charlie said.

"It's a wonder anybody talks to you, for fear of getting a lecture."

"I can hear what she says to her friends about us. 'Devious, cold, single-minded. They're ruining our economy. They're taking over the world.'"

"Such melodrama," Gran said, refusing the provocation. "I'm worried about Naomi. Her son wants to move her to Four Winds in San Jose. He says it's near his tennis club, so he can visit her on his way to getting in a workout. She gave everything to her children— she gave up performing; she was a very good musician—and this is how he repays her."

"Does she have any help at home?"

"A lady comes in, but her son is determined to drag her off to that place. Four Winds. Who names these outfits? They name the cemeteries, too. They're professional namers, but they have so little imagination. *Haven, Peace, Hills, Forest.* All those words that tiptoe around death."

Charlie thought of her father, scattered to the four winds. Gran had not wanted to cremate his body, but her father had insisted, and Les and Charlie had arranged it. She overruled him often enough when they were married, Les told Charlie. Let him have his say at the end.

"For my part, you are forbidden to put me in a badly named graveyard," Gran said.

"Let's talk about something else," Charlie said. Her mother loved to debate about where she should be buried. Sometimes she said Los Angeles, other times Taipei. Millbrae, she said, was out of the question. Charlie always quickly changed the subject. Her father's death had left her full of sorrow. Losing her mother was unthinkable.

"Naomi's been talking to me about her brother," Gran said. "She never used to. The strokes are to blame, I suppose. The oxygen supply gets cut off in the brain. He died in Shanghai. It's a very sad story."

"Like Mu-you," Charlie said with a hint of spite.

"Naomi's brother got sick," Gran said. "Mu-you always had the best of care. Father made sure of it."

"I thought he didn't live with you. Grandpa Wu sent him away."

"It wasn't like that! In China, in those days, everybody in the family helped each other out. It was safer for Mu-you to live outside of Shanghai."

"Not that safe. After all, the war got him." *How can you defend those terrible people?* Let somebody else for a change feel the sting of harsh judgment. Charlie settled herself more deeply into the sofa, though it was sprung so tightly, it threatened to bounce her back.

Gran didn't answer. Charlie's unkindness spread between them like a stain.

"I'm sorry, Ma," Charlie said.

"Poor Naomi," Gran said. Her voice trembled. "Sons can be cruel. Daughters are so much better."

Don't be so sure of that, Charlie buzzed in her head.

AFTER GRAN'S, on her way to Va's place, Charlie stopped to buy an iced lemon cake and two big balloons, one for each of the boys. Joseph was a little old for a balloon, but she didn't want to favor Manu. For Va, she bought a pink azalea in a plastic pot, then she drove to Va's place, her mood lifting. Joseph had said he would make a big banner, WELCOME HOME MANU, with the paints Charlie had given him. He loved to draw; over the weeks she had brought him pencils and charcoal and a set of fine-tipped markers for his sketches of fingers and hands. He was good at thumbs; he drew them over and over, as if rehearsing for a day when he'd hitchhike down the highway. A young Latina woman at Pen and Parchment helped Charlie pick out the right tools for a budding young artist. And a pen, Charlie said, because he likes to write notes to his brother. The salesgirl showed her the different kinds. She chose one with an angled tip for fancy calligraphy, just for fun. She thought of Ari walking around the store, talking to customers and straightening shelves, but she didn't feel her near. She left with a bag stuffed full and the same emptiness she had carried into the store.

I shouldn't have taken my problems out on my mother, she thought. To bring up Mu-you was the small kind of cruelty that Charlie had always abhorred. She resolved to be more patient, and to maybe call Les to apologize for leaving lunch, though Les, not Charlie, was the one who should say she was sorry.

JOSEPH WAS OUTSIDE with kids and adults and Manu. *A welcoming committee,* thought Charlie, glad to see Joseph so happy.

"This is my brother," he said shyly, coaxing Manu forward, his brown arm around Manu's small shoulders. Charlie knelt to say hello, and she and Joseph exchanged a smile. Ela and her husband had set up a barbecue on the sidewalk, and their two kids were wheeling their bikes out front. Charlie carried her cake to the kitchen, where Va was busy at the sink. Cooking smells wafted invitingly through the open window.

"It's a real party," Charlie said to Va, looking about for a place to put down the cake.

"Manu is back," Va said.

"Yes, I know, that's why I'm here. To help you celebrate." Charlie paused. "Didn't I tell you I was coming?"

Va shrugged. Charlie was confused. She thought they had agreed, after the court hearing, that Charlie would come over the first Saturday that Manu was home. Four o'clock. That's what she thought they had said.

"I brought you this." She held out the lemon cake. Va nodded her thanks. She moved a bowl to make room on the crowded counter.

"My family is here," Va said.

"I said hello outside. It's great that you're all together. Is Manu happy to be home? Joseph is thrilled." She laughed. "He's got big plans for the two of them."

"Did you need something from me?" Va asked. "I gave the social worker all the information. She says she's the one who'll be making regular visits."

"Yes, she'll have to do that, as part of the court's order. I—" Charlie stopped. She understood. It had happened to her before. A client got what she wanted and had no more use for Charlie. She had preferred it that way, every single time. It was the only way to get through her caseload. Any defender who took on more than she had to was a fool and a patsy. A bad lawyer, too, if you stopped to think about it.

"I'll just say good-bye to the kids," Charlie said.

Va looked out the window. "They're riding bikes. I'll tell them for you."

Charlie turned abruptly. Her eyes burned; if she hurried to her car, she might make it before the tears fell. For the third time in the day, she rushed out, groping. A young guy wearing a black shirt and holding a beer stood talking to Ela's husband. *The boyfriend*, Charlie thought, but she didn't stop to find out. Va wasn't her friend, and Joseph wasn't her problem. She went home and cried until she couldn't feel her face anymore. At midnight, she walked. The wind was up, the trees like hauntings. The sailboats in the marina moved on the black water, their rigging creaking and slapping. In the morning, Ari was still gone.

CHAPTER 22

LES

The caller on speakerphone was yelling so loudly that Tony, the bailiff, could hear the guy's voice through the door. *Poor bastard*, Tony thought, chuckling. The judge'll eat your lunch in a minute. Maybe she'd yell back; maybe she'd soothe him. All the guys around the courthouse agreed with Tony: Judge Kong had great instincts.

At her desk in chambers, Les let the man rail. His name was Jeffrey Greene. His mother, Naomi, lived next door to Gran. "Your crazy, lunatic, interfering mother," is how Jeffrey Greene had phrased it. She remembered seeing a photograph of him and his wife and their two young children in Mrs. Greene's apartment when Les and Gran were invited to tea. Her son was an investment banker, Mrs. Greene had bragged. The photo was outdated—the son a junior partner, not as rich as he was now, not as self-righteous—but still there'd been a certain cock to his smile that Les had recognized. His wife was surprisingly ugly, a point in the man's favor. Remembering that, Les decided on extra patience.

It seemed that Gran and Mrs. Greene had been in a minor accident, with Gran at the wheel of Mrs. Greene's expensive car. They were headed to a concert in San Francisco, but they didn't get past Millbrae. Les was annoyed at Gran but admired her determination to keep doing the things she loved. Nobody was hurt: Les ascertained that right away. Gran had backed the car into a U.S.

mailbox, scraping the fender and cracking a taillight. What had Jeffrey Greene jacked up—she heard his words smacking; she could picture the spittle flying—was the future increase in his mother's insurance premiums and the potential liability, should, on one of their excursions, Gran mow somebody down. "I'll sue the shit out of you fuckers," was the way he charmingly put it.

He paused for a millisecond to gulp air.

"I do apologize, Mr. Greene," Les said. "You're absolutely right that your mother's health and safety are the most important considerations here. I really sympathize with you. I know how hard it is to take care of elderly parents. You and your wife have two kids, too, if I'm remembering correctly. Your mom has told me how proud she is of her grandchildren. You've got your hands full. It isn't easy."

"She's a menace!" he said. "Where does she get off driving my mother's car? She's as old as my mother is. Older! The whole point of the thing is to get these old drivers off the road. I've told my wife a hundred times we should have my mother give that car to our son, but she won't let me. She's worried about drunk drivers. What she should be worried about is your mother, who somehow has convinced my mother that she shouldn't move to assisted living. I'm only trying to do what's best for her. She can't live on her own anymore. I've got the place all lined up; I've fronted her the deposit. But your mother's throwing roadblocks left and right. I've got a big problem, and it's your mother's fault. If something happens to my mother, I'm coming straight for you."

"I understand," Les said. "We do worry about our parents."

He suddenly stopped. Probably he noticed on his clock's digital readout that he'd spent twenty precious minutes, a full third of an hour, on this ridiculous matter. "Unless we reach some kind of satisfactory agreement," he threatened, "I'm calling my lawyer today."

Les sighed to herself. She would have to do this in person. On the other hand, it would be kind of fun to play lawyer herself for an hour. She missed the thrill of mano a mano. Judging required fairness and balance. Lawyering was what you could get away with.

She made an appointment to meet him at his office in San Jose.

That would give him a sense of command and control. She fully intended to pay no more than his mother's deductible and a pan of her celebrated brownies. She wasn't worried. She had all sorts of arguments to make: permissive user, comparative fault, liability coverage, no emotional distress. But she wouldn't have to go there. He'd tipped his hand while his blood pressure spiked. She had guilt to play with.

YAN TOLD HER EMPLOYER, Mrs. Hsu, that she would be right back, then went down to the lobby and called the older daughter. Her mother was fine, Yan said. A little sore in the neck from when she twisted around to look, nothing to worry about. She had put on an ice pack and made her a special medicine tea that stopped pain and tension. Mrs. Greene wasn't sore at all. The two ladies had laughed about it the whole afternoon. Mrs. Hsu said the mailbox didn't matter since nobody used the post office anymore.

"Oh, Yan," Les said. "Thank you so much. I knew you'd call as soon as you were able."

"It's no problem," Yan said. "She thinks I'm taking out the garbage." The older daughter always remembered Yan at Christmas with a thousand dollars and a huge fresh wreath that came by special delivery. At first, Yan had thought it odd that Lesley gave the money early, a whole month before Lunar New Year, and in a stiff white card instead of a nice red envelope. Yan didn't know what to do with the wreath: she was a Buddhist; Christmas was a workday, like any other. But she had grown used to Lesley's different ways and every year looked forward to the check that Lesley quietly slipped her. Nobody else in the family had the eldest daughter's brains. The younger daughter was kind and friendly but had never given Yan any money. She was a bad mother; her daughter hated her, as daughters often did. Yan had hated her own mother and had been glad to leave her country village, her mother weeping and wailing as Yan skipped away. She had a different name then: Ju-hua, meaning a kind of flower, but it was an ordinary flower and a typical country girl's name, and she couldn't wait to get rid of it when she got to the city. She was lucky to be hired by Mrs. Hsu. When the old lady was dead, Yan was going to take everything that she had saved and go back to her village and spread her money around. She liked to look through Nordstrom catalogs to pick out the outfits she would wear.

"What else is happening at home?" Les asked.

"Your auntie Yifu called," Yan reported. "They had a long talk; your mother got very upset."

"Were they fighting?" Les asked.

"It was some kind of argument," Yan said. "I heard them talking about Mu-you."

"Mu-you? Are you sure?"

"Her brother, Mu-you. Do you know who I mean?" Yan said.

Yes, the older daughter said, she knew. Yan thought it very sad that there was a dead brother, but there were so many dead brothers and sisters and mothers and fathers during the war and after. One couldn't stop to mourn them all. They joined the ancestors, watching over the family's fortunes. Yan's only regret at having left her village was that on Qingming, she couldn't sweep her family's graves. Sweeping the graves and making the proper offerings brought good fortune the whole rest of the year. Still, this year on Qingming, she would light the incense as she had last year and the year before that, light the incense and put fruit on the altar that Mrs. Hsu let her keep on the balcony outside. Her ancestors would understand that that was the best she could do.

"I'll come down to see her soon," the older daughter was saying. Yan quickly made a mental list of the ingredients she would need to serve a nice luncheon. She liked cooking for this daughter, who appreciated the finer things in life.

I SHOULD CALL *Charlie to tell her about the accident*, Les thought, but she didn't. They hadn't spoken for more than a month, ever since Christmas Day. Before that, the last time they had talked was at that bad restaurant. She was still annoyed at Charlie for flouncing out in a huff. She wondered if Ari was checking her e-mail; Les had written her several times but gotten no response. She missed her niece's company. Only Les really appreciated Ari's acid tongue. She liked people with sharp edges. She remembered Ari as a little girl, and how, on lucky days, she had crawled straight to Les. Les had loved the glorious feeling of Ari's weight in her lap.

She looked at the clock. She had briefs to finish reading before the afternoon session, but she pushed the work away. Let the lawyers rattle on; she could fake it from the bench. She tried to rub the stiffness from her shoulders. She hated to admit it, but her mother had been right. Ari's return to China had been an invitation to trouble. Whatever had been brewing in her had boiled over there.

You're your own worst enemy, Burrell sometimes told Les, and Les always replied that it was a family trait. A stitch of regret tugged at Les's heart. To be a Kong woman was to be drawn straight into battle—sometimes with others, more often with oneself.

HIS DESK WAS BLACK and polished, clear of even a single scrap of paper. Twenty-four acrylic tombstones stood in rows on the credenza behind him like a Barbie graveyard, each one a marker of the killer deals he had done. Les's chambers were lined with volumes. In this office, there wasn't a book in sight.

"You see my problem," Jeffrey Greene said.

"I do. I do," Les said.

"My siblings are all in agreement."

"That's good," Les said. "It helps when the whole family is pulling in the same direction. It isn't an easy transition. My mom told me that you've chosen Four Winds for your mother. I've heard great things about it. A friend of mine, a judge, his father moved there last year. It has a great staff-to-resident ratio."

His mouth and nose twitched. "I'm talking about the money." His demand was five thousand dollars. He'd eventually spit out the number, after complaining again about Gran's reckless behavior. The figure was outrageous, as she'd expected. The repair would cost two thousand. The deductible was five hundred. He claimed increased premiums and emotional distress to his mother. And there was the time he'd himself put into it over the past week. That, Les understood, was the most valuable thing of all.

"We'd need a release," she said thoughtfully, eyes lowered, as if talking to herself, then she looked at him directly. "Signed by your mother, releasing my mother from any further claim. It's awkward, I know, especially since they're such good friends, but I'm afraid I wouldn't be much of a lawyer if I didn't at least ask for that."

He fiddled with a pen. "Is that really necessary?" So he didn't have his mother's permission to make his greedy demand. He probably hadn't even discussed it with her.

"I'm afraid so," Les said. "And what shall we tell them about whether my mother may drive the car in the future?"

His face reddened. "No," he said. "No, no. She may not drive the car in the future!"

"That's too bad. They really enjoy their outings, and my mom always does the driving. She doesn't mind taking your mom to her doctors' appointments, either. She likes to be useful. It's good for them to get out once in a while." She gave him a helpless look. "You're probably like me, always knee-deep in work. It's hard to find the time to get everything done."

"I visit," he said coldly.

"There's a sculpture garden at Stanford that's your mother's favorite. They often go there to walk and have lunch at the little café. Do you know it?"

He didn't.

"Your mother loves it there. My mother drives them. She's current on her road test, by the way." Les reached into her briefcase and showed him the DMV paperwork because documents spoke louder than words. "She's the best driver I know."

"So she has a car, right?"

"Yes," Les said, "a really nice one."

"So what was she doing driving my mother's car in the first place?"

"Ah," she said, embarrassed. "That was for your mother's . . . comfort."

"You just said she has a really nice car."

"A Benz," Les said, nodding.

"A Benz. So why aren't they going in your mother's car?"

"A *Benz*," Les said. "Which, as you know, being German-made, your mother would prefer not to ride in."

Jeffrey Greene's mouth fell open. "My mother never told me that."

"She confides in my mom a lot," Les said.

His cell phone rang. His assistant came in as he took the call.

"Can I get you anything . . . Your Honor?"

"A cup of tea would be terrific," Les said. "Thank you!"

The tea came before the call was finished.

"Thank you," Les mouthed again to the assistant, who beamed back and silently shut the door.

"Sorry about that," Jeffrey Greene said—a reflex.

"No worries," Les said. "I'm in no hurry." He looked at his watch. She sipped her tea. "I don't know," she said. "I'd love your advice on how to speak to my mother. Four Winds sounds so great—wouldn't it be nice if they moved there together? How did you convince your mother that it was time for a change?"

"That's still under negotiation. Your mother isn't helping."

"I know what you mean," Les said. "If your mom is anything like mine, she's got a mind of her own."

"She's worse than a two-year-old," Jeffrey Greene agreed, and they shared a joke or two about their mothers' stubborn ways.

"So she's not going to move," Les said.

"Oh, she's moving," Jeffrey Greene said. "We're all in agreement. We're getting her out of there in the next sixty days."

"What are the units like?"

"They're beautiful. It's like a Westin. A big room, lots of light."

"Will she feel isolated, do you think?"

"They have more activities than a college frat house," he said.

"There's a shuttle service that runs every four hours. She can go on her own to her doctors' appointments, shopping, the beauty parlor, whatever."

"She won't have to worry about driving anymore," Les said.

"Nope," he said. "And I won't have to worry about her getting hurt or cracking up that beautiful car. She never should have bought it. It's too much for her to handle. She shouldn't drive anyway, with these little strokes she's been having."

"I suppose," Les said, "that within sixty days, you'll cancel her auto insurance."

Jeffrey Greene balked. The frown returned. "I suppose so."

The assistant knocked softly. "May I bring you another cup of tea?" she asked.

LES PAID IN CASH. "I just went to the bank," she apologized. "I hope this is okay." She took five hundred dollars out of her wallet and put it in an envelope emblazoned with the seal of the San Francisco Superior Court, which she crossed out with a flourish as he watched. She laid the envelope on the edge of his polished desk, not so close to him as to taint their new friendship with lucre. Her mother, she assured him, would never get behind the wheel of Mrs. Greene's car again. Lesley would sit down and have a talk with her and explain that Mrs. Greene's deteriorating health made it imperative that she move to Four Winds, though neither mother was to worry: Lesley would arrange for her mom to make frequent visits. She'd shoot Jeff an e-mail as soon as she got back to the office with the contact info for that VC they had discussed, a good friend of Lesley's who'd been way smarter than the rest of their graduating class when he left his corporate practice to start a venture fund. A written release wasn't necessary. Why make things awkward?

"Thank you for the brownies!" the receptionist chirped as Les was leaving. "I put them in the kitchen, and they're disappearing like magic."

"Thank *you*," Les said, dimpling. "You did me a huge favor. I made a double batch for my niece's soccer team, and so did everybody else.

If I take them home, I'll end up eating all of them myself."

"I know exactly what you mean," the receptionist said. "Soccer snacks are my downfall. 'Bye now! You have a good day."

Jeffrey Greene, relaxing behind his desk, picked up his cell phone to call his brother. "We're doing the right thing," he said. "It's got a great staff-to-resident ratio. Mom will be happy there."

DRIVING HOME ON 280, Les passed the Sand Hill Road exit and thought idly of Stanford. She showed up now and then to serve on moot court panels or to give a guest lecture, but she disliked visiting the campus. Nostalgia was a trap, a cozy armchair that would offer such comfort, one might never leave it. She had learned that from her parents. Her mother's tendency as of late to talk about the old days in China disturbed Les. This business with Mu-you . . . Why rummage through that attic? She hoped when she was old that she wouldn't succumb to the weakness that favored the past over the present. It was a good thing that Naomi Greene was leaving, though it had been good, too, for Gran to have an equal. Who would go with her mother now to walk in the sculpture garden?

Les had been there once, hosting a group of judges visiting from Hubei Province. Somehow Les always got asked to take on the Chinese delegations under the blighted assumption that she, more than Ronnie Hernandez or Grace Swansen, would be able to speak their language. Of course, she couldn't. Instead, she smiled and pointed at the sculptures by Rodin spaced in stately rows, powerful and gleaming. The cameras had come out, clicking madly. The piece she'd liked best was the massive bronze doors by Rodin called *The Gates of Hell*. She remembered those writhing figures caught in various poses of agonizing damnation. Talk about the power of the sentencing laws! She chuckled to herself as she drove up 280. Even federal judges didn't get to do that.

AT HOME, SHE CALLED her mother to ask for Yifu's phone number. Gran's fling of a friendship with Naomi Greene was over. The old connections—with Aunt Rose; Uncle Bennett; Gran's oldest and best friend, Yifu—must be preserved. She didn't want Gran to be lonely. "I have a conference in Los Angeles," she said. "I was thinking of paying a visit to Auntie Yifu and Uncle Robert."

"Why?" Gran said. "Did she call you?"

"I haven't seen her for quite a while," Les said. "My meeting is close to Pasadena."

"Did she ask you to come down?" Gran asked. "Did she say she has something to tell you?"

"Would you like me to take anything to her? A gift or a message?"

Gran was silent.

"Or have you talked to her recently?" She couldn't bring up the subject of Mu-you directly, lest Gran figure out that Yan had spilled the beans, but maybe Gran would tell her what had been discussed between them.

"I'm sure Auntie Yifu would love to see you," Gran said. "Let me give you her number."

LES TRIED CALLING Yifu several times and was told each time that the number was disconnected. It took her a day to realize that she'd been played. Gran had no intention of giving her Yifu's number. Whatever ancient history was unearthed would remain between Gran and Yifu. Les decided that was for the best. If her mother had secrets, Les would rather not know. They were mother and daughter, not friends. Still, she was annoyed that Gran had tricked her. She popped a last bite of brownie into her mouth. She hadn't gotten everything done for Gran that she had hoped to accomplish, but she'd done her duty.

CHAPTER 23

CHARLIE

C harlie stood chatting in Paula's doorway. Down the hall, their boss bellowed in rage.

"The Wilson Ng case," Paula said. "We're waiting for the trial court assignment. I better go see." She hurried out. Charlie trailed behind her, curious.

"Goddamn it!" Hal shouted. "Judge Kong." He glared at Danny and Paula. "Of all the ill luck. First the preliminary hearing and now the trial."

"I'm not surprised," Paula said. "They went through reassignments in January."

"I'm going to dump her," Hal said. Use his one peremptory challenge to knock her off the case. He didn't have to give a reason; he got one freebie. It was a risky move—if he did that, he'd be stuck with the next judge assigned.

"I don't know," Danny said. "We might get somebody bad."

"Who?" Hal said. "Vukasich? Hodge?"

"Vukasich is an idiot, and Hodge is a jackass," Paula said. "Hodge'll play to the media, which isn't a good thing for Wilson. There's sympathy for him locally, but with the trial about to start, the national media have begun to pick this up, and nobody's feeling too sorry for Wilson. We might even get Mullen. That would be a disaster."

"Danny?" said Hal.

Danny shrugged. "It's your call," he said. "Judge Kong is smart. She'll keep the pressure on Riordan."

"Too smart," Hal grumbled. "Too fucking smart to let me try the goddamned case the way I want to try it. She let that sentence-enhancement stand—" He was still complaining about Les's earlier ruling that the case could be tried as a hate crime.

"We knew we were going to lose that," Paula said.

"Kong has to be careful," Danny said. "Her every move will be picked apart. She's under serious pressure from her community. Reynold Low and Stanley Yeung are going to pack that courtroom."

"She's *Asian*," Hal said. "That makes her law and order." He glanced up; he noticed Charlie. His jaw worked, but his gaze didn't flicker. He wasn't apologetic. His job required him to deal in stereotypes because most of the time—not always, but most of the time—they worked. He didn't win cases by being subtle. Charlie turned and walked back to her office. *Her community*, Danny had said. Ha, what a joke. Even Danny, sophisticated as he was, lumped all the Chinese together. Les would no sooner call Reynold Low and Reverend Stanley her "community" than walk through the streets of Chinatown on Autumn Moon Festival Day.

Les would want to keep the case; of that, Charlie was certain. From Les's point of view, the hotter the case, the better. But Charlie was surprised that Hal might challenge Les. Nobody was more fair than her sister.

SHE SNEAKED OUT of the office early; she was flying to Philadelphia to seek comfort from Aunt Rose. Even all these months later, Ari wouldn't speak to her on the phone. Staccato e-mails were all she sent, demanding she be left alone. On Ari's birthday, Charlie had baked and iced a lemon cake—her daughter's favorite—then snapped a photograph and sent it to Ari, but when the telephone rang and Charlie jumped for it, it was only Auntie Rose. "Come for a visit," Rose had said, and Charlie, despairing, said yes.

She sent Les an e-mail saying she'd be back in three days. They hadn't spoken in two months, which felt like a year to Charlie. She was used to talking to Les on the phone every day, but a day had passed and then a week and then neither wanted to blink. The last time they had been together was Christmas Day, a strained and laughable affair. Gran had insisted on cooking her traditional Christmas goose, which meant that Yan and Charlie had had to order and shop and stuff and truss, following a constant stream of instructions from Gran to get the bird in the oven and the multitude of side dishes prepared. The meal was delicious, the mood sour. Maybe Ari will call, Charlie had said when they sat down at the table, and Les had said that it was hard to decide who was more pathetic, Charlie or the goose on that platter.

They were expert practitioners of the Kong family creed: the less said, the better. An outright airing of grievances might lead to an actual fight, and they all preferred festering to open scarring. She wondered if their mother knew of their extended silence. She hadn't said anything, and she doubted Les had, either; but Gran had a way of divining her daughters' moods, of pinpointing where the walls were weakest. Once, when Charlie was fixing a flat on her bicycle tire, she slid the inner tube inch by inch through a basin of sudsy water. Where air bubbles rose, she found the invisible puncture. That's what Gran was like: she could detect the tiniest leak.

On the flight to Philadelphia, Charlie thought of the cozy home where Aunt Rose and Uncle Bennett still lived and how, as children, she and Les had loved visiting every summer. The house was in a Philadelphia suburb on what used to be farmland and woods, so different from Southern California that it seemed to Charlie and Les like a foreign country. Down the street was a small woods where their four cousins took them every day to build rock dams in the creek and search for box turtles. The company of boys was glorious. They didn't talk as much as girls, and when they did, they spoke directly. Their needs seemed simple to Charlie—food, the woods, dirt, investigations. She didn't have to compete with them because they weren't her siblings. She had only to hold the sticks they gave her or screw the lid on the grasshopper jar or throw dry corn from the bucket to lure pheasants out of the grass. Les, too, had loved their yearly visits, and though at home she was too old for childish games, in the woods she dug with the rest of them and flung skunk cabbage leaves in mock battle. In the afternoons, she and their oldest cousin, Bill, grabbed towels and rode bicycles to the neighborhood pool, where they cannonballed off the diving board and baked themselves brown on the deck. They all got along famously, including the grown-ups.

Uncle Bennett was her father's younger brother, and the married pairs of brothers and sisters seemed almost like four siblings, so well did they know one another. They drank cocktails every evening and barbecued in the backyard and called the children to the picnic table while the sky was still light and before the mosquitoes started biting. Charlie liked seeing her father that way. With Bennett, he laughed easily and let the others tease him about their early days in America when they were all poor students eating rice in rented rooms. Aunt Rose was the youngest, and they made much of her youth, telling her that she should borrow Les's bikini. Charlie found it touching that her mother often reached for Aunt Rose's hand, and how Aunt Rose, in turn, sat close to Gran, leaning in for a smile, soaking up every word.

As they got older, their visits stuttered and then ended. Her father worked long hours, and Gran started planning her restaurant, and Les didn't want to leave her high school friends. Gran said that Rose and Bennett's house was really too small to accommodate everyone and why didn't they move? Before her complaint was finished, her father answered with a sharpness that upset Charlie. They had four children to put through college, he said, and Bennett, as a college professor, was worried about how they would manage. We should help them out. Absolutely not, Gran said. Rose would never want the obligation. There's nothing worse than having to be grateful, especially to one's family. What nonsense, Charlie's father said.

Charlie missed her summers in the woods and begged for another visit, and so, when she was thirteen, her parents let her fly alone to see Aunt Rose and Uncle Bennett. She had sauntered through the airport, balloon-buoyant. *Not like today*, Charlie thought glumly, joining the line shuffling through security as if shackled at the ankles. She was touched by Aunt Rose's kindness—Rose, who had been there at the orphanage on Ari's Gotcha Day, and who said she was certain that Ari would come home soon—but it felt fruitless, flying three thousand miles with no Ari at the end of her journey. *I'm Demeter*, thought Charlie, *wandering the earth in search of my missing daughter.* Ari had liked that story when they read from her big book of Greek myths at bedtime. She had wanted to know what a pomegranate tasted like, and so they had bought one at the Chinese market, split it open under water, and worked the red seeds out. *One, two, three, four, five, six*, she had counted—she was five years old, eager for kindergarten. Six bright seeds went into her rosebud mouth. When she crunched down, red juice had spurted, and Charlie, for a moment, had feared she had bitten her tongue. *Now I have to go to the underworld for six months*, Ari had crowed, and climbed under the bed and stayed put, ignoring Charlie's pleas to come out.

Demeter ruined the harvest until she got Persephone back, which had always seemed selfish to Charlie. One woman's sorrow shouldn't be visited upon the whole earth. She knew that her own stubbornness over Ari's disappearance, so infuriating to Les, was inflicting suffering on her sister and on Gran, too, though Gran had kept mostly silent, saying that sometimes it was a matter of survival for a girl to go off and live her life as she was meant to. *I'm being selfish*, Charlie thought, *not delivering Ari home. Laying waste to my family's harvest.*

Uncle Bennett was waving to her at the meeting point. Aunt Rose stood beside him in a bright blue raincoat. Bennett was stooped and gray, but Aunt Rose, like Gran, commanded flourishing health. Charlie smiled at the sight of her aunt's knit hat, worn at a rakish angle. That summer she had visited, she had not played anymore in the woods, but had learned how to sew and crochet and embroider.

Aunt Rose hugged Charlie to her broad rib cage, prompting Charlie to think of the photograph of her grandmother Eugenia with her big Dutch bosom and her squinty Chinese eyes. *What a mishmash we are,* Charlie thought. *If only Ari would understand that there was no such thing as a normal family.*

None of the boys were home, nor were they boys anymore. Charlie sat at the old pine table drinking tea and hearing the family news. The grandchildren were in college or starting careers. Eric's daughter, Sonja, was at Smith, Aunt Rose's alma mater.

"It will be nice for your mother when Ari goes to Bryn Mawr," Aunt Rose said. "That connection is special, between grandmother and granddaughter."

"Maybe next year," Charlie said.

"Do you have plans to visit Ari?"

"She doesn't want to see me. She won't talk to me anymore."

"Are you sure?" Aunt Rose asked.

Charlie nodded. When tears filled her eyes, Uncle Bennett excused himself to go tinker in the garage.

"Maybe she needs you to come to her," Aunt Rose said, "to prove one more time that she's loved."

"There was a man," Charlie said. "I knew him years ago." She had never told Aunt Rose or Gran about Aaron. She had intended to, at some point, but Gran was living in Taipei, and Charlie had dreaded her disapproval; after he was dead—well, what was the point then? She had asked Les to keep Aaron a secret. I can do that, Les had said. Some things ought to stay private.

"What?" Aunt Rose asked.

"Never mind. I'm exhausted. I think I'll go to bed."

THE NEXT DAY, walking through the neighborhood in February gray, Aaron returned, unbidden. His warm mouth. His voice of reason. She almost turned her head to see him striding beside her, so forcefully did she feel his nearness. After Christmas, when Ari hadn't called, Charlie had rooted again through every drawer and file for anything more she might have saved and forgotten, intent on purging the last little scrap of Aaron. She found nothing.

At first, after he left, he called her every night. They talked while

Ari was sleeping, his voice drowsy in her ear. On Saturday mornings, he called very early just to hear Ari's babble. He said he had told Wendy that he'd fallen in love in San Francisco and that he and Charlie were going to marry. He described his midnight hours, imagining her in his bed. When he returned, they would make love every night at the stroke of twelve and, in the morning, put Ari into the little seat on the back of Aaron's bicycle and ride out side by side to show her the beautiful city.

Then his letters began to change. He reported on his work in Juneau and gave her snippets of life with the Ericssons and their kids. The calls came further and further apart; the letters got shorter and shorter. Love turned into appreciation, fervor into haste. She detected dissembling in his voice and told him forthrightly that he was released from his promise. He didn't want that. Give me time, he said. It was too late to guard herself against him. She had already dreamed a family completed, with Aaron as the father of her darling little girl.

The sound of snow tires thudded against the pavement. She looked up to a brightening sky, waved a car past, and turned at the end of the street. The woods were gone, Uncle Bennett had said, cut down for housing, but the creek was still there. She forced her way through a hedge to where she thought the creek was. There was only the mouth of a culvert and the noise of trickling water. Dirty snow humped the ugly ground. She went up on a road she didn't remember and kept on walking.

She had crumbled when he died. Locked the doors and wailed because she knew that he had died without her in his heart. She could barely rouse herself to take care of her toddler and, on more than one night, had fed them both from a box of macaroni and gone to bed at seven, wine-numbed and speechless. One night, she fell asleep in her clothes and didn't come to until she heard the child crying. Ari had vomited all over herself, her cheeks were bright with fever. *I can't go on*, she thought, *but I have to: I have a daughter to raise*. When she woke the next day, Ari sleeping beside her, clammy in the bed, Charlie dug deep and came up with a shard of pride. She thought of it as shrapnel, lodged in her very tissue. She dragged herself from the bed to face the morning.

That flint of pride was digging at her again. However much she wanted to, if she chased after Ari it might feel like humiliation. Les had accused her of giving up. Well, fine, if that's what Les wanted to call it. For once in her life, she was hanging on to *no*.

She tramped the road for two hours. Except for her aunt and uncle's house, she didn't see a familiar landmark.

AUNT ROSE SAID that a great-grandson was due in April. They were in her sewing room with the winter light slanting in, Charlie cross-legged on the window seat and Aunt Rose in her wingback chair. Uncle Bennett was in his lab on campus—*They don't want him anymore*, Aunt Rose had said, *but he doesn't know anything else.*

"Do you think my mother is unhappy that she never had a son?" Charlie asked.

"She had Mu-you," Aunt Rose said shortly. "He could have been a son to her, after Father and Mother died."

"It's sad," Charlie said. Aunt Rose didn't answer. "Ma always talks about how daughters are better, but I think it's a smoke screen. She must have wanted a son."

"Your mother is not conventional Chinese. She always thought girls were stronger."

"She knows men well. They used to flock to her restaurant."

"She had a lot of beaux. There were always boys who wanted to take her out. She was popular with everyone, and she was the best student. At our school in Shanghai, she was the teacher's pet."

"She always got the lead in the school play," Charlie said. "She made Les learn all her speeches from when she played Portia. Maybe that's why Les became a lawyer."

"She didn't play Portia," Aunt Rose said. "She played the boy. The one who wants to marry Portia."

"Really? Are you sure?"

"Of course," Aunt Rose said.

"But Ma always told us that she had the heroine's part."

"She's the heroine of her own life. That's all."

"I guess she's always been independent." It disturbed her to hear such harshness from Aunt Rose.

"There's no such thing as being truly independent." Aunt Rose's voice grew louder. Charlie imagined it trapped against the dormer window or muffled by the quilt hanging on the wall. Something in Rose was fighting to get out. "She always pretends like all she's doing is standing up for herself, but what she does hurts other people. This car accident, for instance. She could have killed somebody."

"What car accident?"

"Her fender bender. With her neighbor in the car."

"Nobody told me about that!"

"Lesley knows. She fixed it all up for your mother. They probably thought you had enough to worry about."

"That makes me so mad," Charlie said. "Of course I want to know!"

Aunt Rose looked away. "Sisters can be difficult. They have special ways of hurting each other." She suddenly began to cry.

"What's happened?" Charlie stood up, alarmed, but Aunt Rose pushed her away.

"Your mother did a terrible thing. Yifu told me."

Charlie backed herself onto the window seat again. She didn't know what else to do.

"She lied to me about Mu-you," Aunt Rose said. "She said he was dead when he wasn't."

"I can't believe that. Are you saying Mu-you's not dead?"

"Dead now, but not dead then."

"I don't understand," Charlie said.

Aunt Rose left the room; Charlie heard her blow her nose. When she returned, her eyes shone clear and bright, as though cold anger had brought youth back to her face. Her voice rode in judgment from start to finish.

"When your mother was a nurse in training, she assisted in the delivery of a deformed baby. The doctor instructed the nurses to let it die. It died in the delivery room. They didn't try to save it."

"That's dreadful," Charlie said. Aunt Rose dismissed it.

"It happened that way sometimes. Doctors made decisions. Nurses did what they were told. Your mother was very disturbed by it." She had bad dreams about the baby for months afterward, Rose went on. By then Rose was in college; she would take the train from Smith to visit Gran in Philadelphia, and her sister's nightmares used to wake Rose in the middle of the night. "It was scary for me, seeing my older sister afraid. She was the strong one. She took care of me after Mother and Father died."

"In the war," Charlie said.

"After the war," Aunt Rose said sharply. "You kids never get these things right." Gran had come to America first. Rose followed. Their parents were making plans to leave, then their mother was killed. It was 1948. "Father died a few months later. I had already left China by then. I was at a boarding school; your mother was at Bryn Mawr. Father was in Hong Kong when he got hit by a car."

Charlie nodded. At least she remembered that part. Grandpa Wu had died in Hong Kong. She'd always been sorry that she hadn't met the handsome doctor hero of her mother's favorite stories.

Aunt Rose paused. "I saw Yifu recently."

"Auntie Yifu?" Charlie said. "Was she visiting from Pasadena?"

"Her husband was giving a talk at Penn, and she came to see me. We were reminiscing about our early days in America, and I mentioned those nightmares that your mother used to have. Yifu got a very strange expression on her face. She told me that she had come for a specific reason. She wanted me to know something. She said she had kept a secret for your mother for many years, but she didn't want to keep it any longer. She had asked your mother to tell me herself, but since she didn't, Yifu had come."

Charlie held still, as if she'd heard a noise in the woods. She didn't want to know her mother's secret. Ari had hurt her, digging into the past. But Aunt Rose continued.

"When Father died, your mother came to see me at my boarding school in Massachusetts. She told me that Father had been hit by a car and died on his way to the hospital. It was terrible news. We had lost Mother a few months before. We were so far from home and alone. I didn't know how I could go on without my parents. And then she told me that Mu-you also had died. He had gotten sick and died at Cousin Pei's house. She had just gotten word.

"For two days, we held each other and cried. At the end of the weekend, your mother got ready to leave. I didn't want her to go. She told me I had to stay and finish my schooling. She and I were the only surviving family, and we had to be strong for each other. And then she left."

"I can't imagine how that was," Charlie said, "losing your parents and Mu-you in the same year."

"It wasn't true," Aunt Rose said. "She lied to me. She told Yifu at the time what had really happened. Mu-you wasn't dead. He was still living with Cousin Pei, near Hangzhou. He died ten years later, of illness, but not when she said. He survived our parents." She put her hands to her face and leaned forward deeply. "I might have helped him," she sobbed. "I might have seen my brother again."

"Auntie Rose," Charlie said, but she didn't go to her.

Yifu told Rose that she had to forgive her sister. Their father had ordered that Mu-you stay behind. He said that Mu-you was too weak to come to America with the rest of the family. He had too many problems. How could they start over if they brought their damaged son with them? Mu-you wasn't little anymore. He was fourteen and strong, but he couldn't talk and couldn't feed himself at the table. He needed constant, devoted attention. Maybe they could send for him later, but he was better off with Cousin Pei. He had given her plenty of money.

"Mother refused to listen to Father," Aunt Rose said. "She was determined that Mu-you should come with them. The government was collapsing, and they had to leave the country soon. If they didn't take Mu-you with them, they might not be able to reach him later." Her parents had fought about it for weeks. In defiance, her mother left Shanghai and traveled to Hangzhou to bring Mu-you home. The roads were still unsafe, especially for a woman. She was killed by gunfire; they never found out whose.

"But why lie?" Charlie said. Her own face was wet with tears. "Why tell you that Mu-you was dead?"

"Your mother was twenty years old," Aunt Rose said. "I was fifteen. We were orphans. She could have gone back to try to bring Mu-you out, but she didn't. Father had told her to go to America and make her own life. She cried and cried, Yifu said, and then she stopped crying and made Yifu swear to keep her secret. She didn't want me to know that Mu-you was still in China. I might beg her to bring him to America with us, or go back myself and try to save him. She didn't want that for either of us, and neither did Father. She did her duty, Yifu said. For years, she sent money, though she had no way to know if Cousin Pei received it. Many years later, she learned that Mu-you was dead."

"Did my father know?" Charlie asked.

Aunt Rose shook her head.

"What a weight she must have carried," Charlie said, "keeping such a secret."

"That baby she helped to deliver. Yifu said it brought up all the bad feelings about leaving Mu-you behind. That's why she had the nightmares." Aunt Rose stood and went to draw the curtains.

"Yifu says I have to forgive her," she said. "But all I think about is Mother."

BEFORE UNCLE BENNETT DROVE Charlie to the airport, Aunt Rose gave her a handkerchief embroidered with tiny daisies.

"Shall I tell my mother that I know about Mu-you?" Charlie asked.

Aunt Rose looked old again in the dawning light.

"That's up to you. Yifu couldn't carry the burden any longer. But you are young. Secrets stay fresh forever."

TRAVELING HOME, Charlie thought of her mother at twenty, and Aunt Rose, and what her mother had done. The revelation didn't shock her. She had seen far worse violations and betrayals in the thousands of cases she had handled over the years. What was most troubling to Charlie was the break between the sisters. She wasn't sure that Aunt Rose could forgive Gran. How painful it would be if they never spoke again. Then the whole family would be destroyed.

I wouldn't know myself if that happened, Charlie thought. *If I lost my family, I wouldn't know where I came from.*

She resolved to go see Les as soon as she got home.

AT LES'S HOUSE, everything was nicer. The sofa was wide and deep, and warm yellow lamplight filled the room. Jazz played from speakers in the ceiling, a woman singing silkily in a foreign tongue. A good Pinot Gris was probably cooling in the refrigerator. And she had peonies by the armful.

Les herself was Sunday casual in corduroy and cashmere. Charlie made a weak joke about showing up like a bag lady and took off her worn boots and stood them up on the hearth. They could have been a decorator's whimsical touch—the antique accent that pulled the room together.

"Ma is mad at me, as usual," Les said. She plopped herself into an armchair sized perfectly for a woman. "Her friend Naomi can't live alone anymore, and Ma blames me for telling Naomi's son to move her. He didn't need my permission. He practically had the moving truck backed up to her bedside."

"Is she okay? Is she moving out soon?"

"This week," Les said. "She had another stroke, and her kids decided it was time."

"I'm sorry," Charlie said. She *was* sorry, though she disliked the old bitch. *China gets clean babies.* She couldn't forgive Mrs. Greene for that.

"So Ma is mad at me. But something else is going on. She's upset, and it's not like her to brood. I think she's been obsessing over Ari. Every time I talk to her, she wants to know when Ari is coming home."

"It's not Ari," Charlie said.

"It is," Les said. "I wish you'd get her back here. She belongs in school. You need to set boundaries."

"It's not Ari!" Charlie said. In a heated rush, she repeated what Aunt Rose had told her. "Isn't it horrible?" she demanded. "Isn't it horrible what Ma did?"

"You shouldn't go around telling that story," Les said. "It's a private family matter."

"We're family!"

"I mean between Ma and Aunt Rose. It's nothing to do with us."

"But she left her brother behind and then lied about it to her sister!"

"What choice did she have? I can understand why she did it. He was being taken care of by relatives. I would've done the same thing."

"Please don't say that. I don't want to believe it."

"You would've, too."

"Oh, Les," Charlie said. "I don't know you anymore."

"On the contrary," said her sister. "You know me all too well. Anyway, there's something else I want to talk to you about."

"I can tell already that I don't want to hear it."

"Ari's living with a family in Juneau. Steve and Peg Ericsson. Aaron's old friends."

"I know that," Charlie said. "Ari already told me."

"What else did she tell you?"

"How do you know about the Ericssons?" Charlie asked. She had held back that fact from her sister, just as she had not told Les at first that Ari had gone looking for Aaron. Not everything had to be shared between them.

"I made some inquiries—"

"You had no right—"

"And you really do need to go up there."

Charlie abruptly stood to leave. For all her trying, nothing was getting better.

"Aaron had a son," Les said, an ugly note of triumph in her voice.

"You're a liar."

"He had a son. His name is Noah. He's two years older than Ari. He goes to school in Juneau, and they've met."

They locked eyes. Charlie knew she was standing—she could feel the plush rug under her stockinged feet and was aware of the mantelpiece at her shoulder—but, impossibly, Les was looking down at her as though from a high seat. The light in the room whirled bright at the corners, but Charlie's view went dim. She heard the woman singing out of the ceiling, her voice caressing syllables that rolled over in Charlie's head. Nothing made sense, and then suddenly everything did. Aaron had a son, two years older than Ari. How fitting, after all, that a child had torn them apart.

"You had no right," she repeated softly, and she bent to put her boots on, her back like an old woman's.

SHE GOT TO THE OFFICE by eight the next morning. She found her boss already standing over his desk, scribbling in a file. "Can I talk to you?" Charlie said.

He looked up impatiently. His shirt gaped where a button was missing.

"Are you going to challenge my sister on the Wilson Ng trial?"

His hand froze. A cunning look colonized his florid face. "Should I?" he asked.

"I would," Charlie said.

He gave a shallow nod, and she turned and strode away.

CHAPTER 24

LES

The news traveled fast. Hal Nugent, the public defender, had stood up in Department 22 and said the magic words: "Your Honor, may I be sworn?" The clerk had stepped forward, Nugent had raised his hand, and ten seconds later, Judge Mullen had been assigned to preside in the Wilson Ng trial.

"It happened so quickly, Riordan forgot to change his expression from slow boat to lucky bastard," her bailiff, Tony, reported to Judge Kong. "The P.D. dropped a huge gift in his lap, and he didn't even realize it until it was all over. There's no way he's going to lose this case now, but if anybody can do it, Patrick Riordan can."

Judge Kong dismissed him with a curt nod. Tony backed out of her chambers, worried. Had he gone too far with his crack about the D.A.? The judge insisted on a certain measure of respect, but she held the office, not Riordan, in high regard. She'd joked with Tony more than once about what she called Riordan's "Botox look": when he didn't understand a legal point that his opponent or the judge was making, his face froze up like a sherbet mold. Tony didn't know why she'd gone so suddenly quiet. Surely Judge Kong didn't care that the P.D. had challenged her. Peremptory challenges happened to every judge from time to time, sometimes by prosecutors, sometimes by the defendant. Judge Kong had never taken it personally, as she shouldn't. "There's always another case waiting," she said to Tony whenever the docket shifted.

She must have other things on her mind, Tony decided. At ten o'clock, he'd bring her a cappuccino and offer to pick up her dry cleaning. She never let him, but he liked to offer just the same.

At her desk, Les slashed a red *X* in the brief she was reading. She got up and moved restlessly around the office, shoving a book into a shelf, flicking a drawer shut. *Your Honor, may I be sworn?* It galled her plenty that Hal Nugent had stood up in court and gotten her bounced from the trial. There probably had been press in the gallery, their knives out for Ng or the lawyers or anybody they could attack. No doubt Reynold Low had been there, rallying Ng supporters. It was humiliating to be challenged in such a public case.

Calm down, Les told herself. She returned to her high-backed leather chair and poured herself a glass of water. Every judge was occasionally challenged. It meant nothing. Counsel had their reasons, and there was no profit in trying to guess why or in taking it as a knock on one's competence or reputation. There was no reason to think that the P.D. judged Les badly. Nobody but Les would give it a second thought. Still, what was Nugent thinking? Les would have considered carefully every evidentiary issue that might save his client or hang him. Judge Mullen wouldn't give him the time of day.

THREE DAYS LATER, Les stood awkwardly by herself in a crowded Chinatown restaurant. She was at the annual luncheon for the local Asian bar. She remembered the day not that many years ago when all the Asian lawyers in town fit into five or six tables. Now the whole banquet floor was full; she swiftly counted more than forty tables. There were bigwigs in attendance from across the spectrum—judges, lawyers, deans, politicians—many of them white, a few black or Hispanic. Every major law firm felt obligated to buy a table. Burrell was here; they'd exchanged a quick hello. Charlie wasn't. Les wondered if she'd skipped the luncheon this year because the tickets had gone up to a hundred and fifty bucks a pop, or because she didn't want to run into Les. She fiddled with a glass of wine and looked around for someone to talk to. Reynold Low stood nearby; he raised his glass to Les, but to her surprise, he didn't approach her. Reynold usually took the time to schmooze with the judges in the room.

"Judge Kong," a hearty voice blared behind her. Reverend Stanley Yeung was holding out his hand. Les had a strong grip, but Reverend Stanley's was stronger. "How much longer will we have you on the state court bench?"

Les demurred. "I love my job," she said. "Every day brings something new."

"I heard you were being kicked upstairs. Next thing you know, I'll be reading your name in the papers as the first Asian American nominee to the U.S. Supremes," he joked.

Les smiled uncertainly. In Reverend Stanley's voice she detected a faint edge—he was usually ebullient to the point of aggression, but she recognized something else. She had heard the same from certain individuals—usually men, though not always—testifying in court: the unmistakable jollity of malice.

I wish my sister were here, thought Les. *Charlie would know how to talk to the people in this room.*

BURRELL CALLED AND ASKED to come over. She met him at home, though she knew the minute she saw him that they wouldn't go right to bed. He sat with her in the living room, his face stern, his bulk on her sofa more obstacle than body.

"It's not going to happen this time," he said directly. "Your name didn't get sent on to the Judiciary Committee."

"Why not?" Les asked.

"We can try again," Burrell said. "There'll be another opening next year when Judge Burch goes to senior status. Or you can try for a federal magistrate position. That might be the way to go."

"We talked about that," Les said sharply. "I want judge, not magistrate. What happened?"

Burrell's baritone sounded wrong in her house, like a cowboy ordering a cattle herd through a tearoom.

"Reynold Low pulled his support. You lost the Chinatown community backing. He made a big deal out of the P.D.'s peremptory challenge in the Wilson Ng case. He said it was an indication that you didn't have high credibility with the members of the bar who appear regularly before you. It was total bullshit, of course. Nobody pays attention to that sort of procedural detail."

"It was one simple case! There's not a judge on the bench who hasn't been challenged."

"You and I know that, but Reynold Low blew it all out of proportion. It spooked the committee." Burrell got up to make himself a drink. The news delivered, his face relaxed, his shoulders softened. "I promise you that we'll try again. Maybe they'll give you a fresh look. There's nobody else with your stellar record, and sooner or later, they're going to have to put up an Asian face. The short list has three white guys on it. Reynold Low just shot himself in the foot."

"Does it have to be this way?" Les asked. "Do I have to be the 'Asian face'?"

Burrell barked a laugh. "You're asking me that question? I'm afraid so. That's the way it has to be." He checked his watch. "Let's go to bed," he said.

Les looked around the room—at what, she didn't know. She wished again that her front windows opened. The air in her house was stale with disappointment.

"I can't," she said.

Burrell made her a drink and put his arms around her. He talked, and she listened, wanting to believe him. His voice, so wrongly pitched a moment ago, reverberated in her ear like the growl of a steady motor. He said they would try again; he said he would help her through it. Be with me, he said. We belong together. They moved into the bedroom. Les undressed and spread herself on the bed. She quickly pulled him on top of her, hiding her face in his neck. Tears came when she finished—ridiculous, silly tears that felt as real as if she were weeping.

He rolled onto his back and held her tightly. "The whole band played that time," he said. "Huh. I didn't think that could happen anymore. It's been a long while."

"You know this is over," Les said.

"No, it's not," he said.

She didn't insist, not yet. Behind her desolation, she felt the heat of rage. Her anger bewildered her almost as much as her loneliness. She pressed herself to her lover's chest and traced his rib cage again and again, the bones faintly visible under his thick flesh and her finger a leadless pencil. It was over at last. She wept true tears as Burrell slept deeply beside her.

CHAPTER 25

ARI

January began with no chance in hell that I'd be turning over a new leaf. I was no more visible to myself than the Northern Lights, which had vanished. The kids returned to day care and the legislature came back to town—Peg said those amounted to the same thing. Everybody but me, it seemed, was focused on new beginnings. Peg read seed catalogs the way Charlie looked after her clients; she was planning her spring garden and dreaming of what would grow. Steve made a list of household projects. I helped him mark a wall in my basement den; he said he wanted to install a bookshelf where I could keep the used books I'd bought here and there for pennies. Peg frowned when he said that and pointed out that the laundry room needed a shelf, too, which Steve said he'd do right after he put one up for me.

A couple of times, Peg and Steve took me skiing at Eaglecrest on Douglas Island. I wasn't very good to start with and didn't get much better. I thought of A.J. skimming down the mountain, attacking the hills with grace. In the evenings, after the Statehood closed, I went to Connor and Shawna's house to watch their little boy, Caleb, while they worked on planning the Dance-Off. I had a lot of sympathy for Caleb. He always backed away in fear, instantly comprehending that my grinning appearance meant his parents were cutting out. I remembered again how I had jumped out of the car on every Whackadoodle Saturday to run to our latest borrowed classroom or church basement or playground. I hadn't wanted to miss a single second because WeiWei had been waiting for me, toe ring displayed, skinny arms open, sardonic smile on her face.

The January Dance-Off was the community's biggest fund-raiser. Shawna and Connor were in the last days of planning, working the phones and directing the volunteers. This year the money was going for youth programs and mobile medical equipment. Sometimes Steve joined them to talk to sponsors and figure out where the bands and extra generators would go, though mostly he enjoyed cooking up a big pot of chili for the committee. When Connor first described the Dance-Off to me, his eyes bright, his fat fingers flying, I had dismissed it in my mind as a corny, small-town event, but after four months of living indoors, I, like everyone else in town, was eager for it to start. Anchorage had its Fur Rondy and championship sled-dog races and Juneau had its twenty-four-hour dance marathon to chase the winter blues.

The crowd gathered early at the Old Armory for a start time of four o'clock. Shawna, in a sparkly silver top, gave me an excited hug and collected my ticket. Friends and neighbors were high-fiving their way through the doors. I was wearing a black tank and hoodie, nothing as glam as Shawna's sequins, and a pair of good running shoes that Peg had loaned me to keep my feet from giving out. I was worried that somebody might bump my finger hard, but I was practiced by then in keeping myself protected.

Inside, people shed their jackets and showed off their T-shirts: Rotary Club members, veterans, Realtors, firefighters. Church groups, jazz band musicians, road runners, the fish ladder crew. A team of tobacco spitters—the top five leaders from the previous Fourth of July, all of whom, Shawna informed me, could hit the twenty-foot mark. The Juneau Jumpers, a championship jump-roping team. A brigade of hairy men dressed in bonnets and diapers. If you weren't dancing, you were there to deejay or emcee or tell jokes or yodel. Anyone who doesn't show up, Connor said, gets hella shit on Monday.

A band started loud and fast with top single hits. I jumped in, trying to get loose but feeling awkward. There were two hundred people on the dance floor, waving their arms and shouting. Every three hours was a block; every block had a theme. The eighties, nineties, hip-hop, and oldies. At one point, Shawna spotted me by myself and shimmied over to draw me into a quick twirl. I let her take my one hand and matched her move for move, though I couldn't summon her beaming smile. Women walked through the crowd, urging us to drink water. I saw Steve and Peg pogoing to the Stones, "Jumpin' Jack Flash" launching solid Steve upright. He couldn't jump very high, but his Chuck Taylors left the floor. Peg looked as serene as ever.

Around ten at night, I spotted Noah. He was in the middle of a teeming group of dancers—by the looks of them, fellow students. He had his eyes closed and his arms in the air. Big circles of armpit sweat soaked his shirt. Gone was his usual tight expression; his brow was relaxed, his mouth slightly open. I didn't think he would know what to do on the dance floor, but his step was easy and his hips moved with the beat. He looked younger and lighter—like his father in the photograph, at home with his place in the world. I didn't go up to him. We hadn't run into each other since our conversation at the Statehood, and I guessed that he, like me, was choosing to keep his distance. When he threw back his head to the music, I saw his long, white throat like a snow print in the dark.

I worked my way to the door. My feet hurt and my finger throbbed and escape seemed the only option. I told myself that I didn't need to stick around for the whole bush-league thing. I'd bought my ticket and shown up for a few hours, and nobody would miss me. A group on break was standing just inside the doorway; somebody grabbed my arm. It was Rick from Wrangell, the guy from the bar before Christmas. He was wearing a green bowling shirt with squiggly black and pink lines and a wide leather wristband and hideous shoes— bright racing flats, the color of traffic cones. He looked about forty, even older than I remembered. He gave me a big wink and yelled into my ear. He had a bottle, he said; his car was right outside, and hadn't I had enough group dancing for one night?

I glanced back as I was leaving. A Native troupe had filled the stage, their leader a great, feathered bird and the dancers striped in green, yellow, and red. I missed the lion dancers of a Chinatown parade, but home was far behind me.

A FEW DAYS LATER, Noah showed up again at the Statehood.

"I saw you at the Dance-Off," he said. "Why didn't you say hello?"

"Why didn't you?" I answered.

He didn't bite back. He'd done some more thinking, he said. He'd come by to see if I wanted to hang out with him and his friends. They were picking him up in five minutes, closing time at the Statehood. "Steve was right. I guess I do have questions. Things I've been curious about that my mother never told me."

I hesitated. Had he seen me leaving with Rick from Wrangell? I didn't want to be Noah's pity project, but I read in his clear eyes behind the black-rimmed glasses the openness he wanted to show me, either because it was there, or because I was horribly lonely. I wanted to say yes. Anything was better than another night in my basement.

"I don't know much," I said slowly. "Steve can tell you what you want to know."

He shook his head. "I can't ask Steve. It's painful for him, don't you think? To talk about my dad?"

I remembered Steve's grief at the kitchen table, but also how happy he'd been describing Aaron's high spirits and the early days of their friendship. "People tell me all the time not to look back," I said. I was thinking of Gran. "Move on. Put the past behind you."

Noah's pale face flickered. "You're probably right," he said. "My mother never has, and it's eaten up her whole life."

"It's the opposite in my family. I guess I'm the one who's no good at forgiveness. I've been known to hold a grudge forever."

"Uh-oh," Noah said. The shadow had passed; he was halfway to a grin. "Then I'm in trouble."

I laughed. I was dying now to shuck my apron and go.

"Forgiveness is overrated," I told him. That, too, sounded a lot like Gran.

A car horn blew. I followed him out the door.

NOAH'S FRIENDS WERE brother and sister, Corey and Brigid. Corey, like Noah, was a junior at UAS, and Brigid a year older. Noah introduced me as a friend of Steve and Peg's. We drove to a house party in Corey's pickup, Brigid and I on the back bench seat and the guys in front with Corey's feathery mutt, Rooster, panting happily between them.

"Where are you from?" Corey asked. I told him San Francisco. He was big and blond with chapped hands, ruddy cheeks, and a goggle-shaped tan line around his eyes, the telltale mark of a skier. Brigid was tall and glowing. They were from Haines, Alaska, a four-hour ferry ride from Juneau. Their parents, she told me, were sailing buddies of Steve and Peg's.

"Are you a student?" Brigid asked. She reached across me to fix my twisted seat belt, an unconscious move that came, I guessed, with being an older sister. It felt nice to be taken care of. I thought again of WeiWei.

"No, not a student. I just came up here to hang out. Work for a while, take some time on my own. I was supposed to start college, but I didn't end up going."

"Most people trying to find themselves, they come up here in the *summer*," Corey said.

Brigid laughed. "Don't listen to him." She gave me an appraising look. I drew my hand into my sleeve so she wouldn't see my missing finger. "How old are you?" she asked.

"Nineteen," I said. It was almost true. My birthday was coming up.

"Okay then," Brigid said, "old enough to party."

I crashed at her place for the night.

WE TOOK ROOSTER the next day to Sandy Beach on Douglas Island, where the air smelled of sea and rain. I prised a stone from the soaked sand and rubbed it clean before slipping it into my pocket. I heard yelling, and turned to see Corey and Noah hooting and hollering to the waves. Rooster circled, barking, then took off again down the beach. Corey loped after him, wheeling and barking in turn. The drizzling mist clung to Brigid's blue cap like tiny sequins. When we walked into a coffee shop, Noah's glasses fogged up.

"We did that all the time as kids," Corey said. "Dad said we were raised by wolves." He punched Brigid on the shoulder. "I still run faster than you."

"But I still beat your ass down the mountain," Brigid said. "Do you have any siblings?" she asked me.

"Baby Bowns," I said. I explained how, when I was a kid, I imagined I had a brother who had shared my orphanage crib. "There was a little tag around my neck. 'Like eating, like the Bowns.' I made up all sorts of stories about what that word could mean."

"That's sweet," Brigid said.

"So you were adopted?" Corey asked. I nodded.

"You could have a sibling that you don't know about it," Brigid said. "That's a weird thought."

"I'll give you mine," Corey volunteered.

"I had a friend who was adopted who found out she has a sister. She had that animated TV show about the adopted Chinese daughter. She did the voice. You know, *WeiWei's World*?" They stared at me blankly. "It was really popular," I said.

"Yeah, among orphans," Corey said.

"It seemed huge to me at the time. This family in Sweden saw a picture of WeiWei and thought that their daughter looked so much like her, there was a chance they were actually sisters."

"Way, way out there," Corey joked.

"Shut up, brute," Brigid said. She had heard my voice change when I named WeiWei.

I told them how WeiWei had arranged for the sister to go to China, where WeiWei was filming a documentary about the orphanage she came from. "While they were in Guangzhou, a Chinese lab tested their DNA and confirmed the girls are full sisters. Now they see each other as often as they can."

"Wow, how lucky," Brigid said. "Have you met her? Are the sisters a lot alike?"

Under the table, I pinched the stump of my little finger. Noah was watching me, a look of concern on his face. "We used to be friends," I said. "I don't know her anymore."

FEBRUARY PASSED. I spent more time with Noah, Corey, and Brigid. The four of us made plans for the spring. I mentioned to Peg that we were talking about hiking the Chilkoot, and she frowned and said that the trail wouldn't be open before I left, so I knew Peg wanted me gone. Steve dropped his chin when she said that, but he didn't correct her. Even Jackson, the cat, stopped sleeping on my bed and stared at me, yellow-eyed, from across the basement room. I'd overstayed my welcome, but I didn't know where else to go. I had enough money to get back to San Francisco, but I couldn't face the thought of going home to Charlie, and although I'd told A.J. that I was saving up for Beijing, I couldn't face that, either. If I left Juneau—my dark, safe wolf den and the suspended life I led—I might make something bad happen all over again, and so I stayed put, pouring coffee at the Statehood and hanging on at Steve and Peg's.

Noah didn't ask me about Charlie and Aaron. He must have seen that I didn't like talking about my mother, or he'd decided that, like Steve had said, it wasn't my story to tell. I told him a little bit about growing up in San Francisco and about my aunt Les and Gran. He showed me the work he'd done on his Juneau project. History absorbed him, especially the old maps he'd found and studied, but he had declared environmental science as his major, a subject that returned that tight look to his face. I wondered if he felt duty-bound to follow in Aaron's footsteps.

A couple of times when Noah and I found ourselves alone, our steps slowed and our bodies drew closer together. Then one of us would flush and fall back while the other stutter-stepped. I could see he was wondering if something was happening between us; I thought maybe it was, and I wasn't sure what I wanted. I liked the way things were. Most of the time, we were easy together, taking short winter walks, hanging out with Corey and Brigid. If I caught him looking at me as if he was thinking of kissing me, I flung a sharp remark to dig at him a little. I even told him about cutting off my finger—to scare him off, I told myself, not because, like Steve, I needed for someone to know.

He recoiled, as I'd expected.

"Are you serious?" he asked.

I nodded.

"It wasn't an accident?"

"No. I had a kind of . . . breakdown. We'd visited our old orphanage, and I was in a really strange mood, and I took a knife from the hotel kitchen and . . . cut."

He stared over my head, then looked back at me.

"Your showing up here has been strange," he said. "I haven't told my mother that we've met, and that feels pretty weird. I think I'd like to meet Charlie, and that feels even weirder. I like hanging out with you. I'm glad we're friends. Sometimes I think you're crazy, but in a normal way, you know?"

I shook my head, hoping I hadn't blown it.

"I mean you're no crazier than anybody else," he said. He lifted my hand and looked long and hard at the stump of my little finger, then he set it down gently.

"WeiWei says we all have little green men living inside our heads, but everybody's green men are different."

"She's right. Maybe we should have your little green men and my little green men tested to see if they're a match."

I laughed and thought, *Baby Bowns*.

A LETTER ARRIVED at the Ericssons' house. I stared at the envelope. It was from WeiWei.

Hiya kid.

Sorry I haven't written. I've been a little busy. I got your address from your mom. She was so happy I called her that she practically climbed through the phone. How are you holding up? A.J. said you ran into a spot of trouble. I wouldn't worry about it. Remember who you are, or if that doesn't work, fake it.

So I have something to tell you. Something bad has happened. I guess you could say I ran into a spot of trouble myself. It's nothing I did wrong. But you're going to read some stuff in the news pretty soon about me. I hope you're not mad about it. I hope, when you read it, you'll give me a call. I could use a friend. Maybe you'll help me blow back the critics. They don't know what it's like to be us, you know? In the meantime, take a picture of a glacier for me and try and be happy. It isn't easy. But it pays.

Love, WeiWei

I read the letter twice. It gave me the sensation that WeiWei was holding on to my outstretched arm, twisting the flesh toward me with one hand and away from me with the other. A.J. and I used to do that to each other, back in Whackadoodle days. I didn't know what else to think. WeiWei was asking for my help, and also asking to be excused—from what, she hadn't told me. *They don't know what it's like to be us.* I had heard that from her before, and it had always been a comfort, but this time it sounded whiny. I raced to the computer. I searched for her name, but all I found was the stuff I already knew, everyone singing her praises. I stumped downstairs to my basement, the letter hot in my pocket. I searched the next day and the day after that and turned up nothing. After a week of distraction, I tried again to forget her.

"HOW'S NOAH THESE DAYS?" Steve asked me. I wouldn't have thought that a burly guy could sound so wistful. The next time I saw Noah, I asked him to come to the house.

"Just to say hi," I said. "Just for a few minutes."

"I don't want to," he said sharply. "Don't push me." He didn't speak to me for the rest of the hour, his shoulders pinned back, his face like a shut door. Other times, he brought up Steve himself, remembering a trail they'd hiked or an old building they'd explored. He said that maybe in the spring he'd ask to go out on Steve's boat. I didn't mind his changeable nature, but sometimes, trying to guess which way the winds were gusting, I felt like Charlie.

Steve's friend Pete asked us to do him a favor. He had a cabin in Tenakee and was sending supplies on the ferry. Could we get the stuff to his cabin? We could stay for a couple of days and check out the hot springs.

The four of us jumped at the chance. Early one morning, we boarded the ferry for the five-hour sail around the north end of Admiralty Island, and south down the Lynn Canal. In the Icy Strait waterway, we saw otters and eagles and the massed clouds of the brooding Southeast sky. When the boat docked at Tenakee, half the town, maybe thirty people, came aboard to load supplies onto two-wheeled carts and then trundle their groceries and booze and thirty-six rolls of Costco toilet paper to the houses dotted along the road. The town itself was four blocks long, making Juneau seem like Manhattan. Noah and Corey borrowed a cart to take Pete's load—a generator and heavy boxes of tiling supplies—up the main road to his cabin. Brigid and I carried the ice chest. Some of the houses we passed stood partially on stilts, but Pete's cabin was set back from the water on the uphill side of town where it didn't need legs to stay dry. We'd been up since six to catch the ferry, so we walked back to the main intersection where the mercantile stood, and bought cold drinks and chips to have with our lunch on the dock. It was drizzling, but we didn't mind; we sat outside in parkas as comfortably as if it were dry. Noah noticed crocuses in a few of the cabin gardens and said that maybe spring was coming a little early.

I'd heard Alaskans rhapsodize about Tenakee Springs and had pictured myself sitting in a steaming blue pool on the edge of the water, gazing up at snow-covered peaks, but the hot springs were in an old bathhouse with a solid wooden door. There were alternating hours for women and men, so Brigid and I went for a long walk while Noah and Corey soaked. We met them back at the cabin; their faces were flushed and they smelled of pine soap and said that they'd almost fallen asleep in the pool. We unpacked the ice chest and made ourselves a feast of salmon and corn and wine and winter apples, and then Brigid and I walked to the bathhouse with one towel between us.

It felt weird to take off my boots. Months had passed since I'd gone barefoot; my toes didn't know how to operate against the concrete floor. There were pegs and painted wooden benches for storing our things, and I stripped down and went through a door and walked naked down the steps.

Three women were already in the water—large, soft bodies bobbing in a rectangular pool in the floor. A fourth woman with heavy breasts and a dark muff was standing on the side, washing. She gave me an empty laundry soap bottle, cut in half, and showed me how to use it to scoop water from the pool for bathing. I wet myself down and soaped my goose-fleshed skin, noticing how pale I looked in the dim light of the bathhouse. The deep brown color I'd acquired the previous summer was completely gone—I hadn't a single tan line— and so I had turned, like every other Alaskan, my version of prize white. I ran my soapy hands over my arms and legs and butt and belly, slicking off the sweat of the morning and afternoon. One of the women in the pool offered Brigid and me her shampoo, pearly green in a clear bottle, and I sudsed my head as well, digging my fingers into my scalp. I scooped and poured warm water over my head, then, completely rinsed, I slipped into the pool.

The water was hotter than I expected, almost too hot to bear, but my feet felt their way across the big rocks on the bottom until I was close to the center and immersed up to my chin. Brigid got in, too, her long legs brushing against my short ones underwater, and ducked quickly, her head popping up like the otters we'd seen from the boat. There were six of us altogether and we chatted as we bobbed, faces shiny. Everyone but me was from Southeast: Tenakee, or Hoonah, or Haines. Brigid and I were younger than the others; they joked about their winter fat and slapped the water with open hands. The noise they made echoed in the room, and the water in the pool spilled out at one end, the pool constantly filling from the hot springs below. I smelled the sulfur as I soaked and felt the heat penetrate my limbs and thought of how, since cutting off my finger, I hadn't looked at my body or cared for it in any way beyond feeding it when hungry and hiding it under layers. Even during sex, I hadn't taken off all my clothes. Kurt hadn't cared; the guy from Wrangell had been in too much of a hurry. I had just about forgotten what my own body looked like.

After a few minutes, I was too hot to stay in the water, and got out to sit on the side. I looked down at my breasts, round and red, and the tops of my thighs as pink as if I had slapped them. I wondered if I would smell like sulfur when I got back to the cabin until I remembered how the guys had smelled of pine soap and how Noah's dark hair had curled above his collar. The only good moment of the night I'd spent with Rick from Wrangell—the only moment that didn't disgust me—was when he had noticed my missing finger. He'd held up his right hand to show me his two missing joints. "Fishing boat accident," he'd said, "but I wasn't as lucky as you. It's a helluva thing to lose your index finger." I'd held up my hand, too, and we'd compared scars and phantom pain stories and, in a funny moment, had tried to link stumps, bumping them instead like little men tapping heads. I slipped back into the water, feeling clean all over.

The next day, Brigid and Corey borrowed a kayak and were gone for several hours. Noah and I swept Pete's cabin and did some weeding in his garden, which was starting to show green. We went back inside to sit and wait for the others. Noah asked if, when we got back to Juneau, I would show him the photograph I had of his father.

"I don't know," I said, thinking of what Charlie had written on the back. "It might hurt you. You might not want to see."

He said he understood. "I guess I'll think about it. I just wish I remembered more about him." His eyes reddened, and he turned slightly away. "I remember him holding me. He used to take me into the ocean. We went fishing one time on a boat with a loud motor. I had a toy football that he gave me. My mother said I slept with it on my bed."

I didn't want to hear more, but he said he kept a picture of his family in his wallet and drew out a black-and-white photo. It was of Aaron, the same as he looked in my picture, in charge and at ease, and a smiling woman with blowing hair and dark-eyed baby Noah. Aaron and Wendy were crouched in lush grass, each holding one of Noah's hands as he high-stepped toward the camera, fairly crowing in his pleasure at taking his first steps. I stared at the picture, and my eyes began to sting. In another few seconds, I was crying.

"Hey," Noah said. He put his arm tentatively across my shoulder. "Hey, hey. It's all right."

I jumped to my feet. "You have this," I said. "You have learning to walk and your noisy boat and your toy football, and I've got nothing. It isn't fair. Look at the love on their faces." I flung the picture to the floor. "I don't feel sorry for you."

"I'm not asking for that." He stood up quickly, sympathy on his face. I felt myself go cold, my stomach an empty pit. My tears were a defeat, a total humiliation. I would have thrust myself at him, the same as I had done with Kurt, Rick, and Niall, except that I had sat in the sulfurous waters and seen my body, pink and solid, and remembered that I had a body, not just a hammered heart. I sat down on the cabin floor and cried for a long minute.

After I recovered myself, Noah gave me a searching look. We might have kissed in that moment, but he didn't press me. He was giving me the choice, and, in that pause, the air cleared between us.

"Let's go out," I said. We walked down to the water and took our turn with the kayak.

Pete flew to fetch us in the morning. We cooked a big breakfast and he showed us his plans for fixing up the cabin. We carried our stuff to the dock and Pete told us to strap in. His floatplane didn't look much bigger than Corey's pickup, and the engine buzzed loudly, but I loved the lift and the shudder and the scape moving beneath us. The forest was so close that we saw grizzly from the air.

When we got back to Juneau, Noah said he had something of his father's to show me. We went to his room, and he brought out a slim box about the length of his hand.

"Open it," he said, and I opened the box to find a fountain pen, a blue Sheaffer Targa.

"It's beautiful," I breathed. It had the signature flat top and clip with the white dot. I had told him before about my job at Pen and Parchment, about Ines and the ten-thousand-dollar pen with the gold nib and the Irish lawyer who came in every day to drool over the Visconti Black Ripple. I had shown him Grandpa Kong's mechanical pencil, but until this day, he'd never mentioned his father's pen.

"Do you like it?" he said. He looked pleased. "My mother says it's proof that beneath the breast of every do-good lawyer beats the heart of a true bourgeois."

I laughed, thinking that I might, after all, have liked Wendy. He fetched a sheet of good paper and tested the ink flow and gave it to me to try. I wrote his name, *Noah Streeter*, and we admired the gorgeous line.

"Write yours," he said, and I did, *Ari*.

"That's it?" he said, and so I wrote the whole thing, *Ariadne Bettina Yun-li Rose Kong*. Noah said it was the longest name he'd ever seen, and I saw it as he did, so long and singular in that beautiful soft blue ink that I felt as if I were reading it for the first time.

CHAPTER 26

ARI

WeiWei's news reached me the last weekend in March. I found out from A.J. Brigid and I had met at her apartment and gone out for Sunday breakfast. The sun had briefly glimmered, raising my sights toward spring, and so I borrowed Brigid's phone to call A.J.

"You heard," she said.

"Heard what?"

"About WeiWei." She was eking out her words, her voice icy. "She lied to us," she said. "She lied to everybody. The whole thing was a fraud. That girl isn't her sister. WeiWei made it all up."

The parents, she told me, had gotten upset at the constant publicity. They accused WeiWei of exploiting their daughter and had the DNA retested. No match was found. WeiWei's handlers were claiming it was a mistake. The Whackadoodles were, to a girl, undone.

"We don't want to believe it," A.J. said, "but the whole thing was total bullshit. And now my mom and Charlie and all the rest of the mothers are saying that they knew all along that something seemed fishy. That's bullshit, too. Everybody believed her." I felt a sharp pain at the bitterness of her tone. "We wanted it to be true," she said. "That's how stupid we were."

"WeiWei wrote to me," I said. "She asked me to call her."

"Don't you do it," A.J. said. "She betrayed us."

"What's going to happen to her?"

She didn't know. "Who gives a shit," she said. She laughed harshly, a rattling, alien noise. "I should've learned what WeiWei told us: 'A bullshit detector is appropriate at any age.'"

"I've never heard you so angry."

"I'm a week ahead of you. Every day I get madder. She let me gush to her on the phone. I fawned over her sister. She was laughing at me behind my back the whole time."

"Is she really in trouble? Maybe I should call her."

"If you do, don't tell me. In fact, don't call me again." Her voice rasped. "You've moved on. You and WeiWei both. I guess I've moved on too."

Before I could say anything, A.J. put down the phone.

WHEN NOAH AND COREY got to Brigid's, I told them all about what WeiWei had done. Brigid was appalled. "She had you and your friend. So why make up a little sister?" I flushed, my jealousy exposed.

"She asked me to call her," I said, "but all my friends are really angry." I couldn't fault A.J. for her bitter tone, but I didn't feel the same as she did. I turned to Noah. "I can't believe she lied about something so important."

He was quiet for a second. "It might have been a mistake," he said, "or maybe it was a lie. If she did make it up, maybe she had a good reason." He looked at me directly. I understood. I would have thanked him but I couldn't get past the words stuck in my throat.

I went to the Statehood and asked Connor if I could use his phone. I closed the door to the back office and sat at the desk and read stories on the Internet about WeiWei's tumble. The comments were uniformly nasty. WeiWei had issued a public apology: it was the Chinese lab's fault, she declared. In no way had she intended to hurt anyone with her actions. She'd done select interviews and renewed her support of adoption causes. The story was a week old. Interest was already fading.

Of course she didn't pick up. I had to leave a message. But to my surprise, she called right back.

"Kid," she said. "You called me. You're my only friend in the world." Her voice sailed toward me, filling me with warmth. I pictured her sunning herself on a deck with an ocean view, wearing a Cal T-shirt and cutoffs with silver rings on her fingers and toes.

"Are you okay?" I asked.

"It's been bad. Really bad." She sounded her cheerful self. "A lot of people are screaming for my head. But don't you worry. I'm taking my medicine, saying what needs to be said. I got out in front of it, you know? I put my hand up and said, 'Geez, I made a mistake, please forgive me, I'll do better.' They all tell me that that should do the trick."

"What happened to the girl? The one you thought was your sister?"

"Yeah, Anna. I feel really bad about that. She's still my sister, as far as I'm concerned. We text. We're friends. I really want you to meet her. Are you coming to see me? I've got loads of room. Bring your mom. Bring A.J. Bring anybody you want. We'll go to the beach. I know you like the water. It's beautiful here. You should see it."

I said I'd be an idiot to leave Alaska just as spring was arriving. I'd lasted the whole winter; summer was my reward. "The days last forever. I've already made plans." I told her how my friends and I were going to hike and fish and sail and kayak. "You should come up for a visit."

"It's not a bad idea. I'll wander for forty days and forty nights. When I get back to L.A., they'll find me a changed woman." She laughed, but I heard the faintest tremble.

"But you're okay, right?" I asked. "You've got friends there? People to talk to?"

"I feel bad about Anna," she said. "But yeah, I'm fine. I don't want you to worry."

The walk home was easy. Until I'd spoken to WeiWei, I didn't have any plan, but now that I'd said it aloud, I saw the months ahead, the summer unfolding with me at the sunny center. I'd done well in calling WeiWei. We were equals now, or if not exactly equals, we were certainly friends. I smiled to myself. I had shown WeiWei kindness in a wilderness of resentment. Compassion, it turned out, didn't always lead to pity. I floated up the hill, my feet feeling bootless. I walked into the house and there was Peg waiting.

SHE WAS SITTING in the living room as chilly and royal as her cat.

"I need to speak with you," she said.

"I'll just—"

"No, now." She pointed to the couch. I sat.

"Your mother called me last night. She needs to hear from you," she said.

"Of course," I said quickly. "I mean, I've been staying in touch like you said, but—"

"She said she hasn't spoken to you since the week after you got here." She narrowed her eyes, as blue as I'd ever seen them, a perfect match to the fleece pullover she'd zipped up to her neck.

"So this is what we're going to do," Peg said. She motioned for me to follow her into the kitchen and led me to the telephone that hung on the wall. It had a long, kinked cord that dangled inches from the floor. The buttons on the phone were crusty with tomato. Steve liked to talk while he cooked. I wondered if he was home, but if he was, he was hiding.

Peg picked up the receiver and handed it to me.

"Go ahead," she said.

"I've been sending her e-mails," I said. "I called when I first got here."

"I think you'll find her at home," Peg said, and she stepped from the room.

AT THE SOUND of Charlie's voice, I pressed myself against the wall.

"It's me," I said, and said again, "It's Ari." At least on the second try, my voice didn't wobble.

"Oh, honey," Charlie said. "I'm so glad you called. I'm sitting at my computer—"

"Phone is fine," I said quickly. If I had to face her, even on a screen, I might not be able to hold the ground I'd staked.

"I hope you got my e-mails," I said more loudly, in case Peg was listening. "Everything's fine here. I'm having a good time. I was going to write soon." As I stalled, I allowed myself a quick peer around the corner, but there wasn't any sign of Peg.

"It's so good to hear your voice."

"Steve says 'hi,'" I added for good measure. He'd mentioned to me a while back that he had talked to Charlie. I heard an odd sound on the line, like a whisper.

"I've been carrying a check for the Ericssons around in my wallet," Charlie said. "I ought to just mail it. It seems the least I could do."

I saw, on the countertop, a jug of red cooking wine that Steve used in his sauces. The long cord easily let me reach it. With a fat glass poured, I was fortified for the moment.

"Aren't you ready to come home?" Charlie asked. The sound of her voice faded, and I heard through the line the squeak of the back door. Maybe, like me, she was pacing as we talked. I drank half the glass and poured it full again.

"I'm doing fine here," I said. "You didn't have to call them."

"Haven't I been good?" Charlie asked. A tiny laugh, high and unnatural. "Les told me to go up there and get you, but I've been so patient, waiting for you to come home."

"You can't fix me, you know," I said. "You and Les. You and A.J. You and all those Whackadoodle experts. I have abandonment issues. Isn't that what they call it?"

"Oh, Ari," she said. Another squeeze of a laugh. Her voice a strangle. The tremor running through my name flowed from her to me.

"Sorry," I said. "I forgot. You never say 'abandonment.' You use a cuter name, like when I was little. The A word. Remember that? How you never wanted me to feel bad about being dumped by my parents?"

"Don't talk to me that way." A sharpness in her voice, more hostile than I expected. I was out of practice knowing how hard I could push. "I'm still your mother. That counts for something."

"You're not coming to Juneau, are you? Because I'm leaving if you do."

"That isn't why I called," Charlie said brusquely. I heard the odd noise again coming at me through the receiver, *hwhuuuuu*, low and faint, as if Charlie were blowing into my ear. I heard a second sound as familiar as taking a breath. It *was* a breath, and then I understood. She was smoking, outside on the kitchen landing, hugging herself against the early spring chill. I could almost smell the cigarette smoke of her drawn-out exhalation.

"I thought for once you could think about someone other than yourself," Charlie said. "For once in your life, you could do that."

"What did you say to Peg? Is she going to throw me out?"

"Babies aren't the only ones left behind, you know. There's the rest of us, too. Have you ever thought about that?"

"Is there something wrong at home?" I asked.

"Everything," Charlie spat, and before I could reply, she hung up.

ALL NIGHT LONG, I huddled like a bug in my basement bed, rescripting our conversation. I could have told her that I missed her, for it was true, some of the time. I could have asked her what was wrong, since I knew she was distressed from the moment I saw Peg waiting. If I had been as strong as I wanted them all to believe, I would have called her right back. But I didn't.

TWO DAYS LATER. Peg and Steve summoned me into the living room and Peg told me it was time for me to move out. Steve looked miserable, but he didn't say a word. I thanked them for letting me stay and then I went downstairs and packed my few things. I was going to leave the books on the shelf above the bed but I didn't like the idea that nobody else would ever read them, so I lugged them in three trips down to the Salvation Army. The next day, after Peg and

Steve had left for work, I hugged Poppy, picked up my duffel, and walked out the front door.

Brigid said I could crash for a few days at her place, and Noah offered to ask around to see if anyone needed a roommate. I couldn't move in with either of them because Noah was in the dorms and Brigid's apartment was full. I searched online for roommate listings, logged into my e-mail to reply to a couple of posts, and saw a recent message from Les marked "Urgent." I'd been ignoring Les's e-mails ever since I left home, but I thought of Charlie, and before I could stop myself, I opened it and read.

Gran had run off, Les said. She'd packed a bag and disappeared without telling anyone, not even her caregiver, Yan. She'd sent one postcard to Great-Aunt Rose from Hangzhou that said, "I've come to sweep their graves." That was her only message. Three weeks had gone by with no word. The morning of Les's e-mail, Rose had gotten a telephone message from Gran. She needed help. She asked for me to come. "Only Ari," her message said. "I want only Ari."

I got up and wrapped myself in my old plaid blanket shawl that still smelled of Poppy and walked the neighborhood for an hour. I knew Les was telling the truth, but I didn't want to go. I told myself that whatever Gran's problem was, Les and Charlie would have to solve it, though it was also true that Gran was too stubborn and too proud to ask her daughters to save her. Something bad had driven Gran to China; I couldn't guess what it was. I knew only that she must have felt the way I did: her mind wouldn't rest until she flung herself into the thicket.

I wasn't going to call Les—I knew to avoid her powerful persuasions—but I sent her a message.

"Sorry, I can't help," I said. "I hope Gran is all right."

She wrote back immediately. Gran was angry with her, and Charlie was, too. Nobody would speak to her. She'd done things to make them both unhappy. There was nothing she could do to take back what she'd done, but at least she could send me to Gran. "Please, Ari, please," she said. "Go and help her."

I closed the computer and made myself a bed, wishing I were still in Steve and Peg's basement with my books all around me and Poppy at my feet.

ON APRIL 5, the anniversary of Aaron's death, I put on my boots and layered up for cloudy weather and met Noah in town. It was one week after Les's e-mail. Noah had asked me to hike the Perseverance Trail. He'd done it twice on that date since moving to Juneau; the first time with Steve, and then alone. We'll make it our first hike of the season, Noah had said, and the summer scenes had rolled before me again.

We went to the store and bought sandwich fixings and assembled our lunch in the parking lot. Heading to Basin Road, we passed close to the Ericssons' house. I'd called Steve that morning to tell him what we were going to do, and he'd given me his blessing and made me promise that if the trail looked dicey, we'd turn around and bail.

Noah stopped and turned to me. "Can I—" he said. The old stiffness was back in his face. "I want to ask Steve to join us."

I nodded, and we walked to the house. Steve came to the door in stockinged feet.

"Come with us?" Noah asked. "We're doing Perseverance." I never saw Steve move as quickly as he did. Ten minutes later, we were out the door.

We walked mostly in silence, with Noah out front and Steve beside me. I heard the wind in the trees and the ripple of Gold Creek. At the start of the trail, a sign warned of danger—sharp dropoffs, a hazard for small children. I thought of Steve living every day with Aaron's absence, and of Charlie trying to fill the hole in my life for me. It wasn't enough to say that children needed protection. Hazards for small children sometimes swept away adults.

Just past the start of the trail, we felt a blast of cold air coming out of an old mine shaft. Noah said that the trail was famous as the state's first mining road. We walked on, smelling the green freshness. Small patches of snow dotted the ground, and branch tips painted my sleeves with water. It was too early for wildflowers, but the willow was starting to bloom.

Up the trail, the path edged along a shelf—cliff face on one side, canyon drop on the other. We walked another few hundred yards to where the trail hooked sharply. At the overlook, we paused. I looked across the valley and saw the waterfalls Steve had described spilling down the mountainsides in long cascades, like tall white towers of sunlight.

I stepped close to both men.

"I'm leaving Juneau soon," I said. "My grandmother needs me."

And so I left and flew to find her.

PART THREE

Qingming

CHAPTER 27

GRAN

don't die at the end of this telling. Although it is true that my
mother and father never saw the age of fifty, that's nothing to
do with me. They died in ways violent and small, whereas I live
in the century of miracles. Who knows what lives they might
have led had they made it to America? What late-stage rockets they
might have fired, how forestalled their deaths might have been?
Mr. Fitzgerald said there are no second acts in America, but he
wasn't speaking of immigrants now, was he? Some people moan
about the tragedy of displacement. I'm not one of them. Rose and I
were lucky, getting a second shot.

I suppose, at the close, one might expect my ignominious end,
or at least a timely passing. The death of the matriarch, a handoff
of the family torch. Miss Havisham disposed of, a wedding for little
Pip. I'm sorry to disappoint. There's no death to report, except for
dear Naomi's. I miss her daily. When the two of us got going, we
defined the word *cackle*. She understood me better than Rose or
Yifu, for she was the eldest, like me, and had made difficult choices.
There was nobody left to do it, so Naomi stepped forward. Her
secrets went to the grave with her. She never breathed them to
me, though one time when we were on a drive together, winding through brown foothills, both of us recounting how romantic
couples used to dance to radio music on Shanghai rooftops and
seeing in our minds' eyes the long rows of rickshaws waiting for

custom and feeling against our skin the lovely silk underwear we wore, Naomi said to me, "Never ask a Jew how he got out."

I never asked. I understood.

This is Ari's story, after all. I'm just along for the drive.

I MADE A PROMISE to myself—in my head, to Father—that once I got to America, I would never look back. The trouble was this: every time I closed my eyes, I heard and saw that baby. A smear of face. A blur of blue. I knew it was my imagination because a suffocating baby doesn't make a single sound. But there he was, gently flailing, like a caught foot, tickled. He didn't fight very hard. He went without a splash.

Yifu betrayed me to my sister Rose. I had told her not to all those years ago, and again when she called me and said she had to speak. If you don't tell her, I will, Yifu said. A fine threat from my oldest friend, a friend saved by Father on his reputation alone. Of course I didn't throw my burden onto Rose, my charge, my *mei mei*, my softhearted little sister. So Yifu flew all the way to Philadelphia and laid out like a cold cadaver what I had nursed as my own. Sixty-three years of my protection smothered to death in a day. I'll never forgive Yifu for that, though I note, and resent, that she's never asked me to.

Why, said Rose, why? I could have blamed it on Father, but I didn't. I reminded her of how it was with our brother. When he was little, we had such times together! Running and splashing in the streams on Lushan Mountain. Kuling was our paradise; we were always happy there. But once he was a big boy, only Mother and Cousin Pei could dress Mu-you, feed him, change his pants when he messed himself, understand his grimaces and gabbles. How could I have taken care of him, even with Rose's help?

You lied to me, Rose said. Yes, that is true, though no judge would hang me for it.

YAN HAS BEEN GOOD to me. She doesn't boss me around like so many other servants who know that with the old and brittle, they've got the upper hand. Naomi, at Four Winds, was bossed to her very death: eat at this time; sign out when you leave to walk three blocks in the park; if you want to get along, keep your opinions to yourself. Yan and I, we understand each other. She has her philosophy and I have mine. But every year on Qingming, I saw how she fretted about how she couldn't go home to sweep her family's graves. She didn't love her parents as I loved Mother and Father, but the duty was there—duty as strong as love. Every year, when she bowed three times at the altar, I thought of Father taking me to visit the family graves, three white headstones among thousands on a high hill on the outskirts of Hangzhou overlooking a beautiful valley. We didn't visit his family often. Father had the hospital, and the war was an interruption, but at least once that I can remember, we made the journey for Qingming.

The baby's eyes fluttered. Then they froze open. Yan helped me pack, but I wouldn't take her with me. I picked up the phone and ordered a visa and ticket. When Mother was shot, when Father was struck dead, Cousin Pei paid in gold to have their bodies wound in white and buried on that same hillside. I never learned where Mu-you was buried, but I knew they must have set him into the ground next to Mother, under her loving gaze.

THE GRAND LAKE shimmered. All else was foreign. A metropolis had multiplied where a beautiful city once stood. In the fine hotel where I was staying, trays danced past me full of morsels like the delicacies that Cook had used to prepare for Father's esteemed guests— shrimp cakes and egg cloud and bean paste tucked into tiny buns, but I could eat none of it, or ride the trolley as I once had, or find my way in the city center. I knew that Hangzhou would be fearfully changed, but I hadn't expected so many vast buildings or the maddening traffic or the Prada boutique in my hotel, none of them improvements as far as I was concerned, and so I was schooled by my sweaty face and knotted stomach and curled lip that I, like everyone I despised, had fallen victim to nostalgia.

I spoke in Mandarin and sometimes in Shanghainese, my

fluency a deep well, but my language was pocked with antiquated phrases that shopkeepers didn't understand. Sometimes they stared at me—my clothing, hairstyle, and face. I had forgotten that stare; after sixty-five years apart, I bristled at its rudeness, until I remembered that staring in China was not a personal matter. *Hey, old woman*, they would ask, their curiosity quickened, *are you from around here? Have you come back for a visit?* Some of them subjected me to minute examination, studying the fold of my eyelids, the prominent nose, the wayward wave in my silver hair. Even in Taipei, I hadn't been scrutinized so fondly. *Are you Chinese?* they would innocently ask, having sniffed out the Dutch blood that Mother dripped into our veins.

American, I would say. Just here for a visit.

Rose had told me that all the family was gone. A distant cousin in Xi'an had reported to Rose that no one was left in Hangzhou, for they were dead, scattered, hounded from pillar to post. Some found protection through political favor—there were stories there that I didn't want to know. Father was the youngest and the most successful, and I had no doubt that the rest of the family's envy had not been extinguished by a mere half century and more.

I didn't need names or addresses. I cared only for the dead.

FOR THE FIRST WEEK. I slept during the day, waking at night to walk around the block or sit in the lobby alone. I had come at last and didn't wish to be hurried by anyone, including my American self. I let my body reset its clock slowly, my bones and joints and arteries and organs sidling up to the idea of day-to-night reversal. In the second week, I ventured out every day into the stabbing light, marking streets and peering into doorways, testing my resolve. At the end of that time, I was sleeping and waking with the darkness and light and had found a shop or two that sold pretty things. Only my stomach and bowels were rebelling, because I could hardly swallow, and what little I ate, raced through me. Tea and toast, toast and tea, were all that I could manage. I shopped carefully in the market stalls for what I needed: soft bread rolls, almonds in the shell, scotch whiskey, American cigarettes. Incense sticks and paper money. Ralph Waldo Emerson. White azalea.

At last the day came: Qingming, grave-sweeping day. I booted and buckled myself for a cemetery visit. It was April 5; the date changes every year with the lunar calendar, and I had looked it up three times to be certain. Rain was falling lightly but I had an enormous umbrella that the concierge had provided and a young, sad-faced driver in a nylon polo shirt who was carrying a striped bag full of my purchases: the incense and paper money and Father's favorite things. For Mother, I had apples and a picture of Rose and me taken in Massachusetts the year that Rose began college. For Mu-you, a ball of yarn, a soft gray, the color of his snowflake sweater, the same as the yarn I had wound into a perfect ball while Mother held the skein and told me that, someday, I would act out of love over duty. I gave the driver directions to the place I remembered well. Others I knew, who had visited Hangzhou, had confirmed to me where to find it. Everything I described recalled my visit with Father. The driver looked skeptical; was I sure I had the right place? Crowds would be there, I pointed out. The cemetery was a large one. Whole families would be gathering, picnicking among the stones. He said it would cost me more to drive so far beyond the city, but after days of haggling in the markets, I was in no mood to bargain and promised him a tip if he handled the drive well.

He put on the radio; I asked him sharply to turn it off. He smoked a foul brand of cigarette while he drove. The car crawled along the congested highway. Father had loved the cigarettes that American visitors brought him—he said the pious parsons always carried the best brands. In the backseat of the car, I had the curious feeling that I was a young girl again, going to visit Father. He was at the hospital, perhaps Mother was with him, for she always helped wherever she was needed. I didn't believe I would encounter them in any real or celestial way—my own faith stretches only so far—but

I had a certain lightness around my heart, a pleasant sensation that lifted me out of the mind of an old woman and into a girl's gladness. *Father, I am coming,* I heard myself say.

Qingming. Grave-sweeping day. Of everyone, Father had chosen me as his companion for the solemn task. I was young, perhaps eight or nine. I remember it was the year of our last summer in Kuling, the last time we were completely happy. I was bold with the relatives, though I didn't know them well. When I asked an apt question, they praised my intelligence to Father. His older brother was away on a trip, and so Father had come home to do his duty. His sisters fussed over him from morning to night; their attentions annoyed me, and I capered when I was with him to make him laugh or fondly swat me away.

He woke me early. The day was clear. Father had hired three cars to drive us, a luxury that set his sisters aflutter. I remember looking up from the bottom of the hill to see row upon row of white headstones winding up the hillside. Mud stuck to my shoes as we climbed the steep path. My aunts and cousins chattered. It was not such a solemn task, I realized, but an occasion for excitement. Among and between the rows, other families gathered, laying out offerings, setting money alight. Groups bobbed their bows in sets of three, and children ran freely. I took Father's hand; he squeezed mine lightly.

"*Jie jie*, I'm glad you're here," he said. Older sister. My heart swelled proudly.

Three graves stood together: his mother, his father, and an older brother who had died at seven. The women scurried about, cleaning the headstones of dirt and leaves and setting fruit and cakes on the ground. Before their father's headstone, they placed the daily newspaper and a tiny bowl of fragrant tea leaves. At their mother's, they laid weedy-looking flowers and a picture of all of her children with Father as a young man in a Western suit and smile. There was nothing for the boy. He had died too young and so long ago, they said, that no one remembered what his favorite things were, so they put extra money in front of his grave and two sticks of incense to curry special favor. A stir in the air thinly fed the burn. I had to sniff hard to catch the scent.

The women stood. Father squared his shoulders. My shoes were muddy, and I was just about to complain when I noticed that quiet had fallen. I made myself as straight as Father, hands at my sides, fingers downward.

"*Yi ju gong!*" Father commanded. He bowed from the waist and everyone followed, my bow a beat late but as low as Father's.

"*Er ju gong! San ju gong!*" Three bows in deep obeisance. Some of the women even got down on their knees and touched their foreheads to the ground, but Father was too modern for that. Still, I was astonished. I had seen him only at church, where he mumbled the Lord's Prayer. I didn't recognize this other version of my father. To my childish mind, it seemed that some unknown hand had led him up the hill, some voice had whispered in his ear exactly what he should do. It disturbed me to know that he had another life in which I played no part. When I took his hand again, he gently dislodged it so he could take the hand of a sister who sobbed on their mother's grave.

I couldn't sleep that night. Finally, in the morning hours, I hit upon an explanation. I told myself that Father's other life was indisputably over. He had often said to his Sunday guests that he and Mother felt very happy and knew that they were lucky to get to know the world through the open doors of Shanghai. Whatever earlier existence he had endured before Mother and Rose and Muyou and me was of no use to him anymore, else why had he kept it hidden?

"Will you take me again next year?" I asked Father on our journey home to Shanghai. I liked having him to myself.

"Oh, next year, my older brother will be back. It will be his turn to follow the old customs," Father said. "Did you like playing with your cousins?"

I nodded, for I had. They were country cousins, impressed by my city ways. I had taught them three swear words in English and two more in French. I showed them how to waltz and how to shoot marbles. I airily presented them with six of my best aggies. The only thing I learned from them was how to sweep the family graves.

I WOKE FROM A DOZE when the car lurched to a stop.

"This is your place," the driver told me. He gripped the steering wheel and leaned forward to peer out the windshield.

"This is not it," I said. We faced a hillside covered in multistory buildings jammed close together. The occupied buildings were windowed concrete; washing hung from balconies; thick cables looped and roped, and tin awnings jutted from lower floors. Other buildings were halfway complete with bamboo scaffolding tic-tac-toed up and over or covered in plastic sheeting striped in red, white, and blue. On the street in front of us, a crowded bus lumbered. Peddlers hawked greens in leafy bundles. It could have been any hillside in any city; surely it wasn't mine.

But this was my hillside, the driver said, where I had directed him to take me. I insisted he had bungled my directions, turned off too early, couldn't read a map. He didn't get angry—arguing, like staring, wasn't a personal matter—but stubbornly held his ground, telling me over and over that if we were lost, it was because he'd been supplied with inaccurate information. I had him drive us up and down the streets, looking for signs that might point us toward the cemetery. The roads weaved in and out. Nothing looked familiar. It occurred to me that he was trying to cheat me. Perspiration beaded on my face and dampened the back of my neck where my silk blouse wilted. I needed a bathroom but was afraid to get out of the car. What if he drove off with all the things I had so carefully collected? I couldn't lug the bag into the toilet with me. I tried to hold myself shut, but cramps seized me.

"Auntie," the driver said. He guessed at my distress and felt sorry for me. He helped me out and guided me to a place—guesthouse, dormitory; I couldn't tell what it was—where a white-haired guard led me to a WC. I groaned and spilt, doubled over. When I tottered out, the guard gave me a chair, and the driver brought me a cup of tea. They hovered anxiously, watching me try to sip it. A stench reached my nostrils; I couldn't tell if it was mine.

"Auntie," the driver said, "he says you are right. The cemetery was there." He pointed up the hill to where more buildings stood. "It was moved five years ago. They needed the land for housing. This zone was selected for development." The guard's wide smile bounced up and down. "It is all new here. The houses are very modern."

"It covered the top of the hillside," I said. I didn't want to believe it. "There were thousands of headstones. Whole families were buried there."

The graves were moved, the guard proudly said. To a much nicer place across the valley. Experts came and selected the best location. Most of the graves went one place, though some went to another. The government paid for everything. If you wanted a new headstone, you had only to request it. Records were kept of who got moved where, but the guard didn't know which department had them. Families from the valley all knew where their ancestors were; they didn't need a bureaucrat to tell them. When he finished work today, he would visit his own mother and father. With the payment he had received for his permission to move them, he had ordered a month of temple prayers, plus hosted his whole family, including nieces and nephews, on a sightseeing trip to Suzhou. They had always wanted to see the famous gardens. I should be sure to go there for a visit.

"Your driver is very good," the guard said. He clapped the younger man on the shoulder. "You should hire him to take you. He is a trustworthy man."

My driver tried for the rest of the day to help me find where they had moved my family's graves. I had a handful of names but not all of their proper characters, and the dates I had were spotty. Offices were closed, records missing. My confusion made the task harder. We grew hungry as we worked and ate the soft bread rolls, the nuts, and the apples. At the failing light, I said the search was over. He said he would bring me again tomorrow, but we both knew it was fruitless. We drove back in silence. I gave him Father's cigarettes and paid him double. All night I sat in my room with the lights blazing and the ball of yarn in my hand. The whiskey burned through me like flaming money. On the balcony outside my room, I set thin paper sheet after sheet on fire until the hotel manager knocked on my door to stop me. I set my hand on top of the ashes, but they were already cold.

THERE'S MORE TO TELL but I'm done with sorrow. Tomorrow, I will read a good book or take Yan for a drive to a place she's never been. If Ari ever comes home, I'll have her read these pages. She's the only one who knows the exact shape of my shame. I yearn for the sound of Father's voice, for the touch of Mother's soft hand. I still have the yarn and the little jade buttons. Their bones I lost the day I abandoned Mu-you.

CHAPTER 28

ARI

Gran was in terrible shape when I got there. She was in a Chinese hospital, dehydrated and jaundiced. She had broken her left foot in a slip on the sidewalk. She was lying in bed like a shrunken mummy. Her eyes were closed, her hair was lank and stringy, her cheeks sucked back into bone. I realized I had never seen Gran lying down before. I had never heard her so quiet. Her big bosom looked collapsed under the blanket. When she opened her eyes, she didn't seem to see me.

"You don't need to look so shocked," she said. "I'm not on my deathbed, to everyone's disappointment."

I gave her a kiss and looked for a place to sit, but the only seat was the edge of her bed, so I stood there awkwardly, my duffel bag making a bulge in the paper curtain drawn around her bed.

"Oh, for heaven's sake," Gran said. "Go find yourself a chair." She struggled to sit up. "I've got to get out of this place. It's driving me mad, listening to all the moaning and groaning. Father never would have put up with it."

"I'm fine," I said. I had noticed, walking in past the long rows of beds, that the other visitors were sitting on three-legged folding stools they had brought for themselves, and were feeding their relatives from little boxes of food carried from home, the patients like hungry babies with eager, open mouths.

"Suit yourself," Gran said, and then she made a crack about

looking so yellow. "It was worse two days ago. The young man who empties the bedpans said my eyeballs looked like a cat's."

"You look good," I said.

"Ha. At least nobody is mistaking me anymore for a foreign devil." She lifted a hand from the blanket. That, at least, looked as large as ever. I took a step closer and clasped it. "Thank goodness you're here," she said, gripping. She shut her eyes tight. "It's been quite awful. Thank goodness you've come."

THEY KEPT GRAN in the hospital another ten days. I spent every day with her, staying until after dinner. I bought my own three-legged stool and a set of nesting containers and filled the snap-lid boxes with meals cooked by the hotel kitchen. The nurses were kind, especially when they learned that I was the American granddaughter, and started calling Gran *"Po Po,"* as though she were their grandmother, too. They had so many patients to take care of that they were perfectly happy to have me feed Gran and wash her and insist she take her pills. Sitting beside her bed, I recalled what I'd seen in the emergency room in Kunming: people arriving at the hospital with six-packs of Pepsi and buckets of KFC, their *guanxi* getting their children and spouses and grandparents much faster attention, patients no more bloodied than I was, who got called to the desk and led behind doors while A.J. and I sat on hard chairs and sang our Whackadoodle song and waited. I started bringing extra food from the hotel buffet every morning and Belgian chocolates from the gift shop. Gran became the staff's most popular patient.

Soon after I got there, I reached out to WeiWei. She was back in Guangzhou, her assistant told me. I sent her an e-mail, and she called me right away, asking how she could help. I'll come see you, she said; it's only a two-hour flight. She'd book her ticket and send me the information. I started sleeping better, knowing that WeiWei was coming.

After a week, Gran began walking the hallway on crutches, her arms surprisingly strong, though her legs looked withered. She was determined to walk out of the hospital under her own steam, but she overdid it and had to go back to bed. The jaundice was past; she had regained her coloring, but now she flushed pink with aggravation at herself and her own stupidity, she said.

"When did I get old?" she demanded. "My weakness bores me."

In the evenings I made my way back to the hotel slowly. I was staying at the fancy place where Gran had a big room, but the hotel air was thick and motionless, the gilt and mirrors too shiny. I preferred to poke my head into crowded storefronts and smell the mix of the city streets, an odor I remembered from Beijing and Kunming, part damp, part green, part garbage. It was wonderful, after the open landscape of Alaska, to jostle with other shoppers and jump across oily puddles and risk my life crossing the broad streets. There was no such thing as pedestrian safety; the cars and trucks and pedicabs and scooters careened and barreled, so the only way I could cross was to attach myself like a limpet to a more practiced traveler. Usually, I chose an old person because anyone younger darted so fast that they were all the way across before I realized that their feet had left the curb. The old folks were saving me every time I crossed the road.

At night, I talked to Charlie or Les and gave them a report on Gran's progress. She had banned them from coming and didn't want to talk to them herself, and so they had to hear it from me. The doctors had done some procedure that fixed a small problem with Gran's liver, I said, which sent them both ballistic. Charlie pointed out that Grandpa George had died of liver cancer, and Les ordered me to move Gran to a Western medical clinic—"Go find some decent doctors, for God's sake, before they kill her," but Gran refused. I think it pleased her to drive them crazy.

"Tell them I have every confidence in my doctors," she said. "Dr. Lin knows all about Herbert's research. He didn't know of Father, but of course he's far too young." The Western hospital, she said, would charge her an arm and a leg. "An arm and a leg and a finger," she said to me as a joke. I brought the man who emptied the bedpans a Big Mac and fries while Gran bragged to the patient in the bed next to her that we'd be leaving in two days.

ONCE OUT, GRAN DEFLATED. She stopped doing her exercises and stayed all day in the room. She wouldn't say much about why she had come to Hangzhou. It had to do with her parents, she said, and her sister, Rose, and her younger brother, Mu-you. I came on a wild-goose chase, she said, and though I said I understood, she retreated back into silence. I asked her if she wanted to go home to California; she shook her head no. The doctor had ordered her to put on some weight, but she ate very little. She wasn't able to sleep at night and dozed during the day in fitful spurts that left her irritable and morose. I tried to amuse her by talking of other things, like books I'd read and my job in Alaska. She wasn't interested. I asked her questions about growing up in China, and she said it was ancient history and not worth telling.

My thoughts, like Gran's, began to spoil. WeiWei moved her dates, then had to move them again. She'd be there, she assured me, as soon as things settled down. She was back on the interview circuit. Her book was doing well: her publisher had changed it from a memoir into a novel.

When I went looking for Aaron, and when I rushed to Hangzhou to rescue Gran, I had a purpose, a mighty distraction, but now, with Gran silent and no clear path before me and the hours lengthening into dragging days, the black ditch reopened by a crack at my feet. I began to hear the old whispers: Who were my mother and father? Did they ever think about me? Were they sorry for what they did? If they had held me in their arms for another day, a week, a month, a year, would they have changed their minds and kept me? In the crowded streets, I found myself studying the flashing faces for some secret message directed only at me, a signal that I was known or recognized or at least taking up space on the sidewalk. Kunming came back to me, though I had tried my hardest the past eight months to barricade against it. The stump of my finger pestered me for attention. In my darkest moments, I imagined cutting it off to finish the job I had started. I wanted to bury it, as I had meant to do the first time, to leave a piece of me behind in the country of my birth. *I am alive. This is where I'm from.*

"Gran," I said, "let's take a trip. Where would you like to go?" The only thing I knew how to do was to keep moving.

"Nowhere," Gran said. "I want to stay right here." She hunched underneath a slippery hotel blanket and refused the good food that the chef sent up on a tray. I paid our bill weekly, nervous that Gran's credit card was going to max out, but somebody—Yan, maybe—was looking after finances on the other side of the ocean. She wouldn't trust Les or Charlie. They might use a frozen bank account to get us to come home.

One afternoon, a white American family with a Chinese daughter got into the elevator with me. I guessed the little girl was about four years old. Her mother looked high-strung and athletic; she reminded me of Robyn. Her father was older, soft-bellied and mostly bald. The little girl was chatting happily to her parents in English. When a young hotel desk clerk got on, she said hello to the little girl and asked her if she was having a fun visit.

"Say '*Ni hao ma*,'" the mother prompted.

The little girl shied away and grabbed for her mother's knees.

"*Ni hao ma*," the mother urged her. "She knows how to say it. She takes lessons every week."

"That's very nice," the young woman said. She bent way down and smiled. "*Ni hao ma?* How are you?"

"We want her to be able to speak the language of her birth country," the mother said. "We think it will give her a real sense of identity later."

The little girl stared in icy hatred straight at her own reflection in the mirror.

I CALLED YAN. I didn't want to call Charlie.

"I'm worried about Gran," I said. "She's very unhappy."

Yan was worried, too. "She's spending too much money. Even a rich lady should be more careful."

I asked her what I should do. Hangzhou was full of sad memories, Yan said. "Take her to Kuling. She was always happy there."

When I told Gran where we were going, she closed her eyes and slept.

SO AT LAST we arrived at Lushan Mountain, called, in Gran's day, the district of Kuling, near the city of Jiujiang, Jiangxi Province. It was early May. Snow draped the rounded peaks of the surrounding mountains. The air was clear and cold. The hotel where I had booked us was ugly and modern, but nearby was a lake with a wide path around and stone benches for sitting and watching the sky in the water. There were many more hotels than there had been before the war, but the low mist and narrow-topped mountains and thick forests drew Gran's feasting gaze. She remembered the morning light and the dark, dripping branches and how swiftly night fell after the sun set. It smelled the same, she said, and the town didn't look all that different from when she was a girl going with her mother from shop to shop to buy paper and ink and tea. We hired a driver one day to take us to the residential section where Westerners used to own summer houses—Gran's father had rented one of those houses several summers in a row—and Gran thought she recognized a few of the gates and rooftops, but most of the houses had been torn down and replaced with modern villas. Her father's house, the one he'd at last been permitted to buy once the war was on and the Westerners were getting out, had stood behind one of those gates. They had lived there just one summer before they, too, had to leave.

"What happened to the house?" I asked.

Gran shrugged. "Gone," she said. "Taken. So much for that dream. But we were happy while it lasted."

Gran was using a cane; for longer distances, she still needed a wheelchair, so she told me to go on a hiking tour without her. I went with an English-speaking guide who took me up and down winding mountain paths on our way to the Cave of the Immortal. The mist hanging above the deep valley and the white, ribboning waterfalls in the distance made me think of Alaska. I got back and found Gran sleeping in the sun on one of the stone benches, a hotel blanket tucked around her in strict violation of the posted hotel rules, so I knew that she was feeling better. We had found a small restaurant that Gran liked with big windows that looked out into a grove of green. Every night, we tried different dishes— mushrooms with thin slices of sausage, egg omelet with tiny local fish, eggplant, spicy cabbage. Gran's favorite was a clear soup with floating dumplings no larger, Gran said, than the tip of her finger. She nudged me when she said that, and I laughed at her sly expression. She said that if we both could laugh at such a tasteless joke, we must be feeling better.

One day, after Gran had told me a story about how she and Rose and Mu-you had gone down the street to an Englishwoman's house to look for their mother and, while waiting for her, had eaten every morsel of food in the poor woman's pantry, I asked Gran if she would tell me what she remembered of Mu-you. He was funny, she said. He had a mischievous sense of humor. He hid himself behind chairs and popped out laughing. Rose didn't like it when he pulled her pigtails, but Gran let him grab at hers, and her father let him tug his forelock, which Mu-you liked to do after taking off his father's hat. "Father used a hair oil that had a strong scent. Mu-you didn't like getting it on his hands. So one time Father put molasses on his hair instead. Mother scolded, but Mu-you jumped up and down." She paused and settled. We were sitting on the hotel balcony, catching the last of the day's sun. "Father loved to laugh when he was with Mu-you."

We told each other a little more after that, and a little more the next day. I talked about Steve and Peg and Noah. Gran told me about Mu-you and the lost family graves. We didn't try to explain ourselves or comfort each other. I asked her why, if I never knew them, I missed my birth mother and father. "Family pain lasts a lifetime," was all that Gran said.

Later, as I was helping her get ready for bed, she brought up my birth parents again. "Draw every breath in their honor," she said, "but remember that air is weightless."

Eight days. Eight was a lucky number. After eight days in Kuling, Gran said she wanted to go home to California. She had made her return. It was time to leave again.

"Saying good-bye to China will be as easy as last time," she said.

"You don't need me anymore," I said, half hope, half suggestion.

She barked a laugh. Lushan had restored her, just as Yan had predicted.

"They'll skin me alive when I come back without you."

ON THE NEXT to last day, while packing, I said, Gran, look what I have with me. I pulled out the leather case for Grandpa Kong's mechanical pencil. I hadn't used it since before I had left Juneau. As I gave it to Gran, I noticed how heavy it felt. She said she was glad I had kept it—"I always knew you were a singular child"— and she traced the imprint of Grandpa George's initials. She undid the flap and tipped the case over; two things slid out into her open hand.

One was Grandpa's mechanical pencil. "Oh," I said when I saw the other. Noah's fountain pen, cobalt blue. I picked it up, and tears sprang to my eyes. "I didn't know this was in there." He had wound a scrap of paper around it: *Keep this for me for a while.*

Gran went out in the afternoon while I made sure of her travel arrangements. We had dinner in our favorite restaurant. The evening was mild and slightly muggy, and when we asked, the proprietor opened the windows so Gran could smell the green of the grove. She was tired, but she looked pleased with herself.

"What have you got there?" I asked, poking her handbag.

"I walked from shop to shop. It took me hours to find what I wanted. They won't let me on the plane tomorrow with these elephantine feet." She laughed her throaty laugh. "I assure you it was worth the effort. Good quality is hard to find, especially here in China."

She gave me blue ink for the fountain pen and cut sheets of cottony paper. "You'll know what to do with this," she said.

After dinner, I tucked her into bed and went downstairs to the lobby. I sat for hours, sipping a beer through nightfall. In the corner of the lounge was a decorative desk fit for a gentleman scholar. A reproduction, Gran had sniffed, but that night it drew me. I asked the lone hotel clerk if I could sit there to write a letter. He brought me a folding chair and an ugly modern lamp and a bamboo wastebasket, "in case of mistakes," he said. I took Grandpa Kong's leather case from my pocket and tipped out Noah's pen. It felt cool in my hand, as though it were made of marble.

Dear Mother and Father, I wrote. The blue line veined from the pen like a taproot seeking water.

Dear Mother and Father,

I write to you from Lushan Mountain, home of the Cave of the Immortal. My grandmother calls it paradise. She lived here when she was a little girl. Maybe you'll visit one day.

Am I a little girl to you or a grown woman? You know exactly how old I am, so I don't need to tell you that. I think of you every hour of every day, in my head or in my heart.

My mother's name is Charlotte Kong. She's a daughter of China. You don't have to worry that all ties between us are broken. My mother would never let that happen. She knows we are bound forever. Everything she does is out of love.

If we were ever to meet, I'd be disappointed if you asked me for forgiveness. It's too small a thing to talk about. I'm thinking big these days. Big mountains, big landscapes, deep, deep holes, and history stretching back. This pen, for instance. The grove outside the restaurant, which Gran said tonight was her childhood come to greet her like Birnam Wood. So maybe paradise isn't exactly heaven.

Anyway, I'm here. Alive and squalling. If I gave you a wave, you'd know me by the missing part of my hand.

I signed it, *Ari.*

IN THE EARLY MORNING, while Gran slept, I walked out and found a driver and asked him to take me to the trail to the Cave of the Immortal. Morning mist filled the valley and clung to the sides of the mountains. The dampness chilled me. The driver waited while I walked alone, not down the trail but to a place off to the side behind some large boulders where few people would wander. I had brought a bottle of water, a plastic coffee cup, and a kitchen knife from the hotel. I squatted in the dirt. My fingers were cold and stiff, so I held them under my jacket until I could feel my joints loosen and my fingertips warm up. I chose a large rock with a flat surface. I heard birdsong above me and the wind high in the trees. *I am alive*, I thought. *This is where I'm from.* I stretched my hand wide on the flat gray surface. Using all my strength, I prised the rock out of the dirt. The soil beneath was packed tightly. With the knife, I chopped at the dirt, hacking steadily until I had dug up enough to scoop it away with the cup. Knife, cup, knife, cup. I worked with steady focus. My throat was parched, my heart thrumming with every strike of the blade. I wanted to go very deep where no animal or person would find it. When I had a narrow trench dug, I sat back on my heels and took a sip of water.

I took the folded letter from my pocket. It felt ample in my hand, like a billfold of money. I laid it in the hole that I had dug and scooped dirt over it. It disappeared quickly. When the hole was filled, I replaced the rock and set it back exactly as it had been, lodged in scrub and earth.

I stood and took a long drink and splashed water over my soiled hands. A bird watched me from a swaying branch. Facing west, I felt sunlight spill over the mountains.

CHAPTER 29

CHARLIE

n April, a few days after Ari had left for China, Charlie got a letter from Noah. *We have never met*, the letter said, *but I thought you might like to have this*. He sent a pencil drawing of two young men on a boat, their arms slung around each other, fishing tackle beside them. Aaron and Steve, smiling. In the distance, a glimpse of a marina. They were bearded and skinnier than when she knew them, and she could see by their T-shirts and the squint on both of their faces that it was a summer day, perhaps on the Atlantic. *I made it from a photograph that I keep with my father's things*. She set the drawing on the altar table, propped where she could see it, and then, with the letter in her pocket, Charlie rode her bicycle up to the lookout beyond the Golden Gate and down the long hill to Baker Beach, just as she and Aaron used to do.

He had loved the tumult of the waves. Some days, if the sun had warmed the dunes and the air was calm, he had braved the dangerous riptide there by swimming straight out into the chilly water. Reaching down to choose a flat stone from the beach, she remembered how he had been waiting for them when she and Ari came home, Ari calm and happy after sleeping most of the flight, and Charlie exhausted. He had flowers for her and a little Giants cap for Ari, and he had gathered both of them into his embrace. She remembered how easily he had buckled Ari into her car seat. She now understood that his were practiced fingers, and that Ari had crawled into his arms in the emergency room the night they took her in for the cut on the back of her head because she had recognized in Aaron a father's strength. She walked from the water's edge back toward the dunes. Grass grew in stubborn tufts in the sand. Aaron was gone and Charlie was standing. For as long as it took, she would wait for Ari.

When she got home, she wrapped the stone in Chinese silk and sent it to Noah, asking him to please place it on Aaron's gravestone. *Until I can visit myself one day*, she said.

SHE EXCHANGED BRIEF MESSAGES with her sister about Gran's situation. They didn't see each other. They didn't speak on the phone. They trusted Ari to tell them how Gran was doing, and she handled that and more. When Gran came home without Ari, Les called Charlie, but Charlie didn't pick up the phone. She opened another file and read another report. On some nights, loneliness heaved itself onto her shoulders or pounded its fists against the cage around her heart, and she struggled to throw it off by cleaning her house again or counting the cracks in the ceiling above her bed or running hard down the Marina Green, her knees stabbing with every step. Other days, she called a friend, and they drove north to the vineyards for farmers' market strolls and patio lunches. When the weather was warm, she swam.

Gran made requests. Charlie met them.

Robyn called her, and they went out for coffee. A.J. visited, and Charlie hugged her tightly, breathing in the girl's scent and resting her chin on top of the bird's nest of her hair. A.J. said that she might go visit Ari at the end of the summer. We talk often, she said. I really miss her.

The county's budget was slashed, and Charlie and her coworkers were asked to take on more cases. The cuts meant that some children were sent back to their parents, children who before might have been detained for their own protection. The police and Social Services and lawyers and judges did their best in difficult circumstances. Charlie didn't make the mistake again of befriending any of her clients.

A social worker she knew stopped her in the courthouse. A former client of Charlie's, a single mother with two boys, had left the boys alone in their apartment. A fire had broken out in the unit below. The older boy had suffered burns over sixty percent of his body. It wasn't the mother's fault, the social worker said. Even if the mother had been home, she probably couldn't have gotten the kids out any sooner because the landlord had padlocked the alley door shut.

That night, Charlie drove to Les's house and screamed for her sister. When Les opened the door, Charlie fell over the threshold.

CHAPTER 30

ARI

My room on campus has a window that opens and looks out onto a green. Students ride their bikes on the pathway, but nobody stops; they're on their way to someplace else. On warm days, if it's not too humid, I bring my book to the grass to study. I eat in the dining hall, but I don't have any roommates. As a foreign student, I was given my own room. Ah, you're so lucky, my classmates tell me. It's crowded in the dormitories. It's much better to live alone.

I live in Nanjing, once the capital of the republic, a city of eight million people. I moved here in the summer when the weather was very hot. Before that, I lived and worked for a year in Beijing. Now it's fall and turning cool in the evenings. My classmates are men and women, but before the war, there was a women's college here famous for educating the daughters of modern China. Later, it reopened as part of this university, so I've almost made Gran happy.

There aren't many American students. Most of them study in larger cities. A.J. says she might study abroad for a semester, but she wants to go to Kunming. I haven't been back. I won't go for a long while.

Gran is well. Her foot is stronger than it was before she broke it. She says she's at rest, which she claims is not the same thing as saying she's ready to go. She's happy that the question of where she'll be buried is settled. Les and Charlie bought her a plot in a cemetery in Bryn Mawr. Finally, she said. There'll be somebody from this family who appreciates the place.

She's given me a set of very specific instructions: I am to find a calligrapher who can help her prepare her gravestone. He's to write her full name in Chinese characters plus specify Hangzhou as her family's ancestral home. By cemetery rules, the stone is twelve by twenty-four inches. It lies flush in the ground. It will also be carved with her American name and the dates of her birth and death and the words BELOVED MOTHER.

"Gran," I said. "There isn't room for all of that. Why not leave out Hangzhou?"

Her voice came through loud and clear on my laptop. "But how will people know where I'm from?"

I miss Noah. We talk, but I haven't seen him. Once in a while, he writes me a letter and signs it "Brother Bowns."

WeiWei never showed up, but I learned to live without her.

Early this year, Charlie came for a visit. I was living in Beijing in a single room with a shared bath and a hot plate to cook on, and though I thought she would disapprove of the arrangement, she liked my neighbors and the easy walk to the subway. We bundled up and walked from market to market, stopping to warm ourselves in noodle shops and cafés. The wind blew hard, clearing out the bad air that was sometimes so thick I could taste it like paste in my mouth. It was too cold to do much touring, but we didn't mind holing up in her hotel where I could watch TV and she could read a book—time is a luxury, she said, same as it ever was. The last night, we curled on the bed together, and I tucked her in like the old days, spreading her hair, penciled with gray, on the pillow. I remembered how, when I was little, she had used to tell me the origin of every part of my name, each piece its own story, until I knew the tale by heart.

Now she's home and busy, she writes, keeping Gran out of trouble and going out with friends. Maybe this spring, she and Les will visit together. She's decided to learn about bonsai trees. Les gave her one in a green glass dish. Charlie keeps it on the kitchen landing. She bought another one last week. I like having the pair, she said. I told her that was an old person's hobby. What do you suggest? she asked. Bungee jumping? She's beginning to sound like Gran.

I'm not going anywhere, at least for the time being. I like the grass outside my window. I walk around the city and look at the interesting faces. I'm not searching anymore for the ones who will look back. There are no answers to *what if* and *I might have been*. But every night, I lie awake in my bed dreaming of row upon row of nursery cribs, all filled with sleeping babies.

Author's Note

The descriptions of an artist's hand that appear in *The Year She Left Us* were inspired by the work of Sheng Qi, born in Anhui Province, China, 1965. The photographs entitled *Memories (Me)*, 2000, and *Memories (Mother)*, 2000, were shown in the exhibition *Between Past and Future: New Photography and Video from China* (co-organized by the David and Alfred Smart Museum of Art, University of Chicago, and the International Center of Photography, New York, in collaboration with the Museum of Contemporary Art, Chicago, and the Asia Society, New York, and which opened in New York in 2004).

Although the photographs described were inspired by Sheng Qi's artwork, the story surrounding them is entirely fictional.

Acknowledgments

I am deeply grateful to my extraordinary mother, Margaret C. Ma, who helped me with history and names and all things in all ways.

Warm appreciation to Geri Thoma and Jennifer Barth, whose brilliance and grace enhance every aspect of our endeavors. I thank my lucky stars for their tireless efforts on behalf of my work.

Thanks with a full heart to Sanford, Emily, Hannah, and Eliza. I am indebted to Louise Ma, Philip Ma, Jennifer Ong, Nathalie Gilfoyle, Alex Wang, and all my family. The poem quoted by Gran was written by my grandfather Chang Fu-Liang.

Thanks also to:

Kyra Subbotin, Diane Cash, and Margaret Carter for unwavering friendship; Tom Scarpino and Mixed Media for inspiration then and now; and True to the Mood for thirty years of books.

Bora Reed, Kirsten Menger-Anderson, and Tony Stayner, who gave generously of time and attention; Liz Nichols and Gary Cohen; and Catherine Alden, Louise Aronson, Natalie Baszile, Leah Griesmann, Susanne Pritchett Jensen, Elena Mauli Shapiro, and Suzanne Wilsey.

The fabulous Lynn Freed for wisdom.

Michael Collier, Margot Livesey, Charles Baxter, and the Bread Loaf Writers' Conference; and the wonderful writers I met there.

For kindness and patience and invaluable help with research, I thank the following, expert witnesses all: Margaret Carter, Susan

Cox, Hon. Lisa Foster, Ed Harman, Dr. Mikiko Huang, Sanford Kingsley (often and throughout), Mrs. Eva Levi, Wayne Lew, Mrs. Mary Loh, Dr. Michael MacAvoy, Hon. Marla Miller, Dr. James Morris, Craig Pinto, Jan Rutherdale, Staci Slaughter, Dr. Marshall Stoller, Dr. Caroline Tsen, Vivian Fei Tsen, Tom Waldo, Mrs. Katharine Wang, and Azeem Zakria (Scriptum in the Turl). For anyone keeping book, all recorded errors should be marked down to me.

I'm grateful to the Carpeneti family, the Cox-Nave family, and the Rutherdale-Bush family for years of friendship and incomparable hospitality in Juneau.

This book owes much to the love of my mother, Margaret C. Ma; the labors of my father, James J. L. Ma; and the integrity of my brother Christopher Y. W. Ma.

Thank you.

About the Author

KATHRYN MA is the author of the story collection *All That Work and Still No Boys*, winner of the Iowa Short Fiction Award. The book was named a *San Francisco Chronicle* Notable Book and a *Los Angeles Times* Discoveries Book. She is also the recipient of the David Nathan Meyerson Prize for Fiction. Before becoming a writer, Ma was a partner in a California law firm. She lives with her family in San Francisco. This is her first novel.

About the author

About the book

Read on

Insights,
Interviews
& More . . .

Meet Kathryn Ma

This article by Georgia Rowe originally ran in Mercury News *under the title "Kathryn Ma mines her own maturity and life experiences to produce a first novel:* The Year She Left Us.*" Used with permission of* San Jose Mercury News *Copyright © 2014. All rights reserved.*

KATHRYN MA clearly remembers the day she started her new novel, *The Year She Left Us*. It was 1999, and she was on a family trip to China.

At her hotel's breakfast buffet one morning, she noticed a large group of Western parents with Chinese babies—an adoption group of the kind that has made the journey to China many times over the past two decades.

"For the first time, the reality of what was happening with international adoption was made visible to me," says Ma, who lives in San Francisco with her husband and three daughters. She instantly saw the situation "as a lens, through which I could look at race, immigration, assimilation, and identity." Those themes come together movingly in *The Year She Left Us*, which tells the story of Ariadne Bettina Yun-li Rose Kong—Ari for short—a Chinese girl adopted by Charlie, an unmarried Chinese-American woman living in San Francisco.

Ari's a teenager in turmoil; as the book begins, she travels with a group to the orphanage where she was adopted, experiencing a trauma that sends her in search of her true identity.

Such orphanage visits are common for adoptive families, said Ma, who did extensive research into the subject.

China enacted its international adoption law in 1992, opening the floodgates for families in the United States and other countries to adopt Chinese children. "I was amazed to learn there are more than 70,000 Chinese children who have been adopted by American parents since 1992," Ma said. "But what was interesting to me was that the oldest of those children are now becoming adults."

The subject was rich with possibility, she adds. "Identity is a theme I'm very obsessed with—for myself, and because I've raised three daughters," Ma said. "I'm very interested in the lives of young women and how they come into lives of their own while keeping family ties." Ma acknowledges that adoption experience varies widely; many adoptees are happy and well-adjusted, she says.

Ari, however, is unable to adjust. "People tell her 'you're lucky—because you're in a Chinese-American family, no one has to know you're adopted. It will be easy for you,' " says Ma. "In fact, everything is harder for her. She's confused and very curious about why she feels so much sorrow and grief."

In alternating chapters, Ma explores conflicts among the other Kong women. Charlie, a public defender, and her sister, Les, a judge, struggle to balance their personal and professional lives. Their ▶

mother, Ari's Gran, faces memories of her own early traumas.

It's a remarkably assured debut novel, and Ma, whose volume of short stories, *All That Work and Still No Boys*, won the Iowa Short Fiction award, says she spent three years finishing it. "I spent a lot of time on the architecture of the book— I wanted it to be seamless," she says. Ari and Gran, she notes, speak directly to the reader; Charlie and Les are written in the third person.

Ma, who was born and raised in Pennsylvania, has roots in China. Her great-grandfather was born there and emigrated to the United States in the 1860s; after working as a servant in Oakland, he became a minister, married a Dutch-American woman, and established the first Chinese Christian church in New York City. Her parents were born in China; that 1999 trip marked the first time in fifty years her father had been back to his hometown.

Ma settled in the Bay Area with her family when she was in college. She studied history at Stanford and law at UC Berkeley, then established a career as a civil litigation attorney that spanned thirteen years.

Still, fiction always beckoned. An avid reader—she lists John Updike, E. L. Doctorow, Margaret Drabble, and Edna O'Brien as favorite authors—Ma was always curious about whether she could write.

"There was that idea buried someplace

deep, and as I got older, that idea grew until it became a kind of urgency," she says. "Finally, I thought, it's time to try." She gave up her law career, rented an office, and started writing.

Now that *The Year She Left Us* is out, she's glad she made that choice.

"I have a bit of sadness that I didn't start writing at an earlier age," says Ma, who is now fifty-seven. "I wonder—where would I be as a writer if I'd started sooner?

"At the same time, I'm enormously grateful that I took my time. I feel like it's a book of substance, and I'm not sure I could have written it when I was younger. All the living that has gone into my life is reflected in those pages. I hope it has a gravity and a maturity to it. And people seem to be resonating with that." ∾

Writing
The Year She Left Us
A Conversation
with Kathryn Ma

How did the idea for your book originate?

My parents are immigrants from China, and issues of displacement, exile, and assimilation have been part of my life story. Those issues became even more important to me when I traveled to China in 1999 and 2001 to tour the country and visit relatives. There I saw many western families with young Chinese babies on their adoption journey. The scenes I glimpsed made me curious to know more about international adoption.

At home in the U.S., Chinese girls with western parents seemed to be everywhere. I knew a number of adoptive parents with children from China, Vietnam, Central America, Russia, and other countries. International adoption has been embraced by countries welcoming new citizens, and by countries giving up their children. American parents have brought home more than 70,000 Chinese orphans—most of them girls—accounting for about one-third of all international adoptions to the U.S.

That so many orphans have found homes is joyful. Adoption has brought together children and parents who have formed new, happy families. But, as a mother, I wondered about the hidden emotional cost. Amidst the joy, there had to be sorrow and longing. For the adopted child, there would be questions about where she had come from, whom she belonged to, and who she would become. An adoption story began to take shape in my mind, a way in which I could explore themes of identity and family.

While mulling over these ideas, I saw an exhibition of new work from Chinese artists at the Asia Society in New York City. The exhibit included a riveting photograph by the Chinese artist Sheng Qi, of a hand missing a little finger. The absent finger spoke volumes about pain, loss, healing, and recovery. I knew immediately that a hand with a missing finger would be part of my novel.

How is international adoption captured in the novel?

Adoption is of course a blessing. Many adopted children are leading very happy lives, and their parents have navigated the adoption waters with love and grace. In this book, I've attempted to portray the complexities that might arise, especially as relates to a child's process of self-discovery. Some of the characters have adjusted easily to their new lives, settling in without conflict. Others, like Ari, are struggling to find their way.

Through the course of the novel, Ari learns to accept the pain and celebrate the blessings, bonding with her adoptive family in a new and profound way. There is struggle and then release. By the end of the book, she has begun to form a ▶

positive identity for herself and to see the possibilities of a fulfilling family life.

What other themes are intertwined in the story?

My novel also explores what it's like to be a strong-minded, independent woman. I'm a lawyer who has worked in the high pressure world of law firms and the courts, where men long dominated until courageous women elbowed their way in. Many of my friends are amazing women who have worked incredibly hard to build careers and raise families. Yet when I read novels that depicted American lives, I didn't see characters like the women I know. There were wives and mothers, but not many women competing in the larger realm. I wanted to write those characters and show them in all their determined, complicated, stressed-out glory. And so I drew on my law background and interviewed women about their jobs to create the characters of Charlie and Les, both lawyers who have to forge their own identities in a sometimes hostile world.

On top of it all sits Gran, the matriarch of the family and a peerless commentator on the state of other people's lives. In telling a multigenerational story, I wanted to explore the power of family legacy, the burden of family myths, and the impact of secrets. The experiences of the older generation shape and shadow the lives of their descendants.

As a daughter, granddaughter, and great-granddaughter, I grew up with ancestors at my back, sometimes beckoning, sometimes pointing the way. All my stories, at some level, begin before my characters are born and end in my imagination, long after their presence on the page comes to a close.

In what other ways did your own life influence this work?

In writing the book, I drew on my travels to China, my experiences living in Southeast Alaska, and my law background. My own family history darts at the edges of the story. For example, the poem I attribute to Gran's father was written by my grandfather in wartime China, and the koi in the hospital courtyard were described to me by my mother, who had seen them as a young girl living in Shanghai. I made writing and research notes for several years before starting. It took about three years to write the book.

What makes your novel relevant today?

April 1, 2015, marks the twenty-third anniversary of the effective date of the Adoption Law of the People's Republic of China, which provided for international adoption of Chinese orphans. As I write this, the oldest of the many thousands of abandoned and adopted Chinese babies are in their late teens and early ▶

Writing *The Year She Left Us* **(continued)**

twenties. The children in this unique generation are just now coming into their adulthood. At the same time, the Chinese immigrants who came to the U.S. in the late 1940s, when World War II ended and revolution was sweeping across China, are reaching the close of their remarkable lives. They've seen the country of their birth go through enormous upheaval, and, for those still living, they are in their final years of being able to make peace with the hardships they faced and the choices they made. I wanted my book to reflect the experiences of those two bookend generations, and to consider the ways in which the old and the young help each other through life. ⌒

The True to the Mood Book Club

LIKE A LOT OF BOOK LOVERS, I belong to a book club. There are eight of us, good friends who met years ago when we were in school. We gather every couple of months to discuss a book we've read. In our first year, we named ourselves the True to the Mood Book Club, after a reference in E. M. Forster's *A Passage to India*. We recently celebrated our thirtieth anniversary. At this point, we've read hundreds of books together. We have widely varying tastes, which means sometimes we argue late into the night, but so far, nobody has thrown anything, and we always come back for more.

None of us kept a complete list of the books we read. We never thought our memories would be anything less than perfect. Eventually, we assembled a partial list, which is posted on my website, www.kathrynma.com. We plan to stay True to the Mood for the next thirty years.

Here are some of the titles that generated particularly memorable discussion.

Henry James, *The Turn of the Screw*: This novella was the first book we read, right around Halloween. The mysterious and perplexing character of the children's governess, as well as the spooky atmospherics, have stayed with us for years. Say the title aloud, and we all start shivering. We went on to read more by James. ▶

The True to the Mood Book Club *(continued)*

Wallace Stegner, *Angle of Repose*:
A dense, encompassing, and absorbing
portrait of a marriage and the American
west, this novel has endured as one of
our all-time favorites. It holds a mythic
power over our group, a fitting position
for a book that itself explores the
mythology of America's drive west.

Pat Barker, *The Ghost Road*: What do
we talk about when we talk about war?
This brilliant, unsentimental novel, the
final volume in Barker's World War I
trilogy, held us fast and, perhaps because
of the distance between us and that
long-ago war, gave us a way to
contemplate the harrowing
unknown.

Margaret Atwood, *The Handmaid's
Tale*: A futuristic fable that entertains,
disturbs, warns and provokes. Not
everyone loved this book, but we all
had a lot to say. Like all good dystopian
novels, this one, published in 1985, has
aspects that hit close to the mark today.

Peter Carey, *True History of the Kelly
Gang*: One of our members is an Aussie,
so maybe that's why we had so much fun
with this book. We loved its rollicking
prose, wild action, fully alive characters,
and the history lesson to boot.

Hilary Mantel, *Wolf Hall*: Ruckus
ensued when we discussed this novel
about Thomas Cromwell, adviser
to Henry VIII. Some loved it, some
strenuously objected to the mash-up
of history, biography, and postmodern
telling. We won't be reading the sequel
together, but the conversation flowed.

Walter Mosley, *RL's Dream*: It's always exciting when an established author takes a leap into new territory. This novel, by renowned detective fiction writer Mosley, reaches deep with its portrayal of an aging blues musician and the tough woman who barges into his life. We liked best its singular prose, and Delta guitarist Robert Johnson whose legend, like the blues, haunts the whole of this book.

Gabriel García Márquez, *Chronicle of a Death Foretold*: Consummate storytelling that offers a meditation on life, death, and how, defying sense, the events of a fateful day can unfold before watchful, unseeing eyes. Reading this book, we were in the hands of the master. ∾